This and every issue of
New Destinies
is dedicated to the memory of
Robert A. Heinlein

Spring 1989

EDITOR IN CHIEF
Jim Baen

ASSISTANT EDITOR
Toni Weisskopf

MANAGING EDITOR
Kathy Hurley

Always gripping. Always new.

This is what NEW DESTINIES is all about . . .

. . . faith in your neighbors, in the honest craft of workmen, and in the human race: testimony from Robert A. Heinlein.

. . . talking to the animals, even those nasty, warlike Kzinti: Dean Ing in "Briar Patch" and "Dialogues in the Zoo."

. . . getting to ftl. Charles Sheffield's "Classical Nightmares and Quantum Paradoxes."

. . . what the space program is really for: port-a-potties in the asteroid belt—"Welcome to Wheel Days."

. . . going out of the fire and into the frying pan: "Origins" by Poul Anderson.

Not enough? Then overturn the government with a bunch of "Kids" and F. Paul Wilson!

JIM BAEN

NEW DESTINIES

The Paperback Magazine
Volume VII/Spring 1989

BAEN BOOKS

NEW DESTINIES, VOLUME VII

Copyright © 1989 by Baen Publishing Enterprises

A Baen Books Original

Baen Publishing Enterprises
260 Fifth Avenue
New York, N.Y. 10001

First printing, April 1989

ISBN: 0-671-69815-X

Cover art by David Mattingly

Printed in the United States of America

Distributed by
SIMON & SCHUSTER
1230 Avenue of the Americas
New York, N.Y. 10020

CONTENTS

Late last year Nasa held a ceremony to grant, post-humously, The Distinguished Public Service Medal to Robert Heinlein. To open the ceremony Robert's wife, Virginia, read aloud an unpublished* essay that Mr. Heinlein wrote nearly forty years ago, something that exemplified his attitude toward his fellows as perfectly in his final days as when it was written. When you are feeling down on yourself, your country, indeed, your species, consider the words of this most insightful of men. This is what he thought of you, and yours.

---

*It was, however, read aloud on national television.

THIS I BELIEVE

Robert A. Heinlein

I am not going to talk about religious beliefs but about matters so obvious that it has gone out of style to mention them. I believe in my neighbors. I know their faults, and I know that their virtues far outweigh their faults.

Take Father Michael down our road a piece. I'm not of his creed, but I know that goodness and charity and lovingkindness shine in his daily actions. I believe in Father Mike. If I'm in trouble, I'll go to him.

My next-door neighbor is a veterinary doctor. Doc will get out of bed after a hard day to help a stray cat. No fee—no prospect of a fee—I believe in Doc.

I believe in my townspeople. You can knock on any door in our town saying, "I'm hungry," and you will be fed. Our town is no exception. I've found the same ready charity everywhere. But for the one who says, "To heck with you—I got mine," there are a hundred, a thousand who will say, "Sure, pal, sit down."

I know that despite all warnings against hitchhikers I can step to the highway, thumb for a ride and in a few minutes a car or a truck will stop and someone will say, "Climb in Mac—how far you going?"

I believe in my fellow citizens. Our headlines are splashed with crime yet for every criminal there are 10,000 honest, decent, kindly men. If it were not so no child would live to grow up. Business could not go on from day to day. Decency is not news. It is buried in the obituaries, but it is a force stronger than crime. I believe in the patient gallantry of nurses and the tedious sacrifices of teachers. I believe in the unseen and unending fight against desperate odds that goes on quietly in almost every home in the land.

I believe in the honest craft of workmen. Take a look around you. There never were enough bosses to check up on all that work. From Independence Hall to the Grand Coulee Dam, these things were built level and square by craftsmen who were honest in their bones.

I believe that almost all politicians are honest . . . there are hundreds of politicians, low paid or not paid at all doing their level best without thanks or glory to make our system work. If this were not true we would never have gotten past the Thirteen Colonies.

I believe in Rodger Young. You and I are free today because of endless unnamed heroes from Valley Forge to the Yalu River. I believe in—I am proud to belong to—the United States. Despite shortcomings from lynchings to bad faith in high places, our nation has had the most decent and kindly internal practices and foreign policies to be found anywhere in history.

And finally, I believe in my whole race. Yellow, white, black, red, brown. In the honesty, courage, intelligence, durability and *goodness* of the overwhelming majority of my brothers and sisters everywhere on this planet. I am proud to be a human being. I believe that we have come this far by the skin of our teeth. That we *always* make it just by the skin of our teeth, but that we will always make it. Survive. Endure. I believe that this hairless embryo with the aching, oversize brain case and the opposable thumb, this animal barely up from the apes will *endure*. Will *endure* longer than his home planet—will spread out to the stars and beyond, carrying with him his honesty and insatiable curiosity, his unlimited courage and his noble essential decency.

This I believe with all my heart.

Introduction

Poul Anderson offers us a tale in the classic speculative mode: What sort of impact could a genuinely spectacular comet have, even without a strike? Could it perhaps transcend any merely physical effect, up to and including multi-species extinction?

ORIGIN

Poul Anderson

"Don't get me wrong," Sanders was quick to add. "This has nothing to do with Donnelly or Velikovsky or any other of those fantasists. It's not only physically possible, I really think it's just about a certainty."

I raised an eyebrow at him. "A comet changing history?"

"Why not?" he countered in his eager fashion. "Put your damn skepticism on the shelf for half a minute and listen, will you?"

Our tones were amiable. They always are; we're old arguing buddies. We'd been at it since dinner, one subject after the next. He'd come by invitation because his wife was off on a family visit, and now mine had sought her pillow. Maybe I'd end up making the spare bed for him, because quite a few Scotches had gone into the glow we felt. Also, the weather had turned foul, wind hooted and dashed rain against windowpanes, driving might not be safe even for a man wide awake.

"Okay, shoot." I rose, pulled the screen from the fireplace, laid on a couple of fresh sticks. The crackling as the wood caught was like small laughter. How snug a house with a hearth is on a wild winter night.

"To some extent, I'm stealing an idea of Fred Jueneman's," Sanders admitted. "I was re-reading his collected essays. You've got that book too, haven't you?"

I nodded. "Uh-huh. Some lively speculations in it. Not that I always agree."

"You wouldn't."

"Haven't looked at it myself for years. What's this particular notion?" I recharged our glasses and settled back into my chair.

"Actually, what he had in mind was an ice cloud from the breakup of a large comet, but I thought the comet itself could have a very similar effect," Sanders began. "Imagine a big one passed quite near Earth sometime in the past. To make the sight as stupefying as possible, have it come in on a retrograde orbit of extremely high eccentricity. Neither characteristic is unusual, you know. Let its perigee be closer than the moon's. Think of it then in the night sky, a broad, forked, filamented, shimmering whiteness across ninety degrees of arc or more. It was seen coming for months, growing, a monster bound for the world of man. After outshining the moon, it swooped by and within a few days vanished— into the sun's glare, but that's something you and I realize with the benefit of scientific hindsight. Wouldn't people be shaken to the core of their being?"

"Well, no doubt."

"The memory of it would become basic to mythology all over the world. And who can say more about the effect of belief systems on how civilizations think, what they do, more than that it's often tremendous? I suspect, myself, it always is crucial, subtle but pervasive."

"What myths are you thinking of?"

"What about Tiamat, the primordial snake of the Babylonians? Or the Midgard Serpent of the Norse? In some cases, since it did no harm, it'd become a benevolent creature, like the Chinese dragon. Or Kukulkan, the Feathered Serpent of the Mayas, Quetzalcoatl to the Aztecs. Watchers may well have seen jets spurt from the nucleus. In Egypt, did that give them the idea of the cosmic Horned One, Hathor? Did it make cows sacred in India? The Hindus believe in a red Third Eye too, the eye of insight; their women put a version of it on the forehead as a beauty spot. Now a star or a planet bright enough to shine through the comet's tail—Sirius or Venus, perhaps—would appear reddened; and in fact ancient records do describe Sirius as red. . . . Oh, the possibilities are unlimited."

I took a smoky sip and murmured, "Extravagant, anyhow."

"Look, I'm not speaking of any global catastrophe. There'd have been terrific meteor showers, heavenly fireworks, leading to concepts of eschatology found world-wide. But actual damage would be confined to those few places where a big rock hit an inhabited area. Maybe those are where the Serpent, the Dragon, is evil, the creature of chaos and destruction. But in general, the comet wouldn't have made any critical difference, except in human minds, which is what really counted."

"What became of it?"

"Oh, either it's got a very long period, so it hasn't been back yet, or else the close encounter with Earth flung it entirely out of the Solar System."

I grinned. "Which makes your hypothesis conveniently untestable."

"Well, not quite. Not quite. A lot of the inferences in science are indirect, aren't they? Look, we know of asteroids that pass pretty near us. We know of meteroids that collide, millions every year, if you count the dust particles, and once in a while a giant. The Tunguska strike appears to have been a comet, doesn't it? If it was essentially a mass of ices, that explains why no debris was ever found. It landed as recently as 1908. So doesn't sheer statistics guarantee that now and then a comet will narrowly miss us?"

My friend is such an enthusiast. "I hate forever throwing the wet blanket on you," I said.

"The hell you do," he retorted.

We laughed together. "Okay," I told him, "physically

speaking, *nihil obstat*. You may even be right about the astronomy. However—"

A female screamed. The He snarled and sprang. In his hand was the leg bone of a zebra. The light from above washed over it. White, white it swung. Wind whirred behind its heaviness.

Barely, Ruu dodged. The club that would have cracked his skull caught him a glancing blow on the shoulder. He reeled aside. The He raised his weapon again. His teeth were bared, the light wet upon them, they were white as the bone. Ruu whirled and fled.

The He chased him just a short way. Not even the strongest of the Folk ventured forth alone after dark. Ruu must.

The He turned back to the little cluster of females, undefiant males, wide-eyed young. He grunted at them. They slipped aside from him. He gestured. They followed him back to the clump of trees. He settled himself comfortably into the nest of grass they had heaped for him. They gathered around to sleep. One kept watch against lion or hyena. If he hooted the alarm, everybody would scramble into the trees.

The female whom Ruu had dared approach stared briefly after him. Light lay like frost over the savannah. Shadows dappled it where bushes stood murky. Shadows ran over the grass as it rippled in the breeze. They were blurred and strange, not like those below sun or moon. A single form was soon lost to sight in that rustling shiftiness.

Ruu slowed his dash to a walk. His hurt shoulder throbbed. He muttered his pain and rage and fear, not so loudly that a hunter beast might notice from afar.

Where to go, what to do? In the morning he might return and abase himself. Maybe the He would let him back into the band. Maybe not. Ill feeling between the two of them had worsened, worsened. Maybe Ruu did not want to go back. He could search for sharp sticks, heavy bones, rocks to throw. As a rogue male, he might live for a short while, all alone.

He did not think ahead in that fashion, not much, although he was given to dreaminess in a way that nobody else was. The visions in him were misty. For the most part, he knew simply pain and rage and fear.

And awe. The sun was down and the White Fire burned on high. Almost from edge to edge of the savannah it reached. Long tongues trailed a round, lion-maned glow bigger than the moon. Nearly all the stars had burrowed down into darkness, terrified. Streaks flew over heaven, tiny lightning bolts, cold and silent as the White Fire itself.

Ruu's memory reached to his first glimpse of it, like a cloud after dark. None had known what it was. They lost the sight for so long that they forgot. Then it came back, larger, brighter, and they remembered and howled. Now it was the He above the whole world.

It had not pounced on them. They set forth haunches of meat, both carrion and kill, hoping that would satisfy it. Instead, the vultures took the offerings; and the White Fire did not care. Slowly, the band ceased cowering, even though the being grew and grew in sight. It was like an elephant, vast, powerful, and indifferent. Yet they could not be sure. They never knew but what it might suddenly turn angry or hungry. That dread underlay their lives, while the waxing lightfulness of the nights troubled their sleep. It made them quarrelsome among each other. At last Ruu went too far.

And so he was going far too far, away, away. Where? Distantly he heard a roar, and shuddered.

Redness flickered on the rim of sight. He recognized a fire and moved toward it. Beasts shunned fires.

Folk ran from them as well, when they went devouring over the savannah; but that was in summer, the grass dry. Tonight the rains were very newly ended, the rivers and pools still full, the land green, the days noisy with birds and insects. Fires were few, not likely to spread. It would be good to huddle by some warmth, safe from teeth, until dawn.

When Ruu got there, he saw that the blaze was indeed small. An old patch of thornbush had caught, as old wood was apt to do. It was burning itself out. Little flames jumped about ash heaps and charred stumps, below which coals still glowered. Smoke blew acrid. Ruu hunkered down and held his palms out.

The heat made his shoulder hurt less and eased the tightness of his whole body. Dreaminess stole into him. That female—the looks she gave him were kindly—the He might have let him mount, had there not earlier been so much snarling between him and Ruu—

The fire sputtered. What had brought it to life? Ruu had thoughts that were half memories, of lightning or high winds, but they were dim. Fire came and went.

Also in the sky. He glanced aloft. It seemed to him that those flames had dwindled since last night. How cold they were. And they did not dance or crackle. A star shone through one of them, coal-red. Would it make the whole White Fire red and hot, till the sky burned?

Ruu shivered and shrank back from the smoldering before which he squatted. When nothing terrible happened, he regained courage. The He yonder must know what he did. He carried the White Fire in his teeth, or in his hand—in something of the vast, maned moon that was himself—to light his way and frighten off whatever beasts prowled heaven.

Ruu's mouth fell open. This was an altogether new dream. To *carry* fire. To *use* it.

He shivered again, but suddenly it was as a male shivers who spies a quarry. He crouched down and stared at the embers and the last flames.

A stick reached out of them. It burned at the other end. Cautiously, Ruu touched it. He pulled his fingers back at once. Shaken, the stick spat a few sparks. It had not bitten him.

Ruu set his jaws tight, reached, clasped the stick again. He picked it up. When he waved it, the guttering fire burned brighter.

He was not the first of his kind who had ever done that much. He was the first to keep hold, and try different ways of grasping and handling the stick—and

at last, when it went out, poking it back in among the
coals to start it burning afresh. He did so because the
sight of the White Fire had given him the dream of a
He who bore it and kept it alive. Grown Folk showed
young ones how to do things. This He was showing
him.

Entranced, Ruu played with his fire throughout the
night. By dawn he knew it must be fed or it would die,
and he knew how to feed it. He knew how to carry and
wield it.

He was hungry and thirsty and weary, but all that
went from him as he set out homeward. In his right
hand, carefully slanted, burned a long branch off a dead
bush nearby. In his left were more branches to make
new torches.

Let a lion or a hyena pack dare threaten him!

Let the He raise a bone to club him. Ruu would
swing the torch, and his enemy would flee shrieking to
become a rogue, and Ruu would be the He of a band
safe against beasts and darkness. What more powers lay
in the red blossom, he did not think to guess. He knew,
deep inside, that the Folk would learn what they were.

He raised his eyes. The White Fire was sinking and
fading as light strengthened from below. He bayed a
farewell to it. Thank you, mighty one yonder. Without
you, this would never have come to be.

I paused for another taste. The smoke of old peat
went gently over my palate. How rich is our world.

"Well?" Sanders asked. "What's your objection?"

I leaned back. "Just this. You can't have your comet
and your myths, not both."

"Why not?"

"Because written history in the Near East goes back
about five thousand years. The Sumerian tablets weren't
lost before the Babylonians had transcribed enough that
we have a pretty good idea of what was on them. If
anything as remarkable as your comet had been seen, it
would be there; they kept excellent astronomical records. And the Egyptians would have mentioned it.

They weren't stupid in those ancient civilizations, you know. Any talk of collective amnesia is an utter crock. We have ample continuity, in clay and on papyrus. Why, I'll bet we'd have found identifiable symbols of the sight on early oracular bones in China."

"But most of the world was still illiterate," Sanders protested.

I nodded. "True. However, those myth systems you were describing—the cultures that produced them originated well within historic times. The Aryans invaded India and got started on Hindu society in, m-mm, the middle second millennium B.C. The Central and South American civilizations didn't arise till well after that, and the Germanic religion later still.

"No, if your comet did pass by, it has to have been in prehistory, so long ago that even so tremendous an experience was quite forgotten." I gazed into the hypnotic flames in the fireplace. "It can't have had any lasting effect."

Whoo-oo, called the night wind.

ROBERT A. HEINLEIN

"Heinlein knows more about blending provocative scientific thinking with strong human stories than any dozen other contemporary science fiction writers."
—*Chicago Sun-Times*

"Robert A. Heinlein wears imagination as though it were his private suit of clothes. What makes his work so rich is that he combines his lively, creative sense with an approach that is at once literate, informed, and exciting."
—*New York Times*

Seven of Robert A. Heinlein's best-loved titles are now available in superbly packaged new Baen editions, with embossed series-look covers by artist John Melo. Collect them all by sending in the order form below:

REVOLT IN 2100, 65589-2, $3.50	☐
METHUSELAH'S CHILDREN, 65597-3, $3.50	☐
THE GREEN HILLS OF EARTH, 65608-2, $3.50	☐
THE MAN WHO SOLD THE MOON, 65623-6, $3.50	☐
THE MENACE FROM EARTH*, 65636-8, $3.50	☐
ASSIGNMENT IN ETERNITY**, 65637-6, $3.50	☐
SIXTH COLUMN***, 65638-4, $3.50	☐

Introduction

Since its inception quantum theory has had an aura of the surreal about it; refutations that depend on paradoxes become laboratory demonstrations. Quantum mechanics is the ultimate triumph of observation over common sense. Herein Dr. Sheffield makes all pellucid, though no less absurd for that, and proposes a method that uses current technology (pun intended) for implementing faster-than-light communication.

CLASSICAL NIGHTMARES AND QUANTUM PARADOXES

Charles Sheffield

". . .the quantum mechanics paradoxes, which can truly be said to be the nightmares of the classical mind. . ."
—ILYA PRIGOGINE.

1. THE MIGHTY ATOM.

The theory of special relativity tells us that we cannot accelerate an object to move faster than the speed of light. Worse than that, it tells us that as we try to accelerate a body to speeds closer and closer to light speed, we must apply more and more energy because the mass of the accelerating object increases and increases. The same theory tells us that we can't send messages faster than light, either.

These results are unpopular with science fiction readers and writers, who need ways to get from star to star quickly, cheaply, and easily, or at the very least to communicate over interstellar distances. This has led writers to seek a variety of loopholes. They include such things as:

  • **warp drives**—largely undefined, though there is usually a suggestion that the drives can warp space-time in such a way that points physically far apart in real space become closely separated in the warped space;
  • **wormholes**—there are singularities in space-time, formed by black holes; wormholes are connections between these black holes and white holes, and the intrepid traveller who enters a black hole will emerge from a white hole;
  • **hyperdrives**—which suppose that there are other space-times, loosely connected to ours, in which either the speed of light is far bigger than in our own universe, or the distances between points are far less. You move to one of these other space-times to do your traveling.

The advantages of these devices are obvious: they let us write and read interesting stories. The disadvantage of all of them is that they have no relationship to today's accepted physical theories (for instance, no one has ever fully defined a white hole, or seen any evidence that such a thing can exist). This does not mean that the devices *cannot* exist—only that they are very, very unlikely. Today's theories will be supplanted by tomorrow's, but surely not in any simple-minded way arranged for the convenience of science fiction writers. Warp drives and their relatives are varieties of wishful thinking.

A much better way to look for faster-than-light travel techniques is to seek the places where today's theories are incomplete or, better still, *inconsistent*. For if two independent theories tell us two different and incompatible things, something must be wrong, and that is fertile ground for discovery.

Where incompatible theories meet, there may be loopholes. We want a particular loophole that allows an object to move from one place to another faster than the speed of light, or permits a piece of information to be transferred faster than light. There is one obvious place to look: at the meeting place of quantum theory and relativity. In the first part of this century, the quantum theory was developed in parallel with, but almost independent of, the theories of special and general relativity. Despite sixty years of effort, the two have never been put consistently together in what John Archibald Wheeler, the physicist who among other things gave the modern name "black hole" to the end-point collapse of massive stars, has termed "the fiery marriage of general relativity with quantum theory."

Moreover, when we explore the bases of quantum theory we are fishing in very strange waters. The techniques allow us to compute the right answers (i.e., they seem to describe the way the universe behaves) but they often run counter to the way we *feel* things should be. That's our problem, of course, and not Nature's. As the late and much-lamented Richard Feynman, one of the sparkling intellects of the century, put it, the problem "is only a conflict between reality and your feeling of what reality 'ought to be.'"

Part of the difficulty is that, until recently, quantum theory seemed to be confined to describing what happened in the world of the very small—atoms and electrons and subnuclear particles far too little for us to have any hope of seeing them. There was thus no direct physical experience to guide us as to their behavior, and a simple extrapolation of intuition derived from large objects was likely to prove false.

In the next sections we will look at quantum theory and ask how the world would appear if atoms were big, say as big as a basketball. Before we roar with laughter at such a silly idea, we ought to look back forty-four years. When the first atomic bomb was dropped on Hiroshima on August 6, 1945, the average citizen knew not a thing about atoms. Even the name, "atomic bomb," was evidence of public confusion. (Every bomb since the invention of gunpowder was an atomic bomb, since it involved the chemical bonds between the outer electrons of atoms. The new bomb should have been called a *"nuclear* bomb"—but the media could get away with the term "atomic bomb" because few people seemed to know about atoms.)

When a poll was made in 1945 asking the general public, among other things, how big they thought atoms were, "about the size of a tennis ball" was one popular answer. And have you ever heard the word "atom" before, Mr. & Mrs. Average Citizen? Well, it is the title of a popular book, *The Mighty Atom*, by Marie Corelli (a book which had nothing to do with atoms in the scientific sense). And how about the word "nucleus" applied to atoms? Sorry, that's new to us.

The bomb was such a sensation that a number of truly amazing rumors made the rounds: e.g., that the bomb itself was far too small to be seen with the naked eye; that Albert Einstein—the one scientist the public had heard of—had personally piloted the plane that dropped the bomb. And my own favorite, the rumor, repeated over British radio, that the container for the first atomic bomb was designed by Bing Crosby. People seemed ready to believe anything.

(Before you laugh, ask if we are smarter now. A country that sends money to Jimmy Swaggart, pays farmers to grow a crop that kills three hundred and fifty thousand of us every year, accepts Jeanne Dixon as a psychic, and tolerates Ed Meese for eight years as Attorney General can't afford to mock anyone. I'd be interested to hear the answers if you held a poll *today* and asked people just how big an atom is.)

My point is this. Most people knew nothing about atoms, and once they found out just how small atoms were, their amazement took a new direction. How is it possible, they said, for anyone to count, measure, and know the properties of objects that we can't even see?

That is a very basic and reasonable question, and in some ways the general public was smarter than the scientists. There is no reason to expect that objects too small to see or touch *should* behave in any way like the large objects of everyday experience. In fact, they don't. And therein lies quantum theory.

Before we can get to quantum paradoxes and faster-than-light communications, we will have to say something about quantum theory itself: where it came from, what it means, why it's needed.

2. THE BEGINNINGS OF QUANTUM THEORY.

Quantum theory has been around, in much its present form, for over sixty years. The basic rules for quantum theory calculations were discovered by Werner Heisenberg and Erwin Schrödinger in 1925. Soon afterwards, in 1926, Paul Dirac, Carl Eckart, and Schrödinger himself showed that the Heisenberg and Schrödinger formulations can be viewed as two different approaches within one general framework.

It quickly became clear that the same theory allowed the internal structure of atoms and molecules to be calculated in detail, and by 1930, quantum theory, or quantum mechanics as it was called, became *the* method for performing calculations in the small world of molecules, atoms, and nuclear particles.

There have been great improvements since that time in computational techniques, and in our understanding of such things as nuclear models, nuclear scattering processes, and subnuclear structure. However, the basic ideas have not changed much since the late 1920s; and the same mysteries that plagued and puzzled the workers of that time are worries now.

It is, in fact, fair to say that although we have *recipes* that allow us to compute almost anything we want to, underneath those recipes lurk deep paradoxes and open questions, and they have been there since the beginning. To quote Feynman again, "I think it is fair to say that no one understands quantum mechanics." We are like people who know very well how to drive a car, but have never looked under the hood and have no idea how the engine works.

If you ask how I have the nerve to write about a subject that I am saying no one fully understands, let me admit the validity of the criticism and point out that such considerations never yet stopped a politician or a preacher. I'm not going to let it stop me.

Harder for me to answer is the need for yet another discussion of quantum theory and its paradoxes, when so many high-quality detailed discussions already exist in the literature. I argue that my objective is rather different, and I will point out here some of the excellent texts that treat in detail what I will only mention: *In Search of Schrödinger's Cat*, by John Gribbin (Bantam, 1984), a text from which I have borrowed liberally; *Directions in Physics*, by Paul Dirac (Wiley, 1978); *Thirty Years That Shook Physics*, by George Gamow (Doubleday, 1966); *Directions in Physics*, by Paul Dirac (Wiley, 1978); *Order Out of Chaos*, by Ilya Prigogine (Bantam, 1984), from which is drawn the opening quotation of this article; and *The Character of Physical Law*, by Richard Feynman (MIT Press, 1967).

On a more technical level, I have drawn from Dirac's classic text, *The Principles of Quantum Mechanics*, (Oxford University Press, Fourth Edition, 1957); the Feynman *Lectures on Physics*, by Feynman, Leighton, and Sands (CalTech, 1965); *Quantum Mechanics and Path Integrals*, by Feynman and Hibbs (McGraw-Hill, 1965; (Al Hibbs, better known to the public as the "Voice of Voyager," served as anchorman at JPL for television coverage of the Voyager encounters with Jupiter, Saturn and Uranus); and *From Being to Becoming*, by Ilya Prigogine (Freeman, 1980), a book which tackles the tough question of quantum theory and irreversible processes, and which should, in its third part, make your head ache.

While in confessional mode, I also have to say that I can't possibly describe quantum theory fully in a few thousand words. There's too much to it, and it's a truly difficult subject. If everything I say seems to be perfectly clear, chances are that either I'm missing the point, or you are.

The need for quantum theory emerged gradually, from about 1890 to 1920. Some rather specific questions as to how radiation should behave in an enclosure had arisen, questions that classical physics couldn't answer. Max Planck in 1900 showed how a rather *ad hoc* assumption, that the radiation was emitted and absorbed in discrete chunks, or *quanta*, (singular, quantum), solved the problem. He introduced a fundamental constant associated with the process, Planck's constant. This constant, denoted by h, is a tiny quantity, and its small size compared with the energies, times, and masses of the events of everyday life is the basic reason why we are not aware of quantum effects all the time.

Most people thought that the Planck result was a gimmick, something that happened to give the right answer but did not represent anything either physical or of fundamental importance.

That changed in 1905, when Einstein used the idea of the quantum to explain another baffling result, the *photoelectric effect*. (1905 was an unbelievable year for Einstein. He produced the explanation of the photoelectric effect, the theory of special relativity, and a paper that provided an explanation of Brownian motion and offered direct evidence for the existence of atoms. The only comparable year in scientific history was 1666, when Isaac Newton developed the calculus, the laws of motion, and the theory of universal gravitation.)

The photoelectric effect arises in connection with light hitting metal. In 1899, the Hungarian physicist Phillip Lenard had shown that when a beam of light is shone on a metallic surface, electrons begin to pop out of the metal provided that the wavelength of the light is short enough. Note that the result depends on the *wavelength* of the light, and not its brightness. If the wavelength is short enough, the *number* of emitted electrons is decided by the brightness, but if the wavelength is too long, no electrons will appear no matter how bright the light may be.

Einstein suggested that the result made sense if light were composed of particles (now called *photons*) each with a certain energy decided by the wavelength of the light. These photons, hitting atoms in the metal, would drive electrons out if the energy provided by the impact was enough to overcome the binding of the electron within the atom. Einstein published an equation relating the energy of light to its wavelength, and again Planck's constant, h, appeared.

Quanta looked a little more real, but Einstein was only twenty-six years old and still an unknown, so the world did not hang on his every word as they did in his later years. (There were exceptions, people who recognized Einstein for what he was from the beginning. Max Born, whom we will meet again in the 1920s, says in the Born-Einstein letters [Walker, 1971]: "Reiche and Loria told me about Einstein's paper, and suggested that I should study it. This I did, and was immediately deeply impressed. We were all aware that a genius of the first order had emerged." Born here is typically modest. *He* certainly knew that a genius of the first order had arisen, but he was himself a genius. It takes one to know one.)

It might seem there was nothing particularly surprising in Einstein's suggestion that light was composed of particles. After all, Newton, over two hundred years earlier, had believed exactly the same thing, and it was known as the *corpuscular theory of light*. However, early in the nineteenth century, long after Newton's death, a crucial experiment had been performed that seemed to show beyond doubt that light had to be a form of wave motion. All the evidence since that time had pointed to the same conclusion.

The key experiment was a deceptively simple one performed in 1801 by an English physicist and physician, Thomas Young. (Young was also one of the men who deciphered Egyptian hieroglyphics, thus allowing ancient Egyptian writings to be understood; he can hardly be given the label of narrow scientist.)

Young took light from a point source and allowed it to

pass through two parallel slits in a screen. When this light was allowed to fall on a second screen held behind the first, a pattern of dark and light, known as an *interference pattern*, was seen. Young's result is explained easily enough if light is a form of wave, but is incomprehensible if light is assumed to be made up of particles. And in the 1860s, Maxwell had gone further, showing that light as a form of wave motion appeared as a natural solution of his general theory of electromagnetism. Thus in 1905, when Einstein published his paper on the photoelectric effect, no one but Einstein was willing to concede that light could be anything but waves. And no one was willing to throw overboard the wave theory of light on the word of a twenty-six-year-old unknown, still working for the Swiss Patent Office.

While Einstein was analyzing the photoelectric effect and reintroducing the corpuscular theory of light to physics, other scientists had begun to put together a picture of an atom that was more than the old Greek idea of a simple indivisible particle of matter (*atomos* = can't be cut, in Greek). In Canada, the New Zealand physicist Ernest Rutherford had been studying the new phenomenon of radioactivity, discovered in 1896 by Henri Becquerel. Rutherford found that radioactive material emits charged particles, and when he moved to England in 1907 he began to use those particles to explore the structure of the atom itself. Rutherford found that instead of behaving like a fairly homogeneous sphere of electrical charges, a few billionths of an inch across, the atom had to be made up of a very dense central region, the *nucleus*, surrounded by an orbiting cloud of electrons. In 1911 Rutherford proposed this new structure for the atom, and pointed out that while the atom was small—a few billionths of an inch—the nucleus was *tiny*, only about a hundred thousandth as big in radius as the whole atom. In other words, matter, everything from humans to stars, is mostly empty space and moving electric charges.

Our own Solar System is much the same sort of structure, of small isolated planets, far from each other, orbiting the central massive body of the Sun. And to many people this analogy, though no more than an analogy, proved irresistible—so irresistible that it was taken to extreme and implausible lengths. The electrons were imagined to be *really* like planets (despite the fact that all electrons appear to be identical, and all planets to be different), and the nuclei really like suns. Each electron might have its own tiny lifeforms living on it, and its own infinitesimal people. And the same argument could be taken the other way. Perhaps, it was suggested, our own Solar System was no more than an atom in the hind leg of a super-dog, barking in a super-universe.

That was perhaps a tongue-in-cheek comment that no scientist took too seriously, but there was a problem with the Rutherford atom, much more fundamental than the breakdown of a rather far-fetched analogy. The inside of the atom, in fact, must be far stranger and more alien than any miniature Solar System. For if electrons were orbiting a nucleus, then Maxwell's general theory of electromagnetism insisted that the electrons ought to radiate energy. But if they *did* lose energy, then according to all classical rules they would quickly have to fall into the nucleus and the atom would collapse.

This didn't happen.

Why didn't it? Why was the atom a stable structure?

That question was addressed by the Danish physicist, Niels Bohr, who at the time was working with Rutherford's group in Manchester, England. He applied the "quantization" notion—that things occur in discrete pieces, rather than continuous forms—to the structure of atoms.

In the Bohr atom, which he introduced in 1913, electrons do move in orbits around the nucleus, just like a miniature solar system. But the reason they don't spiral in is because they can only lose energy in chunks—quanta—rather than continuously. Electrons are permitted orbits of certain energies, and can move from one to another when they emit or absorb light and other radiation; but they can't occupy *intermediate* positions, because to get there they would need to emit or absorb some fraction of a quantum of energy, and by definition, fractions of quanta don't exist. The permitted energy losses in Bohr's theory were again governed by the wavelengths of the emitted radiation and by Planck's constant.

It sounded crazy, but it worked. With his simple model, applied to the hydrogen atom, Bohr was able to calculate the right emitted wavelengths (known as the *emission spectrum*) for hydrogen. No earlier theory had been able to do that. Thus, although the idea that electrons orbit the nucleus, rather than reside outside the nucleus with a certain amount of energy, was found misleading and subsequently dropped, the quantum nature of the electron energy levels within the atom remained and proved of central importance. Electrons jump from one level to another, and as they do so, they give off or absorb quanta of radiation.

How long does it take an electron to move from one quantum level to another quantum level (termed *states* in the vocabulary of quantum theory; any possible unique situation in a system forms one state)?

Here we seem to catch our first glimpse of speeds faster than light. According to Bohr's theory (and subsequent ones), we can't speak of an electron "moving" from one state to another. If it moved, in any conventional sense of the word, then there would have to be intermediate positions that corresponded to some intermediate energy. There is no evidence of any such intermediate, fractional, energies. The electron "jumps," disappearing from one state and appearing in another without any discernible transition. It's meaningless to ask how fast it went.

It may seem natural to ask if there might *really* be a whole sequence of transition states, ones that we are simply unable to observe. Quantum theory is quite insistent upon this point: if we can't *observe* it, it is not a part of physics; it belongs to the realm of metaphysics. "Only questions about the results of experiments have a real significance and it is only such questions that theoretical physics has to consider"—Dirac. This is in contrast to the nineteenth century view of physics, in which Nature was thought to be evolving like some great machine, with all questions about that machine permitted and potentially answerable, even if we could not give answers with present theories.

The next step came in 1923, and it was made by Louis de Broglie. He knew that Einstein had attributed particle properties (Photons) to light waves. He asked if wave properties ought to be assigned to particles, such as electrons and protons, and if so, how. He found that the Bohr "orbits" of electrons in atoms were just right for a whole number of waves to fit into the available space. He also suggested that there should be direct evidence that particles like electrons can be diffracted, just as a light wave is diffracted by an aperture or an object in its path.

His suggestion proved to be entirely correct. If waves behaved like particles, particles also behaved like waves.

The situation in 1924 can now be summarized as follows:

1. Radiation came in quanta—discrete bundles of energy.
2. Those quanta, the photons, interacted with matter as though they were particles, but everything else suggested that radiation was a form of wave.
3. The structure of the atom could be explained by assuming that the permissible positions for electrons corresponded to well-defined, discrete energy values.
4. Particles show wave-like properties, just as waves seem to be composed of particles.
5. One fundamental constant, Planck's constant, is central to all these different phenomena.

The stage was set for the development of a complete form of quantum mechanics, one that would allow all the phenomena of the subatomic world to be tackled with a single theory.

It was also set for an unprecedented confusion about the nature of physical reality, and a debate that still goes on today.

Before we go any farther, let us note a few things about the five points just made. First, the papers which presented these ideas were not difficult *technically*. They did not demand a knowledge of advanced mathematics to be comprehensible. Some of the mathematics used in these ground-breaking papers has a simple, almost homemade look to it. (This was equally true of Einstein's papers on special relativity.) However, the new ideas were very difficult *conceptually*, since they required the reader to throw away many cherished and long-held "facts" about the nature of the universe. In their place, scientists were asked to entertain notions that were not just unfamiliar—they seemed positively perverse. Energy was previously supposed to be a continuously variable quantity, with no such thing as a "smallest" piece of emitted energy—but now people were asked to think that energy came in separate units of precise denomination, like coins or postage stamps. And light was waves, electrons were particles; there should be no way they could both be both, depending on how you looked at them or (as William Bragg once jokingly suggested) on which day of the week it happened to be.

The other thing to note is the power of hindsight.

It is easy for us today to sit back and pick out the half-dozen fundamental papers that paved the way for the development of quantum theory, just as it is easy to point to seminal papers by Heisenberg, Schrödinger, Born, and Dirac that created the theory. But at the time, the right path for progress was not clear at all. The crucial papers and the ideas that worked were not the only ones being produced at the time. Everyone had more or less equal access to the same experimental results, and hundreds of attempts were made to reconcile them with existing, nineteenth century physics. Many of those attempts employed the full arsenal of nineteenth century theory, and they were impressive in their complexity and in the mathematical skills that they displayed.

It called for superhuman brains to sit in the middle of all that action and distinguish the real advances from the scores of other well-intentioned but unsuccessful attempts, or from totally alien and harebrained crank theories. A handful of physicists were able to see what was significant, and build upon it. If we think that the developments of quantum theory are hard to follow, we should reflect on how much harder it was to create.

The same strangeness of thought patterns was there in all the creators of quantum theory*—the whiz kids, Heisenberg and Wolfgang Pauli and Dirac and Pascual Jordan, all in their middle twenties; the wise advisors Bohr and Einstein and Born, men in their mid-forties; the young mathematicians Hermann Weyl and John von Neumann; and the odd man out—Schrödinger, thirty-nine when he published his famous equation in 1926, and an old man for such a fundamental new contribution to physics.

(Of that original legendary group from the mid-1920s, I met only one. Paul Dirac, the most powerful theorist of the lot, taught the first course that I ever took in quantum theory. In retrospect, I think of it as a Chinese meal course. Dirac would derive his results, and they were all so clear and logical that they seemed self-evident. Then I would go away, and a couple of hours later I would try to reconstruct his logic. It was gone. What was self-evident to him was not so to me.

I also met him on several occasions socially, though that may be the wrong word. Dirac was a famously shy man. At cocktail parties in the senior common room at St. Johns College, Cambridge, the professors and the graduate students got together a couple of times a year, to drink sherry and make polite conversation. Dirac was

---

* Einstein, writing in 1926 of Dirac, whom he came to admire, said: "I have trouble with Dirac. This balancing on the dizzying path between genius and madness is awful."

always very affable, but he had no particular store of social chitchat. And we were too in awe of him, and too afraid of looking like idiots, to ask anything about quantum theory, or about the people he had worked with in developing it. Talk about wasted opportunity!)

The logical next step in this article would be to go on with the historical development of the theory. We could show how in 1925 Schrödinger employed the apparent wave-particle duality to come up with a basic equation that can be applied to almost all quantum mechanics problems; how Heisenberg in the same year, using the fact that atoms emit and absorb energy only in finite and well-determined pieces, was able to produce another set of procedures that could also be applied to almost every problem; and how Dirac, Jordan, and others were able to show that the two approaches were just different ways of representing a single construct, that construct being quantum theory in its most general form.

We will not proceed that way. Interesting as it is, it would take too long. Instead we will take advantage of hindsight. We will move at once to what writers from Dirac to Feynman have agreed is the single most important experiment—the one which is totally inexplicable without quantum theory, and the one which is the source of endless argument and discussion within quantum theory.

It is an experiment that Thomas Young would recognize at once.

3. THE KEY EXPERIMENT.

We start, as did Thomas Young, with a pair of slits in a screen. Instead of light, this time we have a source of electrons (or some other atomic particle). Electrons that go through a slit hit a sensitive film, or some other medium that records their arrival. As Louis de Broglie predicted, when we do the parallel slit experiment and look at the pattern, we see a wave-like interference effect, showing that the electron has wave properties.

The problem is, to get that pattern it is necessary to

assume that *each single electron goes partly through both slits*.

This sounds like gibberish. The obvious thing to say is, it can't go through both, and it should be easy enough to see which one it did go through: you simply watch the slit, to see if the electron passes by. If you do that, you will always observe either one electron, or no electron—and when you make such an observation, the interference pattern goes away.

Quantum theory says that before you made the observation, the electron was partly heading through one slit, partly through the other. In quantum theory language, it had components of *both states*, meaning that there was a chance it would go through one, and a chance it would go through the other. Your act of observation forced it to pick one of those states. And the one it will pick cannot be known in advance—it is decided completely randomly. The probability of the electron ending in one particular state may be larger than for another state, but there is absolutely no way to know, in advance, which state will be found when we make the observation.

This "probabilistic interpretation" of what goes on in the parallel slit experiment and elsewhere in quantum theory was introduced by Born in 1926. It is usually referred to as the "Copenhagen interpretation," even though Born worked at Göttingen. (That was because Niels Bohr, of Copenhagen, included Born's idea as part of a general package of methods of quantum theory, allowing anyone to solve problems of atoms and molecules.) The Copenhagen interpretation said, in effect, that the theory can never tell you exactly where something is, before you make a measurement to *determine* where it is. Prior to the observation, the object existed only as a sort of cloud of probability, maximum in one place but extending over the whole of space. And it is the observation that forces the particle to make a choice as to where it is.

Many people found this idea of *"quantum indeterminacy"* incomprehensible, and many who understood it, hated it—including Einstein and Schrödinger. Schrödinger said: "I don't like it, and I'm sorry I ever had anything to do with it," and "Had I known that we were not going to get rid of this damned quantum jumping, I never would have involved myself in this business."

(But one man's poison may be another man's bread and butter. Science fiction writers have regarded the probabilistic element of quantum theory as providing not a problem, but a great deal of license. The logic runs as follows: If there is a finite probability of an electron or other subatomic particle being anywhere in the universe, then since humans are made up of subatomic particles, there must also be a finite probability that we are not here, but somewhere else. Now, if we could just make a quantum jump to one of those other places, we would have achieved travel—instantaneously.

This is a case where the term "finite probability" is true, but totally misleading. If you work out the probability of a simultaneous quantum jump (presumably you want to all go simultaneously, and to the same place—no fun arriving in a distributed condition, or half of you a day late) you get a number with so many zeroes after the decimal that the universe will end long before you could write them all down. As in so many things in science, calculation kills off what seems like a good idea until you look at the numbers.)

It's perhaps a good thing that this probabilistic aspect of quantum mechanics emerged only after people knew that the methods gave results corresponding to experiment. Otherwise, the lack of determinacy that the theory implies might have been enough to stop any further work along those lines. As it was, Einstein always rejected the indeterminacy, arguing that somewhere behind it all there had to be a theory without random elements (perhaps Einstein's most quoted line is: "God does not play dice." He also said, in the same letter to Max Born, "Quantum mechanics is certainly imposing. But an inner voice tells me that it is not yet the real thing.").

Can we dispose of the idea that the electron is in a

mixed-state condition before we observe it, perhaps on some logical grounds?

Suppose that atoms, protons or electrons were as big as tennis balls, or at least weighed as much, as the average citizen was apparently quite ready to believe forty years ago. We could still perform the double slit experiment, and we could watch which slit any particular electron went through. Moreover, a single photon, reflecting off a passing electron, would be enough to give us that information. It then sounds totally ridiculous that the infinitesimal disturbance produced by the impact of one photon could cause a profound change in the results of the experiment.

What does quantum theory tell us in such a case?

It provides an answer that many people find intellectually very disturbing. When we observe large objects, says the theory, the disturbance caused by the measuring process is small compared with the object being measured, and we will then obtain the result predicted by classical physics. However, when the disturbing influence (e.g., a photon) is comparable in size with the object being observed (e.g., an electron), then the classical rules go out of the window, and we must accept the world view offered by quantum theory. Quantum theory thus provides an absolute scale to the universe—a thing is small, if quantum theory must be used to calculate its behavior.

The converse notion, that quantum theory is *only* important in the atomic and subatomic world, is false. Quantum indeterminacy is quite capable of revealing itself at the level of everyday living. For example, superconductivity is a macroscopic phenomenon, but it arises directly from the quantum properties of matter.

However, perhaps the most famous example of the macroscopic implications of quantum indeterminacy, one which has been quoted again and again, is the case of Schrödinger's cat. This paradox was published in 1935.

Put a cat in a closed box, said Schrödinger, with a bottle of cyanide, a source of radioactivity, and a detector of radioactivity. Operate the detector for a period just long enough that there is a fifty-fifty chance that one radioactive decay will be recorded. If such a decay occurs, a mechanism crushes the cyanide bottle and the cat dies.

The question is, without looking in the box, is the cat alive or dead? Quantum indeterminacy insists that until we open the box (i.e., perform the observation) the cat is partly in the two different states of being dead and being alive. Until we look inside, we have a cat that is neither alive nor dead, but half of each.

There are refinements of the same paradox, such as the one known as Wigner's friend (Eugene Wigner, born in 1902, was an outstanding Hungarian physicist in the middle of the action in the original development of quantum theory). In this version, the cat is replaced by a human being. That human being, as an observer, looks to see if the glass is broken, and therefore automatically removes the quantum indeterminacy. But suppose that we had a cat smart enough to do the same thing, and press a button? The variations—and the resulting debates—are endless.

To get out of the problem of quantum indeterminacy, Hugh Everett and John Wheeler in the 1950s offered an alternative "many-worlds" theory. The cat is both alive and dead, they said—but in different universes. Every time an observation is made, all possible outcomes occur, but the universe splits at that point, one universe for each outcome. We see one result, because we live in only one universe.

This suggestion is of philosophical but not of practical interest. It will always get just the same experimental results as those of the Copenhagen interpretation.

We will not try to decide between the Copenhagen interpretation and the Everett-Wheeler many-worlds theory, or other more recent suggestions such as John Cramer's "transactional interpretation," published in 1986. Instead, we will accept that quantum indeterminacy is real, and explore the reasons why some people feel that it could be the key to faster-than-light communication.

4. ACTION AT A DISTANCE.

With waves looking like particles and particles behaving like waves, with energy coming in lumps, with determinacy gone, what was left that the physicists of the late 1920s could rely on?

Well, there were still the conservation principles. In any process, momentum had to be conserved, and so did angular momentum. And energy had to be conserved (though since Einstein's relativity papers in 1905, mass had to be recognized as convertible to energy, and vice versa, according to a precise rule—if "God does not play dice" are Einstein's most famous words, $E = mc^2$ is certainly his most famous formula). Insisting on these general conservation laws within the new quantum theory not only imposed some order on the confusion, it also led to new physical predictions. Wolfgang Pauli predicted the existence of a new particle, the *neutrino*, in 1931, based on the conservation principles. That particle was not actually seen until 1955, but most people accepted its existence during that quarter-century wait.

Angular momentum, or spin, is a variable that quantum theory tells us can take on only a finite set of values. Like the energy levels of atoms, it is *quantized*. If an object with zero spin breaks into two equal pieces, then conservation of angular momentum tells us that the spins of those pieces must be equal and opposite. (By opposite we mean that the spins are in the opposite sense—imagine two spinning tops, that looked at from above are rotating in clockwise and counterclockwise directions.)

Now consider one of the two pieces. Quantum indeterminacy tells us that until we look at it, we don't know the sense of its spin. The two pieces may fly far apart from each other, without our knowing the sense of spin of either one of them, but we can be sure that they must continue to have opposite spins, since their total angular momentum must be zero.

Suppose that, when the two particles are far apart, we measure the spin of one of them. According to quantum indeterminacy, until that measurement is performed, the particle doesn't have a defined sense of spin—it has a mixture of two possible spins, and it is only the measurement that forces it into one particular spin.

But when that happens, the other particle, no matter how far away, must at once take on a spin of the opposite sense to the one that was just measured. Otherwise angular momentum would not be conserved. One particle has affected the other, and the influence has traveled faster than the speed of light.

A version of this experiment was proposed (as a thought experiment, not a real experiment) by Einstein, Rosen, and Podolsky, in 1935. Their objective was not faster-than-light communication. It was rather to assert that the possibility of measuring a property of one of the particles, without affecting the other, undermined the whole idea of indeterminacy in quantum theory, and therefore that quantum theory was missing some basic element.

However, another way of looking at the situation can be adopted: suppose that we accept quantum theory. Then the second particle *is* affected by the measurement we made on the first one. We have achieved "action at a distance," something that most physicists object to on general philosophical grounds. Any theory that allows action at a distance is called a *nonlocal* theory. We are led to one of two alternative conclusions:

a) There is something incomplete or wrong in quantum theory; or

b) The universe permits nonlocal effects, where one action here can instantly affect events far away.

Starting in 1976 and continuing today, experiments have been performed to test which conclusion is correct. They are done by evaluating an expression known as Bell's inequality, first published in 1964, which gives different results in the two situations a) and b).

The experiments are difficult, but they come down firmly in favor of b). The universe is nonlocal; action at a distance is part of nature; and an event here can, under the right circumstances, affect (immediately!) another one far away.

Faster-than-light communication?

Unfortunately, no. To achieve communication, some information has to be transferred when we make our observation on one of the two particles. Say that we created a thousand particle pairs. Half the particles fly away together on a spaceship, and their sister particles stay here. Now we test the ones that are here, and observe their spin. *We* now know what the spins of the other particles must be—but we can't tell our colleagues on the ship! And they don't know if we have done those measurements or not, since when *they* do measurements, they find no pattern to the spins, even if those spins were determined by what we did here. If we could somehow *affect* the spins that we measure, then the other spins, far away, would change, and we would have a message. But that's exactly what quantum indeterminacy tells us we can't do. We have no control over what we will find when we make the measurements.

Let's change the question. Quantum theory seems to give us a nonlocal universe, one in which two events can affect each other unconstrained by the speed of light. Once we accept the idea of action at a distance, is there anything else in the quantum world to give us hope that faster-than-light travel or communication might be possible?

There is. We remarked earlier that the quantum jumps between electron states in the Bohr atom do not take place via a succession of intermediate states. They sit in one state, and then they are, with no time of transition, instantaneously in another state. We also pointed out that quantum phenomena are not, as one might think, restricted to the world of the very small, such as atoms and electrons. Superconductivity is a purely quantum phenomenon. Might there be some sort of "quantum jumping" associated with it, which could allow events in one place to affect events in another, unconstrained by the speed of light?

Ten years ago, I think that every physicist would

have said no. (Just as every physicist would probably have said we would not have superconductors operating at liquid nitrogen temperatures before 1990!) Today, we are at the "could be" stage. If we can, by our experiments, show that *some* events—even one pair of events—far apart in space are coupled, then the universe permits action at a distance. Once we admit that, since *all* the universe was once intimately coupled (at the time of the Big Bang) then it may be just as coupled today, albeit in unobservable ways.

In the case of superconductivity, the theory tells us that the whole superconductor constitutes a single quantum state. If it changes that state, *all* the superconductor changes. However, we can make a superconducting ring or cylinder of any size we choose. If a change of state is induced at one end of it, that state change appears immediately at the other end, and should be measureable.

With the increased availability of superconducting materials, we seem to be just one step away from a great potential breakthrough—a practical test to make one part of a superconducting device respond to another, unconstrained by the limitation of lightspeed.

And if it does not? Then we are back to the drawing board. Quantum theory is even more subtle and complex than it appears today. The soul-searching and agonizing of the world's greatest physicists for the past sixty years will go on.

5. THE COMING TRIUMPH.

We suddenly had a new view of the world, one which was so radically different from all that came before that the older generation of scientists could never fully comprehend it. Many of them would, in fact, spend their remaining years trying to refute it.

The new theory was full of totally unfamiliar concepts; just as bad, it called for the use of mathematical techniques quite unlike any needed for earlier models of the universe. Worse yet, the mathematics contained at its heart deep paradoxes, with processes of thought that defied all logic.

Only the new, upstart generation of scientists were able to master that new mathematics, resolve those paradoxes, absorb and be comfortable with the new world-view, and finally transform it to a subject easy enough to be taught in any school . . .

I am not referring to quantum theory.

I am talking about the theories of motion and universal gravitation developed by Isaac Newton, and presented to the world in the *Principia Mathematica* in 1687.

Newton introduced the concepts of absolute space and absolute time, alien ideas to people who had always thought in terms of the *relative* positions of objects. He suggested that one set of laws—mathematical laws—governed the whole universe. And he spoke a mathematical language that was too hard for almost all his contemporaries.

Before Newton, astronomical calculations and proofs were geometrical or algebraic. He invented the calculus, and then made it a central mathematical tool, to be learned and used if the new system of the world was to be explored and understood. That same calculus, in its notions of limiting processes, brought into existence philosophical questions and logical paradoxes that would take a century and a half to dispose of.

And it was only the later generations who would become totally comfortable with the use of the calculus. Not until half a century after Newton's death did the theory become, in the hands of Euler and Lagrange and Laplace, the easy tool, powerful and flexible, that it is today.

Scientists have been struggling with quantum theory, what it means, and what lies at its roots, for over half a century. If the earlier revolution in thought that took place in Newton's time is any guide, a century from now our descendants will look back at our difficulties, and wonder what all the fuss was about. They will see in the 1980s and 1990s the clear trail of the most significant papers, the ones that removed the paradoxes and made quantum theory so simple. They will have absorbed the quantum world-view so thoroughly and so early that they will be unable to comprehend the source of our confusions.

Hindsight is a wonderful thing.

But there's no need to envy our great-great-grand-children. A hundred years from now, they will surely be struggling with their own surprises, their own paradoxes, their total inability to fathom some new mystery that grew, oak-like, from a small acorn of in-consistency between observation and theory that we are not even aware of today.

Or do I have it completely wrong? Will they be sitting back, with all of nature fully understood and nothing left to baffle them?

I don't know. But as Pogo remarked in another con-text, either way, it's a mighty sobering thought.

Introduction

A truism of science fiction *(first pointed out, I believe, by the late John Campbell)* is that you can't write a story from the point of view of superhumans; all you can do is watch, helplessly . . .

ISOTOPE

Phillip C. Jennings

"This island's all that's left," Morris shouted over the pounding of diesel-powered pistons. "This, and some wheatland near Winnipeg. The Bolsheviks seized Grandfather's Russian investments, and you Yanks struck the final blow in World War Two."

Dr. Cowansky poked a rebellious lock of red hair back under her salt-ruined scarf. She flinched from a plume of spray and moved closer to her companion. "America? What did *we* do?"

"Lend-lease." The ferry-boat heaved and plunged into Scarnay Sound. Morris spread his legs and leaned doggedly into the wind. "British holdings in the States were confiscated to pay for armaments. You weren't in the war yet, and it had to look like commerce . . . forgive me. I'm boring you."

"Oh, no," the woman yelled politely.

"Go on! You came to wander the wilds of Scarnay, not to hear the ravings of a shabby-genteel relict."

Ilena Cowansky turned and thrust her chilled hands into the pockets of the would-be actor's coat. Lacking a foot of his height, she rose on her toes to perch her chin on his shoulder. "I've come to make you richer," she breathed into his ear. "So for heaven's sake don't let McGarrow's ferry toss me into this maelstrom."

Amazing behavior for a matronly scholar with initials

after her name! "I'll keep my grip on you," Morris answered, stifling any exhibition of nerves. His real mother was dead, and it was a little late now to worry about the psychology of this sudden relationship. "Through the bluster, through the crashing surf . . . imagine the weather here during the winter!"

"You Brits! You've been to our part of the world— you *must* have if you've got land near Winnipeg. This is nothing!"

Morris's sales ploy involved dashes of honesty. It was an untested strategem; until last spring no one had shown interest in the Isle of Scarnay since Father's death. Yet with this overnourished American the papers were all but signed. Or was it *her* technique that proved successful? She carried herself as if *of course* men would find her attractive in knee-boots and culottes, and somehow he did! Her cheery eyes, her lush lips, her ample breasts . . .

"Life's no joy without central heat," he continued. "Bask in this weak August sun, because for months it's hidden by cloud, and the effect on one's mood—"

"But till 1961 you had crofters here—Jesus! Those cliffs!"

The ferry veered from a wall of serried slate. "Sorry!" Captain McGarrow bellowed from the pilothouse. "She's nae made this run in many months!"

Five minutes later the sturdy vessel churned into a triangular cove. Mists parted. Along this haven lay a row of stone houses, flanked by unroofed barns and sheds. Those lichened ruins might have been pre-Celtic, but for the tatty reminder of modernity in their midst—a phone booth, with flecks of red paint clinging to its frame.

"It *was* inhabited, therefore it's inhabitable," Morris pronounced. "Is the Isle of Scarnay what far-flung Blenwick University yearns for as a garrison?"

"Almost certainly. Now it's a matter of furniture, repairs, and new construction," Ilena answered.

"Hike and take notes to your heart's content. I shall wait on yon esplanade and spare my shoes."

The ferry bumped up to a dock-embankment. The roar of the engines dwindled to a contented burble. Ilena shook her head. "I've got a better idea."

McGarrow tooted his departure. For the next half-hour Morris followed Ilena through the fields surrounding the ruined village, spading here and there while she noted the depth of the soil. "You're going to *farm* here?" he inquired.

"Probably not. Farm behavior—that's what *we* do. It wouldn't be part of most other matrices."

Morris leaned on his shovel and laughed. "Clipboard behavior; that's your style! Look, I need a fair idea what's on before I let this land. All it's ever been good for is sheep, and for all I know you'll infect it with anthrax. No, don't cozen me— Last night was spectacular, but I've Grandfather's ghost to answer to. You've been leading me by the nose ever since Gatwick—"

Ilena smiled. "I'm shy about telling you. The money's good, you know, and I'm not working with chemicals, or anything of a military nature."

"You could be the maddest crack-pate in these daft islands. I'd not raise an eyebrow—so long as you're harmless. Go ahead, tell me what's up."

Ilena gestured. "Looks like rain. Is that pub open?"

Morris reached into his jacket and pulled out a pint flask. "It is now."

As they walked he patted through voluminous pockets and shook out an oversized skeleton key. He used it on a monstrous equivalent to a Yale lock, swore, and finally freed the door to Scarnay's one public house.

The wind slammed it open. Something black dropped through a hole in the ceiling and chittered out a broken rear window. Morris and Ilena trod gingerly onto the washboard floor as their eyes adjusted to the shadows. Morris found glasses behind the bar, wiped them clean, and poured two gills of amber fluid. "To mystery," he toasted.

"To Model Theory," Ilena retorted, raising her drink. "Whatever *that* is."

"Oh, it's safe," she answered, removing her scarf and

wringing it dry. "—An inquiry into the creative use of
analogy. Take an electric food mixer: the universe is
composed of one's physical environment—that's the bowl;
and then there's the active element, the beaters; and
the passive—the cake mix. So if you think that way,
you're no environmentalist. You're stuck on the conflict
between active and passive, aggressor and victim—"

"Dear lady, perhaps Cambridge trails Blenwick in
these matters, but I *do* understand analogy."

"Okay. Our limited set of models color our world
view. To free ourselves demands new paradigms. Now
I don't say that as a psychiatrist I'm very creative, but I
do take credit for what happened next."

"You emerged from one such exercise, and had a
brainstorm."

"—To do with quantum theory, and whether anything's there when you're not looking. We hunt elementary particles, and say they exist as particles when
we find them, and as waves when we test for waves.
Particles are emitted by radioactive substances, but we
don't act so subtly when we speak of radium, we just
say it exists, although by decay it becomes another
element—"

"Ilena, if your work involves radioactives . . ."

Dr. Cowansky shook her head. "I'm doing badly. No,
this talk of particles and isotopes . . . I've just applied it
to people. Let's say you're an atom. What do you
emit?"

"A rather personal question!"

"Behavior! And what a nice analogy, because we
don't say behaviors exist, not in ordinary English! We
say *people* exist, and that *what* they are depends on
their behavior! Very well, the obvious question is, what
are the human equivalents of what we call isotopes?"

"Obvious?"

"The answer: we don't have any. Everyone in today's
world emits much the same behavior. To create other
isotopes we'd have to break our matrix, and practice
another conglomerate of behaviors until we'd made ourselves into beings of another sort!"

"So you want this dead village to house some offbeat culture? A Synanon, or a Jonestown?"

Ilena smiled. "You think I'm talking psychobabble. Not true. Your behavior affects the growth of glial cells in your brain. By acting like an impoverished Bertie Wooster, you're hard-wiring in that direction!"

"Bertie . . . !" Morris rippled a few chest muscles. "I fancy myself the Roger Moore type."

"God gave you Roger Moore's body, Morris. You've endowed it with your own Wodehousean soul."

"That's a remarkably intimate thing to say on three days' acquaintance. Fortunately, we upper-class drones don't sulk."

Ilena stepped forward. "Words like 'Jonestown' hurt me too. We're not going to have that kind of people here."

"Who *are* you inviting?"

"Up to six resident scientists—neurologists, anthropologists, and psychiatrists. Perhaps six more caretakers, and twenty or thirty very special guests. The world calls them idiot-savants. Does that disturb you?"

"That you're using idiot-savants to create a new isotope of humanity? Why not call them an isotope and be done? What's the reality, when you use odd words in odd places?"

"An inability to function in *our* world doesn't lead instantly to an ability to function in a new community. There'll be pain and confusion before our subjects project behavior that reinforces a social order of their own."

"It could be said that you're segregating them, building a bedlam-house."

"I hope not, but if we fail . . ."

Danny sat on the rug in the middle of the Observation Room, until last week the nave of Scarnay's desanctified chapel. Time passed; the door opened and shut. The twelve-year-old boy ceased his humming. "Daddy?" he asked, raising his face to the crates in this half-furnished hall, and to the red-headed woman who labored in their midst. "Daddy come?"

"Not today, Danny," Ilena answered, as Morris shed his coat and retreated behind a one-way mirror into the old sacristy. She patted the box he'd brought from the esplanade. "But he sent you a present."

"Daddy come," Danny decided. "What-that?"

"A toy robot, Danny," Ilena answered, opening the box and lifting it out. She winced, though the object was hardly heavy. Morris settled into the 'secret' chair, enjoying the privilege of staring holes in the woman he loved. She was out of shape, last night's soccer match proved that, and today her muscles were hardly up to unpacking. It pleased him that he was superior to her, at least physically, though his pride made him easy to exploit as errand-boy and handyman.

His mind returned. What was this? "It's a programmable toy, Danny. If you tell it how, you can make it walk." An extraordinary thing to say to a lad who'd never graduated out of diapers!

Danny frowned, and looked at the floor. Morris had used his backstage talents to repair the chapel's sprung planking, but the boy found fault with his work. Truth to tell, it *was* lumpish, with throw rugs to conceal the worst defects: a freak floor surrounded by massive walls and plastic/steel institutional furniture.

The robot was plastic too, with fake rivets and purposeless lights. But Danny could touch it inside, and shape, and create . . . when he was done the robot toddled in widening orbits.

"No!" Danny shouted. "Bad!" He grabbed the robot, inserted his keyboard plug, and began again. He took only ten minutes. "Pretty," the boy grinned as the robot walked in a pattern designed to test its skills. The child let his eyes close to slits, and watched.

Ilena pulled out a pocket recorder. "Eleven-ten. I can't see any difference between the first and second programs," she admitted, smiling toward the mirror to acknowledge Morris's presence. "Danny never backs anything up, so we'll never know what was wrong with his first attempt. I'll copy his new program while Dr. Gaffarah takes him on a walk."

Fatima Gaffarah was slight and pretty, but the shift in attention—there'd been something hypnotic about Danny's concentration on the toy robot, and Morris felt the boy's shock as the woman invaded his field of vision. She seemed huge, of a vitality that dwarfed the gawky child . . .

Danny was still cowed as she led him outside. He flinched at the sight of gigantic stone buildings, roughly hewn, heavy and cavernous—for so the houses of Scarnay appeared as she tugged him down the chapel steps. By actor's empathy Morris saw the place through Danny's eyes. As he adopted the role of child-imbecile, the village transformed into an Expressionistic movie set: like the background of *The Cabinet of Dr. Caligari.*

"Would you like to go exploring?" Fatima asked. The Syrian anthropologist enjoyed wandering through vacant barns and gardens. Danny shivered, and Morris knew how the boy felt. A perversion to go inside enormous crudities, dark and weathered with age.

They walked toward the lych-gate. Morris felt moved to protest, but how would he explain . . .

Ilena slipped by, and stuck her head outside the old chapel. "It's a bright morning," she shouted. "The first nice day we've had. Why not take him up the hill? Don't hurry. We'll delay lunch."

She turned to address Morris in a quieter voice. "My back's killing me, and we've two arrivals today, by the boat that's taking you home. You've been so helpful . . . could I ask one last favor? How are you at massage?"

Dr. Gaffarah returned twenty minutes after Morris rang the chapel bell for lunch. Her olive face was puffy with weeping. "He won't come back!" she moaned. "He . . . he hit me when I tried to make him—"

Forgetting her stiff muscles, Ilena dropped her plate and ran from the church. She lumbered up the slopes of Scarn Fell at a remarkable pace for one so short and stocky. Fatima shouted directions as she struggled to keep up. Morris loped by, saving his breath as they wasted theirs shouting "Danny! Danny?"

He overshot and jogged back down, a little less the hero. Ilena found the boy where Fatima had left him, lying on ground so overgrown he might have been hiding. "Danny!" the psychiatrist wheezed. "You . . . you—"

Danny crouched, then leapt into the air, arms wide. He landed, and laughed, and crouched again. "He's never done anything this *physical* before!" Fatima whispered.

Ilena bit her lip. "The is the beginning; what I was looking for. Here's where we start pulling back, not imposing our own matrix. It goes against instinct, but maybe we'd best leave him be for a time and see what happens."

II

"—in the middle of the stage, with the cushion still smoldering, I with my fire-hose and John in drag, when the constable burst in with his note pad at the ready. 'Who are you?' he asked. John pulled up to his full six foot five, and answered:

" '*I* am an eNORRRmous virgin!' —Uh, you're not laughing."

Ilena's chair creaked as she raised her glass. "Morris, if they ask, you never once saw my lips touch whiskey."

"Poor girl," Morris sympathized, pouring a tot in response to her gesture. He looked around the former pub. "Ice? Have you Americanized this place in the months I've been gone?"

Ilena snorted. "Bad enough to train myself out of interfering, to let Danny and his friends wander the Fell and choose what to eat, without hovering with blankets and flu shots and chicken soup. Bad enough, and then one of us gets nervous and goes up through the rain to do a body count, and we always come up short and get in a dither . . ."

"You provide shelters—"

"They ignore them. We're going to wire one and put in video games. Maybe that'll do the trick."

"Any signs of, ah, 'culture?' "

Ilena laughed bitterly. "Danny's bunch are given to tonal babble. They're peaceful, disinclined to make tools, and have no concept of past and future. Their memory doesn't work like ours. They look at you, and memory tells them what you're like, but omits the fact that you gave them a toy a few hours ago. They posture and dance, and make music, and program computers, and make plants grow. They'll stare at a plant for hours, and reach out and *do* something, and then watch some more, as if they'd just programmed it somehow . . ."

Morris rubbed his chin. "Is this what you were looking for?"

"Sure, only in a population of seven, with so much being non-quantifiable . . . you don't have to believe me."

"What about the other group?"

"The indoors bunch—the antisocial rogues. They're peaceful in isolation, but clouded by passions when put together. I'm reminded of bulls in rut. Group Two has more skill with language; they're purposive, they use commands. And they make things—rings and puppets!"

"Hmm."

"Group One performed miracles when we introduced programmable robots. We're going to do the same with Group Two, only we'll give them wires and switches and batteries. They've already got that reputation. We're expecting they'll build some pretty exotic toys."

"Cheer up, then! You're on your way."

Ilena scowled. "I'm also ripe for crucifixion. All these kids have parents. No matter that they've signed releases and demonstrated enthusiasm for our ideas: notwithstanding the British tradition of public school child abuse . . .

"These kids were institutionalized for years. That's the standard we're half expected to meet. Instead we're letting them run naked. What can I do? If I put 'em in diapers and stick 'em in dorms it'll be like any old-

fashioned asylum. And yet, without precautions, one of
Danny's lot might wander over a cliff, and I'd be blamed,
because I was so infatuated with *theory* that I ignored
my human responsibilities!"

Morris pursed his lips. "I wonder if the lessor has any
obligations . . ."

"Thinking of betraying me? Kicking us out so you
won't get in trouble?"

Morris closed his eyes. As he opened them again
Ilena smiled grimly. "Try to break that lease. I'll take
you to court, and my victory will make others more
cautious about crossing swords with me."

"I wonder whether you're human! How can you turn
on me after all our intimacies? Well, I've one way of
disinvolving myself. Have you thought of *buying* Scarnay?
I could use the money."

Ilena softened. She gestured him close and gave him
a kiss. "I can't afford it, Morris. Those video games
blew my budget."

"Set up a software house. Those programs your wards
write are pretty spectacular. You might market them."

Ilena blinked at the idea, then frowned. "Another
complication in my life."

"—And there's that goo, that yellow vegetable pig-
ment. Anything that can liquefy fifty-year-old plaster
must have uses. Listen, Ilena. You want to create a new
human subspecies—well and good. Let your cultures
pay their way in this world. Let *them* own this island,
and I'll be free—"

"Exploitation."

"Not if every penny of profit benefits this show here.
Think of it—your own island, your own boat, better
shelters, more supplies! You could afford to put walls
around the Fell!"

"Any energy I divert to these ends deprives my kids
of their rights . . . let me tell you a story. This doctor
was curious about the infant nursing response. At his
urging some young mothers made their babies lap milk
instead of sucking. A year later he moved away—no
follow-up, can you imagine? One of those babies was

me. Now I've launched a program designed to affect peoples' health, and I damn well better SEE that impact. I can't be in London debating ad campaigns!"

"But *I* can. I'm rather well trained for the role," Morris responded. "Does that surprise you?"

"Why sell Scarnay to escape liability, and then reinvolve yourself?"

"Income. Fascination for what you're doing. If I *am* liable for your follies, I might as well take an active part. Given how my stage career's progressing, it's this or wheat farming in Manitoba."

Morris's whirlwind labors bore fruit. Scarnay Enterprises became an entity within the month, while chemists struggled to analyze the various elements constituting the solvent he dubbed 'Plasmuck.' Thanks to the duration of these efforts, the company might have fallen deeply into the red, for the Software Division barely edged toward profitability in a market bled by piracy, and was in no condition to cover research costs. Luckily, one of the rogue savants of Group Two saved the day.

Little Jurgen's toy looked like a mass of gold necklaces, such as burden the necks of certain extravagant Hollywood natives. It weighed ten kilos, and when the top end was flung into the air, its links fell into rigidity in the shape of a helix. In fact, it was a portable stairs, more attractive and easier to carry than a ladder—sturdier too, if care was taken not to trip the crucial link.

Risking nervous exhaustion, Morris motored from Ayr to Cambridge to London, and saw to it that the Loftlace Ladder was quickly patented, a triumph that paid the costs of a re-extension of phone service to Scarnay. Meanwhile, the chemists of Ayr Polytechnic, moonlight employees of Scarnay Enterprises, finally cracked the secret of Plasmuck. Facing its third quarter, Morris's company found itself credit-worthy beyond the actor's dreams, and he was free to return to his island. He moved his office next to Ilena's in an upstairs room in Scarnay's old pub.

He did business by wandering from the Observation Room up to the remote camera stations of the Fell, talking to specialists like Dr. Gaffarah as workmen strung cables through the foliage down to the chapel. Fatima's enthusiasm for Group One's musical talents prompted him to call a London recording studio, and find out what could be done if Danny's group were given proper instruments.

His door was open. Ilena heard talk of sound chambers. She squeezed into his guest chair. After he rang off she shook her head. "It won't work."

Morris stared, and wondered if he was still in love with her. The power to inflame his ardor had been hers to turn on or off, but she'd not used it for so long . . . "Why not?"

"One, staged events are coercive, and interfere with their efforts to build their own matrix. Two, for the last month we've never found more than three of Danny's bunch at a time. We've gotten better at combing Scarn Fell—I could walk the place blindfolded. The problem is, they've gotten better at hiding, too."

"*That* much better? There must be caves."

"They could be using that yellow solvent to excavate a tunnel system. I wish that were true; it would mean they were out of the rain. Besides, what an impressive feat!"

"You're sure they're all . . . there? I mean—"

"They seem to rotate into visibility, if you'll permit such language. When Mr. O'Shea came yesterday to see Colleen, we had the devil of a time keeping him diverted while we ranged the island. Then today little Colleen pops up, vacant-eyed and innocent— I hate parents!"

"It did seem like something was stirring."

"We found a muu-muu and stuck her inside. I don't know if her dad noticed. She's got quite a tummy."

"Pregnant!" Morris rubbed his nose. "This is serious."

"I'm half expecting the O'Sheas to pull Colleen out. If they knew—"

"Are you going to let the Fell kids birth themselves? Are you that far gone?"

Ilena fell silent. "I . . . I don't think so. I'm having second thoughts. What are we learning here? We time them, and videotape them, and nothing we do captures their progress. Now they've begun to tease us, quick-silvering around and making things impossible. What's frustrating is that their ability to dance around us is our only real proof that they're maturing. *Something's* going on—I feel it like tension in the air."

"*Can* you dissuade them? They've gotten more talented this last half year. They're capable of anger. They might make things difficult."

"Difficult!" Ilena snorted. "Colleen's baby—am I really creating a new culture here, or are *we* responsible, in loco parentis? Hell, who am I kidding? These kids would starve but for our jugs of milk and boxes of fruit and nuts. —Please, let's change the subject."

Morris tossed a card across his desk. Ilena plucked it up. "The British Faerie Society?"

"More trouble. One of your workmen's been telling tales, and they think that—well, Britain has fairies—you've harnessed them to slave for Scarnay Enterprises."

"Huh?"

"Danny and his gang. The society have found out they're fairies. They're demanding an Enquiry."

Ilena laughed. "Little old ladies in tennis shoes. I wish . . ."

"What?"

"There's all sorts of precedent for preserving wilderness for animals to live naturally. If we could say that Danny's lot represents Natural Man . . ."

"Naked, grubby, skulking computer hackers with fifty-word vocabularies and no toilet training—a lost population of aboriginal pixies! Only I don't think their parents would play along."

"Dammit! How am I supposed to do my job?" Ilena's mind reverted to an earlier topic. "They flicker in and out of reality like fireflies, and God only knows . . ."

Ilena rose, and muttered off. Morris failed to find her

before the ferry arrived, and set forth on his weekly visit to Ayr full of misgivings. That night he called from the mainland. "Ilena? Do they still drink our milk? Do they still depend on us for food?"

"Yes." Her voice sounded listless.

"Then they need us. Good. Look, we've got to expect shocks now and again—"

Ilena began to cry. "How can I take care of Colleen? I had so little control to begin with, what with their parents and all. Now the kids are playing hide-and-seek, and I have to go along because we don't dare let them perceive us as enemies. It's all blowing up, Morris. I might as well call Colleen's parents and have them come for her."

Indeed, when Morris arrived at the ferry-dock next afternoon he found Mr. and Mrs. O'Shea standing in McGarrow's office. "You have business on Scarnay?" the woman inquired suspiciously.

"I have that honor."

"Don't you recognize the president of Scarnay Enterprises?" Colleen's father growled. "Remember that picture? Sir, I hope your company is prospering. You're going to need a lot of money."

Morris shifted uncomfortably. "Yes, indeed," Mr. O'Shea waved a meaty, calloused finger. "—Child support, maybe for life. What I can't feature is, why did Dr. Cowansky let things come to such a pass?"

"I take it she called you."

"That she did, to come sort out the wreckage."

It was too much. Morris bolted out the door. Enquiries, pregnancies, civil actions, children running naked on the edge of the Norwegian Sea . . . He'd been warned, and yet he'd involved himself for the sake of a fat American psychiatrist too career-obsessed to return his love!

Miserably he waited on the dock for Captain McGarrow to open his boat for boarding. Afterward he took refuge on the foredeck. The ferry's engines thrummed, the vessel churned forward. He heard a few shrill syllables, and turned. To his surprise, the O'Sheas were tottering

in his direction. ". . . stink!" Mrs. O'Shea complained
over the noise of the engines. ". . . can't imagine why . . ."

Acting as if they'd escaped, they carried with them a
foul stench of pig dung. "Sorry!" Morris gasped, and
fled aft toward the interior compartment.

Had it been some stink-bomb prank? But for a mild
mix of pipe smoke, wet wool, and fuel oil, there was no
odor among McGarrow's other passengers. What was
going on? Morris moved to the forward window to
observe the O'Sheas and assess their mood.

Imagine handing them the gentle Colleen! Morris
remembered a girl with eyes rather too widely set,
cowering in her crib, then dancing on Scarn Fell. Now
she'd return to Dublin, to live with her parents and
their restless-tiger moods. Indeed, they seemed to be
snarling now, more than talking. Even their postures
were becoming feral . . .

The ferry moved into the violent waters of Scarnay
Sound. A wave crashed against the prow, filling the air
with spume. Water sheeted down the window, and
then Morris could see again. The foredeck was empty.
The O'Sheas were gone without a trace.

He ran outside and circled forward. It must be true!
"Man overboard!" he shouted, but McGarrow was already cutting power to the engines.

"I tell you, they vanished!" Captain McGarrow repeated to the scientists assembled in the old Scarnay
pub. "They weren't washed overboard: they weren't
even *there*! I saw them pop out of God's air just as the
wave hit. They took me mast bits with 'em! A ton of
metal, clean gone! She's nae the same foredeck she was
before!"

"Morris?"

The young actor-capitalist shook his head. "My van-
tage wasn't as good. All I know is we circled for an
hour. Nothing."

Ilena stood. "We've called the police. They'll know
what to do. Meanwhile, it's time we collect our charges.
The project is over. Done. Kaput."

"We haven't been able to *find* them these twenty hours," Dr. Gaffarah complained. "What makes you think we'll be any more successful—"

"I DON'T KNOW! We're dealing with disappearance as a phenomenon. None of us wanted to admit it, but I'm throwing in the towel. Yes, Danny's bunch can vanish, and it's not just a cute way of saying they know how to hide. They really *can* disappear! So what are the rules? Do they take turns? It seemed like that up until today, didn't it? Let's work on that assumption!" Ilena's shoulders slumped. "It's all we can do."

But since Captain McGarrow was anxious to depart, Ilena felt obliged to monitor the telephone. In her place Morris went out with the rest and joined the hunt. He followed Fatima up the street, past the chapel, through fields blooming exuberantly with vegetation more appropriate to South Devon than to these northern islands.

The scientists climbed Scarn Fell on legs grown muscular, moving at a frantic tempo, crying names ever more distantly, in tones of fondness and anxiety. Meanwhile the wind blew, and clouds piled darkly about the peak.

Once more Morris felt as he had when little Danny had taken over his actor's mind. Empathically he let the gusts transform—yes, they were alive with import, godwinds imbued with terror, manipulation, and the thrill of the hunt; and he was the mad director of some Expressionistic film, a Faustus shouting meaningless demands as they turned into whirling hurricanes of potentiality. Anything might happen, if he only had the strength . . .

But Morris had not spent ten months hiking these slopes. He lagged behind, and sat, and pondered as he caught his breath.

Around him vegetation grew rank. Ilena's team included no botanists, and the miracles twining and blossoming here had never been cataloged, nor even studied. The wind made the branches dance. Webs of light intersected, shadow-structures rose and collapsed as bolts of clipboard-scientist willfulness trudged uphill, shattering crystalline structures and trailing widening wakes of newness. Nodes sparked into actuality while consequences rippled off into the future, swelling into turbulent vastness. Few sequences held solid, and those shifted in value as their environment changed, echoing in multiple versions, manifold futures, none more certain than its predecessor.

Morris stood. He had no words for what was happening, save that time was twisting into a loop around him, a closing trap which would condemn him to live these moments like a scratched record for all eternity. He looked around, saw a nearby vector of normalcy, and stumbled toward it. As he declared his loyalties the wildness spurned him, and he felt more urgently the need to join with his own kind, to repair this great rent in reality, or at least ride out the storm . . . Fatima traced back along her former upward course, and fell into his arms. "What about the others?" she asked.

"They've been swallowed up," Morris whispered, for now the ripples of their passage diminuendoed and were gone. He looked around. The two of them made a reality, and this part of Scarn Fell looked almost normal, an island afloat in howling menace.

Fatima shouted the names of her co-workers. Meanwhile chaos took strength around them. Once more the winds, the dancing shadows, the brachiating webs of manic greenery . . . "Let's go back to the village," she pleaded. "They'll come down and join us if we believe hard enough . . ."

"I don't understand," Ilena repeated.

"Where's your scotch?" Morris asked, tearing off his windbreaker. He felt hollow with guilt: on the way downhill he'd glanced at Fatima, at the wisp of moustache on her lip—a bare act of noticing something out of context—and now the woman was as hirsute as . . . but it wouldn't do to exaggerate in a world where tall tales were coming true! "I need a drink," he gasped, terrified by an idea. She'd looked at him, too. Had she reshaped his features? Was he a caricature of himself?

"The other scientists," Fatima wheezed, still innocent of what he'd done to her. "—Unless they come down soon, I'd say they were gone, into the same . . . place . . . as the O'Sheas. Danny and his gang can deal with couples. They could have swallowed us up if they had wanted to."

"Swallow? But where would we go? Where *is* this place?"

"It's right here," Fatima insisted, "like reality made liquid."

Morris raised the bottle, and Ilena wrested it from his trembling hands. "Come now, you two, there's a storm brewing outside—that's enough to delay our colleagues."

Morris shook his head. "Take us seriously! Your human isotopes, your concentration of idiot-savants—they've done something on Scarn Fell. The place isn't safe anymore."

"The Sound isn't safe either," Fatima pointed out.

"But maybe the village is!" Ilena whispered. "We've got our Group Two kids here, a different isotope, a kind of damper . . . YES! I never went that far before! I never took the analogy all the way!"

"What do you mean?"

"Danny's group is—radioactive! The seven together, concentrated long enough to learn new ways—it's something just short of a fission reaction. Destabilizing behavior, like in a nuclear pile! They've irradiated the neighborhood and weakened reality . . ."

"Now's a hell of a time to play with your theory!"

"Shut up! If we're ever going to fix things—let's trace the implications. First, not everyone is equally real. Life's a series of tests. We exist when we pass, but fifty percent of radioactive atoms decay during their half-lives. Normal people have long half-lives—most of them pass most tests most of the time."

"Except for that electrician we kept trying to get out here," Morris giggled lightheadedly. "Never in his office, never made the boat . . ."

Ilena began to pace. "But there are humans of other kinds, just as there are radioactive isotopes. You know what I'm talking about—the kids out there: elves, fairies—old words for creatures that during their heyday were all too dubious, and now can't be found at all. As time went on they failed our reality tests, first half the time, then half the remainder, until . . ."

"Elves!" Morris suppressed a nervous laugh.

Ilena stood, and pointed up the hill. "I created an environment that's been known before; a soft spot, a concentration. Now we're all irradiated. We're all hot, a little contagious, less real, ready to spread idiot-savantism and propagate new instabilities, unless we stay here and let ourselves be contained."

"Stay?" Fatima shook her head violently. "Never!"

"Consider our options. Danny's gang is gone. So are five scientists, and the O'Sheas. What are the police going to do? Who's responsible? Me! Only I'm not facing the music. I've blown my career. Why shouldn't I go up there? I might put together a new reality . . . even if I can't, things will cool off after a few years, and maybe I'll pop back into our world again. Morris, is there a statute of limitations in this country?"

Morris frowned. "What will you eat?"

"Will I *need* to? I don't know."

"I'm coming along."

"No, Morris. I never loved you enough to deserve that."

"I wonder if you loved me at all."

Ilena's features shifted with a mix of emotions, as if the turbulence outside reached into her soul. She grabbed her shawl and started for the door. Morris took her arm. "Don't! You haven't been out there. You haven't seen . . . it's like taking refuge in the jaws of a wolf. Prison would be better!"

Ilena shivered. "I made this happen. It's gone wrong, but I'm still a little proud of what I've done. Excuse the mad scientist act, but if reality goes plastic, there's a chance I can shape it and tame your wolf. If the phone still works, tell the police I'm off to do my best. Let them think well of me, instead of charging me with negligence. I couldn't stand that!"

She pulled free, and ran out the door. Morris stared after. Would he ever find Ilena again if he lost her now? He stepped outside. Reality was a little soft even here, rippling at the edges enough for him to see two futures segue together in the blue-green evening glow. In one he ran and caught up to her, to live with his love in a dreamscape of chaos, where his unleashed id would shape her into a paleolithic mother-goddess, mammoth and oozing with milk, while he shrank into a baby. No, she wasn't for him—theirs could never be an equal relationship, no more than he could couple with the hairy ape-spider that once would have been Dr. Gaffarah . . .

He turned back into the pub and closed his eyes against the vision of Fatima's mustachioed face. "Let's call McGarrow, and get the Group Two kids together before it's too late."

"I heard your footsteps jogging down the street."

"It wasn't me. All I want is to get out of here."

Escorted by a police boat, the ferry dieseled up to the Scarnay dock. Signal beams swung to ward off the half-formed whimsies that slouched beyond the periphery, as a huddled mass of children and caretakers moved aboard, their way lit by the bonfire that warmed them these two hours, and kept the madness at bay.

Relieved at proof that civilization survived, Morris was chilled by the suspicion that the authorities would make him help in their enquiries, forcing him to troop them up Scarn Fell in this lumpish, archaic dark. Their words dispelled his fear. "Pretty bad on the way across— sirens and sea serpents. Worse here, eh? How long's this going to last?"

"I don't know. Is it safe on the other side?"

"So far. The evidence to date . . . but enough of that." The constable gestured toward a companionway. His superior flipped open his notebook and pulled out a pen. "If you're prepared to make a statement—"

His was a long story. Morris finished on the sane side

of the sound, in McGarrow's office, in the hearing of a deputy from the Ministry of Environment. Mr. Rhys lay down the inspector's notebook and looked up. "How long do you estimate this hole in reality will persist?"

"From the legends . . . the better part of a lifetime," Morris answered hoarsely.

"And meanwhile, those who go and come may infect the rest of us, increasing the chance of new combinations, new concentrations, new holes?"

"That's the theory. Our children—look, rather than be sent back, I'd have a vasectomy."

The deputy sighed. "Quarantine is so expensive. Sea patrols, radar installations . . ."

"Begging your pardon, sir," spoke the constable. "Them old legends—the bad things, the fey things . . . they can be slain. Send in a questing hero—"

"I cut my teeth on green belts, council housing schemes, and motorways," Mr. Rhys hissed. "Now I'm expected to recommend creation of a bleeding Division of Knight-Errantry?" He looked at Morris. "You. You look the part."

"I'm not going to Scarnay. Send me to prison if you like."

"Oh, we can do worse than that! Besides, you're tainted. Where's your public spirit, man!"

Morris stood, weaving slightly from weariness. "Am I under arrest?"

"Don't press us," the inspector warned.

"—Because if I'm not, I'm tired. I want to go to bed. One last warning: send some psychopathic dragon-slayer off to Scarnay, and you'll see things out of his subconscious that'll make what's happened so far look like a picnic."

He stumbled out the door. Out across the water, an auroral mist whirled like a water sprite, lofting into a wraith that glowed and beckoned. Woman? Child? Morris turned, reached in his pants for his car keys, and tottered in the other direction, toward the parking lot. His engine caught. He revved it a few seconds, and then drove off on the first leg of his journey, thinking glad thoughts of farm life in distant Canada.

Introduction

If there was a Big Bang, what preceded it? Everything or Nothing? At age 14 I decided that the answer was self-evident. (I had just discovered Occam's Razor, and so thought I was old enough to shave the Barber.)

After all, to assume that before the Bang there was nothing one must import the otherwise absent entity Creation into one's Universe of Discourse*, and while Creation may be no more absurd than Existence, the latter need not be posited since it is already a given. Thus an oscillating universe (expansion, contraction, Bang . . . expansion, contraction, Bang) is preferable as Least Hypothesis.

Does that logic hold? I dunno . . . but the 14-year old who lurks within is pleased that the physicists have at last come round.

---

*Yes, I thought like that, but as Bob Dylan might say, "I was so much older then; I'm younger than that now."

THE REVERSING UNIVERSE

John Gribbin

Twenty-five years ago, there was a great debate in astronomy about the origin of the universe. Some cosmologists argued that the universe was eternal and unchanging in its overall appearance, and that although it was expanding, with galaxies moving apart from one another, new matter was continually being created in the gaps between galaxies, at just the right rate to maintain the status quo. Others said that the universe must indeed be getting less dense as it expanded; that no new matter was created; that it must have been much denser in the distant past, and had been born in a superdense fireball, the Big Bang, some fifteen thousand million years ago. The Big Bang theory won the day, on the basis of observations that proved the universe was denser in the past, and that theory has not seriously been questioned since the late 1960s. But now, another debate is raging, concerning the ultimate fate of the universe.

In the new debate, the disagreement is between those cosmologists who argue that the universal expansion must continue forever, with galaxies getting ever farther apart as the aeons go past, and with stars eventually exhausting their nuclear fuel to flicker and die as cooling embers, leaving darkness throughout the expanding emptiness. Others argue, by contrast, that there is so much matter in the universe that the pull of gravity acting on everything must eventually halt the expansion and turn it around, so that the universe must collapse back into a superdense state reminiscent of the Big Bang of creation—a "Big Crunch." The difference is like that between a rocket launched from Earth with more than escape velocity that voyages eternally into space, and one launched with less than escape velocity that plunges back to Earth. But which theory is right?

As yet, astronomers have only been able to identify one-tenth of the amount of matter needed to "close" the universe, and make it recollapse. This doesn't resolve the puzzle, since there might be a lot more dark matter out there that we cannot see. But there is a forty-year-old, neglected theory of electromagnetic interactions that tells us the universe *must* recollapse; and this idea is now being revived in the context of the latest cosmological theories of the Big Bang, which independently predict the same thing. The implications for our understanding of the nature of time, however, are too much even for many cosmologists to stomach— and they have notoriously vivid imaginations.

Stephen Hawking, of the University of Cambridge, is widely regarded as the nearest thing we have to another Einstein. He has thought deeply about these mysteries, and has proposed that time has no meaning at what we are used to thinking of as the moment of creation. He makes an analogy with the surface of a sphere, like the surface of the Earth, and points out that even though there is no edge to such a surface, the way we measure directions becomes confused at the poles. There is no direction "north" of the North Pole, just as there is no time "before" the Big Bang. But that doesn't mean, in either case, that there is an "edge" —what mathematicians call a singularity—at the point where we choose to start our measurements. The direction of time, says Hawking, simply corresponds to the direction in which space gets bigger. Extending the analogy, he says our expanding universe is like a series of lines of latitude drawn around the pole, with small circles at high latitudes and bigger circles at lower latitudes. Each circle, a single closed line, represents all three dimensions of space as we know it.

Confused? Things get more confused at the equator. "South" of the equator, the circles get *smaller* the farther we move from the North Pole. Extending the analogy, the arrow of time must reverse in the universe as it shifts from a state of expansion to one of collapse. This is the bizarre requirement that has revived interest in some curious cosmological ideas that relate time, the universe, and thermodynamics in a way that Lewis Carroll would undoubtedly have approved of.

At the North Pole, there is no direction "north," nor indeed "east" or "west;" all directions away from the pole point to the south. At the moment of creation, there is no time "past," and all arrows of time point outwards into the future. The future is the direction in which the universe is expanding. On Earth, we have a similar confusion at the South Pole, where all directions are now "north." In Hawking's universe, however, the arrow of time must *still* be pointing in the direction of expansion, even at the equivalent of the South Pole. Time flows in the opposite sense as the universe collapses.

Or, to put it in slightly more "scientific" language, the universe is finite in both space and time, and is time-symmetric, mirroring its own behavior on either side of the moment of maximum expansion.

From our perspective, the contracting half of such a universe would be strange indeed. Instead of nuclear fusion reactions producing energy that makes stars hot and releases photons into space, there would be a flow of photons *out* from cold surfaces, across space and down onto the surfaces of the stars. The arriving photons would combine with one another in just the right way to break up complex nuclei into their constituent parts. On the surface of a planet like ours, the actions of wind and weather would conspire to build mountains out of sediment, with rivers running backwards. And the behavior of living things would be even more bizarre. The processes we think of as decay would act in reverse, drawing together scattered material to form the living body of an old animal—such as a human being—who would grow younger as time passed, and whose bodily functions would be almost too bizarre to contemplate. (Almost, but not quite, Philip Dick had a brave stab at it in his science fiction story *Counter-Clock World*.)

It *sounds* crazy. But as Paul Davies, of the University of Newcastle upon Tyne, has stressed, it is odd that the description should be so laughable, since it is simply a description of our present world in time-reversed language. The world of the contracting universe is no more remarkable than our everyday world—it *is* our everyday world. The difference in the description is purely semantic. Furthermore, says Davies (in his book *Space and Time in the Modern Universe*, Cambridge University Press):

> A human being in a reversed-time world would also have a reversed brain, reversed senses, and presumably a reversed mind. He would remember the future and predict the past, though his language would not convey the same meaning of these words as it does to us. In all respects his world would appear to him the same as ours does to us.

In other words, any intelligent beings occupying either half of the universe will "see" the flow of time as from a more dense state to a less dense state, as Hawking requires. In each half of the universe, the inhabitants will think that they are living in the first half, the expansion phase, and that this will be followed by a collapse. In that sense, such a closed universe contains *two* beginnings, and no end!

The questions raised by this kind of model are uncomfortable. *How* does time reverse when the universe is at a state of maximum expansion? Does it happen suddenly, all over the universe, at the same instant? How can it know when to do so, everywhere at the same instant, if no signal can travel faster than light? Or could there be a transition period, in which time runs slower and slower, stops, and then reverses? Either prospect worries many physicists, who find these problems sufficient reason to discard the closed universe idea and to accept the idea of a unique big bang, with an eternal expansion and a unique arrow of time pointing always in the same direction, instead of one which circles back on itself. But then they are left with a singularity at the moment of creation, an edge of space-time, and the puzzle of the moment of creation itself and what went "before."

Which set of puzzles you are happier to live with is largely a matter of personal choice at present. But there is independent evidence, largely ignored for forty years—an electromagnetic arrow of time that also points in the direction of expansion and which can best be explained in terms of a model very like Hawking's universe.

ABSORBING THE PAST

Like Newton's laws of motion, the equations that describe the behavior of electromagnetic radiation have no in-built arrow of time. They work as well describing events that move backward in time, from our perspective, as they do describing events that flow forward in time. The best way to see this is by looking at the electromagnetic radiation in terms of waves. Quantum theory tells us that at this level of reality it is possible to treat such phenomena either in terms of waves or as particles (photons), depending on circumstances; the wave description, which is appropriate here, uses a set of equations discovered in the nineteenth century by the Scot James Clerk Maxwell, and named, in his honor, Maxwell's equations. Among other things, they describe how the signal from your local TV station gets from the transmitter aerial to the antenna on the roof of your house.

These equations describe changing electric and magnetic fields moving through space at the speed of light. To get a picture of what is going on, imagine a stone dropped into a still pond. Ripples spread out across the pond, away from the point where the stone was dropped in. In a roughly similar fashion, a wire that carries an alternating electric current, or a TV or radio mast driven by such a current, radiates electromagnetic waves outward in all directions. It takes a certain amount of time for the wave to reach a point in space away from the wire, or antenna, and so physicists call this kind of behavior "retarded" wave motion. Maxwell's equations describe, perfectly, the way waves of this kind propagate. But they do more.

There are, in fact, two sets of Maxwell's equations (strictly speaking, two sets of *solutions* to those equations). The second set describes the time-reversed version of the picture I have just painted, in which electromagnetic waves move in toward a wire (or antenna) from the far reaches of the universe, converging perfectly in step and combining to create an alternating electric current in the wire. Because such waves disturb space far from the wire *before* they reach the wire itself, they are called "advanced" waves. We never see advanced waves in the real world, but the symmetry of Maxwell's equations implies that both are equally valid. The absence of advanced waves is a feature of our universe that defines an electromagnetic arrow of time, seemingly independent of the thermodynamic arrow, but pointing in the same direction. "Forward" in time is the direction corresponding to waves that move outward from their source. And, it turns out, the fact that we never see incoming radiation tells us something fundamental about the nature of our universe and its fate.

I have described the two solutions to Maxwell's equations in terms of waves moving out from, or coming in to, a source. But another way of looking at this is to say that the advanced wave is also moving "outward" from the source but "backward" in time. This is a better way of looking at things, since it emphasizes the fact that the electric current in the wire is indeed the source of the wave, its reason for existence. Many physicists are happy to dismiss the absence of advanced waves in our universe simply on these grounds—"everybody knows" that effects always *follow* their causes, and, indeed, this is a principle dignified by the name "causality." Causes come first, effects later, and so "of course" we don't see advanced waves. But this is no more than semantics, raising the question *why* do effects always follow causes in our universe? We are back, straight away, to the arrow of time!

In the 1940s, two American physicists, John Wheeler and Richard Feynman, were investigating the problem of providing a good mathematical description of the way in which charged particles, like electrons, interact with electromagnetic fields. Their efforts met with only partial success, but led them to develop a mathematical treatment of advanced and retarded waves which gives full weight to both sets of solutions to Maxwell's equations, and lays the responsibility for the electromagnetic arrow of time squarely on the structure of the universe at large. The Wheeler-Feynman theory has never made a major impact on science, although it is often discussed as an intriguing byway of mathematical physics. Perhaps, though, in the light of recent developments in cosmology, it is time it was taken more seriously.

When an alternating current generates electromagnetic waves, it does so because electrons in the wire carrying the current are accelerated. In this case, they are being jiggled back and forth, but they would also generate an electromagnetic wave if they were accelerated continuously in a straight line, or around a large loop. Equally, a charged particle that "feels" the passage of an electromagnetic wave will move in response. For simplicity, the Wheeler-Feynman approach can best be understood in terms of the behavior of a single charged particle (perhaps an electron) being accelerated in the universe, and the response of all the other charged particles in the universe to the wave generated by that electron.

Since there is no asymmetry in Maxwell's equations, Wheeler and Feynman took both the advanced and retarded solutions and combined them, in equal proportions, to provide a description of the way the accelerated charged particle interacts with the electromagnetic field. The accelerated electron creates, in equal measure, a retarded wave moving outward into the future, and an advanced wave moving back into the past. This advanced wave will arrive at other charged particles, and make them move, *before* the original electron is accelerated. But, and now things begin to get complicated, this means that the other particles are accelerated, all at different times depending on when the waves reach them—both before the original electron is accelerated, and, a suitable time later, when the retarded wave eventually reaches them, *after* the original electron is accelerated.

Each charged particle in turn, when it is given a jostle by either the advanced or the retarded wave, will itself generate both advanced and retarded waves. The result, from the acceleration of one electron for a short time, is a complex sea of overlapping electromagnetic waves, both retarded and advanced, spreading out from all the other charged particles and moving both forwards and backwards in time.

But all these waves have a common origin in the motion of the original electron, and are therefore very similar to one another. They will interfere with one another, following well-established mathematical rules, in the same way that the ripples from two pebbles dropped into a pond will interfere with one another to produce a new pattern of ripples. And all of this complexity of interactions will happen instantaneously, from the point of view of the original electron, as a simple example makes clear.

Suppose another charged particle is just far enough

away from the electron that the electromagnetic wave, traveling at the speed of light, takes one hour to cross the gap. This will trigger a response from the second particle, part of which will be in the form of an advanced wave, moving backwards in time at the speed of light, and arriving at the original electron one hour before it left the second particle—just at the instant that the original electron is radiating! The same logic applies to all particles, at all distances from the original electron. How, in these strange circumstances, will the two waves (and all the other waves from all the other charged particles) interact? The great achievement of the work by Wheeler and Feynman was to show, using some rather hairy mathematics, that all of the advanced waves cancel out, under suitable circumstances. The advanced waves from the rest of the charged particles in the universe not only cancel out the advanced waves from the original electron, they exactly double up the strength of its retarded wave, so that instead of a 50–50 contribution from each of the solutions to Maxwell's equations, we are left with a single, full-size contribution from the retarded wave alone. But the cost of doing this places restrictions on the universe, which made the theory look unattractive, until recently.

The Wheeler-Feynman solution to the puzzle of why we don't see advanced waves works perfectly if the universe they are describing with their equations is mathematically equivalent to a closed box, like the closed systems beloved of thermodynamicists. The opaque walls of the box provide the exact response required to cancel out the advanced waves and boost the retarded waves to full strength, but the trick doesn't work if the box is open and energy can get out of it. If radiation can escape from an accelerated particle and disappear into space without ever meeting another charged particle, then, clearly, there is no scope for the production of the advanced waves from the future of that particle which will cancel out its own advanced waves. In technical terms, for the Wheeler-Feynman trick to work, there must be a "perfect absorber" in the future of our

universe—the universe itself must be a "closed box."
And that can only happen if the universe is destined to
recollapse.

What happens to the radiation moving outward from
all the stars in the universe today in such a closed
universe? During the contracting phase of the universe
it must, of course, converge onto cold stars, heating
them up and driving nuclear reactions backwards, and
so on, exactly in line with the description of the strange
behavior of a contracting universe with time flowing
backwards. This is no coincidence; the Wheeler-Feynman
description of electromagnetic radiation works only in a
universe where, as in Hawking's universe, the arrow of
time reverses when the state of maximum expansion is
reached. And the same reversal of the arrow of time
explains why it is the advanced wave that cancels out
and the retarded wave that survives in our universe.
What matters is that *one* of the two solutions to Maxwell's equations cancels out; we see the surviving wave
as the retarded wave in an expanding universe. From
our point of view, the surviving wave could be the
advanced wave in a collapsing universe. But, just as
before, any intelligent beings in *either* half of the universe will see both the thermodynamic and electromagnetic arrows pointing in the direction of expansion, with
retarded waves being normal.

During most of the 1960s and 1970s, however, cosmologists favored the idea that our universe is open and
will expand forever. They did so largely because the
amount of matter we can see in stars and galaxies is not
enough to close the universe. So the Wheeler-Feynman
"absorber" theory was dismissed as flawed, in some as
yet undiscovered way. An example of the way people
thought, quite recently, can be found in Paul Davies's
book, referred to above (pp. 186 and 187):

The ever-expanding Friedmann models (of the universe) are inconsistent with this opaqueness requirement. The recontracting model is, however,
perfectly opaque to radiation. The current evidence

in favor of a low-density, ever-expanding universe should therefore be considered as evidence against the absorber theory.

This appeared in print as recently as 1977. But since then, new theories of the universe—the so-called inflationary models—have appeared. These resolve deep puzzles that have worried cosmologists for decades, concerning the remarkable uniformity of the universe, but require that the universe should contain enough matter to be closed; and Hawking's work has provided a sound theoretical basis for expecting the universe to be closed, and therefore opaque. From the perspective of the mid-1980s, ten years on from that comment by Davies, the success of the Wheeler-Feynman theory in explaining the electromagnetic arrow of time in a closed universe fits very nicely indeed with the best cosmological ideas. Whether this will make the cosmologists any happier, though, must be a moot point.

(John Gribbin is the author of several books about cosmology, the most recent being *The Omega Point* (Bantam). He is currently working on a book about the ultimate fate of the universe.)

Introduction

Though his persona seems rather more consonant with his incarnations as Air Force crew chief, science fiction writer, aerospace engineer, inventor, survivalist, and West Coast Mountain Man, Dean Ing is also the holder of a doctorate in communications, as witness this latest entry in THE MAN-KZIN WARS. Like his previous story, "Cathouse," this one concerns the special problems of inter-species communications, where what we think we are saying may be very different indeed from what is coming across . . .

BRIAR PATCH

Dean Ing

If Locklear had been thinking straight, he never would have stayed in the god business. But when a man has been thrust into the Fourth Man–Kzin War, won peace with honor from the tigerlike Kzinti on a synthetic zoo planet, and released long-stored specimens so that his vast prison compound resembles the Kzin homeworld, it's hard for that man to keep his sense of mortality.

It's hard, that is, until someone decides to kill him. His first mistake was lust, impure and simple. A week after he paroled Scarface, the one surviving Kzin warrior, Locklear admitted his problem during supper. "All that caterwauling in the ravine," he said, refilling his bowl from the hearth stewpot, "is driving me nuts. Good thing you haven't let the rest of those Kzinti out of stasis; the racket would be unbelievable!"

Scarface wiped his muzzle with a brawny forearm and handed his own bowl to Kit, his new mate. The darkness of the huge Kzersatz region was tempered only by coals, but Locklear saw those coals flicker in Scarface's cat eyes. "A condition of my surrender was that you release Kit to me," the big Kzin growled. "And besides: do humans mate so quietly?"

Copyright © 1988 by Dean Ing

Because they were speaking Kzin, the word Scarface had used was actually "ch'rowl"—itself a sexual goad. Kit, who was refilling the bowl, let slip a tiny mew of surprise and pleasure. "Please, milord," she said, offering the bowl to Scarface. "Poor Rockear is already overstimulated. Is it not so?" Her huge eyes flicked to Locklear, whom she had grown to know quite well after Locklear waked her from age-long sleep.

"Dead right," Locklear agreed with a morose glance. "Not by the word; by the goddamn deed!"

"She is mine," Scarface grinned; a Kzin grin, the kind with big fangs and no amusement.

"Calm down. I may have been an animal psychologist, but I only have letches for human females," Locklear gloomed toward his Kzin companions. "And every night when I hear you two flattening the grass out there," he nodded past the half-built walls of the hut, "I get, uh, . . ." He did not know how to translate "horny" into Kzin.

"You get the urge to travel," Scarface finished, making it not quite a suggestion. The massive Kzin stared into darkness as if peering across the force walls surrounding Kzersatz. Those towering invisible walls separated the air, and lifeforms, of Kzersatz from other synthetic compounds of this incredible planet, Zoo. "I can see the treetops in the next compound as easily as you, Locklear. But I see no monkeys in them."

Before his defeat, Scarface had been "Tzak–Commander." The same strict Kzin honor that bound him to his surrender, forbade him to curse his captor as a monkey. But he could still sharpen the barb of his wit. Kit, with real affection for Locklear, did not approve. "Be nice," she hissed to her mate.

"Forget it," Locklear told her, stabbing with his Kzin *wtsai* blade for a hunk of meat in his stew. "Kit, he's stuck with his military code, and it won't let him insist that his captor get the hell out of here. But he's right. I still don't know if that next compound I call Newduvai is really Earthlike." He smiled at Scarface, remember-

ing not to show his teeth, and added, "Or whether it
has my kind of monkey."

"And we must not try to find out until your war
wounds have completely healed," Kit replied.

The eyes of man and Kzin warrior met. "Whoa,"
Locklear said quickly, sparing Scarface the trouble. "*We*
won't be scouting over there; I will, but you won't. I'm
an ethologist," he went on, holding up a hand to bar
Kit's interruption. "If Newduvai is as completely stocked
as Kzersatz, somebody—maybe the Outsiders, maybe
not, but damn' certain a long time ago,—*some*body
intended all these compounds to be kept separate. Now,
I won't say I haven't played god here a little, . . ."

"And intend to play it over there a lot," said Kit, who
had never yet surrendered to anyone.

"Hear me out. I'm not going to start mixing species
from Kzersatz and Newduvai any more than I already
have, and that's final." He pried experimentally at the
scab running down his knife arm. "But I'm pretty much
healed, thanks to your medkit, Scarface. And I meant it
when I said you'd have free run of this place. It's
intended for Kzinti, not humans. High time I took your
lifeboat over those force walls to Newduvai."

"Boots will miss you," said Kit.

Locklear smiled, recalling the other Kzin female he'd
released from stasis in a very pregnant condition. According to Kit, a Kzin mother would not emerge from
her birthing creche until the eyes of her twins had
opened—another week, at least. "Give her my love,"
he said, and swilled the last of his stew.

"A pity you will not do that yourself," Kit sighed.

"Milady." Scarface became, for the moment, every
inch a Tzak—Commander. "Would you ask me to ch'rowl
a human female?" He waited for Kit to control her
mixed expression. "Then please be silent on the subject. Locklear is a warrior who knows what he fights
for."

Locklear yawned. "There's an old song that says,
'Ain't gonna study war no more,' and a slogan that goes,
'Make love, not war.'"

Kit stood up with a fetching twitch of her tail. "I believe our leader has spoken, milord," she purred.

Locklear watched them swaying together into the night, and his parting call was plaintive. "Just try and keep it down, okay? A fellow needs his sleep."

The Kzin lifeboat was over ten meters long, well armed and furnished with emergency rations. In accord with their handshake armistice, Scarface had given flight instructions to his human pupil after disabling the hyperwave portion of its comm set. He had given no instructions on armament because Locklear, a peaceable man, saw no further use for anything larger than a sidearm. Neither of them could do much to make the lifeboat seating comfortable for Locklear, who was small even by human standards in an acceleration couch meant for a two-hundred-kilo Kzin.

Locklear paused in the airlock in midmorning and raised one arm in a universal peace sign. Scarface returned it. "I'll call you now and then, if those force walls don't stop the signal," Locklear called. "If you let your other Kzinti out of stasis, call and tell me how it works out."

"Keep your tail dry, Rockear," Kit called, perhaps forgetting he lacked that appendage—a compliment, of sorts.

"Will do," he called back as the airlock swung shut. Moments later, he brought the little craft to life and, cursing the cradle-rock motion that branded him a novice, urged the lifeboat into the yellow sky of Kzersatz.

Locklear made one pass, a "goodbye sweep," high above the region with its yellow and orange vegetation, taking care to stay well inside the frostline that defined those invisible force walls. He spotted the cave from the still-flattened grass where Kit had herded the awakened animals from the crypt and their sleep of forty thousand years, then steepened his climb and used aero boost to begin his trajectory. No telling whether the force walls stopped suddenly, but he did not want to find out by plowing into the damned things. It was enough to know they stopped below orbital height, and that he could toss the lifeboat from Kzersatz to Newduvai in a low-energy ballistic arc.

And he knew enough to conserve energy in the craft's main accumulators because one day, when the damned stupid Man–Kzin War was over, he'd need that energy to jump from Zoo to some part of known space. Unless, he amended silently, somebody found Zoo first. The war might already be over, and certainly the warlike Kzinti must have the coordinates of Zoo . . .

Then he was at the top of his trajectory, seeing the planetary curvature of Zoo, noting the tiny satellite sunlets that bathed hundred-mile-diameter regions in light, realizing that a warship could condemn any one of those circular regions to death with one well-placed shot against its synthetic, automated little sun. He was already past the circular force walls now, and felt an enormous temptation to slow the ship by main accumulator energy. A good pilot could lower that lifeboat down between the walls of those force cylinders, in the hard vacuum between compounds. Outsiders might be lurking there, idly studying the specimens through invisible walls.

But Locklear was no expert with a Kzin lifeboat, not yet, and he had to use his wristcomp to translate the warning on the console screen. He set the wing extensions just in time to avoid heavy buffeting, thankful that he had not needed orbital speed to manage his brief trajectory. He bobbled a maneuver once, twice, then felt the drag of Newduvai's atmosphere on the lifeboat and gave the lifting surfaces full extension. He put the craft into a shallow bank to starboard, keeping the vast circular frostline far to portside, and punched in an autopilot instruction. Only then did he dare to turn his gaze down on Newduvai.

Like Kzersatz it boasted a big lake, but this one glinted in a sun heartbreakingly like Earth's. A rugged jumble of cliffs soared into cloud at one side of the region, and green hills mounded above plains of mottled hues: tan, brown, green, Oh, God, all that green!

He'd forgotten, in the saffron of Kzersatz, how much he missed the emerald of grass, the blue of sky, the darker dusty green of Earth forests. For it was, in every respect, perfectly Earthlike. He wiped his misting eyes, grinned at himself for such foolishness, and eased the lifeboat down to a lazy circular course that kept him two thousand meters above the terrain. If the builders of Zoo were consistent, one of those shallow creekbeds would begin not in a marshy meadow but in a horizontal shaft. And there he would find—he dared not think it through any further.

After his first complete circuit of Newduvai, he knew it had no herds of animals. No birds dotted the lakeshore; no bugs whacked his viewport. A dozen streams meandered and leapt down from the frostline where clouds dumped their moisture against cold encircling force walls. One stream ended in a second small lake with no obvious outlet, but none of the creeks or dry-washes began with a cave.

Mindful of his clumsiness in this alien craft, Locklear set it down in soft sand where a drywash delta met the kidney-shaped lake. After further consulting between his wristcomp and the ship's computer, he punched in his most important queries and listened to the ship cool while its sensors analyzed Newduvai.

Gravity: Earth normal. Atmosphere, solar flux, and temperature: all Earth normal. "And not a critter in sight," he told the cabin walls. In a burst of insight, he asked the computer to list anything that might be a health hazard to a Kzin. If man and Kzin could make steaks of each other, they probably should fear the same pathogens. The computer took its time, but its most fearsome finding was of tetanus in the dust.

He waited no longer, thrusting at the airlock in his hurry, filling his lungs with a rich soup of odors, and found his eyes brimming again as he stepped onto a little piece of Earth. Smells, he reflected, really got you back to basics. Scents of cedar, of dust, of grasses and yes, of wildflowers. Just like home—yet, in some skin-prickling way, not quite.

Locklear sat down on the sand then, with an earth-like sunlet baking his back from a turquoise sky, and he wept. Outsiders or not, any bunch that could engineer a piece of home on the rim of known space couldn't be all bad.

He was tasting the lake water's very faint brackishness when, in a process that took less than a minute, the sunlight dimmed and was gone. "But it's only noontime," he protested, and then laughed at himself and made a notation on his wristcomp, using its faint light to guide him back to the airlock.

As with Kzersatz, he saw no stars; and then he realized that the position of Newduvai's sun had been halfway to the horizon when—almost as it happened on Kzersatz—the daily ration of sunlight was quenched. Why should Newduvai's sun keep the same time as that of Kzersatz? It didn't; nor did it wink off as suddenly as that of Kzersatz.

He activated the still-functioning local mode of the lifeboat's comm set, intending to pass his findings on to Scarface. No response. Scarface's handset was an all-band unit; perhaps some wavelength could bounce off of debris from the Kzin cruiser scuttled in orbit—but Locklear knew that was a slender hope, and soon it seemed no hope at all. He spent the longest few hours of his life then, turning floodlights on the lake in the forlorn hope of seeing a fish leap, and with the vague fear that a tyrannosaur might pay him a social call. But no matter where he turned the lights he saw no gleam of eyes, and the sand was innocent of any tracks. Sleep would not come until he began to address the problem of the stasis crypt in logical ways.

Locklear came up from his seat with a bound, facing a sun that brightened as he watched. His wristcomp said not quite twelve hours had passed since the sunlet dimmed. His belly said it was late. His memory said yes, by God, there was one likely plan for locating that horizontal shaft: fly very near the frostline and scan every dark cranny that was two hundred meters or so inside the force walls. On Kzersatz, the stasis crypt had ended exactly beneath the frostline, perhaps a portal for those who'd built Zoo. And the front entrance had been two hundred meters inside the force walls.

He lifted the lifeboat slowly, ignoring hunger pangs, beginning to plot a rough map of Newduvai on the computer screen because he did not know how to make the computer do it for him. Soon, he passed a dry plateau with date palms growing in its declivities and followed the ship's shadow to more fertile soil. Near frostline, he set the aeroturbine reactor just above idle and, moving briskly a hundred meters above the ground, began a careful scan of the terrain because he was not expert enough with Kzin computers to automate the search.

After three hours he had covered more than half of his sweep around Newduvai, past semidesert and grassy fields to pine-dotted mountain slopes, and the lifeboat's reactor coolant was overheating from the slow pace. Locklear set the craft down nicely near that smaller mountain lake, chopped all power systems, and headed for scrubby trees in the near distance. Scattered among the pines were cedar and small oak. Nearer stood tall poplar and chestnut, invaded by wild grape with immature fruit. But nearest of all, the reason for his landing here, were gnarled little pear trees and, amid wild shoots of rank growth, trees laden with small ripe plums. He wolfed them down until juice dripped from his chin, washed in the lake, and then found the pears unripe. No matter: he'd seen dates, grapes, and chestnut, which suggested a model of some Mediterranean region. After identifying juniper, oleander and honeysuckle, he sent his wristcomp scurrying through its megabytes and narrowed his opinion of the area: a surrogate slice of Asia Minor.

He might have sat on sunwarmed stones until dark, lulled by this sensation of being, somehow, back home without a care. But then he glanced far across the lower hills and saw, proceeding slowly across a parched desert plateau many miles distant, a whirlwind with its whiplike curve and bloom of dust where it touched the soil.

"Uh-huh! That's how you reseed plants without insect vectors," he said aloud to the builders of Zoo. "But whirlwinds don't make honey, and they'll sting anyway. Hell, even *I* can play god better than that," he said, and bore a pocketful of plums into the lifeboat, filled once more with the itch to find the cave that might not even exist on Newduvai.

But it was there, all right. Locklear saw it only because of the perfect arc of obsidian, gleaming through a tangle of brush that had grown around the cave mouth.

He made a botch of the landing because he was trembling with anticipation. A corner of his mind kept warning him not to assume everything here was the same as on Kzersatz, so Locklear stopped just outside that brush-choked entrance. His wtsai blade made short work of the brush, revealing a polished floor. He strode forward, wtsai in one hand, his big Kzin sidearm in the other, to the now-familiar luminous film that flickered, several meters inside the cave mouth, across an obsidian portal. He thrust his blade through the film and saw, as he had expected to see, stronger light flash behind the portal. Then he stepped through and stopped, listening.

He might have been back in the Kzersatz crypt: a quiet so deep his own breathing made echoes; the long obsidian central passage, with nine branches on each side, ending in a frost-covered force wall that filled the passageway. And the clear plastic containers ranked in the side passages were of three sizes on smooth metal bases, as expected. But Locklear took one look at the nearest specimen, spinning slowly in its stasis cage, and knew that here the resemblance to Kzersatz ended forever.

The monster lay in something like a fetal crouch, tumbling slowly in response to the grav polarizer as it had been doing for many thousands of years. It was black, with great forward-curving horns and heavy

shoulders, and when released—*if* anyone dared, he
amended—it would stand six feet at the shoulder.
Locklear figured its weight at a ton. Some European
zoologists had once tried to breed cattle back to this
brute, but with scant success, and Locklear had not
seen so much as a sketch of it since his undergrad work.
It was a bull aurochs, a beast which had survived on
Earth into historic times; and counting the cows, Locklear
realized there were over forty of them.

No point in kidding himself about his priorities.
Locklear walked past the stasized camels and gerbils,
hurried faster beyond small horses and cheetahs and
bats, began to trot as he ran to the next passage past
lions and hares and grouse, and was sprinting as he
passed whole schools of fish (without water? Why the
hell not? They were in stasis, he reminded himself—)
in their respective containers. He was out of breath by
the time he dashed between specimens of reindeer and
saw the monkeys.

NO! A mistake any Kzin might have made, but:
"How could I play such a shameful joke on myself?"
They were in fetal curls, and some of them boasted a lot
of body hair. And each of them, Locklear realized, was
human.

In a kind of reverence he studied them all, careful to
avoid touching the metal bases which, on Kzersatz,
opened the cages and released the specimens. Narrow-
headed and swarthy they were, no taller than he, with
heavy brow ridges and high cheekbones. Noses like
prizefighters; forearms like blacksmiths; and some had
pendulous mammaries and a few had—had—"Tits," he
breathed. "There's a difference! Thank you, God."

Men and women like these had first been studied in
a river valley near old Dusseldorf, hardy folk who had
preceded modern humans on Earth and, in all probability, had intermarried with them until forty or fifty thousand years before. Locklear, rubbing at the gooseflesh
on his arms, began to study each of the stasized nudes
with great care. He would need every possible advantage because they would be disoriented, perhaps even

furious, when they waked. And the last thing Locklear needed was to start off on the wrong foot with a frenzied Neanderthaler.

Only an idiot would release a mob of Neanderthal hunters into a tiny world without taking steps to protect endangered game animals. The killing of a dozen deer might doom the rest of that species to slow extinction here. On the other hand, Locklear might have released all the animals and waited for a season or more. But certain of the young women in stasis were not exactly repellant, and he did not intend to wait a year before making their acquaintance. Besides, his notes on a Neanderthal community could make him famous on a dozen worlds, and Locklear was anxious to get on with it.

His second option was to wake the people and guide them, by force if necessary, outside to fruits and grains. But each of them would see those stasized animals, probably as meat on the hoof, and might not respond to his demands. It was beyond belief that any of them would speak a language he knew. Then it struck him that he already knew how to disassemble a stasis cage, and that he had as much time as he needed. With a longing glance backward, Locklear retraced his steps to the lifeboat and started looking for something with wheels.

But Kzin lifeboats do not carry cargo dollies, and the sun of Newduvai had dimmed before he found a way to remove the wheeled carriage below the reactor's heat exchanger unit. Evidently the unit needed replacement often enough that Kzin engineers installed a carriage with it. That being so, Locklear decided not to use the lifeboat's reactor any more than he had to.

He worked until hunger and aching muscles drove him to the cabin where he cut slices of bricklike Kzin rations and ate plums for dessert. But before he fell asleep, Locklear made some decisions that might save his hide. The lifeboat must be hidden away from inquisitive savage fingers; he would even camouflage the stasis crypt so that those savages would not know what lay inside; and it was absolutely crucial that he present

himself as a shaman of great power. Without a few
tawdry magics, he might not be able to distance himself
as an observer; might even be challenged to combat by
some strong male. And Locklear remembered those
hornlike fingernails and bulging muscles all too well.
He saw no sense in shooting a man, even a Neanderthal, merely to prove a point that could be made in
peaceable ways.

He spent over a week preparing his hardware. His
trials on Kzersatz had taught him how, when all you've
got is a hammer, the whole world is a nail; and that you
must hammer out a few other tools as soon as possible.
He soon found the lifeboat's military toolbox complete
with wire, pistol-grip arc welder, and motorized drill.

He took time off to gather fruit and to let his frustra-
tions drain away. It was hard not to throw rocks at the
sky when he commanded a state-of-the-art Kzin craft,
yet could not cannibalize much of it for the things he
needed. "Maybe I should release a dog from stasis so I
could kick it," he told himself aloud, while attaching an
oak branch as a wagon tongue for the wheeled carriage.
But lacking any other game, he figured, the dog would
probably attack before he did.

Then he used oak staves to lever a cage base up, with
flat stones as blocks, and eased his makeshift wagon
beneath. The doe inside was heavy with young. Most
likely, she would retreat far from him before bearing
her fawns, and he knew what to do with the tuneable
gray polarizer below that cage. Soon the clear plastic
container sat gleaming in the sun, and Locklear poked
hard at the base before retreating to the cave mouth.

As on Kzersatz, the container levered up, the red
doe sank to the cage base, and the base slid forward. A
moment later the creature moved, stood with lovely
slender limbs shaking, and then saw him waving an oak
stave. She reached grassy turf in one graceful bound
and sped off with leaps he watched in admiration. Then,
feeling somehow more lonely as the doe vanished, he
sighed and disconnected the plastic container, then set
about taking the entire cage to pieces. Already experi-

enced with these gadgets, he would need at least two of the grav polarizer units before he could move stasized specimens outside with ease.

Disconnected from the stasis unit, a polarizer toroid with its power source and wiring could be tuned to lift varied loads; for example, a container housing a school of fish. The main thing was to avoid tipping it, which Locklear managed by wiring the polarizer securely to the underside of his wheeled carriage. Another hour saw him tugging his burden to the airlock, where he wrestled that entire, still-functioning cageful of fish inside. The fish, he saw, had sucking mouths meant for bottom-feeding on vegetable trash. They looked rather like carp or tilapia. Raising the lifeboat with great care, he eased toward the big lake some miles distant. It was no great trick to dump the squirming mass of life from the airlock port into the lake from a height of two meters, and then he celebrated by landing near the first laden fig tree he saw. Munching and lazing in the sun, he decided that his fortunes were looking up. But then, Locklear had been wrong before . . .

He knew that his next steps must be planned carefully. Before hiding the Kzin craft away he must duplicate the airboat he had built on Kzersatz. After an exhaustive search—meanwhile mapping Newduvai's major features—he felled and stripped slender pines, hauling them in the lifeboat to his favorite spot near the small mountain lake. By now he had found a temporary spot in a barren cleft near frostline to hide the lifeboat itself, and began by stripping off its medium-caliber beam weapons from extension struts. The strut skins were attached by long screws, which Locklear saved. The weapon wiring came in handy, too, as he began fitting the raftlike platform of his airboat together. When he realized that the lifeboat's slings and emergency seats could be stripped for a fabric sail, he began to feel a familiar excitement.

This airboat was larger than his first, with its single sail and swiveling double-pole keel for balance. With

wires for rigging, he could hunker down just behind the
mast and operate the gravity control vernier through a
slot in the flat deck. He could carry over two hundred
kilos of ballast, the mass of a stasis cage with a human
specimen inside, far from the crypt before setting that
specimen free. "I'll have to carry the cage back, of
course. Who knows what trouble a savage might create,
fiddling with a stasis cage?" He snorted at himself; he'd
almost said "monkeying," and it was dangerous to assume he was smarter than these ancient people. But
wasn't he, really? If Neanderthalers had died out on
Earth, they must have been inferior in some way. Well,
he was sure as hell going to find out.

If his new airboat was larger than the first, it was also
more unwieldy. He used it to ferry logs to his cabin site
at the small lake, cursing his need to tack in the light
breezes, wishing he had a better propulsion system, for
over a week before the solution hit him.

At the time he was debating the release of more
animals. The mammoths, he promised himself, would
come last. No wonder the builders of Newduvai had left
them nearest the crypt entrance! Their cage tops would
each make a dandy greenhouse and their grav polarizers would lift tons. *Or push tons.*

"Some things don't change," he told himself, laughing aloud. "I was dumb on Kzersatz and I've been
dumb here." So he released the hares, gerbils, grouse
and some other species of bird with beaks meant for
crunching seeds. He promptly installed their grav units
around his airboat seat for propulsion, removing the
mast and keel poles for reuse as cabin roof beams. That
was the day Locklear nearly killed himself caroming off
the lake's surface at sixty miles an hour, whooping like a
fool. Now the homemade craft was no longer a boat; it
was a scooter, and would scoot with an extra fifty kilos
of cargo.

It might have been elation with the sporty performance of his scooter that made him so optimistic, fail-
ing to remember that you have to kill pessimists, but
optimists do it themselves. The log cabin, five meters

square with fireplace and frond-thatched shed roof, needed only a pallet of sling fabric and fragrant boughs beneath. A *big* pallet, he decided. It had been Kit who taught him that he should have food and shelter ready before waking strangers in strange lands. He had figs and apricot slices drying, Kzin rations for the strong of tooth, and Kzin-sized drinking vessels from the lifeboat. He moved a few more items, including a clever Kzin memory pad with electronic stylus and screen, from lifeboat to cabin, then attached a ten-meter cable harness from the scooter to the lifeboat's overhead weapon pylon.

It was only necessary then to set the scooter's bottom grav unit to slight buoyancy, and to pilot the Kzin lifeboat very slowly, towing the scooter.

The cleft where he landed had become a soggy meadow from icemelt near the frostline high on Newduvai's perimeter, protected on one side by the towering force wall and on the other by jagged basalt. The lifeboat could not be seen from below, and if his first aerial visitors were Kzinti, they'd have to fly dangerously near that force wall before they saw it. He sealed the lifeboat and then hauled the scooter down hand over hand, puffing with exertion, letting the scooter bounce harmlessly off the lifeboat's hull as he clambered aboard. Then he cast off and twiddled with those grav unit verniers until the wind whistled in his ears en route to the stasis crypt. He was already expert at modifying stasis units, and he would have lots of them to play with. If he had to protect himself from a wild woman, he could hardly wish for anything better.

He trundled the crystal cage into sunlight still wondering if he'd chosen the right—specimen? Subject? "Woman, dammit; woman!" He was trying to wear too many hats, he knew, with the one labeled "lecher" perched on top. He landed the scooter near his cabin, placed bowls of fruit and water nearby, and pressed the cage baseplate, retreating beyond his offerings.

She sank to the cage floor but only shifted position, still asleep, the breeze moving strands of chestnut hair at her cheeks. She was small and muscular, her breasts firm and immature, pubic hair sparse, limbs slender and marked with scratches; and yes, he realized as he moved nearer, she had a forty-thousand-year-old zit on her little chin. Easily the best-looking choice in the crypt, not yet fully developed into the Neanderthal body shape, she seemed capable of sleep in any position and was snoring lightly to prove it.

A genuine teen-ager, he mused, grinning. Aloud he said, "Okay, Lolita, up and at 'em." She stirred; a hand reached up as if tugging at an invisible blanket. "You'll miss the school shuttle," he said louder. It had never failed back on Earth with his sister.

It didn't fail here, either. She waked slowly, blinking as she sat up in lithe, nude, heartbreaking innocence. But her yawn snapped in two as she focused on him, and her pantomime of snatching a stone and hurling it at Locklear was convincing enough to make him duck. She leaped away scrabbling for real stones, and between her screams and her clods, all in Locklear's direction, she seemed to be trying to cover herself.

He retreated, but not far enough, and grabbed a chunk of dirt only after taking one clod on his thigh. He threatened a toss of his own, whereupon she ducked behind the cage, watching him warily.

Well, it wouldn't matter what he said, so long as he said it calmly. His tone and gestures would have to serve. "You're a real little shit before breakfast, Lolita," he said, smiling, tossing his clod gently toward the bowls.

She saw the food then, frowning. His open hands and strained smile invited her to the food, and she moved toward it still holding clods ready. Wolfing plums, she paused to gape as he pulled a plum from a pocket and began to eat. "Never seen pockets, hm? Stick around, little girl, I'll show you lots of interesting things." The humor didn't work, even on himself; and at his first step toward her she ran like a deer.

Every time he pointed to himself and said his name, she screamed something brief. She moved around the area, checking out the cabin, draping a vine over her breasts, and after an hour Locklear gave up. He'd made a latchcord for the cabin door, so she couldn't do much harm. She watched from fifty meters distance with great wondering brown eyes as he waved, lifted the scooter, and sped away with her cage and a new idea.

An hour later he returned with a second cage, cursing as he saw Lolita trying to smash his cabin window with an oak stave. The clear plastic, of cage material, was tough stuff and he laughed as the scooter settled nearby, pretending he didn't itch to whack her rump. She began a litany of stone-age curses, then, as she saw the new cage and its occupant. Locklear actually had to mount the scooter and chase her off before she would quit pelting him with anything she could throw.

He made the same preparations as before, this time with shreds of smelly Kzin rations as well, and stood leaning against the cage for long moments, facing Lolita who lurked fifty meters away, to make his point. The young woman revolving slowly inside the cage was at his mercy. Then he pressed the baseplate, turned his back as the plastic levered upward, and strode off a few paces with a sigh. This one was a Neanderthal and no mistake: curves a little too broad to be exciting, massive forearms and calves, pug nose, considerable body hair. *Nice tits, though. Stop it, fool!*

The young woman stirred, sat up, looked around, then let her big jaw drop comically as she stared at Locklear, whose smile was a very rickety construction. She cocked her head at him, impassive, an instant before he spoke.

"You're no beauty, lady, so maybe you won't throw rocks at *me*. Too late for breakfast," he continued in his sweetest tones and a pointing finger. "How about lunch?"

She saw the bowls. Slowly, with caution and surprising grace, she stepped from the scooter's deck still eyeing him without smile or frown. Then she squatted to inspect the food, knees apart, facing him, and Locklear grew faint at the sight. He looked away quickly, flushing, aware that she continued to stare at him while sampling human and Kzin rations with big strong teeth and wrinklings of her nose that made her oddly attractive. *More attractive. Why the hell doesn't she cover up or something.*

He pulled another plum from a pocket, and this magic drew a smile from her as they ate. He realized she was through eating when she wiped sticky fingers in her straight black hair, and stepped back by reflex as she stepped toward him. She stopped, with a puzzled inclination of her head, and smiled at him. That was when he stood his ground and let her approach. He had hoped for something like this, so the watching Lolita could see that he meant no harm.

When the woman stood within arm's length of him she stopped. He put a hand on his breast. "Me Locklear, you Jane," he said.

"(Something,)" she said. Maybe *Kh-roofeh*.

He was going to try saying it himself when she startled him into a wave of actual physical weakness. With eyes half-closed, she cupped her full breasts in both hands and smiled. He looked at her erect nipples, feeling the rush of blood to his face, and showed her his hands in a broad helpless shrug. Whereupon, she took his hands and placed them on her breasts, and now her big black eyes were not those of a savage Neanderthal but a sultry smiling Levantine woman who knew how to make a point. Two points.

Three points, as he felt a rising response and knew her hands were seeking that rise, hands that had never known velcrolok closures yet seemed to have an intelligence of their own. His whole body was tingling now as he caressed her, and when her hands found that fabric closure, she shared a fresh smile with him, and tried to pull him down on the ground with her.

So he took her hands in his and walked her to the cabin. She "hmm"ed when he pulled the latchcord loop to open the door, and "ahh"ed when she saw the big pallet, and then offered those swarthy full breasts again and put her face against the hollow of his throat, and toyed inside his velcrolok closure until he astonished her by pulling his entire flight suit off, and offered her body in ways simple and sophisticated, and Locklear accepted all the offers he could, and made a few of his own, all of which she accepted expertly.

He had his first sensation of something eerie, something just below his awareness, as he lay inert on his back bathed in honest sweat, his partner lying face-down more or less across him like one stick abandoned across another stick after both had been rubbed to kindle a blaze. He saw a movement at his window and knew it was Lolita, peering silently in. He sighed.

His partner sighed too, and turned toward the window with a quick, vexed burst of some command. The face disappeared.

He chuckled, "Did you hear the little devil, or smell her?" Actually, his partner had more of the *eau de sweatsock* perfume than Lolita did; now more pronounced than ever. He didn't care. If the past half-hour had been any omen, he might never care again.

She stretched then, and sat up, dragging a heel that was rough as a rasp across his calf. Her heavy ragged nails had scratched him, and he was oily from God knew what mixture of greases in her long hair. He didn't give a damn about that either, reflecting that a man should allow a few squeaks in the hinges of the pearly gates.

She said something then, softly, with that tilt of her head that suggested inquiry. "Locklear," he replied, tapping his chest again.

Her look was somehow pitying then, as she repeated her phrase, placing one hand on her head, the other on his.

"Oh yeah, you're my girl and I'm your guy," he said, nodding, placing his hands on hers.

She sat quite still for a moment, her eyes sad on his. Then, delighting him, she placed one hand on his breast and managed a passable, "Loch-leah."

He grinned and nodded, then cocked his head and placed a hand between her (wonderful!) breasts. No homecoming queen, but dynamite in deep shadows . . .

He paid more attention as she said, approximately,

"Ch'roof'h," and when he repeated it she laughed, closing her eyes with downcast chin. *A big chin, a really whopping big one to be honest about it,* and then he caught her gaze, not angry but perhaps reproachful, and again he felt the passage of something like a cold breeze through his awareness.

She rubbed his gooseflesh down for him, responding to his "ahh"s, and presently she astonished him again by beginning to query him on the names of things. Locklear knew that he could thoroughly confuse her if he insisted on perfectly grammatical tenses, cases, and syntax. He tried to keep it simple, and soon learned that "head down, eyes shut" was the same as a negative headshake. "Chin elevated, smiling" was the same as a nod—and now he realized he'd seen her giving him yesses that way from the first moment she awoke. A smile or a frown was the same for her as for him—but that heads-up smile was a definite gesture.

She drew him outside again presently, studying the terrain with lively curiosity, miming actions and listening as he provided words, responding with words of her own.

The name he gave her was, in part, because it was faintly like the one she'd offered; and in part because she seemed willing to learn his ways while revealing ancient ways of her own. He named her "Ruth." Locklear felt crestfallen when, by midafternoon, he realized Ruth was learning his language much faster than he was learning hers. And then, as he glanced over her shoulder to see little Lolita creeping nearer, he began to understand why.

Ruth turned quickly, with a shouted command and warning gestures, and Lolita dropped the sharpened stick she'd been carrying. Locklear knew beyond doubt that Lolita had made no sound in her approach. There was only one explanation that would fit all his data: Ruth unafraid of him from the first; offering herself as if she knew his desires; keeping track of Lolita without looking; and her uncanny speed in learning his language.

And that moment when she'd placed her hand on his

head, with an inquiry that was somehow pitying. Now he copied her gesture with one hand on his own head, the other on hers, and lowered his head, eyes shut. "No," he said. "Locklear, no telepath. Ruth, yes?"

"Ruth, yes." She pointed to Lolita then. "No—telpat."

She needed another ten minutes of pantomime, attending to his words and obviously to his thoughts as he spoke them, to get her point across. Ruth was a "gentle," but like Locklear himself, Lolita was a "new."

When darkness came to Newduvai, Lolita got chummier in a hurry, complaining until Ruth let her into the cabin. Despite that, Ruth didn't seem to like the girl much and accepted Locklear's name for her, shortening it to "Loli." Ruth spoke to her in their common tongue, not so much gutteral as throaty, and Locklear had a strong impression that they were old acquaintances. Either of them could tend a fire expertly, and both were wary of the light from his Kzin memory screen until they found that it would not singe a curious finger.

Locklear was bothered on two counts by Loli's insistence on taking pieces of Kzin plastic film to make a bikini suit: first because Ruth plainly thought it silly, and second because the kid was more appealing with it than she was when stark naked. At least the job kept Loli silently occupied, listening and watching as Locklear got on with the business of talking with Ruth.

Their major breakthrough for the evening came when Locklear got the ideas of past and future, "before" and "soon," across to Ruth. Her telepathy was evidently the key to her quick grasp of his language; yet it seemed to work better with emotional states than with abstract ideas, and she grew upset when Loli became angry with her own first clumsy efforts at making her panties fit. Clearly, Ruth was a lady who liked her harmony.

For Ruth was, despite her rude looks, a lady—when she wasn't in the sack. Even so, when at last Ruth had seen to Loli's comfort with spare fabric and Locklear snapped off the light, he felt inviting hands on him again. "No thanks," he said, chuckling, patting her shoulder, even though he wanted her again. And Ruth *knew* he did, judging from her sly insistence.

"No. Loli here," he said finally, and felt Ruth shrug as if to say it didn't matter. Maybe it didn't matter to Neanderthals, but—"Soon," he promised, and shared a hug with Ruth before they fell asleep.

During the ensuing week, he learned much. For one thing, he learned that Loli was a chronic pain in the backside. She ate like a Kzin warrior. She liked to see if things would break. She liked to spy. She interfered with Locklear's pace during his afternoon "naps" with Ruth by whacking on the door with sticks and stones, until he swore he would " . . . hit Loli soon."

But Ruth would not hear of that. "Hit Loli, same hit Ruth head. Locklear like hit Ruth head?"

But one afternoon, when she saw Locklear studying her with friendly intensity, Ruth spoke to Loli at some length. The girl picked up her short spear and, crooning her happiness, loped off into the forest. Ruth turned to Locklear smiling. "Loli find fruitwater, soon Ruth make fruitfood." A few minutes of miming showed that she had promised to make some kind of kind of dessert, if Loli could find a beehive for honey.

Locklear had seen beehives in stasis, but explained that there were very few animals loose on Newduvai, and no hurtbugs.

"No hurtbugs? Loli no find, long time. Good," Ruth replied firmly, and led him by the hand into their cabin, and "good" was the operative word.

On his next trip to the crypt, Locklear needed all day for his solitary work. He might put it off forever, but it was clear by now that he must populate Newduvai with game before he released their most fearsome predators. The little horses needed only to see daylight before galloping off. Camels were quicker still, and the deer bounded off like golf balls down a freeway. The predators would simply have to wait until the herds were larger, and the day was over before he could rig grav polarizers to trundle mammoths to the mouth of the crypt. His last job of the day was his most troublesome, releasing small cages of bees near groves of fruit trees and wildflowers.

Locklear and Ruth managed to convey a lot with only a few hundred words, though some of those words had to do multiple duty while Ruth expanded her vocabulary. When she said "new," for example, it often carried a stigma. Neanderthals, he decided, were very conservative folk, and they sensed a lie before you told it. If Ruth was any measure, they also had little aptitude for math. She understood one and two and many. She understood "none," but not as a number. If there wasn't any, she conveyed to him, why try to count it? She had him there.

Eventually, between food-gathering forays, he used pebbles and sketches to tell Ruth of the many, many other animals and people he could bring to the scene. She was no sketch artist; in fact, she insisted, women were not supposed to draw things—especially hunt-things. Ah, he said, magics were only for men? Yes, she said, then mystified him with pantomimes of sleep and pain. That was for men, too, and food-gathering was for women.

He pursued the mystery, sketching with the Kzin memo screen. At last, when she pretended to cut her throat with his wtsai knife, he understood, and added the word "kill" to her vocabulary. Men hunted and killed.

Dry-mouthed, he asked, "Man like kill Locklear?"

Now it was her turn to be mystified. "No kill. Why kill magic man?"

Because, he replied, "Locklear like Ruth, one-two other man like Ruth. Kill Locklear for Ruth?"

He had never seen her laugh aloud, but he saw it now, the big teeth gleaming, breasts shaking with merriment. "Locklear like Ruth, good. Many man like Ruth, good."

He was silent for a long time, fighting the temptation to tell her that many men liking Ruth was *not* good. Then: "Ruth like many man?"

She had learned to nod by now, and did it happily.

The next five minutes were troubled ones for Locklear. Ruth did not seem to understand monogamy in any form. Apparently, everybody took pot luck in the sex department and was free to accept or reject. Some people were simply more popular than others. "Many man like Ruth," she said. "Many, many, many . . ."

"Okay, for Christ's sake, I get the idea," he exploded, and again he saw that look of sadness—or perhaps pain. "Locklear see, Ruth popular with man."

It seemed to be their first quarrel. Tentatively, she said, "Locklear popular with woman."

"No. Little popular with woman."

"Much popular with Ruth," she said, and began to rub his shoulders. That was the day she asked him about her appearance, and he responded the best way he could. She thought it silly to trim her strong, useful nails; sillier to wash her hair. Still, she did it, and he claimed she was pretty, and she knew he lied.

When it occurred to him to ask how he could look nice for her, Ruth said, "Locklear pretty now." But he never thought to wonder if *she* might be lying.

Whatever Ruth said about women and hunting, it did not seem to apply to Loli. While aloft in the scooter one day to study distribution of the animals, Locklear saw the girl chasing a hare across a meadow. She was no slouch with a short spear and nailed the hare on her second toss, dispatching it with a stone after a brief struggle. He lowered the scooter very, very slowly, watching her tear at the animal, disgusted when he realized she was eating it raw.

She saw his shadow when the scooter was hovering very near, and sat there blushing, looking at him with the innards of the hare across her lap.

She understood few of his words—or seemed to, at the cabin—but his tone was clear enough. "You couldn't share it, you little bastard. No, you sneak out here and stuff yourself." She began to suck her thumb, pouting. Then perhaps Loli realized the boss must be placated;

she tried a smile on her blood-streaked face and held her grisly trophy out.

"No. Ruth. Give to Ruth," he scowled, pointing toward the cabin. She elevated her chin and smiled, and he flew off grumbling. He couldn't much blame the kid; Kzin rations and fruit were getting pretty tiresome, and the gruel Ruth made from grain wasn't all that exciting without bits of meat. It was going to be rougher on the animals when he woke the men.

And why wake them at all? You've got it good here, he reminded himself in Sequence Umpteen of his private dialogue. *You have your own little world and a harem of one, and you know when her period comes so you know when not to play. And one of these days, Loli will be a knockout, I suspect. A much niftier dish than poor Ruth, who doesn't know what a skag she'd be in modern society, thank God.*

Moments like this made him squirm. Setting Ruth's looks aside, he had no complaint, not even about the country itself. *Not much seasonal change, no dangerous animals unless you want to release them, certainly none of the most dangerous animal of all.* Except for Kzinti, of course. One on one, they were meaner predators than men—even Neanderthal savages.

"That's why I have to release 'em," he said to the wind. "If a fully-manned Kzin ship comes, I'll need an army." He no longer kidded himself about scholarship and the sociology of *homo neanderthalensis,* which was strictly a secondary item. It was sobering to look yourself over and see self-interest riding you like a hunchback. So he flew directly to the crypt and spent the balance of the day releasing the whoppers: aurochs and bison, which didn't make him sweat much, and a half-dozen mammoths, which did.

A mammoth, he found, was a flighty beast not given to confrontations. He could set one shambling off with a shout, its trunk high like a periscope tasting the breeze. Every one of them turned into the wind and disappeared toward the frostline, and now the crypt held only its most dangerous creatures.

He returned to the cabin perilously late, the sun of Newduvai dying while he was still a hundred meters from the wisp of smoke rising from the cabin. He landed blind near the cabin, very slowly but with a jolt, and saw the faint gleam of the Kzin light leap from the cabin window. Ruth might not have a head for figures, but she'd seen him snap that light on fifty times. *And she must've sensed my panic. I wonder how far off she can do that. . . .*

Ruth already had succulent broiled haunches of Loli's hare, keeping them warm over coals, and it wrenched his heart as he saw she was drooling as she waited for him. He wiped the corner of her mouth, kissed her anyhow, and sat at the rough pole table while she brought his supper. Loli had obviously eaten, and watched him as if fearful that he would order her outside.

Hauling mammoths, even with a grav polarizer, is exhausting work. After finishing off a leg of hare, and falling asleep at the table, Locklear was only half-aware when Ruth picked him up and carried him to their pallet as easily as she would have carried a child.

The next day, he had Ruth convey to Loli that she was not to hunt without permission. Then, with less difficulty than he'd expected, he sketched and quizzed her about the food of a Neanderthal tribe. Yes, they hunted everything: bugs to mammoths, it was all protein, but chiefly they gathered roots, grains, and fruits.

That made sense. Why risk getting killed hunting when tubers didn't fight back? He posed his big question then. If he brought a tribe to Newduvai (this brought a smile of anticipation to her broad face), and forbade them to hunt without his permission, would they obey?

Gentles might, she said. New people, such as Loli, were less obedient. She tried to explain why, conveying something about telepathy and hunting, until he waved the question aside. If he showed her sleeping gentles, would she tell him which ones were good? Oh yes, she said, adding a phrase she knew he liked: "No problem."

But it took him an hour to get Ruth on the scooter.

That stuff was all very well for great magic men, she implied, but women's magics were more prosaic. After a few minutes idling just above the turf, he sped up, and she liked that fine. Then he slowed and lifted the scooter a bit. By noon, he was cruising fast as they surveyed groups of aurochs, solitary gazelles, and skittish horses from high above. It was she, sampling the wind with her nose, who directed him higher and then pointed out a mammoth, a huge specimen using its tusks to find roots.

He watched the huge animal briefly, estimating how many square miles a mammoth needed to feed, and then made a decision that saddened him. Earth had kept right on turning when the last mammoths disappeared. Newduvai could not afford many of them, ripping up foliage by the roots. Perhaps the Outsiders didn't care about that, but Locklear did. If you had to start sawing off links in your food chain, best if you started at the top. And he didn't want to pursue that thought by himself. At the very top was man. And Kzin. It was the kind of thing he'd like to discuss with Scarface, but he'd made two trips to the lifeboat without a peep from its all-band comm set.

Finally, he flew to the crypt and set his little craft down nearby, reassuring Ruth as they walked inside. She paused for flight when she saw the rest of the mammoths, slowly tumbling inside their cages. "Much, much, much magic," she said, and patted him with great confidence.

But it was the sight of forty Neanderthals in stasis that really affected Ruth. Her face twisted with remorse, she turned from the nearest cage and faced Locklear with tears streaming down her cheeks. "Locklear kill?"

"No, no! Sleep," he insisted, miming it.

She was not convinced. "No sleeptalk," she protested, placing a hand on her head and pointing toward the rugged male nearby. And doubtless she was right; in stasis you didn't even dream.

"Before, Locklear take Ruth from little house," he

said, tapping the cage, and then she remembered, and wanted to take the man out then and there. Instead, he got her help in moving the cage onto his improvised dolly and outside to the scooter.

They were halfway to the cabin and a thousand feet up on the heavily-laden scooter when Ruth somehow struck the cage base with her foot. Locklear saw the transparent plastic begin to rise, shouted, and nearly turned the scooter on its side as he leaped to slam the plastic down.

"Good God! You nearly let a wild man loose on a goddamn raft, a thousand feet in the air," he raged, and saw her cringe, holding her head in both hands. "Okay, Ruth. Okay, no problem," he continued more slowly, and pointed at the cage base. "Ruth no hit little house more. Locklear hit, soon."

They remained silent until they landed, and Locklear had time to review Newduvai's first in-flight airline emergency. Ruth had not feared a beating. No, it was his own panic that had punished her. That figured: a Kzin telepath sometimes suffered when someone nearby was suffering.

He brought food and water from the cabin, placed it near the scooter, then paused before pressing the cage base. "Ruth: gentle man talk in head same Ruth talk in head?"

"Yes, all gentles talk in head." She saw what he was getting at. "Ruth talk to man, say Locklear much, much good magic man."

He pointed again at the man, a muscular young specimen who, without so much body hair, might have excited little comment at a collegiate wrestling match. "Ruth friend of man?"

She blushed as she replied: "Yes. Friend long time."

"That's what I was afraid of," he muttered with a heavy sigh, pressed the baseplate, and then stepped back several paces, nearly bumping into the curious Loli.

The man's eyes flicked open. Locklear could see the heavy muscles tense, yet the man moved only his eyes, looking from him to Ruth, then to him again. When he did move, it was as though he'd been playing possum for forty thousand years, and his movements were as oddly graceful as Ruth's. He held up both hands, smiling, and it was obvious that some silent message had passed between them.

Locklear advanced with the same posture. A flat touch of hands, and then the man turned to Ruth with a burst of throaty speech. He was no taller than Locklear, but immensely more heavily-boned and muscled. He stood as erect as any man, unconcerned in his nakedness, and after a double handclasp with Ruth he made a smiling motion toward her breasts.

Again, Locklear saw the deeper color of flushing over her face and, after a head-down gesture of negation, she said something while staring at the young man's face. Puzzled, he glanced at Locklear with a comical half-smile, and Locklear tried to avoid looking at the man's budding erection. He told the man his name, and got a reply, but as usual Locklear gave him a name that seemed appropriate. He called him "Minuteman."

After a quick meal of fruit and water, Ruth did the translating. From the first, Minuteman accepted the fact that Locklear was one of the "new" people. After Locklear's demonstrations with the Kzin memo screen and a levitation of the scooter, Minuteman gave him more physical space, perhaps a sign of deference. Or perhaps wariness; time would tell.

Though Loli showed no fear of Minuteman, she spoke little to him and kept her distance—with an egg-sized stone in her little fist at all times. Minuteman treated Loli as a guest might treat an unwelcome pet. *Oh yes,* thought Locklear, *he knows her, all righty. . . .*

The hunt, Locklear claimed, was a celebration to welcome Minuteman, but he had an ulterior motive. He made his point to Ruth, who chattered and gestured and, no doubt, silently communed with Minuteman for long moments. It would be necessary for Minuteman to accompany Locklear on the scooter, but without Ruth if they were to lug any sizeable game back to the cabin.

When Ruth stopped, Minuteman said something more. "Yes, no problem," Ruth said then.

Minuteman, his facial scars writhing as he grinned, managed, "Yef, no pobbem," and laughed when Locklear did. *Amazing how fast these people adapt,* Locklear thought. *He wakes up on a strange planet, and an hour later he's right at home. A wonderful trusting kind of innocence; even childlike.* Then Locklear decided to see just how far that trust went, and gestured for Minuteman to sit down on the scooter after he wrestled the empty stasis cage to the ground.

Soon they were scudding along just above the trees at a pace guaranteed to scare the hell out of any sensible Neanderthal, Minuteman desperately trying to make a show of confidence in the leadership of this suicidal shaman, and Locklear was satisfied on two counts, with one count yet to come. First, the scooter's pace near trees was enough to make Minuteman hold on for dear life. Second, the young Neanderthal would view Locklear's easy mastery of the scooter as perhaps the very greatest of magics—and maybe Minuteman would pass that datum on, when the time came.

The third item was a shame, really, but it had to be done. A shaman without the power of ultimate punishment might be seen as expendable, and Locklear had to show that power. He showed it after passing over specimens of aurochs and horse, both noted with delight by Minuteman.

The goat had been grazing not far from three does until he saw the scooter swoop near. He was an old codger, probably driven off by the younger buck nearby, and Locklear recalled that the gestation period for goats was only five months—and besides, he told himself, the Outsiders could be pretty dumb in some matters. You didn't need twenty bucks for twenty does.

All of the animals bounded toward a rocky slope, and Minuteman watched them as Locklear maneuvered, forcing the old buck to turn back time and again. When at last the buck turned to face them, Locklear brought the scooter down, moving straight toward the hapless old fellow. Minuteman did not turn toward Locklear until he heard the report of the Kzin sidearm which Locklear held in both hands, and by that time the scooter was only a man's height above the rocks.

At the report, the buck slammed backward, stumbling, shot in the breast. Minuteman ducked away from the sound of the shot, seeing Locklear with the sidearm, and then began to shout. Locklear let the scooter settle but Minuteman did not wait, leaping down, rushing at the old buck which still kicked in its death agony.

By the time Locklear had the scooter resting on the slope, Minuteman was tearing at the buck's throat with his teeth, trying to dodge flinty hooves, the powerful arms locked around his prey. In thirty seconds the buck's eyes were glazing and its movements grew more feeble by the moment. Locklear put away the sidearm, feeling his stomach churn. Minuteman was drinking the animal's blood; sucking it, in fact, in a kind of frenzy.

When at last he sat up, Minuteman began to massage his temples with bloody fingers—perhaps a ritual, Locklear decided. The young Neanderthal's gaze at Lucklear was not pleasant, though he was suitably impressed by the invisible spear that had noisily smashed a man-sized goat off its feet leaving nothing more than a tiny hole in the animal's breast. Locklear went through a pantomime of shooting, and Minuteman gestured his "yes." Together, they placed the heavy carcass on the scooter and returned to the cabin. Minuteman seemed oddly subdued for a hunter who had just chewed a victim's throat open.

Locklear guffawed at what he saw at the cabin: in the cage so recently vacated by Minuteman was Loli, revolving in the slow dance of stasis. Ruth explained, "Loli like little house, like sleep. Ruth like for Loli sleep. Many like for Loli sleep long time," she added darkly.

It was Ruth who butchered the animal with the wtsai, while talking with Minuteman. Locklear watched smugly, noting the absence of flies. Damned if he was going to release those from their cages, nor the mosquitoes, locusts and other pests which lay with the predators in the crypt. Why would any god worth his salt pester a planet with flies, anyhow? The butterflies might be worth the trouble.

He was still ruminating on these matters when Ruth handed him the wtsai and entered the cabin silently. She seemed preoccupied, and Minuteman had wandered off toward the oaks so, just to be sociable, he said, "Minuteman see Locklear kill with magic. Minuteman like?"

She built a smoky fire, stretching skewers of stringy meat above the smoke, before answering. "No good, talk bad to magic man."

"It's okay, Ruth. Talk true to Locklear."

She propped the cabin door open to adjust the draft, then sat down beside him. "Minuteman feel bad. Locklear no kill meat fast, meat hurt long time. Meat feel much, much bad, so Minuteman feel much bad before kill meat. Locklear new person, no feel bad. Loli no feel bad. Minuteman no want hunt with Locklear."

As she attended to the barbecue and Locklear continued to ferret out more of this mystery, he grew more chastened. Neanderthal boys, learning to kill for food, began with animals that did not have a highly developed nervous system. Because when the animal felt pain, all the gentles nearby felt some of it too, especially women and girls. Neanderthal hunt teams were all-male affairs, and they learned every trick of stealth and quick kills because a clumsy kill meant a slow one. Minuteman had known that, lacking a club, he himself would feel the least pain if the goat bled to death quickly.

And large animals? You dug pit traps and visited them from a distance, or drove your prey off a distant cliff if you could. Neanderthal telepathy did not work much beyond twenty meters. The hunter who approached a wounded animal to pierce its throat with a spear was very brave, or very hungry. Or he was one of the new people, perfectly capable of irritating or even fighting a gentle without feeling the slightest psychic pain. The gentle Neanderthal, of course, was not protected against the new person's reflected pain. No wonder Ruth took care of Loli without liking her much!

He asked if Loli was the first "new" Ruth had seen. No, she said, but the only one they had allowed in the tribe. A hunt team had found her wandering alone, terrified and hungry, when she was only as high as a man's leg. Why hadn't the hunters run away? They had, Ruth said, but even then Loli had been quick on her feet. Rather than feel her gnawing fear and hunger on the perimeter of their camp, they had taken her in. And had regretted it ever since, " . . . long time. Long, long, long time!"

Locklear knew that he had gained a crucial insight; a Neanderthal behaved gently because it was in his own best interests. It was, at least, until modern Cro-Magnon man appeared without the blessing, and the curse, of telepathy.

Ruth's first telepathic greeting to the waking Minuteman had warned that he was in the presence of a great shaman, a "new" but nonetheless a good man. Minuteman had been so glad to see Ruth that he had proposed a brief roll in the grass, which involved great pleasure to participants—and it was expected that the audience could share their joy by telepathy. But Ruth knew better than that, reminding her friend that Locklear was not telepathic. Besides, she had the strongest kind of intuition that Locklear did not want to see her enjoying any other man. Peculiar, even bizarre; but new people were hard to figure. . . .

It was clear now, why Ruth's word "new" seemed to have an unpleasant side. New people were savage people. *So much for labels,* Locklear told himself. *Modern man is the real savage!*

Ruth took Loli out of stasis for supper, perhaps to share in the girl's pleasure at such a feast. Through Ruth, Locklear explained to Minuteman that he regretted giving pain to his guest. He would be happy to let gentles do the hunting, but all animals belonged to Locklear. No animals must be hunted without prior permission. Minuteman was agreeable, especially with a mouthful of succulent goat rib in his big lantern jaws. Tonight, Minuteman could share the cabin. Tomorrow he must choose a site for a camp, for Locklear would soon bring many, many more gentles.

Locklear fell asleep slowly, no thanks to the ache in his jaws. The others had wolfed down that barbecued goat as if it had been well-aged porterhouse, but he had been able to choke only a little of it down after endless chewing because, savory taste or not, that old goat had been tough as a Kzin's knuckles.

He wondered how Kit and Scarface were getting along, on the other side of those force walls. He really ought to fire up the lifeboat and visit them soon. Just as soon as he got things going here. With his mind-bending discovery of the truly gentle nature of Neanderthals, he was feeling very optimistic about the future. And modestly hungry. And very, very sleepy.

Minuteman spent two days quartering the vast circular expanse of Newduvai while Locklear piloted the scooter. In the process, he picked up a smatter of modern words though it was Ruth, in the evenings, who straightened out misunderstandings. Minuteman's clear choice for a major encampment was beside Newduvai's big lake, near the point where a stream joined the "big water." The site was a day's walk from the cabin, and Minuteman stressed that his choice might not be the choice of tribal elders. Besides, gentles tended to wander from season to season.

Though tempted by his power to command, Locklear decided against using it unless absolutely necessary. He would release them all and let them sort out their world, with the exception of excess hunting or tribal warfare. That didn't seem likely, but: "Ruth," he asked after the second day of recon, "see all people in little houses in cave?"

"Yes," she said firmly. "Many many in tribe of Minuteman and Ruth. Many many in other tribe."

But "many many" could mean a dozen or less. "Ruth see all in other tribe before?"

"Many times," she assured him. "Others give kill-stones, Ruth tribe give food."

"You trade with them," he said. After she had studied his face a moment, she agreed. He persisted: "Bad trades? Problem?"

"No problem," she said. "Trade one, two man or woman sometime, before big fire."

He asked about that, of course, and got an answer to a question he hadn't thought to ask. Ruth's last memory before waking on Newduvai—and Minuteman's too—was of the great fire that had driven several tribes to the base of a cliff. There, with trees bursting into flame nearby, the men had gathered around their women and children, beginning their song to welcome death. It was at that moment when the Outsiders must have put them in stasis and whisked them off to the rim of Known Space.

Almost an ethical decision, Locklear admitted. *Almost.* "No little gentles in cave," he reminded Ruth. "Locklear much sorry."

"No good, think of little gentles," she said glumly. And with that, they passed to matters of tribal leadership. The old men generally led, though an old woman might have followers. It seemed a loose kind of democracy and, when some faction disagreed, they could simply move out—perhaps no farther than a short walk away.

Locklear soon learned why the gentles tended to stay close: "Big, bad animals eat gentles," Ruth said. "New people take food, kill gentles," she added. Lions, wolves, bears—and modern man—were their reasons for safety in numbers.

Ruth and Minuteman had both seen much of Newduvai from the air by now. To check his own conclusions, Locklear said, "Plenty food for many people. Plenty for many, many, many people?"

Plenty, said Ruth, for all people in little houses; no problem. Locklear ended the session on that note and

Minuteman, perhaps with some silent urging from Ruth, chose to sleep outside.

Again, Locklear had a trouble getting to sleep, even after a half-hour of delightful tussle with the willing, homely, gentle Ruth. He could hardly wait for morning and his great social experiment.

His work would have gone much faster with Minuteman's muscular help, but Locklear wanted to share the crypt's secrets with as few as possible. The lake site was only fifteen minutes from the crypt by scooter, and there were no predators to attack a stasis cage, so Locklear transported the gentles by twos and left them in their cages, cursing his rotten time-management. It soon was obvious that the job would take two days and he'd set his heart on results now, now, now!

He was setting the scooter down near his cabin when Minuteman shot from the doorway, began to lope off, and then turned, approaching Locklear with the biggest, ugliest smile he could manage. He chattered away with all the innocence of a ferret in a birdhouse, his maleness in repose but rather large for that innocence. And wet.

Ruth waved from the cabin doorway.

"Right," Locklear snarled, too exhausted to let his anger kindle to white-hot fury. "Minuteman, I named you well. Your pants would be down, if you had any. Ahh, the hell with it."

Loli was asleep in her cage, and Minuteman found employment elsewhere as Locklear ate chopped goat, grapes, and gruel. He did not look at Ruth, even when she sat near him as he chewed.

Finally he walked to the pallet, looking from it to Ruth, shook his head and then lay down.

Ruth cocked her head in that way she had. "Like Ruth stay at fire?"

"I don't give a good shit. Yes, Ruth stay at fire. Good." Some perversity made him want her, but it was not as strong as his need for sleep. And rejecting her might be a kind of punishment, he thought sleepily. . . .

Late the next afternoon, Locklear completed his air-lift and returned to the cabin. He could see Minuteman sitting disconsolate, chin in hands, at the edge of the clearing. Apparently, no one had seen fit to take Loli from stasis. He couldn't blame them much. Actually, he thought as he entered the cabin, he had no logical reason to blame them for anything. They enjoyed each other according to their own tradition, and he was out of step with it. *Damn' right, and I don't know if I could ever get in step*.

He called Minuteman in. "Many, many gentles at big water," he said. "No big bad meat hurt gentles. Like see gentles now?" Minuteman wanted to very much. So did Ruth. He urged them onto the scooter and handed Ruth her woven basket full of dried apricots, giving both hindquarters of the goat to Minuteman without comment. Soon they were flitting above conifers and poplars, and then Ruth saw the dozens of cages glistening beside the lake.

"Gentles, gentles," she exclaimed, and began to weep. Locklear found himself angry at her pleasure, the anger of a wronged spouse, and set the scooter down abruptly some distance from the stasis cages.

Minuteman was off and running instantly. Ruth disembarked, turned, held a hand out. "Locklear like wake gentles? Ruth tell gentles, Locklear good, much good magics."

"Tell 'em anything you like," he barked, "after you screw 'em all!"

In the distance, Minuteman was capering around the cages, shouting in glee. After a moment, Ruth said, "Ruth like go back with Locklear."

"The hell you will! No, Ruth like push-push with many gentles. Locklear no like." And he twisted a vernier hard, the scooter lifting quickly.

Plaintively, growing faint on the breeze: "Ruth hurt in head. Like Locklear much . . ." And whatever else she said was lost.

He returned to the hidden Kzin lifeboat, hating the idea of the silent cabin, and monitored the comm set for hours. It availed him nothing, but its boring repetitions eventually put him to sleep.

For the next week, Locklear worked like a man demented. He used a stasis cage, as he had on Kzersatz, to store his remaining few hunks of smoked goat. He flew surveillance over the new encampment, so high that no one would spot him, which meant that he could see little of interest, beyond the fact that they were building huts of bundled grass and some dark substance, perhaps mud. The stasis cages lay in disarray; he must retrieve them soon.

It was pure luck that he spotted a half-dozen deer one morning, a half-day's walk from the encampment, running as though from a predator. Presently, hovering beyond big chestnut trees, he saw them: men, patiently herding their prey toward an arroyo. He grinned to himself and waited until a rise of ground would cover his maneuver. Then he swooped low behind the deer, swerving from side to side to group them, yelping and growling until he was hoarse. By that time, the deer had put a mile between themselves and their real pursuers.

No better time than now to get a few things straight. Locklear swept the scooter toward the encampment at a stately pace, circling twice, hearing thin shouts as the Neanderthals noted his approach. He watched them carefully, one hand checking his Kzin sidearm. They might be gentle but a few already carried spears and they were, after all, experts at the quick kill. He let the scooter hover at knee height, a constant reminder of his great magics, and noted the great stir he made as the scooter glided silently to a stop at the edge of the camp.

He saw Ruth and Minuteman emerge from one of the dozen beehive-shaped, grass-and-wattle huts. No, it wasn't Ruth; he admitted with chagrin that they all looked very much alike. The women paused first, and then he did spot Ruth, waving at him, a few steps nearer. The men moved nearer, falling silent now, laying their new spears and stone axes down as if by prearrangement. They stopped a few paces ahead of the women.

An older male, almost covered in curly gray hair, continued to advance using a spear—no, it was only a long walking staff—to aid him. He too stopped, with a glance over his shoulder, and then Locklear saw a bald old fellow with a withered leg hobbling past the younger men. Both of the oldsters advanced together then, full of years and dignity without a stitch of clothes. The gray man might have been sixty, with a little pot belly and knobby joints suggesting arthritis. The cripple was perhaps ten years younger but stringy and meatless, and his right thigh had been hideously smashed a long time before. His right leg was inches too short, and his left hip seemed disfigured from years of walking to compensate.

Locklear knew he needed Ruth now, but feared to risk violating some taboo so soon. "Locklear," he said, showing empty hands, then tapping his breast.

The two old men cocked their heads in a parody of Ruth's familiar gesture, then the curly one began to speak. Of course it was all gibberish, but the walking staff lay on the ground now and their hands were empty.

Wondering how much they would understand telepathically, Locklear spoke with enough volume for Ruth to hear. "Gentles hunt meat in hills," he said. "Locklear no like." He was not smiling.

The old men used brief phrases to each other, and then the crippled one turned toward the huts. Ruth began to walk forward, smiling wistfully at Locklear as she stopped next to the cripple.

She waited to hear a few words from each man, and then faced Locklear. "All one tribe now, two leaders," she said. "Skywater and Shortleg happy to see great shaman who save all from big fire. Ruth happy see Locklear too," she added softly.

He told her about the men hunting deer, and that it must stop; they must make do without meat for awhile. She translated. The old men conferred, and their gesture for "no" was the same as Ruth's. They replied through Ruth that young men had always hunted, and always would.

He told them that the animals were his, and they must not take what belonged to another. The old men said they could see that he felt in his head the animals were his, but no one owned the great mother land, and no one could own her children. They felt much bad for him. He was a very, very great shaman, but not so good at telling gentles how to live.

With great care, having chosen the names Cloud and Gimp for the old fellows, he explained that if many animals were killed, soon there would be no more. One day when many little animals were born, he would let them hunt the older ones.

The gist of their reply was this: Locklear obviously thought he was right, but they were older and therefore wiser. And because they had never run out of game no matter how much they killed, they *never could* run out of game. If it hadn't already happened, it wouldn't ever happen.

Abruptly, Locklear motioned to Cloud and had Ruth translate: he could prove the scarcity of game if Cloud would ride the scooter as Ruth and Minuteman had ridden it.

Much silent discussion and some out loud. Then old Cloud climbed aboard and in a moment, the scooter was above the trees.

From a mile up, they could identify most of the game animals, especially herd beasts in open plains. There weren't many to see. "No babies at all," Locklear said, trying to make gestures for "small." "Cloud, gentles *must* wait until babies are born." The old fellow seemed to understand Locklear's thoughts well enough, and spoke a bit of gibberish, but his head gesture was a Neanderthal "no."

Locklear, furious now, used the verniers with abandon. The scooter fled across parched arroyo and broken hill, closer to the ground and now so fast that Locklear himself began to feel nervous. Old Cloud sensed his unease, grasping handholds with gnarled knuckles and hunkering down, and Locklear knew a savage elation. *Serve the old bastard right if I splattered him all over Newduvai.* And then he saw the old man staring at his eyes, and knew that the thought had been received.

"No, I won't do it," he said. But a part of him had wanted to; *still* wanted to out of sheer frustration. Cloud's face was a rigid mask of fear, big teeth showing, and Locklear slowed the scooter as he approached the encampment again.

Cloud did not wait for the vehicle to settle, but debarked as fast as painful old joints would permit and stood facing his followers without a sound.

After a moment, with dozens of Neanderthals staring in stunned silence, they all turned their backs, a wave of moans rising from every throat. Ruth hesitated, but she too faced away from Locklear.

"Ruth! No hurt Cloud. Locklear no like hurt gentles."

The moans continued as Cloud strode away. "Locklear need to talk to Ruth!" And then as the entire tribe began to walk away, he raised his voice: "No hurt gentles, Ruth!"

She stopped, but would not look at him as she replied. "Cloud say new people hurt gentles and not know. Locklear hurt Cloud before, want kill Cloud. Locklear go soon soon," she finished in a sob. Suddenly, then, she was running to catch the others.

Some of the men were groping for spears now. Locklear did not wait to see what they might do with them. A half-hour later he was using the dolly in the crypt, ranking cage upon cage just inside the obscuring film. With several lion cages stacked like bricks at the entrance, no sensible Neanderthal would go a step further. Later, he could use disassembled stasis units as booby traps as he had done on Kzersatz. But it was nearly dark when he finished, and Locklear was hurrying. Now, for the first time ever on Newduvai, he felt gooseflesh when he thought of camping in the open.

*   *   *

For days, he considered a return to Kzersatz in the lifeboat, meanwhile improving the cabin with Loli's help. He got that help very simply, by refusing to let her sleep in her stasis cage unless she did help. Loli was very bright, and learned his language quickly because she could not rely on telepathy. Operating on the sour-grape theory, he told himself that Ruth had been mud-fence ugly; he hadn't felt any real affection for a Neanderthal bimbo. Not *really* . . .

He managed to ignore Loli's budding charms by reminding himself that she was no more than twelve or so, and gradually she began to trust him. He wondered how much that trust would suffer if she found he was taking her from stasis only on the days he needed help.

As the days faded into weeks, the cabin became a two-room affair with a connecting passage for firewood and storage. Loli, after endless scraping and soaking of the stiff goathide in acorn water, fashioned herself a one-piece garment. She taught Locklear how repeated boiling turned acorns into edible nuts, and wove mats of plaited grass for the cabin.

He let her roam in search of small game once a week until the day she returned empty-handed. He was cutting hinge material of stainless steel from a stasis cage with Kzin shears at the time, and smiled. "Don't feel bad, Loli. There's plenty of meat in storage." The more he used complete sentences, the more she seemed to be picking up the lingo.

She shrugged, picking at a scab on one of her hard little feet. "Loli not hunt. Gentles hunt Loli." She read his stare correctly. "Gentles not try to hurt Loli; this many follow and hide," she said, holding up four fingers and making a comical pantomime of a stealthy hunter.

He held up four fingers. "Four," he reminded her. "Did they follow you here?"

"Maybe want to follow Loli here," she said, grinning. "Loli think much. Loli go far far—"

"Very far," he corrected.

"Very far to dry place, gentles no follow feet there.

Loli hide, run very far where gentles not see. Come back to Locklear."

Yes, they'd have trouble tracking her through those desert patches, he realized, and she could've doubled back unseen in the arroyos. Or she might have been followed after all. "Loli is smart," he said, patting her shoulder, "but gentles are smart too. Gentles maybe want to hurt Locklear."

"Gentles cover big holes, spears in holes, come back, maybe find kill animal. Maybe kill Locklear."

Yeah, they'd do it that way. Or maybe set a fire to burn him out of the cabin. "Loli, would you feel bad if the gentles killed me?"

In her vast innocence, Loli thought about it before answering. "Little while, yes. Loli don't like to live alone. Gentles alltime like to play," she said, with a bump-and-grind routine so outrageous that he burst out laughing. "Locklear don't trade food for play," she added, making it obvious that Neanderthal men *did*.

"Not until Loli is older," he said with brutal honesty.

"Loli is a woman," she said, pouting as though he had slandered her.

To shift away from this dangerous topic he said, "Yes, and you can help me make this place safe from gentles." That was the day he began teaching the girl how to disassemble cages for their most potent parts, the grav polarizers and stasis units.

They burned off the surrounding ground cover bit by bit during the nights to avoid telltale smoke, and Loli assured him that Neanderthals never ventured from camp on nights as dark as Newduvai's. Sooner or later, he knew, they were bound to discover his little homestead and he intended to make it a place of terrifying magics.

As luck would have it, he had over two months to prepare before a far more potent new magic thundered across the sky of Newduvai.

Locklear swallowed hard the day he heard that long roll of synthetic thunder, recognizing it for what it was.

He had told Loli about the Kzinti, and now he warned her that they might be near, and saw her coltish legs flash into the forest as he sent the scooter scudding close to the ground toward the heights where his lifeboat was hidden. He would need only one close look to identify a Kzin ship.

Dismounting near the lifeboat, peering past an outcrop and shivering because he was so near the cold force walls, he saw a foreshortened dot hovering near Newduvai's big lake. Winks of light streaked downward from it; he counted five shots before the ship ceased firing, and knew that its target had to be the big encampment of gentles.

"If only I had those beam cannons I took apart," he growled, unconsciously taking the side of the Neanderthals as tendrils of smoke fingered the sky. But he had removed the weapon pylon mounts long before. He released a long-held breath as the ship dwindled to a dot in the sky, hunching his shoulders, wondering how he could have been so naive as to forswear war altogether. Killing was a bitter draught, yet not half so bitter as dying.

The ship disappeared. Ten minutes later he saw it again, making the kind of circular sweep used for cartography, and this time it passed only a mile distant, and he gasped—for it was not a Kzin ship. The little cruiser escort bore Interworld Commission markings.

"The goddamn tabbies must have taken one of ours," he muttered to himself, and cursed as he saw the ship break off its sweep. No question about it: they were hovering very near his cabin.

Locklear could not fight from the lifeboat, but at least he had plenty of spare magazines for his Kzin sidearm in the lifeboat's lockers. He crammed his pockets with spares, expecting to see smoke roiling from his homestead as he began to skulk his scooter low toward home. His little vehicle would not bulk large on radar. And the tabbies might not realize how soon it grew dark on Newduvai. Maybe he could even the odds a little by landing near enough to snipe by the light of his burning cabin. He sneaked the last two hundred meters afoot, already steeling himself for the sight of a burning cabin.

But the cabin was not burning. And the Kzinti were not pillaging because, he saw with utter disbelief, the armed crew surrounding his cabin was human. He had already stood erect when it occurred to him that humans had been known to defect in previous wars—and he was carrying a Kzin weapon. He placed the sidearm and spare magazines beneath a stone overhang. Then Locklear strode out of the forest rubber-legged, too weak with relief to be angry at the firing on the village.

The first man to see him was a rawboned, ruddy private with the height of a belter. He brought his assault rifle to bear on Locklear, then snapped it to "port arms." Three others spun as the big belter shouted, "Gomulka; We've got one!"

A big fireplug of a man, wearing sergeant's stripes, whirled and moved away from a cabin window, motioning a smaller man beneath the other window to stay put. Striding toward the belter, he used the heavy bellow of command. "Parker; escort him in! Schmidt, watch the perimeter."

The belter trotted toward Locklear while an athletic specimen with a yellow crew-cut moved out to watch the forest where Locklear had emerged. Locklear took the belter's free hand and shook it repeatedly. They walked to the cabin together, and the rest of the group relaxed visibly to see Locklear all but capering in his delight. Two other armed figures appeared from across the clearing, one with curves too lush to be male, and Locklear invited them all in with, "There are no Kzinti on this piece of the planet; welcome to Newduvai."

Leaning, sitting, they all found their ease in Locklear's room, and their gazes were as curious as Locklear's own. He noted the varied shoulder patches: We Made It, Jinx, Wunderland. The woman, wearing the bars of a lieutenant, was evidently a Flatlander like himself. Commander Curt Stockton wore a Canyon patch, standing wiry and erect beside the woman, with pale gray eyes that missed nothing.

"I was captured by a Kzin ship," Locklear explained, "and marooned. But I suppose that's all in the records; I call the planet 'Zoo' because I think the Outsiders designed it with that in mind."

"We had these co-ordinates, and something vague about prison compounds, from translations of Kzin records," Stockton replied. "You must know a lot about this Zoo place by now."

"A fair amount. Listen, I saw you firing on a village near the big lake an hour ago. You mustn't do it again, commander. Those people are real Earth Neanderthals, probably the only ones in the entire galaxy."

The blocky sergeant, David Gomulka, slid his gaze to lock on Stockton's and shrugged big sloping shoulders. The woman, a close-cropped brunette whose cinched belt advertised her charms, gave Locklear a brilliant smile and sat down on his pallet. "I'm Grace Agostinho; Lieutenant, Manaus Intelligence Corps, Earth. Forgive our manners, Mr. Locklear, we've been in heavy fighting along the Rim and this isn't exactly what we expected to find."

"Me neither," Locklear smiled, then turned serious. "I hope you didn't destroy that village."

"Sorry about that," Stockton said. "We may have caused a few casualties when we opened fire on those huts. I ordered the firing stopped as soon as I saw they weren't Kzinti. But don't look so glum, Locklear; it's not as if they were human."

"Damn right they are," Locklear insisted. "As you'll soon find out, if we can get their trust again. I've even taught a few of 'em some of our language. And that's not all. But hey, I'm dying of curiosity without any news from outside. Is the war over?"

Commander Stockton coughed lightly for attention and the others seemed as attentive as Locklear. "It looks good around the core worlds, but in the Rim sectors it's still anybody's war." He jerked a thumb toward the two-hundred-ton craft, twice the length of a Kzin lifeboat, that rested on its repulsor jacks at the edge of the clearing with its own small pinnace clinging to its back. "The *Anthony Wayne* is the kind of cruiser escort they don't mind turning over to small combat teams like mine. The big brass gave us this mission after we captured some Kzinti files from a tabby dreadnaught. Not as good as R & R back home, but we're glad of the break." Stockton's grin was infectious.

"I haven't had time to set up a distillery," Locklear said, "or I'd offer you drinks on the house."

"A man could get parched here," said a swarthy little private.

"Good idea, Gazho. You're detailed to get some medicinal brandy from the med stores," said Stockton.

As the private hurried out, Locklear said, "You could probably let the rest of the crew out to stretch their legs, you know. Not much to guard against on Newduvai."

"What you see is all there is," said a compact private with high cheekbones and a Crashlander medic patch. Locklear had not heard him speak before. Softly accented, laconic; almost a scholar's diction. But that's what you might expect of a military medic.

Stockton's quick gaze riveted the man as if to say, "that's enough." To Locklear he nodded. "Meet Soichiro Lee; an intern before the war. Has a tendency to act as if a combat team is a democratic outfit but," his glance toward Lee was amused now, "he's a good sawbones. Anyhow, the *Wayne* can take care of herself. We've set her auto defenses for voice recognition when the hatch is closed, so don't go wandering closer than ten meters without one of us. And if one of those hairy apes throws a rock at her, she might just burn him for his troubles."

Locklear nodded. "A crew of seven; that's pretty thin."

Stockton, carefully: "You want to expand on that?"

Locklear: "I mean, you've got your crew pretty thinly spread. The tabbies have the same problem, though. The bunch that marooned me here had only four members."

Sergeant Gomulka exhaled heavily, catching Stockton's glance. "Commander, with your permission:

Locklear here might have some ideas about those tabby records."

"Umm. Yeah, I suppose," with some reluctance. "Locklear, apparently the Kzinti felt there was some valuable secret, a weapon maybe, here on Zoo. They intended to return for it. Any idea what it was?"

Locklear laughed aloud. "Probably it was me. It ought to be the whole bleeding planet," he said. "If you stand near the force wall and look hard, you can see what looks like a piece of the Kzin homeworld close to this one. You can't imagine the secrets the other compounds might have. For starters, the life forms I found in stasis had been here forty thousand years, near as I can tell, before I released 'em."

"*You* released them?"

"Maybe I shouldn't have, but—" He glanced shyly toward Lieutenant Agostinho. "I got pretty lonesome."

"Anyone would," she said, and her smile was more than understanding.

Gomulka rumbled in evident disgust, "Why would a lot of walking fossils be important to the tabby war effort?"

"They probably wouldn't," Locklear admitted. "And anyhow, I didn't find the specimens until after the Kzinti left." He could not say exactly why, but this did not seem the time to regale them with his adventures on Kzersatz. Something just beyond the tip of his awareness was flashing like a caution signal.

Now Gomulka looked at his commander. "So that's not what we're looking for," he said. "Maybe it's not on this Newduvai dump. Maybe next door?"

"Maybe. We'll take it one dump at a time," said Stockton, and turned as the swarthy private popped into the cabin. "Ah. I trust the Armagnac didn't insult your palate on the way, Nathan," he said.

Nathan Gazho looked at the bottle's broken seal, then began to distribute nested plastic cups, his breath already laced with his quick nip of the brandy. "You don't miss much," he grumbled.

But I'm missing something, Locklear thought as he

touched his half-filled cup to that of the sloe-eyed, languorous lieutenant. *Slack discipline? But combat troops probably ignore the spit and polish. Except for this hotsy who keeps looking at me as if we shared a secret, they've all got the hand calluses and haircuts of shock troops. No, it's something else . . .*

He told himself it was reluctance to make himself a hero; and next he told himself they wouldn't believe him anyway. And then he admitted that he wasn't sure exactly why, but he would tell them nothing about his victory on Kzersatz unless they asked. *Maybe because I suspect they'd round up poor Scarface, maybe hunt him down and shoot him like a mad dog no matter what I said. Yeah, that's reason enough. But something else, too.*

Night fell, with its almost audible thump, while they emptied the Armagnac. Locklear explained his scholarly fear that the gentles were likely to kill off animals that no other ethologist had ever studied on the hoof; mentioned Ruth and Minuteman as well; and decided to say nothing about Loli to these hardbitten troops. Anse Parker, the gangling belter, kept bringing the topic back to the tantalizingly vague secret mentioned in Kzin files. Parker, Locklear decided, thought himself subtle but managed only to be transparently cunning.

Austin Schmidt, the wide-shouldered blond, had little capacity for Armagnac and kept toasting the day when ". . . all this crap is history and I'm a man of means," singing that refrain from an old barracks ballad in a surprisingly sweet tenor. Locklear could not warm up to Nathan Gazho, whose gaze took inventory of every item in the cabin. The man's expensive wristcomp and pinky ring mismatched him like earrings on a weasel.

David Gomulka was all noncom, though, with a veteran's gift for controlling men and a sure hand in measuring booze. If the two officers felt any unease when he called them "Curt" and "Grace," they managed to avoid showing it. Gomulka spun out the tale of his first hand-to-hand engagement against a Kzin penetration team with details that proved he knew how the tabbies fought.

Locklear wanted to say, "That's right; that's how it is," but only nodded.

It was late in the evening when the commander cut short their speculations on Zoo, stood up, snapped the belt flash from its ring and flicked it experimentally. "We could all use some sleep," he decided, with the smile of a young father at his men, some of whom were older than he. "Mr. Locklear, we have more than enough room. Please be our guest in the *Anthony Wayne* tonight."

Locklear, thinking that Loli might steal back to the cabin if she were somewhere nearby, said, "I appreciate it, commander, but I'm right at home here. Really."

A nod, and a reflective gnawing of Stockton's lower lip. "I'm responsible for you now, Locklear. God knows what those Neanderthals might do, now that we've set fire to their nests."

"But—" The men were stretching out their kinks, paying silent but close attention to the interchange.

"I must insist. I don't want to put it in terms of command, but I *am* the local sheriff here now, so to speak." The engaging grin again. "Come on, Locklear, think of it as repaying your hospitality. Nothing's certain in this place, and—," his last phrase bringing soft chuckles from Gomulka, "they'd throw me in the brig if I let anything happen to you now."

The taciturn Parker led the way, and Locklear smiled in the darkness thinking how Loli might wonder at the intensely bright, intensely magical beams that bobbed toward the ship. After Parker called out his name and a long number, the ship's hatch steps dropped at their feet and Locklear knew the reassurance of climbing into an Interworld ship with its familiar smells, whines and beeps.

Parker and Schmidt were loudly in favor of a nightcap, but Stockton's, "Not a good idea, David," to the sergeant was met with a nod and barked commands by Gomulka. Grace Agostinho made a similar offer to Locklear.

"Thanks anyway. You know what I'd really like?"

"Probably," she said, with a pursed-lipped smile.

He was blushing as he said, "Ham sandwiches. Beer. A slice of thrillcake," and nodded quickly when she hauled a frozen shrimp teriyaki from their food lockers. When it popped from the radioven, he sat near the ship's bridge to eat it, idly noting a few dark foodstains on the bridge linolamat and listening to Grace tell of small news from home. The Amazon dam, a new "must-see" holo musical, a controversial cure for the common cold; the kind of tremendous trifles that cemented friendships.

She left him briefly while he chased scraps on his plate, and by the time she returned most of the crew had secured their pneumatic cubicle doors. "It's always satisfying to feed a man with an appetite," said Grace, smiling at his clean plate as she slid it into the galley scrubber. "I'll see you're fed well on the *Wayne*." With hands on her hips, she said, "Well: Private Schmidt has sentry duty. He'll show you to your quarters."

He took her hand, thanked her, and nodded to the slightly wavering Schmidt who led the way back toward the ship's engine room. He did not look back but, from the sound of it, Grace entered a cubicle where two men were arguing in subdued tones.

Schmidt showed him to the rearmost cubicle but not the rearmost dozen bunks. Those, he saw, were ranked inside a cage of duralloy with no privacy whatever. Dark crusted stains spotted the floor inside and outside the cage. A fax sheet lay in the passageway. When Locklear glanced toward it, the private saw it, tried to hide a startled response, and then essayed a drunken grin.

"Gotta have a tight ship," said Schmidt, banging his head on the duralloy as he retrieved the fax and balled it up with one hand. He tossed the wadded fax into a flush-mounted waste receptacle, slid the cubicle door open for Locklear, and managed a passable salute. "Have a good one, pal. You know how to adjust your rubberlady?"

Locklear saw that the mattresses of the two bunks were standard models with adjustable inflation and webbing. "No problem," he replied, and slid the door closed. He washed up at the tiny inset sink, used the urinal slot below it, and surveyed his clothes after removing them. They'd all seen better days. Maybe he could wangle some new ones. He was sleepier than he'd thought, and adjusted his rubberlady for a soft setting, and was asleep within moments.

He did not know how long it was before he found himself sitting bolt-upright in darkness. He knew what was wrong, now: *everything*. It might be possible for a little escort ship to plunder records from a derelict mile-long Kzin battleship. It was barely possible that the same craft would be sent to check on some big Kzin secret—*but not without at least a cruiser, if the Kzinti might be heading for Zoo.*

He rubbed a trickle of sweat as it counted his ribs. He didn't have to be a military buff to know that ordinary privates do not have access to medical lockers, and the commander had told Gazho to get that brandy from med stores. Right; and all those motley shoulder patches didn't add up to a picked combat crew, either. And one more thing: even in his half-blotted condition, Schmidt had snatched that fax sheet up as though it was evidence against him. Maybe it was . . .

He waved the overhead lamp on, grabbed his ratty flight suit, and slid his cubicle door open. If anyone asked, he was looking for a cleaner unit for his togs.

A low thrum of the ship's sleeping hydraulics; a slightly louder buzz of someone sleeping, most likely Schmidt while on sentry duty. *Not much discipline at all. I wonder just how much commanding Stockton really does.* Locklear stepped into the passageway, moved several paces, and eased his free hand into the waste receptacle slot. Then he thrust the fax wad into his dirty flight suit and padded silently back, cursing the sigh of his door. A moment later he was colder than before.

The fax was labeled, "PRISONER RIGHTS AND PRIVILEGES,"

and had been signed by some Provost Marshall—or a doctor, to judge from its illegibility. He'd bet anything that fax had fallen, or had been torn, from those duralloy bars. Rust-colored crusty stains on the floor; a similar stain near the ship's bridge; but no obvious damage to the ship from Kzin weapons.

It took all his courage to go into the passageway again, flight suit in hand, and replace the wadded fax sheet where he'd found it. And the door seemed much louder this time, almost a sob instead of a sigh.

Locklear felt like sobbing too. He lay on his rubberlady in the dark, thinking about it. A hundred scenarios might explain some of the facts, but only one matched them all: the *Anthony Wayne* had been a prisoner ship, but now the prisoners were calling themselves "commander" and "sergeant," and the real crew of the *Anthony Wayne* had made those stains inside the ship with their blood.

He wanted to shout it, but demanded it silently: *So why would a handful of deserters fly to Zoo?* Before he fell at last into a troubled sleep, he had asked it again and again, and the answer was always the same: somehow, one of them had learned of the Kzin records and hoped to find Zoo's secret before either side did.

These people would be deadly to anyone who knew their secret. And almost certainly, they'd never buy the truth, that Locklear himself was the secret because the Kzinti had been so sure he was an Interworld agent.

END OF PART I

Introduction

Back when I was a civilian, I always read the science-fact articles in the sf magazines before I read the fiction. But the following article on talking to the animals is truly best read after "Briar Patch."

DIALOGUES IN THE ZOO

Dean Ing

In inventing his warlike, tigerish Kzinti to compete against humans for Known Space, Larry Niven did us all a favor. When dealing with a competitor, you'd best understand him at least well enough to communicate. With the Kzinti, Niven has given us a scenario worth studying because it could happen one day, and those big boogers command attention. He's also given us enough of their background and culture for some serious study. Well, *half* serious; nobody said we couldn't have a hell of a lot of fun working out the ways we might screw up when trying to communicate with a Kzin.

The jargon term is "interspecies communication," and we do it regularly with other terrestrial species; but we often think we know what the animal "means" when we haven't the foggiest idea. What happens when a dog confronts a dolphin, or runs with a Russian boar, or when a squirrel is raised with cats? Yes, they can communicate in ways weird and wonderful, and much of their "talk" is silent because it's in pantomime. More on that presently.

Ethologists—animal behavior specialists—say that different species don't converse with the kind of ease described in, say, science fiction. It takes a lot of brainpower, more than most critters can muster, to realize that a gesture or a sound can be a symbol for something else. It doesn't take as much intelligence for animals to mimic what they see or hear. Many species can voluntarily demonstrate or mimic something, behaviors that are clearly deliberate attempts to get some idea across to another species. Niven's fictional Kzinti are plenty smart, but Larry made them emotional and gave them traditional daggers. In writing my Kzin stories for Larry, I found that their emotional states should be pretty easy to decipher from face and body cues, giving us one channel of communication. I also "revealed" how that dagger might be a lot closer to phallic than a mere symbol! Mating cats bite and scratch, right? Maybe a human ethologist, asked to scratch a female Kzin with a dagger, has a right to suspect he's "saying" more than he really wants to say. . . .

The Kzin are easy to communicate with in one way because they're bright enough to have self-awareness. Chimps and other big primates sometimes make what their human friends call "self-referential" comments; they seem to have some small awareness of a self. The gorilla, Koko, is such a creature, who grieved at the loss of a pet kitten. The more self-awareness, the more a critter seems able to "talk" to another species. So much work has been done with chimps and other primates that I propose to concentrate on other species here, chiefly on other mammals. Generally the more forebrain development, the more self-awareness. From studying the brain of a rabbit, you'd guess that cottontails aren't much into communing with horses. And yet, . . .

Yet one afternoon a friend, whose property adjoins a field with horses and a pet rabbit, watched something that put gooseflesh on his arms. The rabbit was mooching around near the front hooves of a horse, which I had seen for myself, amused because the horse was careful to avoid squashing his companion. But this time, the horse pointed its muzzle toward the rabbit—which promptly sat up, placing front paws on both sides of the horse's muzzle. Noses touching, they stood motionless for perhaps ten seconds. Then the rabbit dropped down, and both beasts began to nibble grass again, and my friend began to breathe again.

What the devil was that all about? I can only guess that each was verifying that the other had nothing but foliage on his breath and was willing to coexist with no threat. We can make some other guesses, too. Both animals have highly-developed olfactory bulbs, sections of their brains devoted to scent. And when a critter has a lot of its gray matter devoted to a certain sense organ—eyes among most birds, and ears among dogs—we should expect them to use that sense organ in communication. The horse and the rabbit both have good ears, too. My friend swears he didn't see their lips move, but it's barely possible they might have "said" something that human ears aren't trained to understand.

Benjamin Hunt, an ethologist in the University of California at Davis, cautions, "People want to believe that animals have a very humanlike thought process. . . . but it's really nonsense." Sure, we know they *have* thoughts, to the extent that they can learn new behaviors. But some species can be taught by combinations of reward and punishment, and some evidently can't.

The commonest kind of interspecies communication we notice is the kind we set up when we train animals. Before describing a handful of unstructured events where "lower" animals clearly were communicating with another species, we should check into the ways animals allow themselves to be taught. Ethologists say that demonstration and mimicry are powerful communication tools between human and chimp or dolphin. It's been known for a long time that animals can pick up cues so subtle the trainer doesn't even know he's giving them, and a critter as smart as a dolphin will mimic a demonstration just as a chimp does, within the limitations his body imposes.

Trainers claim that dolphins, like birds, can't be taught by "aversive" (punishment) means. I'll risk a hypothesis on this one: you could use aversive training on a dolphin if you could dominate him in the water. A whale will try to dominate another by resting his "chin" atop the other's head. Makes sense: if the lower whale can't come up to breathe, he's got to flee the scene. If the upper whale is too small to make the gambit work, he can't dominate. Great; now let's see a human trainer try that on a *tursiops truncatus*, the bottlenose dolphin, which is bigger than a human.

The mythical Kzinti, being very catlike, would probably be trained to hunt, or at least pounce, at mama's tempting, furry, twitching tail. So I gave the female Kzin a more twitchable tail and a very haughty attitude toward it. Since cats seem instinctively entranced by moving taillike objects anyhow (cats raised by other animals show the same fascination), and a female might use the appendage more than a male, I let Kzin tails figure in some action scenes. Basically, most action scenes revolve around some form of a basic question: Who's to be dominant? We can bloody-well believe it where the Kzinti are concerned; we might not want to believe it when we have a predisposition to like the critter.

Karen Pryor, an expert on dolphins, insists that they sometimes will strike a trainer's arm aggressively with their dorsal fins, and their rough jostling "play" with a trainer can be a dominance ploy. For some of us, the thread of domination games running through the animal kingdom is philosophically distasteful. Nevertheless, it's more than a thread; practically a hawser. When we meet the intelligent buggywhips from Aldebaran, the first order of business may be to agree on who whips whom—perhaps only symbolically. (Again, Larry's Kzinti spend a lot of energy on status games. Almost as much as humans do.)

Once you've established who's boss, you get to train

your lackeys. Pryor notes that many species—elephant, wolf, primate, even polar bear—want eye contact with a trainer to verify that the trainer is watching what the animal does. But she insists that the dolphin depends on eye contact more than the others. This is social interaction, no question about it! Most trainers claim that a dolphin's intelligence is right up there with the chimp's. The false killer whale, *pseudorca crassidans*, may be even brighter. Pryor described a session where a trainer "told" a *pseudorca,* by giving him half his usual reward, that he was doing the trick half-right. The critter cleaned up his act immediately, and got his full reward.

Dolphin trainers, like trainers of other species including autistic children, must become expert at what B. F. Skinner calls "operant conditioning." Anthropologist Greg Bateson has suggested that, if we want to communicate with extraterrestrials, operant conditioning is one way to do it. You reinforce a behavior by rewarding it so that the behavior is strengthened by its consequences. If the animal wants nothing from you but food, then that's the only reinforcement you can give. If it also wants affection, so much the better. I can't prove it, but I think emotions develop with intelligence. The trick is in making emotion your servant—always a problem for a Kzin. Dolphins may have solved that one, unless someone can prove that their aggressiveness equals anger.

I watched a trainer from concealment once, as she cleaned up a dolphin pool long after a public show. Two of her performers, without orders, fetched the floating sticks and balls and whatnot over a period of several minutes, solely for the rewards of her affectionate pats and gentle words afterward. One of them, thrusting its bottle nose out near her, chattered some quick-march birdlike message as she was leaving until, with the impatience she might have shown to a mischievous child, she knelt at the water's edge to rub and pat its head one more time. No wonder dolphins are so trainable, when they value human attention so much!

A dolphin has no vocal chords in its larynx; it "talks" from its nasal cavities, and projects its echolocating sonar waves the same way. Those sounds are conducted and directed through its "melon," a fatty bulge just below its forehead. The dolphin is descended from land-roving predators which were also ancestors of horses and other ungulates, and horses snort and whistle through their noses too. It might be interesting to study communications between horse and dolphin. Or between horse and Kzin, since Niven provided those folk with highly expressive, umbrella-fold ears. Realizing how those ears could "wink," I went on and made them the Kzin equivalent of a grin. Somehow I didn't think a Kzin, predator that he is, would want to shut one eye even for a wink. But what if you were a dolphin with no external ear appendages, no fingers, no tentacles, no feet?

If dolphins had fingers instead of tough, insensitive flippers, they might be coaxed into really astonishing tasks, maybe including sign talk. The fact is, the male dolphin does have one and only one sensitive digit, and though it's not the kind of datum a trainer tells to a public throng, that male dolphin will sometimes use his penis as an inquiring finger to check things out. This suggests a very special channel of communication which, as you can imagine, might send a lot of botched messages to the dolphin but which might, just possibly, be a source of varied messages *from* him. We view the penis as a digit of rather limited special messages. Perhaps the cetacean takes a broader view, if it's the only highly sensitive tactile organ he's got!

The rapidfire sonar clicks and mimicry sounds of dolphins have been studied by Lilly and others, with some exciting guesses that haven't been fully borne out. Incidentally, the awesome "songs" of whales seem to be sung only by males. For the same reasons that male birds do most of the singing? One day we may know.

Birds, while they aren't exactly geniuses, can learn to count. With training, a budgie loses count after six, a raven after seven or eight. One ethologist, trying to fool a flight of wild crows, took a friend into his toolshed near his garden and then left, alone. The crows stayed in a tree until his friend also emerged and walked away, then swooped down into his veggies. He tried it with two friends, then three. Each time, the crows waited until the last man left.

Then he brought a fifth man. When the fourth man left, the crows happily descended into the corn—and fled with every sign of consternation when that fifth man emerged from the shed. I mentioned this to veterinarian Howard Miller. "Sure," he said. "A crow has only four toes." They just ran out of toes. This doesn't explain the higher counting by ravens and parrots, but given the same experimental lab-learning sessions, the crow might do better. Even in the wild, they can count at least to four. When we learn more crow-talk, we may find that they do it out loud.

Okay, we teach parrots and mynahs to "talk" in *human* words; but do they know what they're saying? Ethologists deny it, for the most part. Our fictional characters in the "Man–Kzin" stories get into a lot of trouble, sending messages that are misunderstood.

On the other hand, and rare among feathered folk, was an African gray parrot that showed a functional English vocabulary, meaning that he literally told humans what was on his mind. He knew nine nouns, three colors, a couple of shapes, and consistently volunteered a loud-and-clear "No!" when faced with anything he didn't like. The bird's trainer claimed that previous failures to get this kind of talk from parrots were because trainers relied on food as the stimulus.

The vet, Miller, knew a mynah that learned to mimic the signal whistle of a garbageman so well, sometimes the garbage truck driver would start away too soon, making an apoplectic garbageman miss the tailgate with thirty gallons of crud. Of course, the bird was repeating a "call" he often heard several times, moments before he responded. The garbageman taught him by accident.

The bird calls are generally territorial claims, though they also have special cries for alarm and so on. I once stole a tiny mockingbird. After my patient Cherokee granny helped feed him for months, I taught him a special warble, unlike any bird call I'd ever heard. Meanwhile he developed his own repertoire of songs. My special series of whistles took ten seconds and he learned it all, though he didn't always repeat it all. We let him go two years later and, after hanging around for a few days, he "lit a shuck," as my granny said. A year later, a mocker perched near our back door and, only when I came outside, he gave that complete ten-second warble. He wouldn't perch on my arm anymore, but it seems very likely he used that particular warble routine as a greeting. I've always wondered if he greeted other humans that way. We can't be certain it was really a greeting, however. It could have been an alarm of sorts: "Watch it, everybody, here comes that damn' bird-stealing kid again!"

Students at the Cal Davis veterinary school were treated to one hilarious proof that birds learn by observation. A tame duck, foraging under a walnut tree in a front yard, found better pickings in the street after the nutshells were cracked by passing cars. The duck couldn't crack the shells himself, so he did the next best thing. He carried more walnuts into the street and deposited them there, then waited at the curb for cars to do the job for him.

A hamster is probably less sophisticated—all right, then: dumber—than many birds. He also lacks a bird's vision. Because hamsters are burrowing rodents, they evolved without needing long-distance sight or much in the way of depth perception. A hamster will, in fact, walk right off your shoulder and whomp his noggin on the floor because he doesn't know any better and doesn't seem able to learn. Let's face it, getting your lights put out by a long fall is pretty aversive training, but it won't work on hamsters. They can, however, learn a few voice commands if rewarded with food. The trick is with the trainer. You learn how the animal behaves, then give a certain command when you see he's about to do something you want him to do: stand, come, go.

Then if he does it right, you reward him instantly, as operant conditioning. Repeat that consistently enough, long enough, and you can train most mammals to obey a few commands.

Domestic cats can be trained this way. Aversive training—such as a light thump on the nose, or grab-the cat by the scruff and shaking it—must be done before he misbehaves. Punishment even moments later will not do any good; you've got to catch the little varmint just as he's about to grab the hamster or do his doo-dahs on the rug. Don't ask me how you'd do that with a young flash-tempered Kzin. Stainless armor, maybe; but one'll get you five Larry Niven would think of a better way.

Some people will go into a rage when you suggest shaking a cat by its scruff. Well, go argue with Pat Widmer, one of the best-known cat specialists in the country. She points out that mother cats discipline kit-tens that way, and an adult cat recognizes the same treatment as the edict of Big Mama.

If you start with a kitten, before the little squirt has learned total self-sufficiency (after that he doesn't need you much and doesn't give a good rat's rump whether he obeys you or not), you can train a cat to obey voice commands. Males seem more willing; I knew one who would run a half a block hell-for-leather toward me when I called his name, would sit up on command, and stop whatever he was doing at "no." He was one of those rare cats that imprinted on a human, and thereby hangs a fact of ethology.

Imprinting is a process where newborn animals, even ducks and geese, quickly accept the sight or scent or combination of stimuli of one individual as Mommy, the good provider. It doesn't have to be the natural mother. Konard Lorenz, the pioneering German ethologist, would raise a gaggle of geese from eggs, exercising them by waddling around in his yard, the goslings peeping and waddling along behind their male human "mother." Lorenz claimed he looked up one day to see a busload of sightseers staring at him in rapt fascination. He was making fowl noises, waddling ahead. His tiny charges were in line behind him, but in high grass. The sight-seers couldn't see the birds; only the great ethologist, waddling around in high grass, looking over his shoulder and making funny noises. Such are the perils of science!

Imprinting really does create a lasting bond from the newborn to the "mother." In the case of our imprinted cat, he was a runt in a big litter. My daughter, who always wanted to Right every Wrong, was visiting kin when the kittens were born and couldn't keep her mitts out of this situation either. Because this tiniest hairless mite (his name, inevitably: Babe) was always out-struggled for a teat, my daughter would pull one of the bigger kittens loose and guide Babe to the milk. The day his eyes opened, she took him away from the litter and then to Oregon.

By this time, of course, Babe associated the girl's odor and touch with food. He slept against her cheek until he was half-grown. *And whatever "mommy" did, was worth copying.* My daughter loved taking showers and lunching on vegetable salads. As an adult with a face uncannily like that of a black panther, Babe still took showers with a kind of "Why the hell am I doing this on my own?" bemusement, and would ignore meat to eat an entire green salad. The girl's favorite? Mushrooms. The cat's? You guessed it, with tomatoes a close second. Notice that Niven has modern Kzinti spurning veggies, though I claim they once ate them and still could.

But as to Babe: who taught him about ownership-marking? Not spraying with urine; that's a territorial sign which Babe never bothered to learn. A cat has scent glands near the hairs above its eyes and, even though even a winetaster is unable to detect that scent, cats can smell it. After "mommy" went away to college, Babe quickly transferred his loyalty to me. Just as he had done with "mommy," he would seek me out each morning and gently bump his forehead against mine. I thought for a long while that Babe was communicating only, "this is my human," but when cats do that, they don't usually seek your forehead. It's *their* own unique scent they want deposited on *you*, not something from *your* forehead on *them*. When they voluntarily swap forehead bumps, it may be their intent to get your scent on them too, the feline equivalent of, "you're my human, and I'm your cat," which is about as near an assurance of affection as a human is ever likely to get from a cat. I have Kzinti doing a neck-nuzzle as a close analogy.

You thought rubbing against you was affection? Ethologists say it's a holdover from kittenhood, a ploy to stimulate milk flow. In other words, "feed me, fool." Kittens knead the belly of their nursing mother because that, too, stimulates milk flow. It's almost certainly built-in, instinctive behavior, though many adult cats continue to knead things and people. How about purring? Well, they do it when happy. Or sad. Or hungry, or full, or—actually, they do it while breathing regularly. An old dictum of communication theorists is, "If it can mean anything, it means next to nothing." When your cat purrs, you know he's breathing. Period. Sorry 'bout that.

The various ploys cats use to get scratched and stroked are often viewed as signs of affection, and you may believe it if you don't mind getting nicked by Occam's razor. The ethologist will tell you the cat isn't showing pleasure; he's stimulating you so you *will* give him pleasure. (Hey, he's not as emotional as a Kzin!) And in truth, the cat does deliberately communicate his desires to you. In a way, *he* has trained *you*. Widmer says that many a cat dominates his master this way, ignoring your commands while you innocently obey his. Oh, yes: if your white cat has blue eyes, don't expect to train it with voice commands because the poor bugger is stone deaf. You may not have noticed because, with or without hearing, the cues cats give and take are more subtle than most. You don't believe it? Your vet is as near as your telephone. Blue-eyed white cats are deaf. And thanks to that famous self-sufficiency, some of them trained to voice command will often ignore you as if they *were* deaf.

Dogs, on the other hand, are highly trainable, welcoming communication with humans because they seem to genuinely want to please us. This may have something to do with the fact that dogs developed as pack animals, living in a true pack society with a leader. Few cats are pack animals, though the cheetah is an exception with behavior that's part feline, part canine. A cheetah's shoulder ruff is coarse doglike hair and its paws, closely resembling a dog's, have claws that are not retractile. And though they purr, they also bark. I've heard them doing it while strolling among cheetahs in a wildlife preserve, and once had one as a houseguest. They definitely show some canine behavior, in addition to operating in social packs.

Some breeds of dog behave more like jackals than like wolves. The wolf is the very model of a pack animal, with absolute loyalty; the jackal and the hyena are more flexible, with pack behavior we might label as "treacherous." If you could ask the jackal, he might tell you he was simply more clever with situationial ethics. Because the Kzinti are so rigorously ethical, I think the males are pack animals. Which doesn't mean the females have to be. . . .

Some dogs get labeled as treacherous because we've bred them to be high-strung; and when they panic, they do it with violent aggression. The dog simply doesn't know what he's doing momentarily. Miller says it can be worth your arm to approach an already fearful German shepherd from above. It interprets your looming above as a dominant, aggressive display—which, among his own kind, it certainly is. Of course a dog has a lot of aggressive display cues, including a show of teeth and bristling hair. Believe them; they aren't usually *symbols* of his outlook, they're *signs* of the real thing. By the way, most dogs will trust their noses and ears instead of their eyes, though a few breeds such as whippet, borzoi, and greyhound depend on good eyesight for the chase as a cheetah does.

A dog will mimic your demonstration for his reward. Given enough intelligence (e.g., chimp and dolphin), the trainer doesn't have to dominate so constantly, but the dog isn't quite that bright and won't learn much unless you dominate. Look, he's a pack animal who adores a leader; let him adore you!

A dog's displays aren't tough to read, but we misread them all the time. A dog can learn he's done something wrong by punishment, but only if he gets punished in less than a minute. After that, he tends to get vague on the details of just what the heck he did.

Scenario: you come home to find that Fang has trashed your parlor and eaten the sofa, and the electric clock cord was pulled loose an hour ago. But Fang is looking awfully sheepish, head down, tail between his legs, so you figure he's ashamed because he remembers bloody well what he's done. And you wallop him good.

Bad decision, the trainers say. They claim Fang's display with the head and tail at half-mast are not shame: the are *submission*. I've heard impassioned argument about this one, but I'm running with the trainers who claim the dog is trying to tell you he is your follower, even though (for example) you kept him inside when he wanted to be out. And being no Einstein, he has forgotten the snack he made of the sofa because he did it, oh, ages and ages ago, at least an hour. He probably won't go for your jugular if you punish him for his mystery sin. But maybe he ought to.

While we're at it, a dog's ears are very expressive—forward and up for amiable alertness; flat back and out of harm's way for readiness to fight—with subtle gradations in between. The ear display is important for many another animal with prominent ears, including the horse and our Kzin and that newest fad beloved of the yuppie at heart, the llama. Don't get me wrong, I've enjoyed a trek along a Siskiyou range trail with a llama (one of a fleet owned by Cordwainer Smith's daughter, Rossana Hart, but the Hart mountaintop menagerie is a story in itself). Everybody knows a llama will spit an awful clam of glop at you if you irritate it, but did you know how they fight for dominance? They raise their heads and slam their long necks against each other in a frontal jolt. That doesn't sound even a little bit funny if you've ever felt the neck of a llama. The dermal layer in front, where that impact will land, is fully a half-inch thick. The side of his neck is all muscle, so unbelievably hard it feels like oak under the rough fleece, and the back (dorsal) of his neck is corded with tendons like bone. With the current interest in the llama, we may soon understand much more about communicating with them. Meanwhile, let one carry your pack for a weekend, but don't try to ride unless you crave a message that makes tobacco juice seem like nectar.

The scents that animals use to communicate suggest that our human noses are pretty pathetic organs. Insects and other bugs disperse a tremendous variety of particular chemicals, pheromones, which are detected and interpreted as distinct messages. Even the lowly aphid, when attacked, exudes tiny droplets of a pheromone that broadcasts alarm to other aphids. After laying eggs, the apple maggot fly deposits a "keep out" pheromone that prevents other females from laying eggs there. The sensors that "taste" pheromone molecules in the air are, in bugs, usually on their antennae and they are incredibly sensitive to certain pheromones. A single molecule of female sex pheromone from the silkworm moth can trigger the antennae receptors of the male. More molecules suggest he's on the right track; his system is literally a molecule counter. (There might be a story waiting for the guy who convinces Niven that Kzin ears are also pheromone receptors. But for what special kind of message?)

At the insect level, pheromones carry many messages: the identity of an individual, its status, membership in the group, its home and range; an alarm, a stimulus for copulation or even an inhibition against aggression. You can communicate with ants in a basic way by detaching the abdomen of an ant and drawing a trail with it. Its nestmates will follow that trail. (For a delightful essay on ant behavior, read *Surely You're*

Joking, Mr. Feynman!, by Nobel prizewinner Richard Feynmann.)

In vertebrates, the pheromone receptors are in the nasal cavity. Ethologists believe rabbit droppings may carry a "keep out" pheromone, a territory marker to warn other rabbits away. H. H. Shorey suggests that certain volatile fatty acids in women are human sex pheromones. Do we respond to them? Some say we probably do without knowing it.

We don't know all the pheromone messages carried, accidentally or deliberately, by a cat's spray or a dog's urine marker. What if they can vary the message at will? I suggested an experiment to one ethologist: anoint a few well-known "signal posts" with puppy urine, but direct the eye-dropper three feet up the post. If the next dogs to visit that post turn tail and run, it *might* mean they think the pup's the size of a pony and might grow as big as a dray horse. What sensible pooch would hang around for dominance like that? Between guffaws, the ethologist admitted that something of the sort might tell us more about pheromone messages.

We've already glanced at a lot of "talk" between humans and various species. That's easy enough because we can be fairly sure what's going on in one side of the conversation. The human can tell us in our own language. With the Kzinti, they can tell us in theirs and, in fact, one of my Kzin characters does exactly that when guiding a human through rituals. When we get into messages between other terrestrial species, however, we're out on a very shaky limb.

Most of the social "talk" that we notice between species is the result of our own good-hearted goofiness. We collect pets that wouldn't ordinarily get along, and we dominate their interactions so the fur won't fly. The easy way to do this is to get them very, very young. If you raise only one of each species together, there's a very good chance they'll grow up tolerant of one another, touching noses often, sharing warmth and maybe even food dishes. If one animal is less able to enforce its wants, it may tend to mimic the actions of its more powerful pal. Could your dog help you train his step-brother cat beyond the cat's usual repertoire? Might be worth a try, one vet said. There's also another Kzin story hiding in that idea.

I knew a Nubian nannygoat who seemed to understand the barks of the three big dogs she led. She never hurried, but the dogs always waited for her before they crowded too near a stranger. If a dog seemed too antsy, the goat would butt his ribs a quick hearty thump and he would calm down noticeably. Perhaps the fact that she was taller and could look down on the dogs helped her dominate them. As soon as she ceased paying attention to the stranger, the dogs lost interest too.

Being smaller doesn't necessarily make a species less dominant. One gray squirrel, that nursed with a litter of kittens, rode the neck and head of his long-suffering tabby "mother" when he was small and utterly dominated the whole menagerie when he grew up. He was so hyperactive and quick, the cats couldn't lay a glove on him and were reduced to hissing when he felt like teasing them. In his more placid moments he would snuggle with the cats, or with his human friend. He absorbed none of the other common feline traits because he was the dominator. The cats evidently absorbed none of his because they were a group, reinforcing each other's cattiness. The dogs in the household never ceased chasing him but never once caught him. God knows he caught *them* often enough. He would ride their backs whenever he took the notion, the dog running, howling, rolling over to exorcise this demon, the squirrel hopping off until the dog jumped up. Whereupon the squirrel would remount. The squirrel ran off, never to return, the first time he found another of his kind. He was not missed.

A Great Dane of my acquaintance grew up on a ranch with piano prodigy Merritt Schader. As a pup he had his own kitten, to which he remains solicitous although it's grown now. But growing up with him was a Russian boar which was allowed inside as a piglet, and the Schaders still let the boar inside to meet friends. The

boar, well over three hundred pounds and still growing, tends to dominate the dog amiably by shouldering
him. The dog accepts this unless the boar eats the dog's
food. The dog then bites him. The boar accepts this
rebuke calmly, bleeding a few drops into the snow as if
to prove the Dane meant business. Five minutes later,
the dog is frisking outside around his huge pal, luring
him into a race over the snowy hillside. The boar will
give chase briefly, but seems not terribly interested in
the game for long.

Much of their communication seems to be pretty
raw: bumping, biting, feinting a playful lunge, chasing.
These guys play rough with each other, though they
treat Merritt and other humans with care. The boar's
use of his barrel-sized bulk to shoulder the dog is a
pretty mild reminder of dominance, considering that
the boar has razor-sharp tusks and could carve himself a
mural on the dog's ribcage if he wanted to. It's my
guess the dog *has* to bite now and then, merely to hold
his own, because he's basically a good-natured beast.

Which suggests something about the, uh, underdog.
When you dare not really try to dominate, you can fake
it a little, or a lot if you have the nerve. I've seen a little
dog try this to get breathing room around cats. He
would also make a very serious game of feinting as if he
were *going* to do something, to see if any of the feline
tribe had any objections. After six months of this, the
little thief knew when he could steal a few bites of
catfood. His feints were mimicry; but observers knew
he'd risk the real thing if he wasn't stopped then and
there. This kind of display probably couldn't be done
successfully by a little dog that was growling and bristling. It's done by a bucketful of tailwags, eye contact,
and other displays of good nature.

Another dog lost his good nature entirely when left in
a small boat near the Isle of Man while his owner was
scuba diving. Witnesses saw a dolphin, familiar to local
divers, lift its head clear of the water to study the dog.
The dog promptly began to challenge, with snarls and a
show of teeth. The dolphin then opened its mouth (that

famous fixed smile is built-in) and began to snap its own toothy jaws, with sounds that may have been the dolphin's mimicry of a snarl. The dog panicked at this, and the dolphin leaped high over the boat before leaving the scene.

Because dolphins threaten with a display of teeth (Niven has taught us to beware of the Kzin "grin"), this dolphin probably understood the dog. And because he showed bigger teeth before demonstrating his ability to vault clear of the water, I suspect the dolphin's message was roughly, "Anything you can do, I can do better." This same bottlenose, never trained or captured, chummed around with divers and discovered that the manfish liked capturing lobsters. He then did the job of a bird dog, circling tightly around a lobster until a nearby human collected it. He also found a missing camera, hovering vertically, nose pointing straight down at the device, until the camera owner realized what the dolphin was trying to tell him. Friends of this dolphin claim that closing his eyes indicated a docile or tender mood. Wide-open eyes meant mischief.

Dolphins, which often hunt as dogs do in packs, need a lot of social messages to do it. It seems sure that a species that hunts in packs is likely to be a better candidate for interspecies communication.

Cheetahs were said by North Africans to hunt with dog packs. Because the cheetah's attack dash exhausts him after a few hundred yards, I suspect a cheetah would let the dogs exhaust the prey and then do his patented, seventy-mile-an-hour sprint to bring the prey down. Marco Polo claimed that the hunting cheetahs of Kublai Khan rode on special saddles behind their trainers, *on horseback*, leaping down for their attacks. Now, it stands to reason that no horse is going to let a hundred-pound cat ride him without a lot of cozening by a very patient trainer. I can only guess how man and cheetah persuaded horses to permit this curious arrangement, but we have to list it as an amiable relationship between horse and cheetah.

Amiable social relations between dogs and cats are

fairly common. When they groom each other, it's a message of acceptance within the family. Dogs, especially, seem willing to cooperate with other species when playing or hunting. Very often, though, we see messages that imply domination ploys. No surprise there; that's a fact of life for all earthly species. We may not like to admit it, but a brief study of children on any playground shows that our domination games are so natural, we have to teach our kids where the limits are. In fact, animal trainers tell us we must make most animals feel dominated before we can train them properly. This is all very well for us, the species with all kinds of tricks for dominating bigger, less intelligent critters. It might not go so well wth us after we meet the first intelligent, tough, BIG aliens who don't bluff all that easily. I wrote that one, too, as "Vital Signs." The title, of course, was a serious pun. How did you think they would negotiate?

So maybe Dr. Hunt was only 95% right when he said it was nonsense to expect humanlike thought processes in animals. They all get hungry, many use mimicry to get a point across, and one of the most important points that is established straight away is, who's top hog. Or Kzin. Or human. That may not say nice things about us, but it's something to build from. Gradually, we can create communication bridges so that, when the Kzin lies down with the lamb, they *might* both be able to get up again.

Copious pharmaceuticals . . . absolutely spherical ball bearings . . . nifty science experiments . . . wondrous structural materials for further space construction . . . Let us count the reasons heretofore given for funding a multi-trillion dollar Space Program. Surely it is significant by now that nobody has figured out a way to make money at it? Could it be there isn't one, at least not in the short-to-medium term in which one can make sensible investments?

On the other hand, so what? Do we really care about that? Trillions of dollars worth? Not if we're sane, we don't. There is only one reason that makes a national space program worthwhile: that it is our destiny as a species to grow beyond this planet. To go out there and have kids who themselves have kids. Lots of kids. Trillions of kids. The reason we must go to space is that we must; Earth is only our beginning. . . . Welcome to Wheel Days. . . .

Welcome To Wheel Days

Elizabeth Moon

Murray and Steve were down under the floor, digging out last year's leftover flyers for the festival when the speaker clicked. I slammed my hand on the OFF button and continued what I was doing, calculating how many porta-potties we could afford to hire from Simmons Sewer Service. Our Ecosystems Chief Engineer insists that he can't let the festival crap (the technical term in this colony) run through the usual pipes, just in case some idiot visitor eats lead or mercury or some other heavy metal that would poison the weedbeds. So every year we have this problem. You just can't run a festival without porta-potties, and with the gravity gradient in LaPorte-Centro-501, that means three separate sets of them, sexed. We never have enough, and we always have complaints, chiefly from uptowners near the core, who go into jittering fits if some stranger in a hotsuit knocks on their door and wants to use the inside can. I will admit, low-gray mistakes are the hardest to clean up, but still you'd think they'd understand why the festival is so important. If LaPorte-Centro-501 continues to grow, we all benefit.

Copyright © 1988 by Elizabeth Moon

Murray crawled out with the dance flyers. All we had to do was change the year and the day; we were having the Jinnits again for lead band, and Dairy and the Creamers for backup. Some people complain about that, but Murray's old buddy Conway is the keyboard man for Jinnits, and they'll come here without a guarantee. We don't get soaked if a solar flare keeps everyone home. So far that's saved us a bit more than I'd like to confess, when we're talking here about a successful annual festival that draws crowds from all over the Belt. And Dairy's local; the Creamers play at Hotshaw's all year 'round, and everyone likes them well enough. The flyers looked pretty good; I nodded and Murray racked them into the correction bracket and went to work. Steve was still out of sight, but I could hear him scrunching around in the insulation.

That's when the speaker clicked on again, and I didn't get my hand on the OFF button in time. "Radio relay message" said the voice, and I sighed. Nobody I wanted to talk to was going to be calling me for another week. I punched for a hard copy, rather than voice, and watched the little strip of paper come zipping out the groove. It's not really paper, of course—paper is precious—but it acts like paper. You can write on it. I tore it off and crammed it into a pocket without looking at it. That was a mistake.

The parade flyers Steve had gone after were all unusable; something had leaked and frozen into them. We had the old master, and we refilled the crawl space with insulation, then set up the master for a print run. I crossed my fingers, assumed 5% more attendance than last year, and ordered another set of porta-potties. Next up were the day's parade and display entries.

I don't want to overdo this about how hard it is to do things in the colonies—that's not my point—but a simple little annual festival like you'd run with maybe fifteen or twenty volunteers back on a planet is not so simple on the inside of a hollow ball with a gravity gradient from zip to norm. Take parades. LaPorte-Centro-501 was built in two helices, like most of the

cored colonies. The only way to route a parade all
through town is rim to core to rim again in the other
helix pattern, and that means everything has to go
through all the gravity gradients twice. Ever try to
design a float for variable gravity, not to mention spin?
We keep the kiddy parades in near-normal gravity, all
around the base of Alpha Helix one year, and Beta the
next, and run the main parade from 0.25 to 0.25 through
the core. That way the floats really float, but they don't
have to contend with heavy stress.

Right now the parade entries were looking a bit thin.
Central Belt Mining and Exploration would have a float:
they always did. Usually it was something "pioneering,"
an adventure still-life. FARCOM would bring a communications satellite mounted on a robotic flying horse
(they alternated that one and a float with two robots
using tin cans and a string). Holey Bey, our nearest
neighbor (and a nasty neighbor, for that matter) was
sending two floats, they said. I scowled at that, and
wondered if they were going to try to smuggle in another gang of ruffians. Four years ago they'd disrupted
our parade with screaming youths in blood-red hotsuits
who made off with parts of other people's floats. Almost
cost us the whole profit of the festival. (I know, you've
seen Holey Bey's brochures in the colonial offices: that
fake beach, with luscious bathing beauties backed by
handsome neo-Moorish arches. Forget it. Their chief
engineer was a drunken incompetent who couldn't hook
one helix with another, their plumbing leaks, and they're
infested with mammalian vermin. Even dogs. I know; I
took our float over there for "Back to Bey Days" and it
was disgusting.)

Anyway, we had to have at least sixty entries to make
the main parade work. Sixty full-size entries. No matter
how you handle core, it's big, and a parade can look
pretty damn puny out there, drifting across the very-
low-gee gap. Back on Earth you get horse freaks to fill
in the gaps with horses (at least I suppose that's why
they're in parades, to fill up the gaps: they have that
advantage of turning sideway to take up less room, or

lengthways to take up more). But of course we don't have horses on LaPorte-Centro-501, and even Holey Bey wouldn't harbor big dirty mammals like that. I called up the parade file, added today's entries, and muttered. Thirty-nine, and five of those were small marching groups. I looked at the schedule for our float to see who might come.

That's how it works, of course. We send our float ("Miss LaPorte-Centro-501 and her Court . . . Rolling Along to Wheel Days") to other colonies' festivals, and they send theirs to us. Back to Bey Days. Rockham Cherry Festival (they don't have cherries, but it sounds good). Pioneer Days (two a year, one at each end of the settlement, and very different: Vladimir Korsygyn-233 is a Soviet colony). It's about like you'd see on Earth: every colony has its festival, and everybody sends a float. There are differences, to be sure. We don't actually *send* our float everywhere; the shipping fees would break us. We send a holo of the new design each year and hire a construct crew in whatever colony it is. Miss LaPorte-Centro-501 and her Court do travel to the nearer communities; beyond that we audition and pay standard rates to local talent.

You may wonder why our festival is "Wheel Days." I don't want to grab credit from anyone, but actually that was my idea. The whole Belt, it's like a big wheel, and the Settlement like a smaller wheel riding its rim. Our conviction that LaPorte-Centro-501 will grow into its motto: "The Hub of the Industrial Center of the Solar System." You don't need to laugh . . . it could happen. Something will be the hub, and it might as well be us. We have talent, room to grow, resources, skilled labor, willingness to work . . . and most of all, we have *vision*.

That's how come we have Wheel Days, and nobody's laughed for the last nine years. We have the most successful annual festival for a community our size in the Settlement. And that's a big job. Everyone has two major assignments and half a dozen little ones, and of course we're all still employed, though some of our employers cut us some slack now and then. As for me, being junior vice president of Mutual Savings & Loan, I could spend pretty much my whole time on it, which is good because it took that and more. If you aren't a Chamber member, wherever you are, then you can't understand just how frantic those last weeks are. No matter how you plan all year (and if you don't plan all year, you don't have a good festival) something always comes unglued. Several somethings.

Our float came apart in a spin vortex at Rimrock, and we were charged with Insufficient Construction. (Luckily our insurance company's lawyers found we had a case against the designated construct company for fraud, and none of the young ladies on the float were hurt.) Still, the accident might deter some parade entries at our end. Simmons Sewer reported that they couldn't fill all the porta-potty order because they had just gotten a contract from Outreach Frames (the big shipbuilding firm). Conway, Murray's friend in Jinnits, broke up with his wife and threatened to leave the band; the band leader called Murray and said that if Conway left him in the lurch he wasn't about to do any favors for Conway's buddies. And so on.

It wasn't until three days before the opening that I wore the light blue zipsuit again, and heard something crackle in the breast pocket. I fished it out and found the message tape I'd never read. Now I read it.

In-laws are an old joke, right? That's because so many of them are just like the stories. My wife Peg is sweet, loving, bright, independent, and not half-bad-looking, either. But her brothers—! There's James Perowne, who's a drunk, and Gerald LaMott, who's probably the reason why James is a drunk, and then there's Ernest. Ernest Dinwiddie, if you can believe it, which I couldn't when I first met him, and I laughed, and he never forgave me. He suits his name, is the best I can say for him, and it isn't much.

The way Peg and I get along, you'd think I'd like her brothers and they'd like me, but that's not how it is. James will fling a half-pickled arm around my shoulders and breathe beery sighs at me about his lovely little sister while I hold my breath and try not to slug him. Gerald sits hunched behind something (table, computer, desk . . . a pillow if all else fails), staring at me with little bright eyes out from under his dark brows and expecting me to make an ass of myself. Peg says she never could play a piece on the piano (and she's good) when Gerald was staring at her. He has that way of looking at you, expecting you to fail, almost *longing* for you to fail, and then you do. And then there's Ernest.

Ernest is in middle management at Central Belt Mining & Exploration. He's told us about it, and about how important middle management is, and how important Central Belt Mining & Exploration is. Well, I know *that*. Anyone in finance in the Belt knows how important CBM&E is. He explained to Peg exactly why she shouldn't marry me, and to me exactly why I wasn't worthy of her, and from time to time he shows up to explain what we've done wrong between the last visit and this one. He asks detailed questions about every aspect of our lives, and gives the impression that he'd like to hire investigators to verify our answers.

Also he can't take a hint. Most people, if you tell them that you're going to be busy the weekend they want to visit, will shrug and say too bad and go on. Not Ernest. He showed up in the middle of our honeymoon, to see how things were going. He brought his whole family ·to help celebrate my fortieth birthday (when Peg and I had planned to spend a weekend alone, having farmed Gordie out with her best friend Lisa). For the past three years or so, we'd managed to avoid him by being "gone" when he came to LaPorte-Centro-501. This time we were stuck.

He was coming, the message strip said, on August 24, the day that Wheel Days opened, because he was *sure* we'd be there for Wheel Days. He was on his way In-system for a management seminar, with his wife Joyce and their three kids. They wanted to see us and would be there sometime during Dayshift. Even in hard copy from a radio relay, Ernest's usual accusing tone was coming through. And by this time they were four days out from Central Station One (the Company's own headquarters colony, as he made sure we knew), and there was no way I could stop them. That's what I got for not reading that message the month before.

I called Peg, and she reacted about how I expected. She's often said she married someone as unlike her brothers as possible. I held the earphone a foot away until she calmed down a little.

"We can hide out in the Wheel Days confusion," she suggested finally.

"They know where we live; they'll just camp outside the door."

"We could stay with Lisa . . . "

"Lisa's already having company, remember?" So were we, for that matter, and Peg and I both said "What about the Harrisons?" at the same moment.

"I can't tell them not to come," Peg wailed. "I *want* to see them. We have *fun* together. Not only that . . . we won't have *room*."

"I'll find Ernest's bunch a room somewhere else," I said, but I was worried. We really haven't built our tourism industry up where we'd like to see it, Wheel Days filled the hotels—overfilled them—and by this time I doubted I could find anything but the most expensive suites still available.

"They are *not* coming here," Peg said, with a hint of Brother Ernest's heavyhanded determination. Then she hung up. Murray came to tell me that Conway had rejoined the Jinnits, but had gotten drunk in the ship on its way from Gone West and given his ex-wife two black eyes. She wasn't filing charges, but the ship's captain was, and wouldn't release him without a guarantee from an employer: the ship's captain was a Neo-Feminist, and wouldn't tolerate spouse (or ex-spouse) abuse. The band didn't count, because apparently the captain considered them a contributing influence, and had already fined them. And of course without Conway, the Jinnits wouldn't sound like the Jinnits, and our main stage attraction would be no attraction at all. Murray wouldn't meet my eyes, even though it wasn't his fault, and we both knew it. But everyone also knew that he was why we had the Jinnits at all.

By the time I'd straightened that out, it was six hours later and the last hotel room was long gone, at any price. I leaned a little on Bennie Grimes, manager of the Startowers, but he knew and I knew that the favors he owed me weren't worth kicking a corporate executive out of his room and alienating the entire company. And no one I knew—*no one*—had room at home. Everyone with spare rooms invited guests or rented them out; the last of the home-rentals had cleared the computer weeks ago.

That left the Campground, and I knew exactly what Ernest was going to say about that. You can't run a festival by turning people away, so when rooms were full we signed transients into the Campground . . . a vast, barren storage bay aired up for a week (it takes that long to get it above freezing), and divided into "campsites" with bright plastic streamers. For about the cost of a cheap room in town, we rent bubbletents, furnished with cheap inflatable seats and sleepsacks. Big tents, too—bigger than the rooms you'd get in most hotels, plenty of room to sleep the whole family. It's kind of a long walk from the Campground in toward the core, so we have some extra entertainment out there. A few clown/juggler acts, a little carnival with rides for the kids, that sort of thing. And we have one day of the games right next to the Campground: the penny toss, the ring-dunk, the disk golf tournament.

Some people even prefer the Campground, and reserve a favorite spot ("Aisle 17, lot D, next to the big bathroom with the sunken tubs") year after year. You can be sure you'll be next to friends. The traffic isn't as bad. It's less expensive than anything but the cheapest Portside hotels. One group of oldtimers from Wish & Chips holds reunions there; they say it's like going back to the old days before the shells were built up, and they sit around singing sentimental pioneer ballads.

But Ernest in the Campground . . . we'd never live it down. Yet it was that or have him and his family crammed into our place with us and the Harrisons and only two toilets. The memory of my fortieth birthday, when instead of a long, relaxed bath and bed with Peg I ended up defending the right of independent investors to organize savings & loan associations, while Ernest's kids tore into Gordie's things and trashed his carefully-organized Scout files, hardened my resolution. I reserved the best space I could find (Aisle 26, lot X), and paid the advance on a deluxe camping outfit so that it would be set up and waiting. I didn't figure that having a two-room inflated habitat with full cable connections would really soothe Ernest down, but it was the best I could do. I also recorded a message for him and left it in the Port message center. It would tell him where to go, and apologize for this inconvenience.

Then I went back into battle with Simmons Sewer Service. Our contract predated the one they had with the shipbuilders, I said firmly, and they had no valid legal reason to back out. We went back and forth awhile, and came up still three complete sets of porta-potties short (eighteen units: three grav levels, both sexes) even after they said they guessed they could haul some on tomorrow's oreloader from Teacup 311, where they had just finished a contract. At least I'd originally ordered more than last year, so we weren't behind as far as it seemed.

Then it was only two days to go. By this time, of course, the main structure is in place. Anything that isn't is lost, and you can't change it till next year. Main Parade was still a little skimpy, a bare sixty entries with those seven (by now) marching units, but we usually picked up a few extras the last day, as people came in and saw the competition. In fact, we kept three or four blank floats set up in storage, ready for last-minute spray-painting and decoration as desired. The Kiddy Parades always had problems, but none you could anticipate, since any child who showed up at the beginning could join the parade: that was the rule. All the ribbons and trophies for the games had arrived on schedule.

The candidates for Miss LaPorte-Centro-501 were even now being interviewed by the judges for poise and personality; we had enough entrants for a good pageant, and plenty of contracts for the losers to ride floats representing distant colonies (which keeps losers happy. And unlike some colonies, we don't let outsiders haggle over our girls: we have them draw lots for the available contracts). The Scoutmasters had their assignments for traffic control and information booths. We've found that strangers will accept direction from a neatly uniformed kid when they'll argue with an adult cop. We started that about ten years ago, and now most colonies use the kids as traffic control and guides during their festivals.

Going through all this and checking what still had to be done took several hours, interrupted by calls from everyone who could find a line. Or that's what it seemed like, with people asking things like "When are the opening ceremonies?" (on the flyers, not to mention broadcast on video!) and "What are you going to do about the construction mess behind the middle school on Alpha Helix?" which had nothing to do with us, or the festival, and was the sole responsibility of the Alpha Helix School Board. It did look tacky, but it wasn't my fault. Peg's a Board trustee, not me. I gave that caller her work extension, and went on to someone who demanded to know why the official garbage pickup was two hours late.

Sometime after lunch the ship from Gone West docked, and my earlier fix of that band problem came unglued again. Seems that the Jinnits agent on board got into an argument with the captain about how much fine had been assessed to the band, rather than to Conway personally. By this time the captain was fairly tired of the Jinnits band, from drums to keyboard and back again, and she expressed this in my ear with some force, offering to space the lot of them if I didn't do something. Murray, of course, had disappeared as soon as he saw me mouth "Jinnits . . ." I swore up and down that the Jinnits did indeed have a contract engagement, that they had a good record on this colony and had never been in a fight that I knew of, that we would guarantee (how I didn't know) that they wouldn't cause any trouble for the ship's crew should the crew stay for Wheel Days. To which, of course, I lavishly invited them.

Somewhere in the next 24 hours, which you might think would be the worst, is a lull—never at the same point two years running—when for six hours or so everything seems to hang on a knob of time and wait. All the committee chairs were exhausted but triumphant. What could be done had been done, and we all looked at each other and wondered what we'd see four days later, when the whole thing was over. A hush settled over the Chamber offices. Peg and Gordie and I had a last quiet meal (no ringing phones!), and I even lay down with my shoes off for a brief nap.

Finally it was opening day, with two hours to go before the Chairman cut the ribbon for the official start of Wheel Days, and everything I'd worked for as President of the Chamber this past year was out there on the line. I had already been in the office for three hours, checking in that last shipment of porta-potties, and making sure that they got where they needed to go. Checking on the bands (Dairy and the Creamers were peacefully eating breakfast; the Jinnits hadn't come out of their suite yet). Checking to make sure that the Scouts had picked up their armbands (green wheels on a blue background) and directional flags (green arrows on blue). Taking a look into the low-gray storage bays where the floats constructed here are aligned for the parade start. Finding an emergency ground crew to help with someone's unexpected float being unloaded at the Port, and entering it into the parade as entry 62 (61 had come in overnight). Racing home when I realized that I'd never changed from my worksuit the night before, and had to be in some kind of dress outfit for the Opening.

I got to the opening ceremonies just in time, and was glad to see that Connie Lee (our veep this year) was standing by in case I didn't make it. Last year's Miss

LaPorte-Centro-501 posed gracefully beside the large silver wheel tied with a bright green ribbon. First came the Colony Chair's speech (short: that's one reason we elected Sam), then my speech ("Welcome to Wheel Days"), and then he cut the ribbon and Lori Belhausen took a good hold on the wheel and shoved it into motion. And then I went on with the rest of the welcome: "Rolling into the future with the Wheel of Progress, right here at LaPorte-Centro-501, the Hub of the Industrial Center of the Solar System." And it doesn't sound a bit silly, coming over the speakers like that, with the silver wheel flashing in the lights and Lori grinning for all the cameras.

It was when the candidates for this year's Miss LaPorte-Centro-501 honors came out to be cheered and photographed, and to toss handfuls of little gilt wheels into the audience, that I remembered that I'd forgotten to include something in my message to Ernest. I hadn't warned him about the wheels.

It's nothing unique. Lots of festivals have visitor requirements of the same sort. If you don't carry a six-shooter (a paper cut-out is enough) at Gone West's Pioneer Days, for example, you'll be put in "jail" until you're ransomed. They have a cute little cage you have to stand in, just outside the Lily Langtry Saloon, and everyone giggles and teases until you can persuade one of the honkytonk girls (if you're male) or bartenders (if you're female) to accept a donation for a kiss. They make a big deal of being persuaded, too, and the hapless prisoner has to do more than wave some money out the jail's window. All proceeds go to the Vacuum Victims Fund, and most people take it as it's meant, a big joke and a good way to earn money for the Fund.

At Wheel Days, we "arrest" everyone who enters the central festival area without a wheel . . . a pin, a dangler, something in the shape of a wheel, a circle with spokes. Most people simply pin on one of the hundreds of free wheels tossed into the crowd at the opening ceremonies, or handed out by any of the Miss LaPorte-Centro-501 contestants. It's true that no one is told what the wheels are for, but most people know (or find out quickly). We're lenient—we let a Shakespeare-revival streetdancer get by with a ruff—but we make a sizeable donation to the Vacuum Victims Fund every year. Anyway, I hadn't warned Ernest . . . and I knew his attitude towards "commercial junk." He would be the last person to pin on a cheap plastic gilt wheel for the fun of it.

I really meant to call the Port, but even before I left the platform a long snaky arm in cerise, fringed with silver, had wrapped firmly around my shoulders. "We got a problem, son," said the raspy voice of the Jinnits lead singer, just as the crowd realized who that was and started oohing. I hardly had time to gulp before the Jinnits, all of them, whisked me away and into the nearest doorway.

I don't pretend to understand musicians. I like music, sure, and Peg and I love to dance. But the way musicians think is beyond me. Murray's had us over when Conway was visiting, and I always felt a little uncomfortable, knowing that he's never sat behind a desk from nine to five in his entire life. Now I was surrounded by them, strange-looking people in bright, shimmery suits, with gold and silver fringe on arms and shoulders and hips and ankles. Cerise male and female, tangerine male and female, caution-yellow male and midnight blue male. All bright-eyed, all very alert, and all very upset about something.

As it turned out, they had three problems. Someone had put only two porta-potties in the cubbyholes off Main Stage, and they needed at least four (three M, one F) because they'd brought along a whole new stage crew, much bigger than last year. I gave myself a pat on the back for sequestering one set in the Chamber offices, and said I've have someone bring the others right away. That got me a nod from the female in cerise and the male in tangerine, but the band leader didn't budge.

There was this ship captain, he said. I had formerly heard all of this from the ship captain's point of view; now I heard it from the band's. Conway, they agreed (patting Conway, whom I hadn't recognized with this year's hair-color and a shimmering yellow catsuit) had gone a little overboard with Zetta (the ex-wife), but it was mostly Zetta's fault. She'd threatened to leave him for a fat-cat management type at Central Belt Mining & Exploration, who was going to get her a permanent position there. So Conway had put the moves on a corporate wife, being hurt and lonesome and willing to make some CBM&E husband unhappy in return, and then Zetta had had a row with her new lover and come tearing in to find Conway embracing what'shername. Some brunette with plenty of miles, the cerise female said admiringly, but a lot of horsepower under the hood. Conway nodded, at this point, and said she was made for more than a middle manager's wife. No one said a word about the corporate wife's *husband*. I thought of Peg, who in a hotsuit and hood could pass for twenty, and decided to keep her far away from Conway.

Zetta had already filed divorce, but apparently she still considered Conway her property, because she had sent the brunette away in tears. Then on the voyage across, she had started a row with Conway in the ship's bar, expressed herself in highly colored terms on the subject of his ancestry, his anatomy, and his eventual destination, and finally had thrown his own drink in his face. That's when he hit her, but actually it was Shareen (the tangerine female) who blacked her eyes, because Zetta had elbowed Shareen in sensitive places and said "nasty things" about Shareen's lover, who worked backstage. "Zetta deserved it," said the band leader, and everyone else nodded.

"I was drunk," said Conway, sadly.

"She deserved it anyway," said the band leader, and everyone nodded again. "But this damn captain . . ." Seems the captain, as a Neo-Feminist, considered any female who wouldn't file charges when assaulted to be in need of protection at best and permanent re-education at most. She wouldn't believe that Shareen had blacked Zetta's eyes, and assumed that Shareen was another of Conway's lovers, trying to take the rap for him. Zetta didn't like being hit, but she liked even less being treated like a nincompoop. Shareen was furious because she'd never had an affair with Conway—she was gay, and proud of it. And now the captain was going around LaPorte-Centro-501, telling everyone that the Jinnits were a sexist band that no self-respecting Neo-Feminist would listen to, and the band were under a peace bond order (guaranteed by the Chamber, as their employer) and couldn't fight back.

"I could kill that bitch," said Shareen, looking me straight into the eye until I nodded agreement, "But it would break the bond, and our contract both, and you'd have no lead band, and we'd have no gig."

And besides (third problem) there was Conway, who was depressed and miserable, and needed a girl to cheer him up so he could do his best. Nothing else would do, and brunette was preferable. Somebody (they all looked at me, intently) had to do something to stop that captain from ruining their reputation and their business, and somebody had to get Conway cheered up so he could play. Then they patted my arms and told me they'd be in their suite when I got it all straightened out.

I started by calling the Chamber offices and arranging to have the porta-potties moved. The captain hadn't sounded very understanding on the radio, and I wasn't at all sure how I could deal with her. We do have laws about libel, and also about inciting a riot, but what with the way colonies depend on spacers, you just can't afford to alienate the people who run the ships. And for all I knew she'd claim it fell under religious freedom or something. I looked up Sarah Jolly Hollinshead, the Chamber's top lawyer, on the schedule. She had volunteered to handle Campground registration this year. This was too important for a call: I'd have to go myself.

The Campground was already filling up. Colorful bubbletents sprouted from the storage bay floor. Sarah had a line maybe seven families long, and I knew better than to break in, even though she caught my eye and nodded to me. Justice must be *seen* to be done, as she keeps telling us. I stood there catching my breath after the droptube ride, and admired Sarah's organization. She had two gofers with her, and really kept things moving along without seeming to hurry anyone. I moved up behind the family in front of me (by their T-shirt designs, recently from Teacup 311's "Tea for Two Days").

It wasn't until I heard Joyce's voice that I realized she was two families ahead of me in the line. I peeked. There was the back of her smooth dark head, looking very much as I remembered the back of her head looking, and there were the three kids (one niece, two nephews), some inches taller. They all held small travel bags. She was asking Sarah where to find Aisle 26, Lot X, as they had a reservation (which Sarah checked, before handing them a map), and then she asked where she could find me.

"Mr. Carruthers?" asked Sarah, as if she hadn't heard that name before, but she said it loud enough for me to hear, in case I wanted to.

"My brother-in-law," said Joyce. I started to back up and bumped into someone behind me, someone who turned out to be large and solid.

"Andrew Carruthers?" asked Sarah. I think she was trying to give me time to escape.

Joyce said "He's the President of your Chamber of Commerce," in a tone of voice that implied Sarah was too far down the list to know that, and I saw Sarah stiffen.

The giant behind me read the name off my presidential seal and said, all too loudly, "I think someone's looking for you, Mr. Carruthers." And grinned at me. His gimme cap was from Holey Bey, and that figures. Troublemakers, that's what they've got over there. Perverted humor.

I stepped out of line and went forward as if I hadn't seen Joyce. When she turned around, I had a big smile ready.

"You came," she said, as if she really wanted to see me. "I didn't know if you'd find time . . ." But for once it didn't sound accusing.

"Had to check on you," I said genially, trying a smile on the kids. The girl, Cynthie, was looking around with some interest.

"What is this place?" asked the older boy.

"It's a storage bay," I said. "We make it a campground for Wheel Days."

"It's big," said the girl. "We don't have things like this in Central Station One."

"We're all built up," said the boy. "This is great. I hope our tent is a long way across." He pointed. Harris, that was his name, and the younger one, presently examining his toes, was Elliot.

"Andy, I hate to bother you," began Joyce. "It's about Ernest . . ."

"I'll be with you in a second," I said, "but I have to ask Sarah about something first—just came up on the way down." Joyce nodded, collected the children, and moved off a few feet. Tactful of her, I thought, and then launched into a very fast precis of the Jinnits problem for Sarah. She folded her lip under her upper teeth, and hummed . . . a sound known to strike terror into the hearts of opposing attorneys. When I finished, she nodded once, and pushed back her chair.

"I'll take care of it," she promised. That was that. One did not ask Sarah *how* she planned to do things; she was not a committee sort of person. I went back to Joyce and the kids, and (for no good reason other than the manners I was brought up with) picked up her travel bag and led them toward their bubble. I *should* have been somewhere else, but what could I do?

To my surprise, the kids continued to show a livelier interest in the Campground than they ever had in our place. A strolling juggler chucked Cynthie under the chin and gave her a momentary crown of dancing colored balls, then moved on; she was delighted, and flushed, and altogether not the same girl who had demanded a different brand of breakfast cereal and insisted that our house smelled funny. Harris came to a halt outside one of the bubbletents, eyes fixed on the logo hanging from a snatchpole.

"That's . . . that's John Steward's First Colony badge," he said, breathless with adolescent awe.

"Some of the pioneers hold a reunion here," I began, but he wasn't listening. Steward himself had ducked out the door of his bubble and paused, finding himself impaled on Harris's gaze. He nodded to the boy, gave me a half-wave, then ducked back inside. "He doesn't talk to strangers much anymore," I said, softening the blow. Harris didn't notice.

"He nodded to me. Mom, he *nodded* to me. John *Steward*!" Then he turned to me. "You know him?"

"Not really," I had to admit. "The oldtimers stick together pretty much. But I've listened to him at the Tall-Tale contest, and bought him a drink once or twice."

"I didn't know you knew *John Steward*," Harris said. "I wish we came here more often. Does Gordie know him?"

"Probably better than I do," I said, relaxing. The kids weren't as bad as I'd thought. "John does a program for the Scout troops every year."

Harris subsided, newly impressed with his cousin. Elliot had acquired a spring in his step, which indicated that things weren't too bad for him, either.

"About Ernest," Joyce began again. I tensed. "He's in jail," she said. "And I wondered . . ."

"I'm sorry," I said, and started explaining about the wheels and the festival jail.

"I understand," she said. "But it's not that jail. It's a real jail."

"Ernest?" My mind fogged.

"It's—I hate to explain—" She looked away. I glanced around, and saw that we were nearly at their bubble. Pointing it out and settling them into it distracted us both. Then she sent the kids to the nearest foodstand for a snack, and went on. "It's not what it sounds like," she began. "I met this musician . . ."

Lights flashed in my mind. "Conway?" I asked. "Of the Jinnits?"

She blushed. "How did you guess?" she asked. I couldn't have explained, and nodded for her to go on.

"Well, anyway, he was sad and lonesome—his wife had just run out on him with another man, he said. And I suspected that Ernest was having an affair."

"With—?" I had a glimmer, but it seemed wildly improbable.

"I didn't know, then. Someone younger, blonder, whatever. I thought maybe I could make him jealous, and Conway was so sweet, so . . . pathetic . . ." Her lashes drooped, and I felt a rush of sympathy. "Then . . . we were just relaxing together, there in the sauna, and in rushes this blonde viper!" Joyce's voice had thinned and hardened; I could imagine it making holes in steel. "She grabbed my arm and *threw* me out, and screamed the most terrible things at us . . . threatened to tell Ernest . . ."

"Did she?"

"Not that I know of. Anyway, I went home, and Conway shipped out that night. And I was glad we were coming here, because I knew the Jinnits would play, and I might see Conway. Not anything serious, but . . . but he doesn't think I'm too old . . ."

"Of course not," I said gallantly, but worriedly.

"So when we got here, Ernest was—well, frankly Andy, he wasn't too happy with this—the idea that you'd stuck us out here in the Campground. I tried to tell him you'd probably done it for the children—much better than a crowded hotel, where they wouldn't have many people their own age. He kept insisting it was only because you hadn't bothered to find us a place until the last minute." I tried to look innocent as she glanced at me, then she went on. "We stopped on the way down to have something to eat. That's when I saw the blonde—Conway's friend or ex-wife or whatever she is—sitting up at the bar with two of the biggest black eyes I've ever seen. Frankly I was glad: she left bruises on my arm when she yanked me around. I wanted to hurry Ernest out of there, but he caught sight of her too . . . and he left me sitting there, just walked off, to go up to her."

"Mmm." Joyce had tears in her eyes when she looked at me.

"That's right, Andy. *She* was the tart he was having an affair with. Ernest demanded to know who had blacked her eyes, and a spaceship captain across the room yelled 'That bastard Conway,' and Ernest—" She paused, looking down. "You know, Ernest really doesn't get along with lots of people."

"Who hit him?" I asked, not surprised at that revelation.

"He told the captain to mind her own business—he really doesn't like women in authority—and she said it was her business since it happened on her ship. By this time she'd come up to the bar, and she said that the blonde—whatever her name is—"

"Zetta," I said.

"I never knew," said Joyce. "Anyway, that she— Zetta—was too enslaved to admit it was a man who hit her, and was trying to blame it on a woman. And Ernest said it was probably the captain, since she looked like the type, and she swung first, but he got in a couple of blows before he fell down. She filed charges, and he filed countercharges, and they're both in jail."

"Oh," was all I could think of to say.

"I'm sorry," said Joyce. "I guess I knew we shouldn't come. We always seem to be in your way, somehow, and you're awfully busy. I know you have important things to do. It's just . . ."

"Oh, that's all right." It wasn't all right, but for some reason the tight knot of apprehension that had bothered me since I read Ernest's note was loosening. Ernest in jail—a real jail, and for brawling in a bar—was something I felt I could handle. Suddenly I wished Peg were there with me. I wanted to see her face when she heard that holier-than-anyone brother Ernest had started a fight in a bar.

"I'm really sorry," said Joyce again. "I know we're causing you a lot of trouble, and at the worst time. If it hadn't been for me wanting to see Conway again . . ."

"Don't see why not," I said, suddenly reckless. Running any festival is a matter of dancing tiptoe on a tightrope with people throwing waterballoons at you.

Crazier ideas than the one that came to me then had worked for others. "I can't get Ernest out immediately," I said, "not if he's really assaulted someone. And in the meantime, the Jinnits tell me Conway isn't playing up to his level because he's lonesome."

Her eyes began to sparkle. "I couldn't . . . I mean, to seriously—"

"No, not seriously, but you certainly could go to the core dance tonight. After maybe eating dinner with the band. Couldn't you? It would solve a big problem for me."

"But the kids—"

I grinned at her. "Harris is crazy about oldtimers, right? I'll bet he'd be glad to sit in on the first round of the Tall Tales Competition, which is just three aisles over, where that big teepee is."

It was not really that simple, of course. It never is. But anyone who can organize the annual festival of a growing community which is going to *deserve* to be called the hub of the industrial center of the solar system can finagle or squinch or maneuver his way past a few difficulties. With Joyce radiantly at his side (in a silver-lame suit she'd borrowed from Zetta, after a tearful reconciliation), Conway didn't even glance at Peg when she and I whirled past the Main Stage, with every curve of hers showing in her new scarlet hotsuit, Jinnits had never sounded better . . . and they'd already renewed their contract for next year, because, as the lead singer said, "I guess Murray's not the only friend we've got on this colony." Ernest would be out on bail the next morning; he had been pitifully grateful for my visit and promise of help, once he found that his Company legal insurance wasn't good in our jurisdiction. And when we finally escorted Joyce back to the bubbletent, in the short end of Nightshift, we found four cheerful and excited youngsters—her three and our Gordie—who had been invited to share snacks with the oldest of the oldtimers, John Steward himself.

If I do say so myself, it was a good start to Wheel Days.

Introduction

As most readers of New Destinies *are doubtless aware,
I don't have a lot of faith in the appropriateness of
government solutions to most any problem but the
preservation of domestic tranquility. Still, if it is true
that government and only government can accomplish
the settling of space, an end we hold to be self-evidently
desirable, then Dr. Woodcock's prescription makes a
great deal of sense.*

WANTED: PIONEERS FOR THE SPACE FRONTIER

Gordon R. Woodcock

"To lead the exploration and development of the space frontier, advancing science, technology, and enterprise, and building institutions and systems that make accessible vast new resources and support human settlements beyond Earth orbit, from the highlands of the Moon to the plains of Mars." Thus opens the report of the National Commission on Space, issued May 1986. It is a bold new outlook, capturing for the first time in an official document of the U.S. Government the visionary dream of human settlements in space. So now, we space enthusiasts can relax and watch NASA move out to pioneer the space frontier, right?

WRONG!

For one thing, the commission's report has already been criticized by some Congresscritters for suggesting that we double or triple NASA's budget to do all these good things. To a red-blooded space cadet that may seem reasonable: perhaps even a bit stingy. To many Americans, however, even those that support the space program to some degree, spending a lot more on it is not a good idea. Especially if it might make their taxes go up.

We have been through this before. The Apollo program peaked out at about $10 billion annually in 1986 dollars; the total NASA budget reached about $18 billion (in 1986 dollars) in the peak Apollo year. This was about 1% of the U.S. GNP in that year. The present NASA budget is about $7.8 billion, roughly 1/5 of 1% of current GNP.

During the mid-1960s, the Apollo development years, space planners in NASA believed that space funding would continue at about 1% of the GNP. Accordingly, they developed detailed technical plans for permanent lunar bases and manned missions to Mars. They believed we would go from the Apollo landings right into a small but growing lunar base, and that a manned Mars landing would occur by 1985! More money was spent on engineering studies of manned lunar and Mars missions during the late 1960s than has been spent in the entire period since.

What happened? The Vietnam war led to a general souring of the national mood and a severe strain on the federal budget. When Nixon ran for president in 1968, he asked Spiro Agnew, his running mate, to prepare a "Nixon space plan." A group was formed, called the Space Task Group (STG), consisting mostly of NASA people. It was not as prestigious as the Space Commission, because it was not presidentially appointed, but the personnel had a very similar assignment and they came up with a very similar plan. Drawing on the extensive NASA studies, they recommended a space transportation system (today we would call it "infrastructure") for routine manned access to space, including the Moon and Mars as well as low Earth orbit.

By 1968, the NASA budget had already fallen significantly from the Apollo peak and the STG recommended it be restored in order to afford the new ventures. Sound familiar?

It didn't happen, of course. There was the war, the sourness of national mood, and this terrible budget deficit. The only thing that survived from the STG plan was the space shuttle, and it was considerably scaled down in scope from the original plan. NASA's budget continued its slow decline for several more years.

So now we have a new plan from the Space Commission. What's different? Well, for one thing, after years of what Jimmy Carter called "national malaise," we are short on optimism. It's going to take longer under the new plan than was proposed by the STG plan. Apparently, the longer we wait to start these ventures the longer it's going to take to accomplish them.

On the positive side, the new plan talks about "enterprise," "new resources," and "human settlements." These are all new themes that were missing from the STG plan. They came not from NASA, but from the "space movement," Gerry O'Neill's space colonization studies, his Space Studies Institute (SSI), the L5 Society, the "Mars Underground" and others. NASA has funded some work on these subjects, including summer studies, where university professors and graduate students work with NASA scientists and engineers for about eight weeks to develop a report on a topic such as space colonies or search for extraterrestrial intelligence (SETI). In this way, NASA is able to provide some support to frontier research, on subjects that might get them one of Senator Proxmire's "Golden Fleece" awards if funded as mainstream research. But NASA has definitely been following, not leading.

It's a sad commentary on the state of the U.S. space program that most of the significant research on space settlements, use of extraterrestrial resources, manned Mars missions, and such has been done by the "Mars Underground," a loosely organized group of space professionals who care enough to do such work on their own time, or which has been supported by SSI from voluntary contributions.

It's a sad commentary on the state of the U.S. space program that the main excitement in space transportation development is a prospective resurrection of the old Saturn V Moon rocket, scaled down to launch commercial satellites, now that NASA has been directed not to accept new commercial customers for the shuttle.

It would be easy to get discouraged, to say "what's the use?" Some people have. Some say that after Challenger, America is a second-rate space power; that the American space program is over. But in fact there are many positive signs, indications that this time, if space advocates get together and get the message out, we can make something happen. To begin with, there wasn't a discernible space movement at the time of the STG report; space had no constituency. And the nation was on a downward path into the malaise of the Carter years, where now it seems to be on an upward path. Sometimes it seems like we don't know which way is up, but at least that is the direction people want to go.

MOON BASE ALPHA

Unfortunately, the Space Commission report has a "someday" far-future quality to it. Like don't hold your breath. But a lunar settlement program could begin tomorrow. In fact, it could have begun twenty years ago, when the Apollo planners wanted to start it. There is no clear distinction between a base and a settlement. When we return to the Moon, we will establish a base; it will grow gradually in size and sophistication. Eventually we will call it a settlement, never knowing exactly when the change occurred unless we decide upon some particular event like the first human birth on the Moon.

Most politicians and too many space planners equate a return to the Moon to the high cost of Apollo, in total about $80 billion in today's dollars. That's like equating the cost of a home computer to the cost of the ENIAC.

We don't have to repeat Apollo to return to the Moon in an age of space shuttles and space stations. A mere return, that is, one or more isolated landings after the manner of Apollo, is a relatively easy job, once we have a space station. Moon rockets would take off from the space station and return to it. The entire moonship would weigh about 200,000 lb.—that's about four shuttle payloads—and about 160,000 lb. of this would be hydrogen and oxygen fuels. The ship would be assembled and fueled at the space station. It could use the venerable Centaur engine, the RL-10. (The RL-10 has been around for twenty years; it might be nice to have a new engine. But the RL-10 would work.)

Our biggest problem may be how to get the fuels to orbit, since NASA has decided that, at least for now, it is too dangerous to put liquid oxygen and liquid hydrogen in the shuttle payload bay. We would probably have to use expendable rockets, or a new heavy cargo rocket that has been talked about for years. We could even make the fuels at the space station by water electrolysis (breaking water into its constituent hydrogen and oxygen by passing an electric current through it). That way the cargo to orbit is just water. But electrolysis takes quite a bit of electrical power, about 2 kilowatt hours per pound of water. We would have to add a couple of extra solar generators to the space station.

Our moonship would take four or five people to the Moon for a two-week stay. The first couple of trips would be devoted to checking out the operation of the system and selecting a site suitable for a permanent base.

There are a great many details to work out; the shuttle spacesuit, for example, isn't really designed to be used on the Moon. It would have to be modified or we'd need a new one.

After a few prospecting flights, perhaps one or two a year for two years, we could begin to build a permanent base. Fortuitously, we selected the size of our prospecting vehicle so that it can also deliver base cargo, about 40,000 lb. per trip. We need habitat and lab modules, adapted from the space station, a twenty-kilowatt solar power generator, a thermal control system (a heat pump and radiators to control the habitat and lab interior temperature; it gets hot during the long lunar day), and some construction and scientific equipment. Six delivery trips in all, and then we are ready for permanent occupancy with an initial crew of six.

In a crew rotation and resupply mode, our lunar ship, now used as a lunar shuttle, can carry up to ten people; the crew are in the shuttle only about four days each way instead of three weeks or so on the prospecting flights. The early crews will surely not want to stay too long; we will probably go for 120-day stays initially and gradually adopt longer stay times. We will also want to keep up some flight rate for continuing base buildup; three per year is a reasonable figure, for six per year overall. After a few living amenities and plenty of backup and emergency handling capabilities are added, we will probably go to a crew of 10 and a six-month staytime, for two crew rotation and four buildup flights per year.

Now, you may have noticed a problem here. I want six flights of the lunar shuttle per year, and it takes about four space shuttle flights (or equivalent) to support each lunar shuttle flight. That's 24 equivalent shuttle flights per year, and NASA presently estimates they can only provide fifteen total for everybody! Space station, the military, space science, you name it, they all somehow have to share only fifteen shuttle flights.

I probably don't have to tell you that fifteen shuttle flights isn't much of a space program. In fact, our entire space future is hostage to the inadequacy of our space transportation capability. The military would like eight or ten, the space station eight, the space science community four to six, and the commercial satellite people about four. That adds up to twenty-six, which may explain why NASA has thrown the commercial guys overboard. And now there are these return-to-the-Moon nuts who want another twenty-four! Well, you see what the problem is.

Without the Moon program, there might be some hope of patching it up with a few expendable rockets. That's for today's projected demands. Of course, if there come along some folks who want to go to Mars (the Mars underground, remember?) or if someone experimenting with making electronic crystals or whatever in orbit has a resounding commercial success, we're in the soup even if the Moon people would go away. And oh, by the way, there are some ambitious projections for growth of the space station: building big telescopes in orbit and lots of other things. They want more flights too.

Fact is, fifteen flights a year just aren't enough to go around. It's important for all the future users to be heard now. If twenty to twenty-five flights are enough, then crutching the shuttle with expendable rockets is the right answer. You can't justify a new reusable system on 25 flights a year. You couldn't when the shuttle was proposed, either, which is why NASA then forecast sixty a year. Trouble is, when NASA got around to picking a system, they chose one that had no hope of delivering. NASA had some help, from Nixon and the Congress, on how much money they could spend to develop the shuttle; it just wasn't enough for a sixty-per-year system. But NASA did claim they could deliver that flight rate with the system they picked. Ah, well, hindsight is always clearer than foresight.

The important thing here is that Americans should pay attention to whether we want a growing space program that opens the frontier with such things as a return to the Moon. Because if we do, we should step up to a next-generation shuttle, one that can make the flight rate. We should plan in terms of a "class 100" system: 100 thousand pounds to orbit, 100 dollars per pound (marginal cost, and I'll explain what that is), and 100 flights per year rate capability. Actually, we should build that vehicle anyway. It would blow Ariane, the Japanese, the Chinese, the Russians, and everyone else right out of the space transportation marketplace. With the shuttle under our belt, we can do it. And no one else can!

SPACE TRANSPORTATION

Many observers of the space scene believe space transportation services should be provided by the private sector. There is ample reason to think the private sector could offer them at lower cost. "There are things which the federal government cannot do no matter how hard it tries. One is it cannot contain costs let alone save money," says Tom Rogers, who directed the Congressional Office of Technology Assessment study of civilian space stations in 1983. The French believe it. Their Ariane is "commercial"; although developed entirely by government funding, the Ariane is operated by Ariane-Space, a quasi-commercial company. It is apparently subsidized to some degree, as is the shuttle.

Some U.S. companies, now that the shuttle is not a major competitor in the commercial marketplace, are planning to offer commercial versions of their expendable rockets. This is the slow road to low cost, but it may be the only road. If one or more companies are successful and become profitable in space transportation service, one might expect that competition would start to drive costs downward. But the investments required to attain really low costs are huge, more or less equivalent to that of another shuttle program. It is hard to imagine the private sector making such investments unless a substantial part of the government marketplace can be garnered. This is what has motivated a proposal for a "Space Commercialization Incentives Act": legislation that would guarantee government business to any private provider of space transportation that could deliver enough payload to orbit at low enough cost. It is a subsidy of a sort, as were the mail contracts offered to the fledgling air transportation industry about fifty years ago. But just as that industry provided the service at less cost than the government could for itself, the cost targets of this Act are low enough that if a private operator were successful in achieving them, the government would be getting a bargain.

The other possible route to low cost is for the government to directly develop a new, second-generation shuttle. With the experience of building and operating the present shuttle under our belt, we could undoubtedly make a success of the "class 100" system I mentioned above. It would have the attributes once planned (before the budget was cut) for our present shuttle: complete reusability, design for routine operations, and fast turnaround.

Had we built the present shuttle with these features, it probably would not have worked very well at all—too big a technical step at one time. Many technical "firsts" don't work well; they turn out to be as much an educational experience as anything. Quite often, the second time around we get it right. In space transportation it's time to try again.

To understand why space transportation costs so much, one must know that the nation pays a high institutional cost for it. This is the cost of all the people on the shuttle payroll; their cost is incurred whether the shuttle flies or not. On top of that is marginal cost, the cost of flying one more shuttle flight.

The difference in these costs is the root of all the arguments about the cost of flying the shuttle. If you want to paint it expensive, quote the total cost—the annual cost of the program divided by the annual number of flights. If you want to make it look economical, quote the marginal cost; it's much less.

The essential points of this are two: first, there is a significant fixed cost of maintaining the institutional base (the minimum team of people) to operate a space transportation system. Perhaps NASA overdoes it, but it is costly because of its complexity. For that reason, low total costs of space transportation operation are only possible at high traffic rates, where the institutional cost is spread over many flights. Second, the cost of adding flights, e.g. for a lunar program, can be far less than the average cost per flight for the number of flights without a lunar program. This is especially true if the space transportation is designed, as in the "class 100" system, for low marginal cost. With a low marginal cost system, we can plan to expand the lunar base to at least 1,000 people without having to come up with still further space transport developments.

SETTLING IN

If we want to have enough people living on the Moon to think of it as a city or a settlement, we must overcome a few "choke points" along the way. We can start the base buildup with about a half-dozen trips to the Moon per year. The first choke point is that the present space shuttle isn't adequate to support that many trips. A short-term, and possibly attractive, solution is to back up the shuttle with an unmanned heavy-lift system; it's good enough for the first few years. The longer-range solution is the new class 100 system; it is the only way we can grow to hundreds or more people on the Moon.

Dividing six trips a year between base buildup and crew rotation, with a 10-person crew cab, permits us to build up to ten people with four-month stay. At this crew exchange rate, we would need 300 trips per year for 1,000 people. A larger crew cab doesn't really help, since it will cost more about in proportion to its size. Crew transport is the second choke point. Its resolution is simply to permit (ask? demand?) base crews to stay longer on the Moon. For one-year tours of duty, our three trips per year are sufficient for 30 people. Five years, 150 people.

At some point, probably this side of one-year stays, we will need to allow accompanied tours, i.e., with family, as the government presently does for diplomatic postings, and as companies do for extended overseas duty. Accompanied tours might seem a wasteful transportation cost, but I would remind our readers that in a frontier community, everyone works.

Accompanied tours are, of course, a beginning step towards a true settlement. Before we can take that step, we will have to answer some questions, and perhaps solve some problems, about long-term health effects in one-sixth gravity. We know there are problems in zero g and we know there are not at one g. No one has been on the Moon long enough to find out how it is at one-sixth. We need to know how long people can stay on the Moon and still be capable of returning to Earth's stronger gravity. And children born and raised on the Moon—could they ever return to Earth?

Long tours would not eliminate short ones. Crew trips to the Moon three times a year would continue, and the rate would likely increase after a few years. Some people would have things to do, like special scientific investigations, that don't take years. The important thing is to get the average stay up to years rather than months.

Once people begin to stay a long time, transporting their food will become the dominant cost burden. Air will be revitalized and water recycled on the space station now being developed by NASA. The equipment to do this is relatively well understood and compact. The equipment to grow food in space is neither well understood nor compact. For a space station a few hundred miles up, it is easier to just send up food and bring the trash back to Earth for disposal. On the Moon, this will be very costly. We will have to learn to grow food, and recycle everything.

Whenever I take the garbage out, I think about how hard recycling will be, and how beneficial to the folks here on Earth when we learn to do it efficiently. On the Moon, biological and organic substances containing carbon, hydrogen and nitrogen will be precious, because those elements are very scarce there (oxygen is plentiful). There won't be waste paper or plastic trash on the Moon, any more than there is waste gold here on Earth.

What we have to learn to do on the Moon with food, agricultural wastes, and any wastes containing the precious volatile elements is to recycle efficiently and quickly. On Earth, the natural environment does it for us, in ways we don't completely understand, with glacial slowness and with a huge inventory of material in the process "pipeline." We can't afford those luxuries up there.

Another choke point right in there with food and waste recycling is construction of facilities. It takes about ten cargo trips to house and gainfully occupy the people carried by one flight.

The answer is to build our facilities from Moonstuff. Ordinary lunar soil and rocks contain plentiful amounts of common engineering metals, especially aluminum, iron and titanium. Natural asteroidal steel (nickel-iron) is present in lunar surface fines at about 1% concentration and can be separated using a magnet. Industrial processes for winning iron and aluminum on the Moon are analogous to certain processes used here on Earth. Titanium is more difficult, but possible. When building facilities on the Moon for use on the Moon, there really is no reason to get excited about weight; steel will do nicely. But it's hard for aerospace types not to get excited about weight. Making things weigh less is their lifelong occupation.

There are also a number of proposals for making lunar analogs to concrete, and for making very good fibrous reinforcing materials. Lunar feldspar, with a bit of processing, might make fibers about as good as the best glass fibers made on Earth. Silica and sapphire fibers should also be possible; these are theoretically the strongest known. One imagines fiber-reinforced "lunar-crete" structures made entirely of indigenous materials.

Lunar construction must be far more sophisticated than the proverbial mud hut or grass shack. Anything people live in will be pressurized—there is no atmosphere and no pressure on the Moon. Pressure forces will run into hundreds and thousands of tons. Structural failure of a pressurized building on the Moon would be immediately fatal to its inhabitants. We must develop superior materials production and construction techniques, and we must prove them capable of consistent high quality. But if we can build pressurized structures on the Moon and do enough metals production and fabrication to outfit these structures with basic plumbing, wiring, and furnishings, we can get over the facilities choke point.

Facilities and food are the tough ones. If we can do those, we can eventually have a lunar settlement as large as we like. You can bet that developing these capabilities will be high priority for the early base. In the early years, all the facilities and all the food will come from Earth. We will also deliver pilot plants for food and materials processing, and learn how to do the engineering the hard (but only) way: by trying it. Tuning up the pilot plants and designing and building the real ones will take several years, probably at least ten.

The lunar base will grow slowly at first: six, then ten people, then twenty and eventually thirty. We'll do a lot of science. There is much excellent science to do on the Moon that can't be done as well anywhere else, but that's a subject for another time. We'll develop techniques for food growth and for construction. Gradually we will put food and facilities into production, as we also learn to operate an efficient recycling economy.

Despite glowing predictions of artificial intelligence and self-replicating machines, I believe that nearing self-sufficiency on the Moon will be a difficult, piecemeal struggle won only through human dedication and ingenuity. My guess is that it will take ten to fifteen years of hard work on the Moon, backed up by all the Earth-based research we can muster, before we are able to do simple things safely and reliably. For instance, build a pressurized habitat and feel safe living in it.

But then, Katie bar the door! We can start growing the lunar settlement as fast as we can send people. After fifteen years getting to about thirty people, we can begin adding that number every year; if we increase the trip frequency to, say, 20 per year, we can accelerate to something like two hundred per year. The time to go from thirty to 1,000 will likely be less than that to get up to thirty.

The potential for so-called economies of scale is

remarkable. When we get to thirty people, we will have averaged, summing up all costs (including a "class 100" launch system), about a million dollars per man-day on the Moon. Apollo was a thousand times more. We will, at thirty people, be at about $100,000 per man-day marginal cost; that is, we will be accumulating more time on the Moon at that figure. By the time we get to a thousand people, the marginal cost will have dropped below $10,000 per man-day.

The cost of supporting a thousand people on the Moon will be much less than the peak funding of the Apollo program! The cost of a trip to the Moon will be down to a few millions, a level where a more or less wealthy adventurer could afford to pay his or her own way. Commercial transport to the Moon will be available or at least in the talking stage. We will be approaching the economic takeoff for true settlement, where someone who wants to emigrate to the Moon can afford the fare to get there.

AND ON TO MARS?

Why would anyone want to live on the Moon? Without belaboring the fact that American families live in such places as Libya because the pay is good, the sorts of challenges one would expect to find in our frontier community are attractive to people with a pioneering spirit. Observatories on the Moon will have the edge on astrophysical research. The Moon offers decades of challenges to planetary geologists. Physicists and other scientists will think of novel ways to use the cubic miles of extraordinarily high vacuum for unique research projects. Engineers will be challenged to develop new processes, materials and construction techniques suited for high vacuum and one-sixth gravity, and to build novel machines like mass drivers (electromagnetic catapults) for launching lunar products into space to supply propulsion systems or space construction projects.

Science and engineering are not the only reasons and probably not the most important ones for developing the Moon. Industrialization and settlement are very important economically. When the Virginia Company founded the Jamestown colony, its first export was tobacco. Timber, becoming scarce in England because of extensive shipbuilding, was also seen as profitable. Of course, no one then foresaw the industrial revolution, let alone the fact that industrial innovations in America would change the world by creating untold wealth. What innovations might occur in a lunar colony? Obviously we don't know, nor do we know for sure that any would. But it's a good bet. And it's a good bet that the long-range economic benefits will be far greater than any imaginable sums spent on space development.

"Frontiersmen" will emigrate for the challenge of carving an existence out of a remote and desolate wilderness. Jim Lovell on Apollo 8 described his view of the Moon: "Essentially gray, no color, like plaster of Paris or a sort of grayish beach sand." "It certainly would not appear to be an inviting place to live or work," said Frank Borman on the same flight. But Buzz Aldrin described the Moon as "beautiful, beautiful— magnificent desolation." Harrison "Jack" Schmitt referred to the "unique visual character and beauty" of the Taurus-Littrow Valley.

People go to Alaska with the idea of making a lot of money, but most that stay do so because it is a wild, majestic wilderness, a frontier. Antarctica is certainly as desolate as the Moon, except for the blue sky during the summer when it is daylight. People "do Antarctica" for science, but many do it simply because of the challenges. Some day people may settle there, too. (Antarctica is presently a scientific preserve.) So why should the U.S. government, probably in cooperation with other governments (Canada, Europe, and Japan are international partners in the NASA space station project), spend the taxpayers' money for developing the Moon? Why spend money "up there" when there are so many problems "down here"? To begin with, of course, we don't spend money "up there." All of it is spent here on Earth. If there were a settlement there, we might indeed "send money," but it would be to purchase products. Wherever the money is spent, what we get for it is a valid question. What's in it for "Joe Taxpayer"? Where's the return on investment?

Space development and the much-maligned "spin-offs" from it have created major new industries: space communications and microchip digital electronics, to name two. These return more in taxes on the income they generate than ever was spent on space development. Development of the Moon may lead to new techniques in ceramics and composite materials, creation of a large-scale space manufacturing industry, and discoveries in space medicine with broad application here on Earth. Development of the Moon will provide a source of raw materials and finished products for use in space at very low transportation cost compared to shipping them from Earth's deep gravity well. It will create business opportunities in transportation service between the Earth and the Moon for people and products. Long before the lunar population reaches hundreds, we can look forward to the beginnings of economic exports: oxygen for refueling rockets in orbit; later, construction materials for space projects; still later, specialized products exported to Earth.

It is very hard to place a definite economic value on knowledge gained in pure science, but one can argue convincingly that all technology and increased productivity flow ultimately from fundamental science. No new science? Technological advance will soon wither.

Finally, human cultures in new settings often develop new art forms and social innovations such as representative government. Western democracy cannot hope to continue leadership here on Earth if we abrogate it in space. Freedom and liberty cannot survive in an economic and cultural backwater. The space frontier will attract the best minds and the strongest spirits; the societies that develop space will control the destiny of mankind.

This, of course, is an argument for developing the space frontier, not necessarily the Moon. There are those who think we should press on to Mars and forget the Moon. After all, we've already been on the Moon! There are even those who think we should go to Mars with the Russians. Mars is certainly the most exciting site for manned exploration we can contemplate reaching with foreseeable technology. Other places are either too hot or too far away. Mars is a real planet, not "just" a moon.

There are, however, lots of reasons for doing the Moon first. It is a much less expensive proposition to get started on—probably about an order of magnitude less. When the space station is in place, we could do a one-time return to the Moon for about five billions. A one-time visit to Mars will cost ten times more. A lunar program with a future will cost more than this, but the same is true for Mars.

The Moon is relatively close at hand. A trip there takes three to five days, and a complete round trip can be made in two to four weeks. We can go to the Moon more or less any time; the propulsion requirements are always about the same. There are launch window considerations, especially if departing from a space station orbit, but the worst possible case offers a departure opportunity every other month and we will probably pick mission parameters that give us more than one opportunity per month. Mars, on the other hand, involves trip times of six months or more each way and total round trips of at least sixteen months. The departure window is only open two months at most every 26 months. (With very high energy space propulsion, one could go to Mars more or less any time, but we would need at least a very good fusion engine.) Mars missions need to be meticulously planned because there is no room for "I forgot's."

Because the Moon is close and accessible, one can do the Moon with many small trips and incremental programs. Considerable mission flexibility exists. Safety is enhanced because opportunities to return to Earth, or mount a rescue from Earth, are frequent. The Moon is well situated to be an industrial supply port for Earth and all Earth orbital space. Stations in Earth-Moon space, such as at the L2 or L5 libration points, can be used as staging depots for Mars missions, with a ready supply of lunar oxygen for the massive fuel loads needed for trips to Mars. Because Mars is relatively inaccessible, the mission emphasis there will probably be on exploration and science for a long time, at least until high-energy space propulsion systems are in service.

Once we have gained practical experience on the Moon in operating, surviving, and being self-sufficient on a planetary surface, we can essay Mars with much higher confidence and less risk. We will know how to make our systems dependable enough for the long Mars missions, and we will have enough experience to avoid the deadly "I forgot's."

In some ways, Mars will be easier. It has everything including the organic volatiles. Self-sufficiency on Mars could reach one hundred percent, not a likely prospect on the Moon. Because of the Moon's slow rotation and consequent long days and nights, people will mainly live indoors; the Moon will be something like Antarctica in this respect. Although Mars' atmosphere is much too thin to get by without a spacesuit, the day there is just over 24 hours, and the sky has color (apparently it's pink). Some planetary scientists are optimistic that Mars has enough frozen atmospheric gases someday to be thawed and make a real walking-around shirt-sleeve atmosphere.

What about the Russians? Are they going to Mars? Will they beat us there? Should we have a cooperative program?

The Russians have announced that they will launch unmanned planetary probes to orbit and explore Mars and its moons Deimos and Phobos in 1988. They have for years described indefinite long-range plans for manned planetary missions. They appear to be about as far from manned Mars landing capability as we are. Landing requires building a spacecraft in Earth orbit of two million pounds or more total weight, committing crews to a mission of 1½ to 2½ years' duration, development of a Mars lander more difficult than the Apollo lunar lander, proving out an Earth return capsule capable of very high speed entry into our atmosphere, and probably a Mars atmosphere fly-through capability to slow down on arriving at Mars. The Russians are cautious and methodical in their space developments; they are also persevering and make steady progress. We can expect to see them test most of these things long before they are ready to launch a manned Mars landing mission; so far they have tested none of them.

The Russians are rumored to be about ready to begin flying a large Saturn-class launch vehicle. This would give them single-launch manned lunar landing capability, but they would still need a half dozen or more launches to put up a manned Mars landing vehicle. If the Russians are contemplating a near-term, surprise manned planetary mission for political reasons, they might think seriously about a planetary flyby. A flyby doesn't have much scientific value because there isn't much the crew can do that can't be done as well by elementary robotics. But a flyby could have great political effect.

The prescription for a planetary flyby is simple: a Salyut-class space station launched on a planetary flyby trajectory that returns to Earth; and an Earth entry module capable of slightly higher velocity than for lunar return. Flyby trajectories are well known. The practical Mars one is two years in duration; the practical Venus one, one year or slightly less. The rumored Saturn-class Russian launcher could put up a manned Venus flyby mission in a single launch. The Russians have already had people in orbit as long as 237 days. All they really need is a test of the return vehicle, a rather simple and quick test to run. In fact, they did such a test in 1968, getting ready for a manned Russian lunar flight that never occurred because Apollo 8 got there first. They would probably want to update it.

There is one final concern: dangerous radiation from solar flares. A spacecraft on an interplanetary trajectory is unprotected unless heavily shielded, and the radiation from a severe flare could be fatal. However, during each eleven-year solar cycle, there is about a three-year period during which no flares have been seen; a flight during one of these periods would be fairly safe. The next such period starts about this year. I suspect that if the Russians are planning a manned planetary flyby as a surprise, it will be Venus and it will happen soon.

Should we go to Mars with them? There is a certain appeal to the idea of a bold and dramatic space mission such as a manned Mars landing to foster better cooperation and relations between the superpowers. However, I suspect it would divert our attention from the realities of the U.S.-Soviet international competition more than it would theirs, and that they know that. It is clear from Soviet writings that they see the international competition as a long-term struggle between two fundamentally incompatible ideologies; further, that they believe democracy and free enterprise represent flawed systems, that theirs is superior and that they can outlast us.

It's not clear that the Russians want a joint manned Mars mission with the United States. If they do, and if we were privy to the reasoning behind their desires, we would probably not have much enthusiasm for the idea.

At any rate, I would strongly favor a less ambitious trial balloon, such as a joint automated mission where we land a remote-controlled surface vehicle with a Mars soil sampler, and they supply the means of returning the samples to Earth.

THE FUTURE

It's essential that we have a "planning horizon" that looks far enough ahead. Until recently, NASA was not looking beyond the space station. The National Commission on Space report attempts to look ahead fifty years, and this longer view seems to be filtering back into NASA. At least, NASA is now again funding studies of manned lunar and planetary missions.

The only mention of the size of bases or settlements I could find in the Commission report was a reference to twenty people on Mars. The pictures in the book give the impression of large, ambitious installations, but I suspect the actual planning doesn't look beyond tens and twenties of people.

A thousand people on the Moon doing scientific research and developing a self-sufficient industrial settlement is totally foreign to the way we think about space bases and projects. Science communities of a thousand or more people are commonplace here on Earth. Any major national or international laboratory is certainly that large. A more familiar number to space planners, however, would be a dozen or so. This is because they think we can't afford more, and if we do things "business as usual"—that is, designing only for an initial capability—they will turn out to be right.

If we are serious about settlements, and we should be, we must start by building an adequate transportation system, one that can grow affordably to at least a lunar trip per week. We must follow through by stepping up to accompanied tours and long stay times, agriculture on the Moon, refueling with lunar oxygen, and production of habitation, scientific, and industrial facilities on the Moon from lunar resources.

Each of the advanced basing technologies, from long stays to lunar construction, leverages our ability to operate on the Moon by at least a factor of two. By making the best of all of them together with a class 100 transportation system, we can look forward to lunar operations two orders of magnitude bigger than most space planners have in mind—operations that evolve naturally to true settlements.

Mention of space settlements brings forth, in the minds of many, images of O'Neill's space cities drifting majestically at a lunar libration point, rotating in slow motion and tracking the Sun like gargantuan sunflowers. A grand vision of a human future in space, entirely free of the onerous "limits to growth" so faddish a few years ago, these space cities are about as similar to the earliest space settlements as modern Manhattan Island is to the Jamestown of 1610. Just mentioning very modest settlements, however, jars the tranquility of the "business as usual" thought process about space futures.

A settlement is merely a natural product of increasing industrial and scientific operations on the Moon. The reason is economics: the same one that has always been behind the establishment of colonies and settlements.

The economic benefit of a settlement is in its self-sufficiency. We could create a "company town," i.e., a large base on the Moon. Governments and companies would pay to send people there, pay for all the facilities they live in and work with, pay for all their logistics support (food and supplies), and pay all their salaries. Economic returns from lunar activity would have to bear all these costs. If we have a true settlement or colony, people will sooner or later pay their own passage, build their own facilities, have their own local economy, grow their own food and produce most of their supplies. What they need or want from Earth, they will trade for by exporting what Earth wants from them. This is the normal pattern of foreign trade. The United States, for example, gets a lot of stuff from Japan (too much, some people say!). Imagine if, to get it, the U.S. had to pay the salaries of everyone in Japan. We simply would have no trade. No one would pay the prices.

But isn't all this very "far out"? Why worry about it? Isn't it for future generations?

There is no rational reason to believe that a return to the Moon, once we as a nation decide upon it, should take any longer than going the first time: eight years. Ten to fifteen years after the initial return, we should have mastered the basics of self-sufficiency, after which it will take another ten years or so to build up to the thousand-people level. We could have a real settlement by the year 2020, if we get started soon.

The first steps are not expensive. They are things we should be starting anyway if we want leadership in space. An automated lunar polar orbiter is needed to prospect the Moon by remote sensing; its mapping is vital to base site selection. It would also return valuable scientific data. We need an advanced space propulsion engine for lunar vehicles. Our only hydrogen-oxygen space engine is thirty-year-old technology! We should start an unmanned cargo launcher derived from the shuttle propulsion systems. While we also need the Class 100 system, the cargo launcher can be ready in just a few years, is needed anyway, and is adequate to support the first few years of manned lunar flights.

All of these have been studied for years and are well understood. Hardware development should begin at the earliest opportunity, at least by Fiscal Year 1988.

We should begin a preliminary design (NASA calls this "Phase B") of the lunar transport vehicle in FY 1989, with partially parallel hardware procurement starting in FY 1990. These activities would permit initial manned landings in 1997 and opening a small permanent outpost by the year 2000. A Millennium Project!

The first challenge to prospective space pioneers is to get something started soon. Although a lunar base and settlement program can be much less expensive than most policy-makers suppose, a significant long-term investment of government funds is needed before returns start to come in and the beginnings of self-sufficiency are attained. Policy-makers must be convinced, by a vocal and numerous space constituency, that America must not give up space leadership and that space leadership means having a program of goals and missions, not merely one of building "infrastructure" like the shuttle and the space station.

America's first "space crusade," which culminated in Apollo, began with the publication of a book, *Across the Space Frontier*, by Cornelius Ryan and Wernher von Braun, in 1952. This book set off a public debate on the feasibility, cost, and worth of beginning the exploration of space. The crusade gained great impetus from Sputnik and the impressive string of Russian "firsts" that followed; the American public literally demanded that their leaders do something to regain U.S. leadership and prestige.

The U.S. is on the verge of losing space leadership once more and losing it badly; not only the Soviets, but also Europe and Japan have aggressive programs. Public support must be galvanized if we are to retain leadership (or get it back—it may already be too late to avoid losing it temporarily). "They" won't do it; "they" can't; there is no political mechanism I know of in this country, other than public demand, to create conditions under which a bold, imaginative space program can emerge and move ahead.

It's tough for an aspiring space pioneer, who would really like to be homesteading the Moon or Mars or designing spaceships, to get involved in the political process. But space programs are made in the minds of political leaders who respond to public pressure. The struggle for adequate funding occurs every year in each of several Congressional committees. And public funding is only part of it. We also need legislative initiatives that will make it possible for free enterprise to exist and prosper in space. Some nations would like to make the space frontier off limits for free enterprise.

Politics is where the pioneering has to happen today, so that it can happen on the Moon tomorrow; on Mars and elsewhere the "day" after. It's important and it's urgent. H.G. Wells once said, "It's the universe or nothing." The choice is ours and the time for choosing is upon us.

Introduction

This is a writer's plaint against those who, skillfully or not, vivisect his creations. Who asked them to? What gives them the moral right, with or without actual malice, to do such harm? Another question: why should we read their deconstructions?

(After you have finished Larry's broadside, you will come to an example of a very different kind of writing about writing. Since the two were not planned as a set—indeed, neither was commissioned—perhaps it was Fate.)

CRITICISM

Larry Niven

On a Thursday afternoon in 1978 I read a well written, convincing review in an amateur press magazine.
It chopped one of my books into hamburger.

Thursday nights are LASFS meetings, and Joe Halde-
man was visiting. After the meeting Joe and I and Jerry
Pournelle went to Jerry's house to drink and talk shop.

I was still worried. Not angry: worried. It wasn't my
first bad review, but this one sounded too plausible.
Maybe I was doing everything wrong. After a few years
of writing I was still the new kid on the block, and I
knew I had a lot to learn.

So I told my friends of my fears. "Does this guy
Richard Lupoff know what he's talking about? He's a
writer, isn't he?"

Joe said, "He wrote *Sacred Locomotive Flies*."

I laughed and we changed the subject. But I'll never
forget the relief that swept over me.

Critics are self-designated. Nobody licenses critics—it
would be illegal under the First Ammendment—and
nobody votes for them. New writers hear it constantly:
*Don't read your own reviews. If you do, don't take
them seriously.*

Everybody hears it. Nobody does it. Nobody can.

A successful critic needs something to explain. Thus a
lucidly written, easily understood book is likely to escape critical attention.

Writers are communicators and translators. Our whole careers are spent learning how to write more lucidly. This is most difficult with science fiction and fantasy, where the pictures a writer must put in a reader's mind are of things never yet seen, or of things impossible. The most complex ideas need the simplest prose. Kurt Vonnegut writes almost in baby-talk, and he can talk to *anyone*.

Any story that needs a critic to explain it, needs rewriting.

Can you say "Conflict of interest?"

Many critics avoid science fiction and fantasy as demons avoid holy water. And why not? A science fiction work that needs explaining may or may not be trash, but the standard-issue critic is not likely to know the difference, and not likely to be able to explain it either.

Many teachers of science fiction end up letting the students run the classes; many critics end up ignoring science fiction for fear of looking foolish. They are *right*. They *have* looked foolish:

An author of recognized literary worth tries his hand at SF. He confuses infrared with ultraviolet, or loses all track of sociological principles. Everybody notices except the critic.

A critic praises a brilliant new idea brilliantly handled by an author already honored in literary circles. It turns out to be Heinlein's "Universe" ship, decades old and universally imitated.

The standard-issue critic stands some chance of understanding and appreciating Carolyn Cherryh or Ursula Le Guin, and that can make him cocky. (You give *The Left Hand of Darkness* to an English teacher who hates science fiction. It's good by his standards, and short enough that he'll keep his promise to read it.)

But Le Guin and Cherryh tend to step lightly around physical laws while playing with sociological implications. What chance has the same critic of knowing whether Poul Anderson is any good? Anderson is a poet with a solid grasp of every science a mainstream critic can spell, and many he can't. The standard-issue critic took English Lit because Physics was too hard for him!

It's modern criticism that has ruined modern poetry. Any budding poet will be attracted by the freedom and the discipline of science fiction. Kipling saw no reason not to write science fiction and poetry both. Dante Alighieri wrote science fiction *in* poetry. But the critic sees only that Poul Anderson or Chip Delany or Roger Zelazny write sci-fi. So their poetry, if they write poetry, never gains them wealth or recognition.

Then again—

Gene Wolfe's writing has depths that only an English teacher or another writer is likely to probe. It was hours after "The Doctor of Death Island" before I understood what had happened at the end. *The Book of the New Sun* was more lucid than anything Wolfe had written previously, yet it can still benefit from a critic's attention.

Often I've wanted to tell Gene what his multilayered style is costing him . . . and then I decide not to. We need something to read too, you know.

At a SFRA gathering—that's Science Fiction Research Association—I met a man who had written a critical review of *Ringworld*. He told me that my story line was based on *The Wizard of Oz*. I listened as he explained—

The Scarecrow is *Speaker-to-Animals*. (Fear of fire; searching for intelligence.)

The Cowardly Lion is *Nessus*. (Fear of everything.)

The Tin Woodman is *Teela*. (Looking for a heart, for emotions.)

The Wizard is *Halrloprillalar*. (Posing as a goddess.)

Tourism in fairyland, with dangers and a lethal puzzle to spice the adventure. But the solution is much closer than the illusory goals Dorothy (Louis) has been chasing . . .

He must be right. It fits too well. I surmise that *Ringworld* seemed to be plotting itself nicely, all those years ago, because it so resembled a book I had loved as a child and then forgotten.

Algis Budrys praised my early work in the *Galaxy* magazines. Richard E. Geis decided I was good, and has sent me his fanzine for twenty years or more. Their praise came when I most needed it.

I *do not* want all critics hanged alongside the lawyers and tax collectors. The good ones serve a purpose. I myself have felt the critic's compulsion.

An article by Joanna Russ complained that the Ringworld is unstable. That's true, and it's one reason I wrote a sequel: to put the attitude jets in place. But she implied that this is obvious; that she noticed it herself! Joanna's education doesn't reach that far. The instability was obvious to MIT students, and they talked.

In his review of *World out of Time*, Robert Silverberg wrote that my method for moving the Earth would wreck the biosphere. When I asked him about that, he told me that the review was in the mail before he remembered that tidal force varies as the inverse cube. He didn't bother to write to the magazine correcting the error. It didn't seem important.

Ursula Le Guin didn't like my short story "Inconstant Moon." She was apalled by my callous murder of half the Earth's population. Yet I'm intensely proud of "Inconstant Moon." I don't write all that many love stories, and it did win a Hugo Award.

None of these events caused me to write letters of protest.

I once caught Jerry Pournelle writing a coldly reasonable answer to a bad review. I lectured him thus: "You're giving the publisher free material of professional quality. You're rewarding him for trashing your book!" (Jerry makes a wonderful audience. He quotes me later, and gives credit!)

Then came a copy of Richard De Lap's *Science Fiction Review*, with a review of *A Mote in God's Eye*.

It was an exercise in vandalism. I say that not only because the critic (named Burk) didn't like the book, but because we found twenty-three factual mistakes! Burk quoted Rod Blaine's full name and titles, *wrong*, and wrote *(sic)* after it. He quoted me as saying that there has not been a new breed of dog in hundreds of years. Species, dammit! *Species!*

We wrote a letter pointing these things out. We were sarcastic, we were cutting, we were brilliant. "If you *do* write a reply to a bad review," I pontificated, "at least make the publisher regret it!"

De Lap had an answer. He refused to print our letter.

De Lap and his magazine have vanished and I haven't. But there is no defense against bad reviews, and I'm still twitching from that one.

Sacred Locomotive Flies isn't the book that enraged me most. It's a cheat, of course; the author reminds you frequently that this is fiction, that he is not bound by physics or reason or even self-consistence. But worse has been done, by better writers.

Sometimes I feel silly, getting mad because I didn't like a book. These days I don't even pay for them! Books arrive because I might put a cover blurb on one. I read one in five, maybe, and too often I wait for other reviews and choose from the best; which isn't fair.

No point in demanding my money back, then. But who's going to return my *time?*

Gather in the Hall of the Planets, by Barry Malzberg, still has me boiling. It's half of an ancient Ace double; Malzberg may not consider it his best work, so I'm *really* taking it too seriously. But—

It opens as a science fiction detective story. An alien species has been exterminating worlds occupied by intelligent beings for as long as they can remember. They always test a randomly chosen member of the species first; but no species has ever passed their test. Now it's the protagonist's turn.

At the end, we are asked to believe that the aliens have been exterminating whole worlds after testing *not* members of the target species, but *each other!*

Of symbolism and character development and deep psychological exploration within the novella, I will say nothing. Why bother? Malzberg posed us a puzzle story when he didn't have a solution. Regarding matters of symbolism and metaphor, I was told early: Moby Dick doesn't work as *anything* unless he works as a *whale*.

Brian Aldiss does consider a certain book to be among his best, or so he's said in print. All I have to judge by is my own awful experience, which was not entirely Aldiss' fault.

There was a World Science Fiction Convention in Heidleberg in 1970. A block of American fans arranged for a charter flight to fly from New York to London and return from Amsterdam. We thought we'd like the company of our own. In practice, we got little of that. We were packed like sardines; there was no way to circulate and converse.

In Amsterdam I went looking for a book. There'd be precious little of other entertainment on the flight home! I found one in English, by Brian Aldiss. The critics liked him. I remembered fondly *The Long Afternoon of Earth*. I walked aboard that plane carrying one book, unopened, and that was *Report on Probability A*.

I found the opening a little slow . . . massively slow . . . I got as far as page 38 or so, pushing myself, desperate, unbelieving, before I could accept the fact that *nothing was going to happen in this book*.

Later it came back to me: the reviews by critics who were admiring but a little bewildered. *Report on Probability A* uses techniques developed by French novelists, a sub-genre of stories in which nothing happens. As for me, stumbling wide-eyed into a New York City morning after ten hours of sensory deprivation, I had a fixed opinion as to what had been done to me.

An author is always an egotist. Writers who are not egotists can be easily recognized by the fact that they never send out a story to be bought. Only an egotist will believe that he can be paid money, serious money, for writing down his daydreams.

In my paranoia I pictured a brilliant, literate, egotistical Brit with a vicious sense of humor. The critics love him, but he's never loved them. One or another critic may think that he's wonderful, but for superficial reasons. Again, there are critics who *don't* love him. Death is too good for them; he intends worse.

To this imaginary Brit comes a brilliant, literate, vicious idea:

Write a book in which nothing happens at all. Justify it by reference to a French tradition (real or imaginary) of books in which nothing happens at all. One or two critics may guess that it's a jape; they can be brought in on the joke. The rest . . . well, they've never understood the Brit's writings before, and they're far too daunted to admit it. They'll praise the book, because if they don't, the brilliant Brit will somehow make them look like idiots.

I was not comforted by this notion. I was infuriated. We trusted a novelist who has dealt fairly with us before, and with that result? We are readers; we have rights!

Worst case of jet lag I ever had.

Once you know about critics, you know about literature. Literature is whatever survives the critics.

Melville lasted long enough to reach critics willing to research whaling. (The standard issue critic is typically willing to do endless research, though he avoids the hard subjects.)

Shakespeare survived the critics of Victorian times. Bowdler missed some of his best off-color references.

Dante wrote the first hard science fiction. His best-known work was a trilogy set in an artificial structure larger than the Ringworld. Like the best of the hard science fiction writers to follow, he used extensive knowledge of the sciences of his day: theology, the Greek and Roman classics, early attempts at chemistry and physics, and astrology.

In Dante's age, surviving the critics was more than a matter of bad reviews. Dante survived the wrath of the Church and the passage of centuries, and censors: parts of *Inferno* have been judged obscene in every age. His success may be measured by how often his work has been stolen by writers, newspaper cartoonists, animators, you name it.

The test of time has at least the virtue of being unambiguous.

The final critic is a schoolteacher, and schoolteachers are not interested in changing a verdict. Safer to talk about H. G. Wells, Jules Verne, or Mary Shelley. Wells didn't use anything too complicated, and a lot of what went into his work was pure fantasy. Verne didn't know the physics of his own time. Old science becomes fantasy.

Therefore classes in science fiction typically start far back in history, with stories unlikely to be interesting to the students. They move toward modern times, losing students all the way, and never quite get there.

Introduction

Algis Budrys, the exceptional critic who defies the rule, presents here, with the help of a wild-eyed inventor and his imperious lady, a brilliant dissection of the SF story—complete with all the hope and discouragement a would-be writer needs. Budrys is a Free Lithuanian citizen, author of Rogue Moon, Falling Torch *and assorted other novels, review editor for* The Magazine of Fantasy and Science Fiction, *and the co-ordinator of* L. Ron Hubbard's Writers of the Future *contest and its associated programs for nurturing new talents.*

—T.W.

Writing Science Fiction and Fantasy

Algis Budrys

Technically, science fiction and fantasy—lump them together as "speculative fiction," and call it "SF"—are a bit harder to do well than general—"descriptive"—fiction is. But not that much harder. Furthermore, the difference doesn't come into play until fairly late in the process of learning how to do fiction at all.

Considering that the creation of fiction predates the writing of history, you would assume that learning its techniques is a process that has been refined over the centuries and is now readily graspable by anyone of at least average intelligence.

Not so. Most people become writers despite being encouraged to go about it in a confusing and tortuous way.

One way to get a stone elephant is to take a block of marble and chip away everything that isn't part of an elephant. That's also a way to produce a notable quantity of gravel, especially since most apprentices will go through several repetitions before they understand the animal passably. There we see why novice writers are apt to be eyebrow-deep in elephant chips before they attain professional publication.

So we get a useful indication of why the final stages preceding success must usually consist of unlearning. The fact is that trial-and-error can hardly be the best possible method, but most of the instruction and advice directed at novice writers boils down to variously subtle, often effective venerations of it.

Being a publishable author is not that difficult a thing to sustain. For instance, it's obvious from looking at what's on the best-seller lists that a high level of literacy and a close approximation of life are not required for attracting legions of enthusiastic readers. And in examining the works of "classic" authors who are still being recycled to the public, it's clear this has always been so. There's also something to be learned from the fact that Shakespeare, a consummate melodramatist, plays very successfully in Japanese, as well as any number of other languages quite foreign to that English in which he turned so many apt phrases. It isn't language *per se* that seizes and holds the audience, nor is it deft syntax. It's something called "story," which exists almost independent of its wording and—go look—often proceeds without very accurately depicting what people actually do or how they do it.

Storytelling, as distinct from the other known forms of fiction, is the time-proven means of attracting the largest audience. Furthermore, the prevailing tradition in modern SF has educated most of its readers to expect a "story," as distinguished from a vignette or a jest. And so it seems logical for a beginning writer in search of an audience to learn the fundamentals of storytelling, however he or she may depart from them later . . . although all the work done over the millennia since Homer has not sufficed to exhaust the possible subtleties and power inherent in the story form.

* * *

Story affects the reader through a balance between an engineered series of events and an artful depiction of what they mean to the characters involved in them. Without the art, the engineering is empty hackwork. Without the engineering, the art can't be communicated clearly.

The chances are overwhelming that almost all the instruction and advice you've ever received on writing has concentrated on composing words. Good; you are going to need a sound grasp of what words mean and how they link themselves into effective sentences and paragraphs. But *writing* does not primarily consist of stringing words together, as Japanese Shakespeare proves. Writing primarily consists of forming a series of events in your mind and somehow transmitting them into the mind of the reader. Writing things down in letters and words is a traditional way of accomplishing this transmittal, but stories exist in illiterate cultures, and there was a time when all cultures were illiterate. Nevertheless, stories are "written" in those cultures, and somehow "read" by their audiences. Stories are also transmittable through staged drama, but audiences do not read the scripts and screenplays; they observe the events. Similarly, some forms of the graphic arts are storytelling forms. Consider not only the comics, with their sparse dialog and captions serving mostly to string the graphics together, but such things as billboard photographs, greeting-card art, and paintings like *Custer's Last Stand*. Looking at them, a "reader" finds a story forming, and reacts to its significance.

The reader does this by comparing what the eyes can see to everything like it the reader has ever seen. The reader's mind supplies the crash of gunfire, the whinny of the horses, the outcries of living creatures locked in mortal combat, the baking summer heat and the stench of sweat, gunpowder, and spilled blood. There was no way the artist could have put them into the mute canvas. What the artist *has* done is provide the reader with cues that stimulate the reader's search through his or her own experience, and the selection of what the reader finds most appropriate to the depicted situation. Similarly, what a reader of words sees is marks on paper; the reader's experience turns those marks into words, and those words into events. Encouraging the reader to create particular events is, by some slight margin, more important than which particular words you choose to write down, and, by some slight margin, more important than the elegance with which you do it. The first purpose of a chair is to enable someone to sit in it; the carving of the wood, the comfort and color of the padding, are by some slight margin subordinate to that purpose.

So unlearn the idea that the words—the "style"—are what makes writing. What makes writing is your ability to arrange imagined events purposefully, transmit them, and transmit their meaning. When you do this as efficiently and engagingly as possible at the time, your personal "style"—whether it be in prose, words and gestures, or telepathic image-modules—will emerge automatically.

All right, how do you arrange imagined events purposefully? The most direct way is to follow a leading story-character through a chronological sequence of happenings. The first happening introduces the character, and the last happening reveals the character seen in some crucially different new light. In between those two ends, you place the minimum number of happenings required to achieve this alteration. This string is called the "storyline." The story's various events, or scenes, occur along this line.

If you wrote out a description of each of these events in order, you would have a detailed outline of the story—a "scenario." Events in a scenario occur at points along the storyline as it progresses, like longitude and latitude positions plotted along a vessel's course on a chart. So the storyline is often called the "plot," and the creation of individual scenes, and their placement in relation to all the other scenes, is called "plotting."

Contemporary SF still depends heavily on its mid-century traditions as a mass literature, so very often the "new light" in which principal characters are seen at the end is one created by having them experience crucial change, and having the reader experience it with them. That is, most central figures in SF are admirably heroic, and discover crucial things about themselves and the world while solving an immediate physical problem, and the next most populous class are the villains who ultimately fail to prevent this.

There are other ways of doing fiction, as can be seen by looking at the minor but strong tradition of pieces with revelatory last lines . . . "For you see, Darling, as I strip off this outer skin, you will discover that you have come to love a being from another galaxy . . ." but this mode has inherent limitations that prevent it from ever becoming the most popular, or the most useful to a writer's career.

So it is possible to launch and sustain a highly successful SF writing career by learning some science or some magical lore and then setting a rather straightforward story against it. Even the other sorts of story can be seen as twists on the basic story. Furthermore, though it is *possible* to be stupid and clumsy and still do well, it is even more possible to be subtle and craftsmanly in one's art. And in the long run it's advisable to be the latter; your books rarely stay out of print for any great length of time, your stories are frequently anthologized, and a nice permanent structure of both royalty checks and reputation builds up to underpin you in bad times. It is even possible that as a consequence there will be no bad times. This may not seem so important at the beginning of a career. However, few good SF writers die young. (No one knows why this is, but you should keep it in mind.)

Remembering those cautions, let's look at the minimum needed to introduce and establish a strong central character:

Obviously, a character must have characteristics; a specific physical appearance and a particular way of going about things. While it's possible for a master storyteller to handle characters in a variety of indirect ways, my strong advice to a beginning writer is to get that character out where the reader can see him or her plainly, and do it as early in the story as possible. "Haugiser was a wiry man with scarred lips" is not a bad opening line.

But simple, static description will not tell you all of a character's salient traits. Nor will it tell you where the opening scene has found him. So a good second line is "He moved toward the gate as if already beyond the suddenly wary guards; as if in his mind he was even now within the courtyard, and they tumbled dead or maimed on the weathered gray planks of the drawbridge." And a good continuation for the scene is: "Hautereine watched him from the keep; she saw him and the guards come together in a knot, and heard his shout of furious surprise as they knocked him into the moat with the flats of their swords. 'Bitch!' he cried out distinctly. 'The kingdom needs my artifice!'

" 'Ah, hero, hero!' she muttered, and turned back from the window to what her counsellors were telling her now."

Character is delineated not so much in physical appearance as in actions. And a principal character in motion is automatically someone with a destination. Destinations imply plans and purposes, and difficulties to be overcome. Named characters are automatically interesting. Named characters shown interacting with each other imply the existence of major cross-purposes, which implies that none of them may get to their original destinations, or at least will not arrive by the route they first selected. It certainly promises contention. And so in an opening paragraph a story can set the stage, introduce principal players, and intrigue the reader into going on to see how it all comes out.

But of all these important things to do, the key thing to do is to introduce interesting characters who assert their individualities, or the reader will not care what happens to them. Conversely, if the reader is intrigued by the characters, there will be strong urge to read on.

You will notice that it's not really possible to characterize without also moving along the storyline. Questions that arise as the characters bloom into life are: What in particular does Haugiser want in the castle? How does Hautereine know him, and why, in her position of power, does she not in some way intervene personally in what happens to him at the gate? Or is her apparent nonintervention actually the deliberate response it seems likely to be?

But asking these questions implies that a context and problem are already emerged in the story. We find these characters contending over some medieval thing; we have an idea of what sorts of things are possible in a medieval setting, and now we are almost as ready to find out which of these the author will work with as we are to find out more about the characters. We are, in other words, building a bridge over from the beginning of the story toward the middle.

"In the guttering lamplights, Haugiser's apprentices cursed and sweated in the cavern, clambering over the impossible framework, lashing strutwork in wet rawhide, shrinking it with torches, levering portions off the floor while something . . . wheels the height of a man's shoulders; spoked oaken wheels with knobbed iron tires . . . was fitted onto blunt axle ends dripping with grease. The stench of men and hide, torchlight and lamp-fat, raw wood, and some other substance, fuming in huge pots along one wall; the hammering of mallets, the imprecations and gesticulations of foremen; and hurry, hurry, hurry while Haugiser pointed here to this portion and there to that segment of the great, hulking thing, his keen voice driving through the tumult to cause action there, redirect it here. . . .

"Gradually, Hautereine's senses took in the shape of this device as her eyes widened. It had a belly, this creature aborning, and in the belly, benches and footrails, for men to sit braced while they clutched the ash-and-iron crankworks that would turn the wheels. Already, as she watched, other swarming apprentices were draping the bent oaken ribs with Haugiser's stone-cloth fabric, and the looming creature was growing its indurate hide, turning gray, taking on substance and . . . she frowned . . . plausibility.

"But it was at the snout-works that Haugiser directed the main of his vociferous attentions. There, within the bulbous skull, distended ballonets of sewn-and-tarred hide bulged with the leaden cold vapors hosed in from the fuming pots. There, frost rimed into flower on the ballonets, and there the fastidious layings and uncrimpings of hoses and brazen valvings, there the wrapping of cord around the control wheels before they grew too cold to touch, there the fluted silvery nozzle, as though the device sucked on the bell end of a trumpet and the mouthpiece, disconcertingly, pointed outward at the end of the nearly lance-like flute. There—

"She turned away. She could not bear it. 'What do you think of my contradragon now?' Haugiser demanded, plucking at her sleeve, capering pop-eyed, and she tore herself free and fled. 'Hero! Hero!' she cried out to the waiting Council. 'He will kill my beast!' "

And so, scene by scene, the story grows. But it is not *about* a compulsive inventor and a powerful female contending over a dragon. The purposeful accumulation of incidents that further and flesh out the contention along the storyline is what forms the scenario—which is not the story. The *story* is in what Haugiser and Hautereine make of the incidents, and ultimately in what the reader makes of what becomes of them as a consequence of what they make of it. It is necessary to have the characters do more than walk through the incidents, make motions, and speak lines. It is necessary for them to be alive at the time.

And so there is a name for the quality called "drama," a classical Greek word derived from the verb *dran*, to do, to act. It is possible to depict a living character who does not do or act very much, and the Greek dramatists could accomplish that, but they preferred to reach their audiences through vivid actions by their characters.

Communication with a reader is more easily attained by this means, it is part-and-parcel of the modern SF tradition, and I advise you against disdaining it until after you have done some of it in the professional arena, if then.

The ultimate reason for this is that only through vivid action is a character seen to have been fully tested. Stories in which the characters hold long philosophical discourses about the events, and reach intellectual conclusions, may in fact verge on or even attain the ideal of revealing some important truth about life. But they are by definition abstract intellectual propositions, rather than concrete emotional experiences. What happens to their characters may be of intellectual interest to the reader—compelling interest, in some cases—but the experience of reading them is ultimately not different from reading a persuasive textbook. That is, this cannot be what fiction is truly for, since textbooks can and do exist independent of fiction. Thus, the for-you-see "story" reveals itself in the end as an intellectual proposition. It is limited in its ability to give the reader the feeling of having changed what the reader is, as distinguished from what the reader knows.

What you know may be *important* to your survival as a self-aware, thinking being, but existing is *essential* to that condition. It's in dealing with essentials that fiction fulfills its unique artistic role and provides its readers with the greatest satisfactions.

But if the reader's existence is to change, or convincingly appear to change, as a result of a merger with the existence of the story's characters, then that existence must have a point. And so, when all's said and done, there has to be a rounding-off; a convincing demonstration that all of the preceding events have had significance. This is commonly called "the ending," but does not occur in the last paragraph of the manuscript. In fact, it doesn't occur at any particular place in the manuscript.

Usually, toward the end of the manuscript there is a

climactic event, in which someone wins or loses defini-
tively; then there is an "anticlimax," or "post-climactic
event," in which the energy of the characters is seen to
have been drained, and in this last scene someone or
something authoritatively validates the worth of the
climax, and thus the worth of the winning. This sequence, which is mandatory for satisfactory drama, is
the reader's cue to perceive that the story has ended.
With the dawning of that perception, *every* event in the
story is reviewed, reassessed, and made to fit a new
meaning. So in fact the "ending" begins with the first
word of the manuscript, and continues through all the
other words until and including the last. The ending is
everywhere.

It's important to remember that. It all hinges on the
concept of validation.

Validation during the anticlimactic event can consist
of the most simple-minded ritual signal, as in "Who was
that masked man? I wanted to thank him," uttered over
the background cry of "Hi-Yo, Silverrr, away!" and the
fading sound of hoofbeats. This only apparently redun-
dant exercise tells the audience that (1) The victims are
satisfied the hero has rescued them, (2) That they feel
grateful, (3) That the hero sees his service to them as a
duty, and thus a service to an ideal, for which it would
be improper to receive personal thanks, (4) That the
hero is alive and well, and launched in pursuit of the
next wrong to be righted, (5) That the world is a better
place for such actions, and (6) That this episode is indeed over, and its villain thereby crushed never to rise
again, thus revalidating the worth of this sort of hero.

There are subtler forms of anticlimactic validation;
Dorothy exclaiming "Oh, Auntie Em, there's no place
like home!"; the medal ceremony at the end of the first
Star Wars film (and of Leni Reifenstahl's *The Triumph
of the Will*), the heroine's gasp as her lover's skin comes
off, or the dazed Haugiser, blackened and shocked,
reacting to Hautereine as she stands regarding the in-
terlocked monstrosity of dragon and contradragon life-
less on the mutilated plain below: "They have died,"

she utters lowering her frost-charred eyelids. "Your monomanic child and mine." Haugiser extends his remaining hand to touch the faded Stone of Creation dangling in her necklace, and the seemingly devitalized thing suddenly emits one faint spark, then subsides. "While we, my Lady," he gasps from his seared lungs, "must yet live on, in recollection of ourselves."

That last is not quite up to the standard either of "Our revels now are ended" or "flights of angels sing thee to thy rest," but it works the same dramatic work, as does "Hi-Yo Silverrr!"

But you can see from this, I hope, that validating the climax will have no effect if we never saw what the individual events meant to their participants, and if we then can never add up what they meant under the surface. Last-paragraph eloquence will not *per se* repair that. Eloquence comes not from the words but from what they refer to. So, it also seems reasonable to declare that the effectiveness of the ending is in direct relation to the series of running validations that have linked one event to the next along the storyline, and every action within an event to all the other actions within it.

Put it another way: A science fiction story, however otherwise good, will not be fully good if it contains a starfleet captain whose author is clearly shaky on the difference between a solar system and a galaxy, or who thinks a solar system is perhaps as much as a million miles across, or who thinks a light-year is a unit of time. Gaffes of this sort obviously destroy all trust in their author. But make it something subtler; make it a science fiction engineering-problem story whose solution to the problem is utterly plausible to anyone who does not know the exact Rockwell hardness of the cast-iron frying pan with which the hero improvises the key component. Nevertheless, for a few readers, the story is a disappointment, because in the anticlimax all those dunderheads are standing around congratulating each other, whereas that reader knows full well their new turboencabulator is inevitably going to pieces unheeded behind them.

In fact, the same thing happens in all forms of fiction, but is particularly prominent in mass-market fiction. Mass-market fiction tends toward ritual; in order to interest the broadest possible audience, it keeps its characters and their problems within a rather simple, rather narrow range. In order to attract intensely interested readers, it purveys a great deal of technical detail and jargon. Thus, in a standard Western there is more discussion of the horse than its rider, in the standard crime story the detective is detached from his procedures, and woe betide the sports-story writer who not only cannot ingeniously turn victory on some abstruse rule of the game but, worse, gets a well-known rule wrong. In *all* mass-market fiction turned out by technicians, the story is about essentially interchangeable people but a particular rule. (You will recall we do not encourage you to write simply as a technician.)

This situation imposes particular burdens on the SF writer. Speculative fiction, unlike the Western, is not a "genre," although it is often casually called one. But because of the way SF has been marketed since the 1926 appearance of *Amazing Stories* on the newsstands in competition with genre-fiction periodicals, its body of published work abounds with genre trappings—ritualization, jargon, simple plots full of conventionalized events—and readers have been trained to expect the SF writer to do the equivalent of knowing the difference between a rimfire revolver and a cap-and-ball pistol.

But the SF writer's purview is not some narrow slice of time in the history of the West, or an equally researchable segment of social interaction such as baseball or police work. The field of play for speculative fiction is the entire known universe, plus all the scientific and magical explanations of it. It is a world wider than that of "mainstream"—ie., "descriptive"—fiction. And there will always be readers who know more about some part of it than you do, and who are attracted to reading by genre trappings.

My advice is to never include anything you don't know. This advice is patently sound in genre terms—if your laser works in some way that is known to be out of accord with the laws of the physical universe, or if you do not know the difference between a necromancer and all the other sorts of wizard, you will be scorned for being ignorant of facts. But it is also sound advice in literary terms. Never include *anything* you haven't thought through. Or you will be scorned for your ignorance of life.

The genre-verisimilitude problem is only a special case of the general literary problem, which is to avoid invalidation of all sorts, in favor of building validation toward the climax. Some readers will never be satisfied, and that probably can't be helped. But with each uncharacteristic act by a character, each line of tinny dialogue, each assertion of rationality when in fact the character has chosen a stupid course into the next event—or a blatantly clichéd one—with each such micro-invalidation, another component of the total potential readership falls away. Too many of them, and those dunderheads at the end will be uttering meaningless speeches while soberly taking seats on a mirage. At these junctures in a manuscript, editors sigh and clip on the rejection slip, much wearied, and sustained only by the knowledge that they have once again stood between their readers and disappointment, as well as between their paychecks and dwindling readership.

Let's work through this:

In SF, it has been possible to dazzle the specialized readership by shifting attention from wooden characters and their obviously concocted personal concerns to the drama inherent in deft use of the laws of science or of magic. But as noted above, in that case you had better have done your homework exhaustively, which is exhausting, and in any case that day is fading into the past.

SF—science fiction in particular—has been cited with some justice for its acceptance of shallow characters with trivial emotions. Accordingly, many professional litterateurs in academe and elsewhere have disdained the field in its entirety and regard its study as frivolous.

The standard defense from SF's intellectuals has been that SF is "a literature of ideas" and that "the idea is the hero." But that's just a fancy way of agreeing with the attack, and furthermore is the same defense Western fans could make. The standard pragmatic defense has been that the most widely distributed new SF after 1926 and before 1958 was done by professional technologues who wrote as hobbyists, their creativity sparked by technological notions that had occurred to them in the course of their day jobs, and their style conditioned by a bent toward abstract problem solving. In this response to criticism from promulgators of descriptive fiction, the assertion was that these authors were not interested in "doing literature." This defense boils down to "So what?" That attitude has its attractions, but it is simply an aggressive rephrasing of the intellectual defense, and, like it, agrees with the judgment that SF is *intrinsically* a ghetto within the arts.

There are better responses to the condemnatory propositions of the descriptive-fiction establishment. For example, such works as Ursula K. LeGuin's *The Left Hand of Darkness* clearly indicate that while the idea is a central operating part, the standard armamentarium of mass-market SF writing is powerfully capable of exploring the human condition in ways that are forever inaccessible to descriptive fiction. One such example suffices to invalidate the generality of the standard attack, and since this is not a critical essay we can leave it at that; for our functional purposes here, the more important aspect is that if one form of conditioning was imposed on a field, other forms can be brought forward to stand beside it. Clearly, what the establishment scorns for its imbalance between artifice and art is only a portion of what is *possible* in the literature, and only a portion of what the audience can perceive.

It's also important to remember that the "So what" defense is artistically valid. If the writer does not work offhandedly, and if the audience enjoys delving into the artifice, then the artifice, like Kabuki theater, has become the art. In SF, ritualized writing has been brought forward through a number of generations of authors, has grown in sophistication with each generation, and finds copious creative validation in such works as William Gibson's *Neuromancer*, with its punning title. *Amazing*'s founder, Hugo Gernsback, might have considerable difficulty in recognizing Gibson as a descendant of his, but Gibson's work could not have been created in a universe without Gernsback in it.

However, this stage of your interest in writing is not the time at which to limit your explorations. If you want to become a writer, then insightfully and intelligently try everything; what have you got to lose? Historically in this field, as in all literatures, there are the promising new writers who do very well what has been done before, and there are the writers who validly do what has never been seen. That is, they produce new forms of SF which validate themselves largely through self-consistency rather than by reference to existing models. These become the landmarks in the literature.

Of course, to do that you have to know yourself, know your field, work hard and work smart. It may be that for some reason you will find yourself opting to simply work well for a long period of time, validating your career and garnering those various rewards. And who is to say which of these is preferable, which adds more to the art in the long run, or which more justly bestows honors on its creator? Well, as a matter of fact, you, and only you, are who is to say.

Introduction

We are all of us agreed that the proper function of government is to guarantee the rights of its citizens to life, liberty and the pursuit of happiness. (What constitutes the foregoing, *and how to achieve it once it is defined, is of course the very essence of modern political discord.) But what makes somebody a citizen rather than an unauthorized person, and who has the right to declare him so? F. Paul Wilson here takes that question to the max with the urchins and clones in this final story of* Dydeetown World.

KIDS

F. Paul Wilson

What can you say about a client who didn't exist?

Further, what can you say about a client who didn't exist who paid you in hard to find someone else who also didn't exist?

Severe neuronal dysfunction, right?

But that's what had happened. Earl Khambot, as he called himself, had lied to me about his own name yet had paid me in advance in good metal to find the fictional daughter he had supposedly given over to the urchins as a babe.

Why?

Couldn't think of a single reason.

Couldn't complain, either. Had his gold, and that was not exactly what one would call a heavy burden. Of course, on the downside, along the way I'd met B.B. the urchin who'd attached himself to me like a limb graft. Not that B.B. was so bad, he was just *around*. Do you know what it's like to have a skinny energetic twelve-year-old *around* all the time after you've spent years aclimating yourself to being alone?

Not easy.

Became clear to me after a while that I was going to have to find the guy who'd called himself Earl Khambot or go crazy. Not that I'd have a great deal of trouble squeezing the search into my busy schedule. After all, I'd been out of the business for a pair of years, and hadn't been all that terribly busy when things were in hyperdrive, relatively speaking. Passed the word around that I was taking clients and doing searches again, but there wasn't much shaking besides Ned Spinner coming around every so often to harrass me about his missing Jean Harlow clone.

So I used my copious slack time to apply my sector-renowned tracking skills to hunting down Earl Khambot. Knew it wouldn't be easy, but I was getting first hand experience with the concept of *obsession* and had to keep going. It wouldn't let up on me.

Why?

Everybody tries to gain in some way by whatever they do. Even if they give a trinket to an urchin beggar, they're getting a feelgood in return. Even crazy people have their reasons for doing things. Plenty of times they're rotten reasons, but at least you could see what they were after. With Khambot I couldn't even guess. The trail was cold but it didn't matter. I had to know. And to know, I had to find him.

Wished I could have traced him through his thumb, but that was out because he'd paid me in gold. That had impressed me at first as a gesture of trust and good will, and a sure sign that he didn't want our business relationship recorded in Central Data. Perfectly fine with me. And perfectly consistent with the job he wanted me to do: Locate a supposedly illegal child.

Supposedly.

Well, couldn't find her. And when he didn't contact me again, I went looking for him. That was when I found that he didn't exist. Which led me to the obvious conclusion that his kid didn't exist either.

Started driving me crazy.

What had been Khambot's angle? What did he get out of our little transaction?

Didn't know, but was damn sure going to find out.

Or so I thought.

Came up blank all over the Megalops. No one could recollect ever hearing his name before; and although a fair number said he looked vaguely familiar, no one

could say where they'd seen him. B.B. even had a
couple of urchingangs looking for traces of Earl Khambot
but they came up null score.

Looked hopeless.

So imagine my surprise when I find him in my home.
Right. Was sitting in my polyform chair in my cozy
little compartment, the picture of modern domestic
tranquility: Me, the urch, and the iguana around the
vid.

That was where I found him. On the vid during good
ol' Newsface Four's datacast.

It was a VersaPili commercial. The one where the
guy up front starts off swaying back and forth in completely hairless holographic splendor, then grows a little moustache, then some chest hair, then a heart-shaped
pubic bush, then starts with hairy designs all over his
body while the back-up chorus dances and chants,

"It's automatic,
It's enzymatic,
So pragmatic
You'll be ecstatic!
Stimulate or numb your hairy molecules!
Hirsutize or dormatize those follicules!"

A certifiable classic. Everyone remembered it because it used real people instead of digital constructs.
And guess who I spotted prancing around in the chorus?

Right.

Started shouting like a black holer: "It's him! Damn
the Core, it's him!"

Scared the hell out of B.B. who was visiting again
after one of his periodic sojourns home to his old
urchingang, the Lost Boys. He spilled half a cup of
green FlavoPunch all over himself.

"Wha? Wha?" he said, twisting that boney body this
way and that, bright brown eyes popping. "Who's him?
Who?"

"That guy there in the back on the right! The one
with the cubed hair! It's him! Khambot! Earl dregging
Khambot!"

"Sure?" he said. He was trying to wipe the green

goop off him but succeeded only in smearing it deeper into the fabric of his jump.

"Pretty sure."

Moved closer for a better look but the commercial faded from the holochamber to be replaced by Newsface Four again. Told it to retrieve the commercial and ordered it to freeze when the guy in question stepped forward for a spin. Checked him from a couple of different angles.

Khambot all right. Or his clone.

Told the vid to relocate the leading edge of the datastream, then sat back in the chair and considered: mystery man Earl Khambot—low odds that was his real name—was really a song-and-dance man. Wasn't too sure how happy I was with that revelation.

"How you gonna find him, Siggy-san?" B.B. said.

Sometime during the past week he had stopped calling me Mr. Dreyer. Wasn't something I liked but wasn't about to make an issue of it, either. He had found a way to clean the green gook off his jump by letting Iggy lap it up with his big coarse tongue. Never dreamed an iguana would take to FlavoPunch. Maybe it was a nice break from the compartment's roaches.

"Could be I'll go into the commercial business."

-2-

Finding Khambot wasn't as easy as I'd thought. Took me days to snake my way through the various departments of the VersaPili division of the Leason Corporation until I got to someone who had the name of the company that had produced that particular commercial for them. Turned out to be one of these avant guard artsy groups that was dedicated to using live actors. From them I got names of the five guys in the chorus—nobody there seemed to remember the name of the second guy from the right so I took all five names and began searching them out.

Got lucky with number three.

Earl Khambot turned out to be Deen Karmo. Lived

alone in a small compartment in an old complex in
Queens. A small building, holographed up to look like
the top half of the old Chrysler Building. That alone
told me it was old and seedy—the classic Chrysler had
been the most popular of the very early envelopes—
and the lobby confirmed the impression.

Waited til he left one morning, then let myself in.
Easily. His security rig was rudimentary. And once
inside I knew why. The guy didn't have anything worth
taking. Made my place look like a palace.

Being a flesh-and-blood song-and-dance man these
days obviously didn't pay well.

Made myself at home and waited for him to come
back. Was resigned for a long haul but he surprised me
by showing up in a couple of tenths.

Didn't even look up as he came in. He was humming
a tune and dressed in the latest style just as he'd been
when he showed up at my office that one time. A real
pretty-boy. The door had already slid completely shut
behind him before he spotted me. He dropped the
package in his hand.

"What are you doing in here! I'm calling security!"

He reached for the panic button. Obviously he didn't
recognize me.

"You shock me, Earl," I said quickly. "Throwing out
your old friend without even a hello."

His finger stopped about a millimeter short of the
button. "My name's not—"

He gave me a closer look. Came the dawn:

"You—you're that, that, that—"

"Investigator."

"Right!" He smiled. "How have you been, Mr . . .?
Forgive me, I forget your name."

"Really? How could you forget the name of the man
you hired to find your daughter?"

The smile faltered and his hand still hovered over the
panic button.

"I'm not sure I know what you're talking about."

"The name's Dreyer. Sig Dreyer. And what shall I
call you? 'Mr. Khambot' or 'Mr. Karmo?' "

"Mr. Karmo will do fine."

"Good. Let's talk, shall we, Mr. Karmo? I'm not here to cause you any trouble. You paid me well for my time so I've got no quarrel with you. But I *am* curious."

Finally, he dragged his hand away from the button and took the only other seat in the tiny compartment.

"I don't think you'll be too happy with what I have to tell you, Mr. Dreyer."

"Why not?"

"Because there isn't much."

"Let me decide that. You can start by telling me if you have a daughter."

He laughed but it didn't seem to relax him. "Oh, no! Of course not! That was just part of the story!"

"But why any story at all?"

"I really don't know. I'm an actor. I was hired to act." He shrugged expressively. "So I acted."

"Who hired you?"

"I don't know. He was wearing a holosuit."

"Isn't that just bloaty!" I said, getting annoyed and showing it.

Karmo cringed. "Sorry."

"What was the image?"

"Joey José."

Wanted to throw something. Had high hopes since tracking Karmo down, now they were going up in smoke. He'd been hired by a guy hiding inside the holographic image of the Megalops' most popular entertainer. It was the number one holosuit on the rental circuit. Every holodashery had twenty Joey Josés in stock. No way of tracing the mystery man through that!

"What about the voice? Any accent?"

Karma cringed again. "He was using a Joey voicer."

A holosuit and a voicesizer. Whoever he was, he was taking great pains to cover his tracks.

"And he just came up to you and handed you that gold piece and said 'Go find somebody to search for your imaginary urchin daughter' and you picked me out to—"

"Oh, no. He was very specific. It had to be Sigmundo Dreyer and nobody else."

"But I'd been out of business for years! I'd only opened up a couple of days before you showed up!"

Another shrug. "What can I say? Maybe he'd been waiting for you to reopen. All I know is that he gave me two goldies, told me to use one to hire you and keep the other for myself. If I was successful in getting you to take the job, there were two more coins in it for me." He smiled briefly. "Needless to say, for that kind of fee, I put on my best performance."

He shrank back as I stood up.

"That you did, my friend. That you did."

Would have loved to give the jog a dose of Truth but had a feeling I'd learn nothing new. Somebody pretty glossy was behind this: left no trail, and dangled a pay schedule that not only kept Karmo from roguing off with the goldies, but insured he'd give the performance his all.

"No harm done, I hope," Karmo said.

Clapped him on the shoulder and he almost came apart.

"Nope. No harm at all. Just want to know what's behind it all. And you're no dregging help."

Left a very relieved and very sweaty actor behind in his compartment.

-3-

"Eat your soyshi."

B.B. made a face. "Needs more cooking."

"Not so. Supposed to be raw."

"Raw fishee?"

His repulsed expression was something to behold. All I could do to keep from laughing. He was pulling me out of the trough I'd slipped into since my talk with Karmo.

"Not real fish. Only looks that way. It's veg. Pseudotuna on vinegared rice. Watch." Finger-dipped one into the nearby soy-wasabi mix and popped it into my mouth. "Mmmm! Filamentous!"

B.B. grabbed his throat in a stranglehold and treated me to the sound of a melodramatic retch as he toppled off his chair.

The other customers in the dinnero were starting to stare.

"Get up before they kick you out of here!"

He returned to his seat. "H'bout soysteak—"

"Pardon?" I said, cupping my ear.

"How about a soysteak?" he said carefully.

"How about broadening your horizons? There's more to eating than soysteaks, cheesoids, and speed spuds."

"Dun like this dreggy stuff."

"How would you know? You haven't tasted any. What kind of parent would I be if—"

"Not my parent!"

That stung more than I would have imagined it could. Don't even know why I'd referred to myself as his parent. Didn't want to be. Truly. But felt the jab anyway. The sting must have shown on my face, because he added:

"Wendy parent to all Lost Boys."

Could have added that you're allowed more than one parent but that would have slipped me into a position I didn't particularly care for so I kept quiet.

"Right. Forgot."

The black mood was settling on me again.

"You fren, Sig. Not parent."

"One way of looking at it, I guess. And friends don't make other friends eat soyshi, right?"

"Right."

Ordered him a soysteak with his habitual trimmings. Every time I took him out to eat he ordered the same dregging meal. Urchins must have a high threshhold of boredom.

"Who is this Wendy, anyway?" I said as we waited for his meal.

"Mom-to-all."

"B.B. . . ." I said tiredly.

"Know, yes, know, Sig. Not biomom, but real mom. Readee us, teachee us, fixee clothes an food. Do tuck-in a'night f'babes."

His eyes shone as he spoke. There was adoration there. Why did that irk me? What did I care about some crazy femme playing Mamma to some urches?

"What's she look like?"

"Byooful."

"Of course. Aren't all mothers? But give me some details. Her hair, for instance? Blonde?"

He shook his head. "Brown straight."

"Fat? Thin?"

"Thin like us, course."

"Why 'course'? When she leaves you at night, she probably goes home to a big meal."

"Wendy live w'urches."

That gave me pause. Who in their right mind would want to live in the tunnels with a horde of kids, eating begged food and cooking rats?

"What's she get out of it?"

He beamed. "Family. Allus family."

"All?"

"Huh. Sh'go lots gangs. Mom-to-all, but sh'come back Lost Boys most. We her *firs* famly."

B.B.'s urchingang, the only family he had ever known until he hooked up with me. Urchins—these were the Megalops' castoffs, the kids who were beyond replacement value. The Replacement Law went into effect long before I was born, back when we were up to our nostrils in people. It said for the sake of population control, you could only replace yourself childwise. No more. After that it was sterilization time. Any child conceived beyond replacement level had to be aborted; any child born live beyond replacement level had to be terminated on the spot.

Some people couldn't accept that. They had extra kids and kept their above-and-beyonders alive by hiding them away. Eventually the urchingangs sprung up and became a self-perpetuating society—new babes raised into cute little beggers by the older kids who eventually grew up and left the tunnels to join the shadow economy.

An endless cycle.

And unnecessary, too, I guess. Attrition had whittled the population down to a level where everybody could eat, but still the Replacement Law stayed in effect. Probably because the C.A. feared a rebound population boom of monstrous proportions. So the urchins hung on, alive but officially nonexistent.

See: all Earth residents are citizens, and the genotypes of all citizens are registered in Central Data. If you're not registered, you don't exist. Urchins aren't registered. Therefore there are no such things as urchins.

Get it?

"Wendy never leaves the tunnels?"

"Sometime, but n'f long. Always come back with special giftees."

Now I was really suspicious. This Wendy was either a true disequillibrated non-comp, verging on black holedom, or there was a roguey angle to this that I wasn't seeing. Either way, I wasn't comfortable having B.B. involved with her. Not until I knew more.

"Sounds like a wonderful person," I said. "When can I meet this Wendy?"

He started as if he'd just received a shock.

"Meetee? Oh, no. None upside ev meetee Wendy. Sh'say n'even jaw 'bout her to any not urch."

"You told *me*."

"You friend f'life, Sig. Trust."

"Yeah. Well, see if you can arrange it. It's very important to me to meet such a unique person."

"I ask, b'tell now, sh'nev say 'kay."

The food arrived then and no further conversation was possible. You can't talk to B.B. when he's got a meal in front of him. You can barely watch him.

-4-

Two days later, sitting in my office, got treated to the pleasure of another visit from my favorite procurer and clone slaver, Ned Spinner.

"What do you want, Spinner?" I said as he stood in front of my desk, staring at me.

His hair was in his usual curly blond Caesar cut and he was dressed in the same dark green pseudovelvet jump he always wore. As he spoke in his nasal whine, he began strutting back and forth, doing his oversized rooster routine.

"I just wanted to check up on you and make sure you were okay."

"Your concern is touching."

"Truth, Dreyer. After all, you're probably the only one who knows the whereabouts of my missing clone."

The jog still thought I was hiding his Jean Harlow clone somewhere. Thought I'd stolen her from him. He'd been hounding me for two years. Some guys never learn.

"You can go now."

He hesitated. "Look, Dreyer. I'll make a deal. I know you've put her in business somewhere, but the take you're getting off her can't be anything near what she could earn back in Dydeetown. She was dregging good, one of the top earners in the whole—"

"The door is behind you, Spinner."

"I'm offering you a cut, you jog!" he screamed. "Tell me where she is and I'll go get her. I'll set her up in her old spot in Dydeetown and give you a percentage! What could be fairer? After all, she's my dregging clone!"

Stared at him.

"Well," he said. "What do you say? Attractive offer, no?"

"No. Because then I'd be like you, Spinner. And I don't find that the least bit attractive."

The sneer that he tried to pass off as a smile crawled across his face. "All right, Dreyer. Play your roguey game. But keep in mind that I'm always around. I'm always watching you."

"Each night I rest easy knowing that."

"Don't rest easy, Dreyer. I'm the guy that's going to cut you down. Remember: every day, I'm watching. And one of these days, you're going to lead me back to my property."

"Your clone is on one of the Outworlds, Spinner. And since I don't plan on heading off-planet soon or ever, you've got a long wait ahead of you."

"Keep lying, Dreyer. You'll end up on the South Pole if I catch you with her."

"Look," I said, trying to talk some sense into him so he'd leave me alone. Doubted that was possible—after all, he'd made a good living off his Jean Harlow clone and now he was on the dole without her—but figured I'd try. "Even if you got her back, she'd be no good to you. She'll refuse to whore a Dydeetown slot for you. So why don't you face facts? You lost. She won. She got away and she's staying away. Give it up."

His eyes blazed as he slammed a fist on my desk.

"*Never!* She's Earthside! Probably right here in the Megalops! And I'm gonna find her! And if she won't cooperate, I'll memwipe her and we'll start all over again from scratch! But I'm *never* giving up, Dreyer!"

Good thing he left on his own then. The thought of him wiping Jean's memory and sticking her back in Dydeetown had me itching to go for his throat.

Was just about calmed down when B.B. popped in. He looked dazed as he plopped down on a chair.

"Something wrong, kid?"

He shook his head slowly as he spoke, as if not fully understanding what he was saying.

"Har b'lieve, Sig, b'Wendy say sh'jaw you, see you."

B.B. was definitely spending too much time with his old urchingang. Had to work on getting him to do some time in front of the datastream before his speech got stuck in pure urch pidgin again.

"Well, I assume you gave me a bloaty recommendation."

"Bloaty, yeh, b'she *nev* see toppers."

"She's gotta see somebody when she disappears topside."

He thought about that one. "Mayb. B'when sh'go way, nev f'long. Allus back morn."

Understandable. No matter how overdone she was on urchins, even this Wendy had to crave some adult chatter once in a while. Maybe that was why she'd agreed to meet me. She'd know from B.B. that I wasn't some dregger out to stake some sort of claim on them, especially after taking that pair of vultures from NeuroNex off their backs.

"When do we meet this lady?"

"Now, today, ri'way."

"Whoa, little man. I've got business to tend to."

Not true, but I wanted to have some say in how and when this meeting took place.

"Sh'say now or nev. Or leas nah f'verlon time."

Wasn't happy with the ultimatum, but the meet had been my idea, in the first place. She was agreeing to it, but on her own terms.

"Where?"

"In downbelow."

"In the tunnels?"

"Wendy n'like upside."

"Bloaty." Last place I wanted to spend a day was in the old trans tunnels. "I'll get a handlight and then you can lead the way, B.B."

We tubed across to the Battery area, back to the foundation of the Okumo-Slater Building where I'd met my first urchins, then shot north two stops. From there it was all on foot. We walked further north until we came to a middle-sized office complex. B.B. led me through the subbasement to an old sealed up subway entrance. The kids had unsealed it long ago. B.B. ducked within, I squeezed through behind him. Out came our lights and we began our crawl into the Megalops' nether regions.

Down concrete steps with our handlights reflecting off old tiled walls, along rubble-strewn corridors, hopping down concrete embankments to follow steel rails through passages crudely hacked through the living granite. Moisture had collected in puddles, some small, some wide enough to block our path so that we had to creep along a raised ledge to get by. Something splashed in one of the bigger puddles as we passed and I felt my hackles rise.

"Chilly down here," I said.

Ahead of me, I could see B.B. shrug. "Allus same. No matter what upside, allus same in downbelow."

After a long, seemingly endless tunnel, I noticed a faint glow from up ahead. It grew as we moved toward it, becoming almost blinding as we rounded a bend.

It was a station, an old subway stop. What wall tiles that remained sparkled in the light. In one spot, some blue and orange tiles formed a sign: W.4TH. In a far corner, green things were growing. The platform was lined with a motley assortment of little shacks made of epoxied scrap vinyl and polymer. They looked like they'd been slapped together, but the overall picture was one of neatness and order. Saw a few urchin toddlers sitting and playing in a group while some nine- or ten-year-olds swept the platform floor between the shacks. Cleaning the place up. Almost like they were expecting company.

"The Lost Boys," I said.

"Ri'!"

As we got closer, I squinted up at the bright ceiling over the platform and saw that it was lined with Ito daybars. Nudged B.B. and pointed to them.

"Where'd you get those?"

"Stealee long time go. Two-three urch life."

"Yeah, but you need power—"

"Stealee tha, too." He pocketed his handlight. "Come. You meetee my frens."

B.B. led the way up a short run of steps to the platform. A couple of the kids waved as they caught sight of him, then froze when they saw me. One of them let out a yell and suddenly there was a torrent of urchins of all shapes and sizes spilling out of their shanties. Only in a few cases could I tell the boys from the girls. They were all thin, all dressed in castoff clothing, all had hair of about the same length.

And all the older ones were armed and looked ready to fight.

B.B. hurried forward, waving his hands. "No, no!" He pointed back at me. "Siggy! Siggy!"

Saw their eyes widen as they all stared at me. Suddenly the platform was silent. They began to move toward me, slowly, as if unsure of themselves.

Wasn't too sure of myself either at the moment. There was an awful lot of them—fifty at least—and I was pretty much at their mercy. Couldn't even run if it came to that. Didn't know how to backtrack from here. So I held my ground and let them come.

Their faces . . . their expressions were all the same. Could that be *awe*? Of me?

They crowded around, cut me off from B.B., encircled me, but kept a distance of about a meter. Until one of the toddlers broke through the others and came up to me. He or she looked up at me for a moment, then grabbed my leg in a bear hug, saying,

"Thiggy."

That broke the ice. The rest of them crowded closer, some patting me on the back, some gently punching me on my shoulders, others hugging me, and all of them saying softly, almost reverently,

"Siggy, Siggy, Siggy."

What was going on?

Looked around for B. B. but couldn't find him in the press. Then the crowd parted to let someone through. An adult. A woman. Slim, with straight, light brown hair flowing over her shoulders. Nice figure.

When she smiled, I knew her. The platinum hair was gone, and so was all the make-up. But by the Core I knew her.

"*Jean!*"

"Hello, Mr. Dreyer," she said, calm and as matter-of-fact as if we had just had lunch together yesterday.

She put a hand on my shoulder and kissed me on the cheek. All around us, the urches giggled and whispered.

"They like you," she said.

With the toddler urches clinging to my arms and legs, I could only gape at her.

"B.B. has spoken so much of you, about how you almost died catching the ones who were snatching our toddlers. You're a hero here, Mr. Dreyer. All the urchingangs have heard of you."

Finally found my voice.

"It's been two years, Jean. Thought you were Out Where All The Good Folks Go."

"I was. I went to Neeka and settled there for a while. I thought it would be all right. I thought I could fit in. But it didn't work out."

"You didn't tell them you were a clone, did you?"

"No. That wasn't the problem. There were many men interested in me."

"I'll bet."

No shortage of food on the Outworlds, but they were always short on women.

"But I quickly found out that I would never be considered a suitable mate for anyone there."

"Why not?"

She shrugged forlornly. "I'm sterile."

"Oh. Right."

Had forgot about that. All clones, male and female, are routinely sterilized at birth—at deincubation, rather. Injected with something that keeps the gonads from producing gametes without interferring with their hormone output.

As far as Outworlders are concerned, a woman who can't breed is not a real woman.

"So, I came back home," she said with forced brightness. She put one hand on the shoulder of a nearby urch and tousled the hair of another. "And found some people who really need me."

"Yeah, but you were free to come and go as you pleased out there. Earthside you're—"

"A mother—something I can't be anywhere else."

The realization hit me then. I'm a little slow, but eventually I get there.

"You're Wendy!"

She curtsied. "At your service."

"Hear you're a real mother to them."

"I try."

"Wendy bes mom ev!" It was B.B. He had squeezed in beside her and was grinning up at both of us. "An Sig bes fren. Protectee."

Circuits were beginning to come to life, correlations were beginning to be made in my pitiful brain.

"You hired that actor to hire me to . . . to . . ."

She nodded, smiling. "Of course! Me and my Joey José holosuit."

It all fit. Someone had been snatching her children and returning them damaged. She had wanted it stopped and so she came to me—or rather, sent someone to me.

"Why me?"

"Because you don't quit."

Shrugged that off. Probably just trying to get on my good side.

"Why didn't you come yourself?"

"I wasn't sure you'd take the job from me. I know how you feel about clones. Besides, Spinner was always hovering about. I couldn't risk him spotting me."

"Doubt he'd recognize you."

"This is the real me," she said, twirling a strand of brown hair around her finger.

"You look nice," I said before realizing it.

"Why, thank you, Sig." She was staring at me, her eyes soft and wondering. "You've changed, haven't you?"

Shook my head. "Not a bit. Why should I?"

"I don't know. And I can't say exactly what it is, but you're different."

"My hair—combing it different."

"No, I mean different *inside*. And by the way, I've been wanting to ask you for two standard years now—"

That was a giveaway that she'd spent some time on the Outworlds—only Outworlders talked about "standard" years.

"—about that greencard you returned to me at the shuttleport."

Felt myself tighten up inside. Didn't want her figuring out that I'd done something stupid like changing the worthless phoney card Barkham had given her to a genuine counterfeit Realpeople card. She'd probably get all sorts of wrong ideas then.

"What about it?"

"It felt . . . different."

"It worked, didn't it? So don't complain." Then I thought of something: "Wait a bit. How'd you get back Earthside without Spinner finding out?"

"Simple," she said with a mischievous smile. "I declared citizenship on Neeka, changed my legal name, and came back on a visitor's pass."

"But that only gives you a limited stay."

"As far as Central Data is concerned, Jean Double came to Earth as a visitor and disappeared."

" 'Jean Double,' huh? You've gotten pretty glossy since you left."

"I'm not as naive as I was two standards ago, if that's what you mean."

Laughed. "Nobody is!"

She laughed, too, and I liked the sound.

"But is this it?" I said, looking around at the Lost Boys' tunnel village. "This is it for the rest of your life?"

"It's not so bad." She hooked her arm around mine and I felt a strange tingle run up to my shoulder. "Come on. I'll give you the tour."

The kids fell back, then followed us in a herd as she led me toward the greenery. Watched her out of the corner of my eye. She thought *I'd* changed? *She'd* changed! This was not the dumb woman-child clone of two years ago walking at my side. This was a grown-up— content, assured, self-confident. More than her hair had changed. Seemed to me she'd made major changes *under* that hair.

"The daybars were here before I came, but the children never took advantage of the artificial sunlight. I had them collect some soil from the upper tunnels, steal seedlings from a few choice window boxes, and here we are: fresh vegetables."

"Filamentous," I said, and meant it.

She led me through the old station, showed me the various models of hut. Did my best to appear interested, but couldn't get a certain question out of my mind. Finally, when she stopped and showed me her own hut, I asked it:

"How come you're wasting your life down here?"

She turned on me like a tiger. "*Waste?* I don't call this *wasting* my life!"

"Bloaty. What do you call it then?"

"Doing some good! Making a difference! And I don't need your dregging Realpeople seal of approval to make it matter to me, either!"

"Making a difference?" She was getting me riled. "What difference? They're still going to grow up and move upside with no legal existence and try to scratch out a living in the shadow strata."

She turned away. "I know. But maybe they'll be just a little bit better people because of what I've done for them down here. And maybe . . . just maybe . . ."

"Maybe what?"

"Maybe they won't all have to move into the shadow strata. Maybe some of them can go somewhere else."

"Like where?"

"The Outworlds."

Too stunned to speak as she turned around and faced me with all this hope beaming from her eyes. Jean Harlow the clone had a Big Idea. A Dream.

That can be dangerous.

"Did they make you travel back and forth from the Outworlds in an unshielded cabin or something?" I said when I'd regained my voice. "Being out there must have affected your mind."

"I'm not crazy!" she said with this beatific smile. "Farm planets like Neeka are *crying* for settlers—the younger the better! They need hands!"

"But these are little kids here! They can't—"

"Little hands quickly grow into bigger hands!"

"And how are you going to get them off planet?"

She frowned. "That's the problem."

"That's not the only problem," I said. "Who knows how they'll be treated out there? Some dregger could turn them into slave labor, or worse."

"I know, I know," she said in a miserable voice. "But look at this." She gestured at the platform around us. "Something has got to be done. These are *babies*! This has got to stop!"

Stood and stared at her, not really understanding her. As usual.

Guess there are two ways of looking at things like the urchingangs. Me, I've always accepted them. The urchin problem was swept under the carpet long before I was born and I've always taken it for granted that they'd still be there long after I died. Urchins: Everyone knows they're there, but as long as they stay out of sight in their assigned niche, no one has to bother about them.

Then there's the other way: someone sees the lumps in the carpet, lifts it up and says, Hey, what's this dregging mess doing here?

This has got to stop.

Well, sure. Now that I really thought about it, yes, it *should* be stopped. But who was going to do the stopping? Not an everyday jog like me. And certainly not a renegade clone of Jean Harlow.

This has got to stop had never occurred to me because I knew it would never stop.

And what you can't change, you accept.

At least that was what had always worked for me.

"Don't go stirring things up," I told her. "You might get hurt."

She shrugged. "I'll risk it."

Pointed to the kids standing and staring at us from a distance. "*They* might get hurt."

"I know." She turned those big eyes on me. "Will you help me?"

Shook my head. "No."

"Please, Sig?"

That startled me. She never called me by my first name.

"With all your contacts, you could help me find a way to get some of these kids out of here."

Shook my head again, very slowly so she couldn't confuse it with anything else. Knew if I got myself involved in this one it would make me crazy.

"Double no. And let's change the subject."

She gave me a long, reproachful look. "I suppose you want the rest of the payment for ridding us of those NeuroNex snatchers."

"We're even," I said. "Consider it a favor for a friend."

She smiled. "So I'm a friend? How nice of you to say so."

That took me back. The friend I'd meant was B.B., but I didn't correct her.

"Better be getting back," I said. "Is there a shortcut out of here?"

"Only if you're B.B.'s size."

"But they must have had lots more entries and exits in the old days."

"Of course, but they've long since been sealed up and built over. The nearest adult-sized entry is the one you used to get here."

"You going to lead me out?"

"B.B. will do that. Good-bye, Mr. Dreyer."

She turned and walked away.

-5-

Strangely enough, about a week later I was sitting in my office with my feet up on the desk, thinking of Jean—nothing personal, just wondering what she was going to do with all those kids—when B.B. raced in. His eyes were bugging out of his ashen face.

"Got uh! Got uh! Got Wendy!"

My insides did a flop to the right, then to the left as I got my feet down and shot upright.

"When? Who's got her?"

Already knew the answer to the last part. What a dregging jog I'd been not to remember what Spinner had said about watching my every move.

"Yellows!"

That stopped me.

"You mean M.A. Types?"

He nodded vigorously. "Four!"

What 'round Sol were Megalops Authority police doing arresting Jean?

"Where'd they take her?"

"Dunno! Dunno!" B.B.'s face skrinched up and he started to blubber.

"Hey, little man. Calm down."

Seeing him break up was upsetting. Motioned him over by my chair and put an arm over his shoulder. He slumped against me and sobbed.

I said, "I'll find out what's going on. If the yellow-jackets took her, she'll be down at the Pyramid. Probably all a big mistake."

He seemed to take heart from that. "Think?"

"Sure."

Biggest lie of my life.

"Y'get Wendy out, ri', Sig? Get back Mom-to-all?"

"Do my best."

"Cn'do, Sig. Know it be filamentous soon. Cn'do any!"

"Yeah."

-6-

THE PEOPLE'S PYRAMID—
OPEN TO ALL THE PEOPLE ALL THE TIME.

Megalops Central really is a pyramid—no holo envelope. The real thing, squatting in the middle of a huge plaza. Hollow inside with all the governmental offices in the outer walls. Supposedly a showpiece but actually a colossal waste of space. A golden Cheops model, sloping up stepwise to a transparent apex. The steps provide landing areas, making up for the lack of a flat roof, I guess. Always bustling. Never closed.

Took me a while—had to answer lots of questions and go through a genotype check—but managed to get a short visit pass to the detention area. Sat there in a booth facing a blank wall. Noticed recorder plates overhead. Every word, every move was going into Central Data.

The wall cleared and there was Jean. She looked surprised. Shocked, in fact.

"You? You're the last one I expected to see."

"Sorry to disappoint you."

"No—no! It's so good to see a familiar face."

"B.B. asked me to see what I could do."

She looked scared. "I don't think anyone can help me now."

"Tell me about it. Couldn't get much from B.B. He was almost incoherent."

"Not much to tell. I came upside last night and the yellowjackets were waiting for me."

"What's the charge?"

"Illegal alien. I guess I didn't do such a good disappearing act."

"Maybe, maybe not. Was it the same entry I used?"

She nodded. "It's one of the few big enough for an adult."

Suddenly I knew: "Spinner did it!"

Jean blanched. "Oh, no! How can you be sure?"

"He's been following me! What a jog! Led him right to you!"

"But you didn't know you were going to meet me!"

True. But somehow I still felt responsible.

"Well, Ned Spinner can go sit on a black hole. He's out of luck. I'm a citizen of Neeka now. He's got no lein on me any more!"

Wasn't so sure of that. Wouldn't be hard for Spinner to establish by genotype that she was a clone of Jean Harlow. When he did that, all her rights—to emigrate from Earth, to take citizenship on Neeka—would go null. The M.A. would treat her like Realpeople until the genotyping was confirmed and Spinner's ownership of her genotype was established. But once that was settled, she'd be property again. Ned Spinner's property.

"Just for the sake of argument," I said, "let's suppose you wind up in Spinner's clutches again. What'll you do?"

She shrugged. "Nothing. And I mean *nothing*."

"And if he forces you?"

Her expression was grim. "He'll own one dead clone."

Was afraid she'd say that. And knew she might not get a chance to make that final gesture if Spinner had her personality wiped. The clone I knew as Jean, the person B.B. knew as Wendy—"Mom-to-all"—would be gone, but her body would go on working for Ned Spinner.

Wondered briefly which was worse, then realized it really didn't matter.

"Just a thought," I said. "Don't worry about it."

She looked scared enough already. Didn't need me injecting a worse reality into the nightmares she was probably having as it was.

The transpanel began to opaque between us. Time was up.

"Be back when I find out what's going on. Don't go anywhere."

She smiled—could tell it was forced—and faded from sight.

-7-

"Don't look so grim, Dreyer," said a nasal voice to my left as I stepped from the downchute onto M.A. Central's ground level. "You should be feeling lucky."

Ned Spinner, grinning like a shark.

"Feeling pretty murderous at the moment, Spinner. Don't press your luck."

"I'm not scared of you. Especially here."

Looked at him hard, letting my face show him what I wanted to do to him.

He took a step back. "You'd better be careful, Dreyer. You got lucky last night. If they'd caught you with her, you'd be in your own cell on grand theft charges."

So that was why he had her grabbed by official types—he wanted me, too.

"Tough luck, dregface."

"You're not off yet. You may still wind up spending

lots more time here than you want when they start
investigating how her genotype status got switched from
clone to Realpeople in Central Data. The M.A.'s gonna
be *real* interested in that!"

Felt a spike of uneasiness when he said that, but
showed him nothing.

"Do your worst," I said, knowing he would, and
headed for the exit.

Became aware of an awful lot of kids around as I
crossed the Pyramid's cavernous inner space. Dirty,
skinny kids of all sizes in ragtag clothes.

Urchins.

Hadn't noticed them when I came in, but then, I'd
been in a hurry at the time. Maybe this was a good
begging place. Wouldn't think so, but how would I
know? Was a habit of mine to avoid M.A. Central at all
costs.

Right now I had to get to Elmero's. Potential trouble
brewing and he had to know about it.

-8-

"I think we're safe," Elmero said after a moment's
consideration.

His skeletal body was embedded deep into his
polyform chair. He smiled with what he no doubt thought
was friendly reassurance, but a smile from Elmero is
never a pretty sight.

"Not so sure," I told him.

"Where's the link? My contact in Central Data is an
old hand at this sort of thing—as you should know. He
can add genotypes or subtract them, or change a genotype status from Realpeople to clone and back again
without anyone connecting him to the foul deed. And
even if they did, all my dealings with him are blind,
paid for with hard. Even under Truth he couldn't finger
me."

"What about Jean—I mean, the clone?"

"If they Truth her, she'll just tell them what she truly
believes: that her old boyfriend Barkham fixed the

databank for her. We're safe." His brow suddenly furrowed. "She does still think Barkham did it, doesn't she?"

"Well . . . yeah."

His face grew stern and distant, which was better than seeing him smile again.

"You didn't play hero and tell her you paid for the switch, did you?"

Felt myself redden. "Course not! But she mentioned that she thought the card I returned to her was different than the old one, but she wasn't sure how."

"Even so, this could be bad," Elmero said after a moment's thought. "When her clone status is confirmed, they'll be in a dregging frenzy to find out how her genotype got switched over. When they bang her with Truth, you'll fall under suspicion because she'll tell them you had the card for a while. And when *you* get Truthed . . ."

His voice trailed off.

"Yeah," I said.

"Isn't this just bloaty," he said after a while. "Why'd you have to get involved with a lousy clone anyway?"

"Leave it alone, Elm," I said in a low voice and he knew I meant it. "She was leaving for the Outworlds—wasn't supposed to come back."

We sat in uneasy silence for a while, then Elmero said,

"There's only one thing to do."

Knew what he was thinking, so I said it for him:

"Put in a block."

He nodded, then spoke to his intercom: "Find Doc."

-9-

"Now," said Doc, the overheads reflecting gleaming highlights on his black skin, "I want you to think about the greencard the clone received from Barkham. Picture it in your mind. Think about getting it from her, then think about giving it back. Getting from . . . giving back. Got it?"

Saw the card coming into my own hand, then being
handed into Jean's. Some foggy memories tried to slip
into the picture but I pushed them away.

"Got it."

My scalp tingled and then light exploded in front of
my eyes. Felt my arms and legs jump and spasm, then
it was over.

"That the last?"

Doc nodded. "I believe so."

Doc had popped a dose of Dyamine through my scalp
a little while ago, then had begun working from the
middle outward toward both ends of the memory chain
he wanted to block. The procedure was tricky but Doc
was an expert at it. Illegal as all hell, too. Which was
partly why Doc's license to practice was presently on a
three year suspension.

"Try me."

"Do you know Jean Harlow-c?"

"Sure."

"Did she ever show you her greencard?"

"Yes."

"Did she tell you where she got it?"

"From Kel Barkham."

"Did she ever give it to you?"

"Yes. To help find Barkham."

"Did you alter the card in any way while you had it?"

Something *zipped* through my brain. Tried to catch it
but it was moving too fast. Gone in a blur before I
could latch onto it.

"Course not."

"And you returned it to her unchanged?"

"Right."

"Think, now. Are you absolutely sure?"

Nothing churned in the background this time. The
card had been in my possession for a while but that was
it.

"Absolutely."

Doc smiled. "Excellent! The other memories are completely blocked."

"What other memories?"

He laughed and so did Elmero, who'd been watching the whole thing from behind his desk.

"The effect should last about a month," Doc said as he removed the stim unit from my head. "After that, the Dyamine will begin to break down and free up those memories."

Really weird. Had no idea what memories he was talking about.

"And the real beauty part of this," he went on, "is that since Dyamine is a partial analog of acetylcholine, you can't form any new memories during the procedure or for an hour or so after. So you won't even know you had this done."

"Just make sure you've got a mouth along when they Truth you," Elmero said.

"No fear."

Crazy to go through a Truth session without some legal type there to limit the scope of the questions and keep the interrogators from going off on a deepspace mining expedition through your private life.

"Turn on the datastream, will you, Elm?" Doc said as he packed up his equipment. "I want to see if there's an update on the doings down at the Pyramid."

Thought of Jean. "What's going on?"

"Something about a bunch of kids clogging all the lower levels in the place. Just caught the end of the blurb as I came through the bar before."

"Kids?" Remembered all the urchins I'd seen as I was leaving the building earlier. "Urchins?"

"I didn't hear."

The datastream filled the big holochamber in the corner of Elmero's office. Newsface Two, a baldy, recited the usual boring dregs about politics, traffic, entertainment, sports, reminders that this was a skip day for the four A.M. rain, news from the other megalops around the world, all interspersed with lots and lots of visuals.

"Must've cleared up," I said. "She never mentioned M.A. Central."

"It was graffiti," Doc said.

Just then the holo warped and suddenly we were looking at a very bizarre-looking Newsface—this guy had leaping flames where his hair should have been, and spiraling pinwheels for eyes. Central Data's policy was to keep its computer-generated Newsfaces attractive but ordinary looking, and to rotate them frequently—in case the public got too attached to one of the nonexistent things. But we all developed favorites. Newsface Four was mine. This roguey guy was a sure sign that we were watching a graffiti capsule someone had slipped into the datastream.

Flamehead didn't waste any time getting to the meat:

"They're calling for help down at M.A. Central. Seems the lower levels there have been invaded by a small horde of kids. Or maybe I should say, a horde of small kids."

A quick cut to a wide angle shot of the groundlevel lobby of the Pyramid. It was filled—*jammed*—with urchins, milling about, moving up and down the arched stairs along the perimeter, playing in the up- and downchutes. The announcer continued in voice-over:

"For those of you who manage to keep yourselves securely insulated from groundlevel, these are what are known as urchins. Maybe you've heard them mentioned at a party. You certainly didn't hear of them on the official datastream."

Noticed the angle of the sunlight coming down through the Pyramid's apex and realized that this was recent vintage vid.

Moving right into the crowd of kids now. The graffitist must have had his hidden recorder strapped to his lower chest because we were winding through them at eye level—*urchin* eye level.

"Officially, the kids you're watching are not a problem. Their genotypes aren't registered in Central Data, therefore they don't exist. And none of you are concerned about kids who don't exist, right?"

"Proud of yourselves?"

All those big deep eyes looking right at you and then shifting away. There was sadness in them, a sense of

loss, as if they were searching for something or someone who had been taken away from them. The effect
was devastating.

*"Nobody knows why they've come or what they want.
They're just there, clogging the aisles and stairs. Mostly
they're quiet, but every so often they begin to shout—"*

The image warped and suddenly we were back in the
official datastream.

"They sure yanked that one fast!" Doc said.

Right. Usually a graffiti capsule got to run through
the stream a couple of times before it was culled. Central Data tended to view the radical journalists as more
of an annoyance than a threat—hecklers on the fringe of
the Big Show.

Elmero said, "They're embarrassed by all those kids
there," as he stared reflectively into the holochamber.

"Going down there," I told them.

"Yeah?" Elmero said. "Be sure to tell me all about
it."

Could figure what was running through his mind:
How can I make out on this?

Elmero's instincts were pretty astute when there was
credit to be made. He sensed something big brewing.
So did I. And Jean and B.B. were right in the middle of
it.

-10-

Either M.A. Central had become more crowded with
urchins since the datacast, or the graffito I'd seen hadn't
done the crowd a bit of justice. Mobbed. They were
everywhere. Could barely move through the crowd. All
the kids were babbling to each other, to anyone who
would listen. The sounds mixed and mingled into a
constant susurrous hum, an irritating white noise.

They'd brought the M.A. Central Pyramid—at least
its lower levels—to a standstill.

Made finding B.B. just about impossible.

Felt a tug on the sleeve of my jump. Looked down to
see a little red-headed urch. A boy, I thought.

"Sig?" he said, pointing up at my face.

Picked him up and looked him over. Didn't recognize him.

"You from the Lost Boys?"

He nodded proudly. "Lost Boy me."

"Know where my friend B.B. is?"

He looked around, then began screeching at the top of his lungs as he pointed at me.

"B.B.! Siggy! B.B.! Siggy!"

Was about to tell him that there were scads of urches named B.B., that even with his considerable volume, only a small fraction of the crowd was going to hear him, when I noticed that those around us were falling silent and staring at me. The silence grew, spreading out like a ripple in a puddle. It moved up the big arched stairways and across the balconies and arcades on the inner walls.

Soon the whole floor was quiet except for this one persistent squealy voice.

And then from fifty meters or so away came an answering cry.

"Sig! Here me! Ov'here!"

Looked and saw B.B. jumping up and down, waving his arms to get my attention. As he began moving my way, the noise picked up again, but it wasn't the formless hum from before. Now it was a word: my name.

"SIGGY! SIGGY! SIGGY! SIGGY! . . ."

They were all looking at me, raising their hands each time they said my name. Seemed to go on forever. B.B. finally broke through and hugged me around the waist.

"Filamentous, Sig, yeah? Filamentous!"

Barely heard him over the chant. Pushed him to arm's length and got a good look at his shining eyes.

"Yeah. Filamentous, all right. But what's going on? What do you kids think you're doing here?"

"Ge'Wendy back."

Simple as that. If only they knew.

"But where'd all these kids come from?"

"Wendy Mom-to-all."

"So you've told me. But she couldn't have tucked every one of you into bed."

"Evbod hear Wendy. Come togeth."

"*Every*body? They're all here?"

He shook his head. "More come. From all ov."

More coming? The place couldn't hold them. All the urchingangs in the Metalops were united, probably for the first time in history.

"Evbod hear Sig, too."

His smile showed how proud he was to know me. Damn rattly thing to have a kid look at you like that. Could make you want to run and hide. Or move mountains.

While I was wondering where I could hide, a hand tapped me on the shoulder. Turned and found myself looking into a datastream reporter's recording plate.

"Excuse me," he shouted over the noise. The plate was mounted on his forehead and I could see my reflection in it. "But am I correct in assuming you're this 'Siggy' fellow."

Didn't know what to say. B.B., however, was at no loss for words. He patted me on the arm as he piped up:

"Oya, san! Siggy him! Filamentous fren!"

"I'm Arrel Lum," said the reporter. He had black hair, dark eyes, and a round face. "I'm with Central Data."

Knew that. Looked for ways to keep his questions away from me until I could duck out. Tried sidetracking him.

"The datastream's ignoring this. Kind of a waste of time for you to be here, isn't it?"

"Not at all. Central Data records *everything* for the record. What's fed into the datastream for public consumption is another matter."

His frankness was engaging, but something about his diction, the rhythm of his voice. Familiar.

"You remind me of Newsface Four."

He smiled. "You've got a good ear. I've been writing his casts and doing his voice for the past five years."

"He's—you're my favorite Newsface."

"Why, thank you. But tell me: Who are you, and what's your connection with these kids?"

So much for sidetracking.

"Know one of them."

"What do they want?"

"You mean you don't know?"

He shook his head. "Nobody can figure it out."

Interesting.

"Embarrassing, isn't it?"

"Not for me," he said with a grin. "I think it's a bloaty show. Just wish I knew what it was all about."

Turned to B.B. "Tell him what it's all about, Beeb."

The urch started shoving his fist into the air and crying, "Wendy! Wendy! Wendy!"

The other urchins around us picked it up immediately. The Siggy chant had been dying out anyway—thank the Core—so now they substituted two new syllables in the same rhythm.

"WENDY! WENDY! WENDY! . . ."

Lum's eyes roved the mob, searchingly, I thought.

"They've been doing that off and on all day," he shouted above the din.

"Well," I said, "then you know why they're here."

"No, I don't. I—" He looked past my shoulder. "Don't look now, but I think you've just become important."

Turned and saw a squad of yellowjackets—six of them—coming my way. My bladder got a sudden urge to empty itself but I stood my ground and held my water. No place to run.

Lum stood back and trained his recording plate on the scene as the yellowjackets bullied their way through the kids. The leader led them around me, brushing B.B. aside like a bug. Found myself enclosed in a yellow elipse.

"Come with us," he said.

"What if I don't want to go?"

He had beady little eyes, close set and mean.

"The boss says he wants to speak with you. You'll come."

"Bloaty," I said.

Lum peered between two of the security men and called to me over the chant:

"But what do these kids *want?*"

"They want their mother," I told him.

Encased in yellow, I was marched off toward the upchutes, leaving him standing there looking like someone had punched him in the throat.

-11-

"Are you behind this, Mr. Dreyer?"

Regional Administrator Brode was giving me a hard look as he stood over my chair. Natural silver hair, crinkle cut, square jaw, piercing silver eyes, perfectly matched to his hair. Looked almost as good in person as he did in the holochamber. His stare was supposed to carry all the weighty authority of his office, I guessed.

He needn't have bothered. After all, the C.A. had put him in charge of this Megalops, so he didn't have to do anything special to get me nervous. Passed nervous on the way up here when I learned the R.A. wanted to see me himself. In person. Never knew anyone who'd met him in person.

Yeah, way past nervous. Slipping over into twitchy now.

"Behind what, sir?"

"These urchins all over the place."

Couldn't resist: "Been told there are no such things as urchins, sir."

"Don't you *dare* get—"

"Don't know a thing about them, Mr. Administrator."

"But they know you. Why? How?"

"A long story."

He let my words hang as he walked in a slow circle around his desk. His office decor was surprisingly lean and spare. Everything cool and functional. The only sign of extravagance was his big ungainly pet dodo bobbing and pecking around the furniture and weaving between his hovering aides.

"Who's this Wendy they keep chanting for? Central Data says there's no one with that name anywhere in the Pyramid."

"That's because Wendy's not her real name. She's a prisoner here."

"Oh, really? And just what is her real name?"

The sudden light in his eyes told me something: the urchinmob had our dear Regional Administrator worried. Why?

"What's in it for me?"

His eyes went hard and cold. Knew right then I'd made a large mistake as he barked to one of his attendants:

"Get some Truth!"

"Not asking much!" I blurted.

He glared at me, as if daring me. "Go on."

"Just want to be left out of this, that's all. Don't have anything to do with this, don't *want* anything to do with it. Just know a couple of urchins and ran into this Wendy a few years ago. That's it."

Brode smirked. "Central Data says you know a lot of wrong people, some of them suspected black marketeers."

"Wouldn't know anything about that, Mr. Administrator," I said. "Private investigations are what I do."

"So I understand. Very well. I won't hound you or Truth you. I sincerely doubt you would be worth the trouble."

"Thank you. Her name's Jean Harlow-c. She's a former Dydeetown girl, here as part of a property dispute."

He was suddenly furious.

"Well, isn't that just bloaty! M.A. Central is clogged with urchins in search of a renegade clone! This gets more ludicrous every second!" He turned to one of his aides. "Get him out of here! Then fill me in on this clone!"

No one had to hurry me out the door. Headed straight for the first downchute and jumped. Was coasting fast and alone in the center lane when someone pulled up alongside.

"I need to talk to you."

It was Lum, the Central Data man. Didn't recognize him without his recording rig and wasn't in the mood for talking to anybody.

"What about?"

"What you said before . . . about the kids looking for their mother. What did you mean?"

"Nothing."

"Off the record?"

"Nothing's 'off the record' in this place."

He smiled thinly. "Don't believe everything you hear. Follow me."

Thought about this. Why should I trust a Central Data man, even if he was Newsface Four? Why tell him anything at all?

"Please," he said. "It's important to me."

"I'm thinking."

Had a suspicion about reporter Lum. Wanted to know if I was right.

"Lead the way," I told him.

-12-

Lum was furious.

"You told Brode about her? You dregger!"

We were on level 48 in what Lum called a "blind alley"—a lounge used by the Central Data reporters and technicians between shifts. They had it fixed so the recording plates in the walls could be jammed when they so desired. Told him an edited but fairly complete history of Jean and her involvement with the urchins and how she wound up a prisoner here, candidate for a memwipe. Then related my friendly little meeting with the Regional Administrator.

"You've got it wrong, Lum—"

"Now she's in more trouble than ever!"

"Don't be a jog! What's more trouble than a memwipe?"

He cooled quickly. "I guess you're right."

"Course I'm right. That's why I told him I knew who Wendy was—figured it might buy her some time."

"It might," he said, brightening. "It might pay Brode to give her back to the urchins!"

"What do you care?" I said. "You've never even met her."

"But I want to. More than anything. She's special. I mean, we regularly get data on people and groups wanting to 'do something' about the urchins. They make some noise, they're ignored, and after a while they go away. But this . . . this . . ."

"Clone."

"Right. This clone gave up the freedom she had on the Outworlds to come back here and be with those kids. Actually *be* with them, go down in the tunnels and *live* with them. I've never heard of anybody doing that!"

"So?"

"So it makes the rest of us Realpeople look like dreggers."

"Speak for yourself, Lum. Urchins are out of sight, forgotten. How many times in a year do you think the average Realpeople even *thinks* about urchins? Once? Maybe half a time?"

"I think about them every single day," Lum said in a thick, low voice.

Patted myself on the back.

"You've got a kid with the urchins, don't you?"

As he nodded, a tear collected in one of his eyes. He rubbed it away before it could slide down his cheek.

"And the idea of going down in the tunnels to be with them never even crossed my mind. Do you know how that makes me feel?"

Didn't say anything, just let him rattle on.

"That could have been my little guy with you today, my son holding your hand and looking up at you like that, like you were some kind of hero! I'm going to find this Wendy and talk to her. Where's she being kept?"

"Don't know."

"That's all right. I'll find . . . Brode's probably with her now. I can view the ▓▓▓ ing of the interview later, maybe get an idea what he plans to do with her, or with the kids."

"And then what?"

"I don't know. I'll think of something."

"Let me know what you find out. My number's under 'Investigations.' "

Lum nodded absently. Didn't know if he was really listening.

"Got to find her," he said again.

"Don't get carried away. She's only a clone."

"Really?" His eyes scanned my face. "Then why'd you try to help her?"

Didn't like the scrutiny, or the question.

"She was a client a couple of years ago. You know how it is: once a client, always a client."

Lum nodded but didn't look convinced.

"Just let me know," I told him.

"I'll try," he said.

We left the blind lounge and returned to the downchute. At the lower level we were met by yellowjackets. A bulky officer boomed at us:

"M.A. Central is closing. Unless you work here, you must exit."

Lum said, "The Pyramid never closes!"

"Tonight it does," said the officer. "Move!"

Lum showed him his Central Data ID, but since I had nothing like that, I had to go. Fine with me. Suddenly came a lot of yelling from the main floor. We ran to see.

The yellowjackets were clearing the urchins from the lower levels, and they weren't being gentle about it.

Lum's face was grim. "I'm going back up to get my recorder. I want some close ups of this!"

"What for?" None of this would ever get on the official datastream. "You a graffiti journalist on the side?"

"Not yet," he said, and ran off.

-13-

Spent much of the night in the front room of Elmero's, whiffing with the crowd. Almost all the regulars were there. Minn had to hustle to keep up with demand, and she didn't like that. Wasn't used to being busy.

Doc was around but he was acting weird. Kept asking questions about Jean's old greencard, like did I ever have it and what did I do with it. Told him all I knew: had it for a while, then gave it back to her, and nothing more. The answer seemed to delight him. Must have asked me two or three times.

Everybody was talking about the urchins down at the Pyramid and, Elmero's clientele being the sort it was, laughing about how the kids had glitched a few sectors of officialdom today. Caused a bit of a stir when I told how the yellowjackets had booted the kids out as I was leaving. Everyone was shocked that M.A. Central had shut down its public areas, even for a few minutes.

And everyone was keeping half an eye on the datastream playing in the life-sized chamber in the corner. No hologames, no drama or comedy tonight— just the Newsfaces and everyone waiting for a graffiti capsule on the urchins.

"Hey, there's Four!" I said as the familiar newsface rotated into view. Hoped maybe he'd slip in something about the urchins. "Listen to this guy."

Newsface Four's square-jawed, blond-haired, straight-nosed visage, which couldn't have looked less like Arrel Lum, stared out of the chamber at us in silence for a moment, then began to speak in his resonant baritone.

"The Eastern Megalops' human garbage backwashed into the lower levels of Megalops Authority Central this morning. Here's how it looked."

Newsface Four dissolved into a panoramic view of today's mob scene at M.A. Central.

"The children you see here," he said in voice-over, *"are what we call urchins, in case you've had any doubts about their existen this vid dispell them.*

This is the real thing. Those are real children, and they were all over M.A. Central today.

"*Look closely. Some of them might be your nieces and nephews. One of them could be your grandchild. You can't be sure can you? Of course, there are some of you watching who may be looking at your own child. My heart breaks for you.*"

"Core!" Minn shouted from behind the bar. "He's showing urchins on the datastream! Really showing them!"

"It's got to be graffiti!" said someone else.

"It's not! It's Newsface Four!" another voice cried.

Recognized Doc's voice from the other side of the room. "If it's not graffiti, that means this is going out system-wide! The whole dregging *world* is seeing it!"

The whole dregging world! What a thought!

"Somebody's ass is going to be shot to the South Pole for this!" Minn said with her usual delicacy.

Thought of Arrel Lum—he was saying good-bye to his career and putting his whole life on the line with this move.

"*But what do these children want?*" said Lum in his Newsface Four voice. "*Why did they come to M.A. Central?*"

The chamber filled with one earnest little face after another, each chanting a single word. The sound filled the barroom at Elmero's:

. . . "*WEN-DEE! WEN-DEE! WEN-DEE*" . . .

"*And who is this Wendy?*" he said as the faces continued to roll through the chamber. "*This reporter has learned that she is a young woman who has been living with the various urchingangs in the central area of the Eastern Megalops, reading to them and teaching them to read, cooking for them and teaching them to cook, tucking them in at night. Mothering them, you might say.*"

He paused and more faces crowded into the chamber.

"*They want their mother!*"

Jean's face suddenly filled the chamber. Her eyes had a hollow, hunted look. She looked frightened.

Newsface Four's words hit the room like cannon shots.

"And here she is. Real name: Jean Harlow-c. A Dydeetown clone. Yes, a clone! A sterile underperson. Down in the tunnels. Taking care of our kids! The ones we cast off, whose existence we were forced by inhumane laws to leave to chance.

"And what is her fate?"

The holo cut to a high angle longshot of Jean sitting before Chief Administrator Brode. She looked small and frail while he looked huge and imposing.

"This was recorded earlier today."

Brode: *And just what was your plan for these urchins?*

Jean: *No plan, really. They needed me and I needed them. That was all.*

Brode: *Organizing them for your own purposes? Disruption of official business—wasn't that part of your scheme?*

Jean: *I told you, I had no—*

Brode: *I don't believe you! Truth her!*

There were some quick cuts showing her being dosed and then we were back to the two-shot.

Brode: *Now. What were your plans for the urchin-gangs?*

Jean: *Well, I . . . I know it sounds stupid, but I wanted to find a way to get some of them to the Outworlds.*

Brode's derisive laugh sounded uncomfortably like mine when she had told me that.

Brode: *The Outworlds! You little idiot! What were you thinking of?*

Jean: *I was thinking of sunshine and fresh air and futures for them. The Outworlds need able bodies. They'd be treated as Realpeople there. No more living in sewers and tunnels.*

The barroom was dead silent as Brode paused and looked around at his aides who were out of the frame. Finally, he spoke.

Brode: *You know you're scheduled for memwipe first thing tomorrow, don't you*

Heard a sharp intake of breath nearby. Doc had moved up beside me. His jaw was set.

In the chamber, Jean only nodded sadly.

Jean: *I know. And after that, I won't remember any of the kids. I'll be working Dydeetown again for Ned Spinner. I won't be any good to them anymore. But Mr. Brode, sir—*

She looked up at him here and her big blue eyes shone in the harsh light of the interrogation room.

—Do you think you could do something for them?

You're powerful. Can't you help them get a fresh start someplace? I won't be able to.

Heard a loud sniff from behind the bar. There was Minn, wiping her eyes. Never thought there was a single tear in her whole body. She shot me an angry Don't-look-at-me look, so I turned away. Looked around. Saw Doc and a few of the regulars puddling up. Not all, of course, or even most. This was a tough room to play. But you had to believe Jean—she was on Truth. For a heartbeat or two, even Brode looked moved. Then his features hardened.

Brode: *That's impossible. We—*

The vid skewed, twisted, turned to confetti, then Newsface Seven appeared. Her oval, eyebrowless face smiled reassuringly.

"We are experiencing technical difficulties—"

Her face dissolved into confetti and the chamber filled with scenes of the urchins' eviction by the M.A.'s none-too-gentle yellowjackets. Four's voice-over sounded strained:

"(garbled)—let me finish! This was how they treated the kids today! Tomorrow might be worse! Do something about Wendy! Call your—"

More confetti, then Newsface Seven again, her expression bland.

"There now. All difficulties have been cleared. This is Datastream Host Seven. On with the news . . ."

We waited to see if Four would get back onstream, but apparently he had been shut down for the night. For good. Pretty clear that as a Newsface, Four was dead. They'd have to generate a new face to replace him. That was easy. Four was just a program.

But what about Lum? Arrel Lum was real. What were they going to do to him?

"Since when did Four turn into an ooze?" said someone near the center of the room. Looked and saw it was Greg Hallo. Nice guy, but he tended to overdo the vape-ka.

"Yeah," said somebody else. "What's he starting trouble for?"

"Maybe he thinks we'll vote for clones' rights on the next referendum," someone yelled.

There was laughter, but not much.

"I find nothing funny in the prospect of a beautiful woman being memwiped," Doc said.

"Not a woman, Doc," said Hallo. "A *clone.*"

Doc was getting hot. "One who's done more for urchins than any Realpeople I know!"

"Urches are urches, clones are clones," Hallo said. "That's the way it was, that's the way it is, that's the way it's gonna be. We don't need the boat rocked."

Hallo spoke for a lot of people, in and out of Elmero's.

"We know you're an old oozer, Doc," somebody yelled, "but we love you anyway!"

The room broke up into arguing factions. Wasn't interested in what they had to say, so I left.

Tubed home. B.B. wasn't there, only Ignatz. Was tired, lonely, and down. Could've used a button real bad now. But even that avenue of release was closed to me. Felt like a dissociator grenade about to explode and I didn't know why.

Flopped on the bed and listened to the fuze ticking in my head.

Sleep was a long time coming.

-14-

Was already awake when the doorbuzzer sounded. Was watching a bit of gr___ on the datastream. A simple piece: Jean's face and a voiceover: *"A modern Joan of Arc? Don't let it happen!"*

Turned and through the door I saw two impatient looking yellowjackets. My stomach did a free-fall drop.

"Administrator Brode wants to see you immediately," the bigger one said as soon as the door slid open.

"And a good morning to you, too," I said. Was still in the jump I'd worn all yesterday. "Mind if I change?"

She grabbed my arm and pulled me out into the hall. " 'Immediately' means just that."

Didn't fight them. No percentage in that. We chuted straight to the roof and flitted for the Pyramid at top speed in the official lane. Brode really did want me there fast.

The Pyramid gleamed golden in the morning sun. As we banked toward one of the landing decks, I saw the crowd.

The entire plaza and all visible spaces around the structure were filled with people. *Filled.* There didn't seem to be room to breath down there. The crowd trailed off into the dark tunnel-like feeder streets. Looked like a million sugar ants around a giant honeycomb.

"Core!" said one of the yellowjackets. "There's even more than before!"

Saw the look of concern pass between them. They were worried. They'd been trained in crowd control but I was sure neither of them had ever seen anything like this. Doubt if anyone on Earth had.

"They can't all be urchins," I said.

The shorter yellowjacket, the male, turned to me. "It started off all urchins—they're the ones crowded around the entrances. We've kept them out of the complex. But the largest part of the crowd is all adult Realpeople."

Couldn't believe my eyes and ears. "Realpeople? Why?"

"A show of support, I guess. We anticipated a few oozer groups showing up, and maybe some independents. But nobody figured on anything like this!"

"Maybe you should have," I said, but didn't explain. Had figured in a flash why there were so many

Realpeople down there. It was geometric. Every urchin had a couple of parents and a legal sibling or two. And two or four or more aunts and uncles and grandfolks to boot. You get all those guilty-feeling people, and maybe a few of their friends and neighbors along for the fun of it, coming down to the M.A. Central Pyramid to make sure the little kids didn't get bullied like they did on the vid last night, and you've got yourself a crowd of astronomical proportions.

After we landed on the topmost flitter platform, the doors popped open, and that was when the noise hit. Even way up here you could hear it. Eerie. A deep, almost subliminal sound, coming to you not just through your ears, but through your skin and the soles of your feet as well. If an angry, stormy ocean could talk, it would sound like that crowd.

"WEN-DEEEEE! WEN-DEEEEE! WEN-DEEEEE!"

They hustled me inside, down a chute, through some halls until I was deposited in a bare room where Administrator Brode waited. His mouth was set in a grim line. He looked tired. We were alone except for one beefy aide by the door. In a far corner, the datastream was playing.

"Over here," he said, motioning me to his side.

He deopaqued the wall and there we were, looking down on the roiling mob in the plaza below.

"Surprised you haven't slimed them," I said.

"Don't think it hasn't occurred to me. But there are too many Realpeople, some of them no doubt influential. We can't risk any of them getting smothered."

Could see what he meant. Slime could produce hilarious results. Seen vids of some of the old food riots when it was sprayed on the mobs. The silicone emulsion allows for *zero* traction. Once it gets on you or on the street, you are *down!* You can't stand, can't hold onto your neighbor, can't even kneel. Really funny. But in a crowd like the one in Pyramid Plaza, some folks were bound to get smothered.

"I want you to send them home," he said to me.

Couldn't help laughing.

"Of course! Just say when!"

"Now. Immediately."

He wasn't joking.

"Not too much disrespect intended, sir, but have you busted up a few synapses since yesterday?"

He was about to answer but stopped and stared past me at the datastream. Looked myself and saw a close-up of Jean's face as she spoke to Brode—a graffiti rerun of a piece of Newsface Four's unauthorized transmission. Her voice came on loud:

"*—Do you think you could do something for them? You're powerful. Can't you help them get a fresh start someplace? I won't be able to.*" And then the voice-over: "*Madonna of the Tunnels, pray for us!*"

It replayed immediately—a graffiti loop. Brode turned to his aide and screamed,

"Get her off there! *Now!*"

The aide said something into his throat mike. The loop disappeared in the middle of its third play.

"As I was saying," Brode said, again training his gaze on the crowd below, "I know you can do it. I saw yesterday's vid from the lower level. For a while there they were chanting your name instead of hers. You can get them chanting your name again. And then tell them their dear clone will be released from the complex as soon as they are completely dispersed."

Bit my lip to dispell the sudden light feeling that swept over me. Wasn't buying it yet.

"That true?"

He finally pulled himself away from the window and looked at me. His eyes were flat and cold.

"Of course it is."

"She'll be free to go?"

"In a way."

"What's that supposed to mean?"

"She'll be free to go with her owner."

Jean back with Spinner—the sudden rage that ripped through me was barely controllable. If he hadn't been Regional Administrator . . .

"You think that's going to end this? It won't!"

"Oh, but it will. They'll come to her but she won't know them, won't know who or what they're talking about. There will be a few more rumbles, and then it will be over. Things will be back the way they used to be."

"She gets memwiped and you'll never hear the end of it!"

"That was a judicial decision. It's out of my hands."

"What about executive clemency or reprieve or some such dregging garbage!"

He turned back to the window.

"It's a little too late for any of that now."

Just stood there staring at him, feeling a wind as cold and dark as deep space howl through the hollows of my heart. The air seemed thick. Couldn't draw it through my constricted throat. Gravity doubled, tripled. Stumbled to the nearest chair and sat there trying to breathe.

Because when I caught my breath, I was going to put Brode through that window.

The single aide in the room with us must have been trained in reading postures. Big guy. He walked over and stood half way between Brode and me.

"Want to see her."

"Impossible. You know as well as I do that memwipe subjects are comatose for hours after the procedure, and disoriented for weeks."

There was silence for what seemed like a long time. My own mind felt like it had been wiped. Finally Brode said,

"Well? Will you speak to them?"

"You must be out of your dregging mind! I'll tell them to dismantle this place panel by panel, block by block!"

He turned to me. A smug look on his face.

"Will you? I don't think so. You seem to have a good thing going for you, Mr. Dreyer. Not much of a life to most people, but you seem to be enjoying it. You've got your hidden stash of gold, you've got your roguey friends such as the owner of that seedy tavern, your sometime roommate urchin, and that vsician with the suspended license." He smiled thinly. "Just the kind of acquaintances I'd expect of a former buttonhead."

Didn't blink. Didn't even flinch. Too mad now to let any kind of insult get to me. But it was clear he'd had a deep probe done on my life.

"I can change your pitiful life, Mr. Dreyer. I can reopen the investigation into the deaths of those two NeuroNex employees who were sliced into pieces in your compartment. Your urchin friend was involved in that, wasn't he? I can shut down that tavern and send its owner to the South Pole for so many offenses he'll never see the sun at zenith again. I can see to it that your doctor friend's license is permanently revoked. I can make you wish you'd never been born, Mr. Dreyer."

"Don't count on it. Already been there and back."

"I can make your friends wish the same thing."

We stayed silent for a while, glaring at each other. We both knew I was going to lose. He was threatening Elmero and Doc and B.B. Couldn't take them down with me.

But something wasn't right here. Didn't know what it was, but sensed other players in this game. Had an idea.

"Let me talk to Lum."

"Lum?" he said, fury etching lines in his face. "*Lum?* He's in detention, awaiting sentencing—and it will be an interminable sentence if I have anything to say about it! He can't help you."

"Want to talk to him anyway. Not a major request."

Brode sighed. "Very well."

He nodded to his aide who spoke into his throat mike.

And then I waited, with the aide watching me as I watched Brode watch the mob outside.

-15-

Noticed a thick, odd-looking silvery cuff on Arrel Lum's right wrist when he was led in. They let us go off to a corner to talk, but first they activated his cuff.

"What's that?" I said.

Lum grinned sourly. "If you paid closer attention to my datacasts, you'd know. It's a gravcuff. I'm now locked to an azimuth through the earth's center of gravity. Plenty of vertical movement—" he moved his wrist up and down as far as he could reach—"but nothing laterally."

"Real bloaty," I said, then explained what Brode wanted. Knew every word of what we said was being recorded but didn't care. Lum listened for a while, then turned toward Brode.

"You know, Mr. Administrator, this could be your big chance to show you're more than just a politician. With a little creative thought on your part, you could actually come out on top here. You could prove yourself a real statesman. We haven't seen one of those in ages. We can clone out dinosaurs and dodos and Jean Harlows, but—"

"They memwiped Jean," I said.

Lum reeled as if I'd punched him. Only the gravcuff kept him from stumbling back. He covered his eyes with his free hand. Thought for a moment he was going to break down, but he didn't.

"I really wanted to meet her," he said softly, pulling himself together and glaring at Brode.

"She's not dead," I told him.

He stared at me. "Yes, she is."

Knew he was right but tried not to think about it.

"What's Brode trying to get from me?" I asked.

Lum's smile was tight and predatory. "Political salvation. Thanks to my datacast last night, the Harlow clone and the urchins have received worldwide attention. He's been getting heavy pressure from the Central Authority to defuse this bomb as quietly as possible. That's the main reason he hasn't slimed them. His political future is on the line."

"Good. But how'd you learn all this?"

"I'm allowed visitors. And all my friends are datapeople. So what's happening is he's passing the pressure. You're it. He's counting on getting you to cooperate."

And I had friends counting on me to cover for them.
"He's succeeding."

"Well, Mr. Dreyer," said Brode from across the room.
"I'm waiting. Time is critical."

"All right," I called back. "Let's do it."

Lum's eyes were wide. "Do *what*?"

"Don't know yet."

The big aide was motioning me toward the door. As I
headed his way I heard Lum say to no one in particular:

"What about me?"

"You and I are going to have a talk, Mr. Lum,"
Brode said.

"I'd rather be in my cell."

"Nevertheless, we are going to discuss your ideas on
statesmanship."

Then the door slipped shut behind me and closed
them off.

-16-

They coached me on what to say, made me repeat it
over and over until I had it down perfectly. Then they
fitted me with a transparent, thumbnail-size chin mike,
a finger control toggle for on/off, and placed me on a
float platform. Another of Brode's seemingly endless
supply of aides piloted the thing. From far below, the
chant continued:

". . . *WEN-DEEEEEE! WEN-DEEEEEE! WEN-
DEEEEEE! . . .*"

As the platform hove into view and started its de-
scent, the chant broke up and died. When we reached
the ten meter level, I could make out a clear division in
the crowd—ragtag urchins in the front, better dressed
Realpeople toward the rear. The two groups weren't
mixing much. Behind me, the entrances to the Pyramid
were blocked with armed yellowjackets.

Waved to the kids and toggled my chin mike on.

HELLOOOO, URCHINS! boomed into the air from
speakers somewhere in the Pyramid's wall.

Some of them must have been Lost Boys because a

murmur ran through their ranks. It grew into a new
chant, shorter, choppier than the other:

"*Sig-gy! Sig-gy! Sig-gy! . . .*"

Nowhere near as loud as the Wendy chant because
the Realpeople weren't joining in. Probably asking themselves who or what 'round Sol was this Siggy? After all,
he hadn't been on the datastream last night.

But the kids knew the name. All those little faces and
big hopeful eyes looking up at me. Gave me a chill.

"*HAVE A MESSAGE FOR YOU ABOUT WENDY.*"

The volume of the ensuing mad cheer rattled the
platform and then the Wendy chant started again.

Hated myself for what I was about to do. To put it off
a little longer, I let the chant build. Turned off the
mike and said to the aide:

"By the way, how can you close M.A. Central?
Thought it was supposed to be open to all citizens all
hours of the day."

The aide's smile was smug. "True, but we found a
forgotten ordinance that prohibits children unless accompanied by an adult."

"Well, well," I said. "Isn't that bloaty."

The urchin part of the crowd began shifting, squirming, and flowing, and suddenly there was B.B. on somebody's shoulders, waving and beaming with pride. Could
see it in his eyes: *Siggy's here. Siggy won't let us down.
Siggy can do anything.*

That was the moment I made my decision.

"Take me down to get that kid," I said.

"That's not in the script."

"Let me improvise a little. What I've got to say will
be a lot more effective if I've got one of the Lost Boys
sitting on my shoulders."

The aide talked to the Pyramid. They must have had
a conference in Brode's office because the answer took a
while coming. But apparently he got the okay because
we began to descend.

Motioned to the kids below to clear a spot around
B.B. They backed away from him when we got down to
a height of about two meters.

That was when I jumped ship. Over the rail and onto the ground.

"Hey!" the aide yelled. "You can't do that!"

Ignored him. Scooped up B.B. and hustled him toward the nearest entrance to the Pyramid. The cheering urchins made way for us.

The aide followed us above and behind on the platform. He shouted to the yellowjackets at the door I was approaching.

"Stop him!"

This was it. This was where I put the blaster to my head and pulled the trigger. Was endangering Doc and Elmero and even B.B., but that couldn't be helped. Nobody could memwipe a client of mine and rub my nose in it and figure they could bully me into saying, Thank you sir and yes I'll help cool some of the heat you're getting.

Dreg that.

Don't mind getting pushed around some. Expect a certain amount of it. That's life. Not a rad, not an oozer, not a mal. But there were limits. Brode had found mine.

And I was going to bring him down if I could.

The yellowjackets closed ranks ahead of me. Flicked on my chin mike, wheeled it to max, and shouted at the top of my voice:

"*I AM A CITIZEN OF THE MEGALOPS AND DEMAND ENTRANCE TO THE PYRAMID! THAT IS THE LAW!*"

The sound was deafening. Like hearing thunder up close from inside a cloud. Like the voice of God. All the urchins around me cringed and bowed and slapped their hands over their ears. Was almost knocked to my knees by my own voice.

The yellowjackets were clearly shaken. Could barely hear the nearest as he spoke:

"No urchins."

"*HE IS ACCOMPANIED BY AN ADULT! STAND ASIDE NOW!*"

As they winced at the noise, I slid between them

before either of them could grab me. When I reached
the inner floor, I raised my voice and said,

"ALL RIGHT, EVERYBODY! FOLLOW—"

My mike was suddenly cut off. But as I turned, I saw
it didn't matter. Realpeople were pushing through the
crowd carrying urchins in their arms, on their shoulders. The yellowjackets made half-hearted attempts to
stop them, but the Realpeople were adamant. They
were incensed. And the law was on their side. Even
saw one of the yellowjackets pick up a kid himself and
march inside.

Like water through the floodgates of a dam, they
poured in on all four sides of the ground level, washing
along the floor, choking ground level and rising to fill
the perimeter arcades on the second. It wasn't long
before the chant began again, echoing through the air,
rattling the cavernous interior of the Pyramid:

"WEN-DEEEE! WEN-DEEEE! WEN-DEEEE! . . ."

Held B.B. on my shoulders and let him chant away,
but didn't join in myself. What was the use? The Wendy
he knew was dead. Brode wasn't going to bring her
down and show her hollow remains to the crowd. But if
things went the way I hoped, maybe this crowd would
bring him down—not down here, but *down*. And out of
office.

He ruined a client of mine. Now I was going to ruin
him. Or go down trying.

The chant went on forever with no signs of diminish-
ing. More people were squeezing in from outside—there
were still lots more out there than in here—and pushing up to higher and higher levels on the inner walls.
Given enough time, we'd soon occupy every square
centimeter of the Pyramid. Brode was going to have to
do something, and quick.

And he did.

A floater platform like the one I'd been on outside—
maybe the same one—glided out from one of the upper
levels and began descending along the wall to my right.
Looked like it was riding the huge shaft of midday

sunlight pouring through the apex. Squinted into the glare. Made out four figures on it.

The chant died as we all watched and waited to see who was coming.

"Hoodat, Sig? Wendy come?"

Poor kid. Didn't want him to get his hopes up.

"Don't think so, Beeb. Let's just hope they're not carrying slime guns."

We watched it sink lower. Suddenly B.B. screamed.

"Her, Sig! Wendy! Her! *Her!*"

He was right. Couldn't believe my eyes, but there she was, Jean Harlow-c herself, standing at the front rail of the platform, looking dazed as she stared at the crowd. Couldn't believe Brode had the nerve to do this. What was he planning? Did he really think he could get away with it?

The urchins went wild but the Realpeople around me held back. Knew why, too. They had all seen the datastream last night. They knew she had been scheduled to be wiped first thing this morning. They feared they were looking at a shell.

They were right.

Then I looked at her companions on the platform and almost dropped B.B. off my shoulders. It was Brode himself, one of his aides at the controls, and Lum.

What was going on here?

A million thoughts screamed through my mind. Was this a scam? Had they made a Wendy holosuit? Was there an actress in there? But no, it didn't look like a holo—the outline was too crisp. And what was Lum doing up there with Brode? Had they bought him off somehow? Or twisted his arm to the breaking point like they tried with me?

The platform stopped at thirty meters. Jean still looked dazed. They must have taught her a speech. One that would send everybody home. This was going to be bad.

She leaned forward and her soft voice, amplified hundreds of times, filled the Pyramid:

"Hel—hello. They say I'm free to go. Are my Lost Boys here?"

And then she smiled, and behind her Lum smiled, and I knew it was her. Couldn't explain how this could be, but it was really her. Suddenly found myself weeping like a dregging baby. Me, Sigmundo Dreyer, who never cries.

And around me: bedlam, pandemonium, delirium, ecstatic chaos. Never seen anything like it before or since. Normally staid, reserved people were laughing, crying, screaming with delight, leaping and waving their arms like maniacs. They cheered, they jumped up and down, they hugged and kissed each other and danced in circles. Could swear I heard church bells ringing.

For a while, at that time, in that place, we were all Wendy's Lost Boys.

-17-

Took a long time, but things finally quieted. Guess the human voice box can only take so much abuse and then it starts to shut down.

During the commotion I'd noticed Brode and Lum with their heads together more than once. Now Brode stepped up beside Jean and raised his hands. His deep rich voice boomed through the hollow insides of the Pyramid:

"My fellow citizens. Due to confusion as to the exact status of her citizenship, and to avoid giving offense to the sovereign world of Neeka, I have used the emergency powers granted to me by the Central Authority in the Megalops Charter to extend Realpeople status to Jean Harlow-c, the woman you know as 'Wendy.'"

Cheers and roars of approval rose on all sides of me as I wondered what Brode was up to.

"That status is only temporary, however. Within a month's time she will have to return to the Outworlds."

As a murmur of disapproval ran through the crowd, Brode hurried to explain.

"But I don't want to see her return there alone. Like you, I want to see Wendy's dream come true."

Never would have believed such a huge crowd could

grow so silent. Not even a foot-shuffle could be heard. We were all holding our breaths, wondering if he was going to say what we never dreamed we'd hear.

"We can't use public credit, of course, so I am empowering the First Bosyokington Bank to open a trust fund: the Lost Boys' Trust. The funds will be used to provide transportation to the Outworlds for the unfortunate children we call urchins."

A noise, more like a seismic rumble than a cheer, began to rise from the crowd. Brode raised his voice to be heard.

"To open the trust, I am personally donating the first ten thousand credits. If we work together, we can make Wendy's dream a reality!"

That was it. Forget any more speechmaking. He tried to say something else but the Pyramid's speakers were overwhelmed by the celebratory roar of approval, amorphous at first, but soon taking form:

"BRODE! BRODE! BRODE! BRODE! . . ."

Watched Lum's grinning face and realized that Brode's bold move was not of his own devising. Lum had found a way to impart vision to an ambitious, high-ranking politico, turning him into a statesman, a man who could grab the reins of history and alter its course.

Didn't join in the chant myself. Let B.B. sit on my shoulders and shout for both of us. Just stood there and watched Jean's stunned, tearstreaked face as she beamed down at all her Lost Boys.

Clone lady, I thought, *Do you have any idea what you've done?*

-18-

"So Brode was lying about the memwipe," I said to Lum as we sat at Doc's table in Elmero's.

"Of course. He was putting heavy pressure on you and didn't want her to be any part of the bargain. So he took her out of the picture by telling you, in effect, that she was dead. But he was protecting her, holding her back as a last resort."

A lot had happened in the two days since the show-down at the Pyramid. The Lost Boys' Trust was ballooning with donations. And after Brode played and replayed the vid of his performance on the datastream, the citizenry of Chi-Kacy, Tex-Mex, and the Western Megalops were demanding trusts for their own urchins. Same in Europe and elsewhere.

"Can the Outworlds handle all those urchins?" Doc said.

Lum nodded vigorously. "As many as we can send them. The farm worlds will set them up on big tracts and supervise the kids until they're old enough to homestead the land on their own. They'll all be landowners sooner or later. Me, too."

"You?" I said. "Thought you were Brode's new top aide."

"Right. But only for a while. There's a lot of change in the wind and Brode's the man who's going to spearhead most of it."

"Sure. Because he's been such a true-believing oozer all along, right?"

Lum shrugged. "Brode believes in taking Brode to the top. Before the Wendy affair, he was just another magalops chief administrator, a regional big shot. Now he's *sui generis*—the only politico standing up for clones and urchins. He doesn't have universal support, of course, but there's enough pent-up emotion behind these issues to carry him a long, long way. He's now a world class contender for Central Authority. If clone rights and urchin emigration are going to get him where he wants to go, then he'll champion them with all his heart."

"And if the opposite stands would get him there?" Doc said.

"Then he would damn clones and urchins with equal passion and sincerity." Lum shook his head. "An amazing man—the very soul of pragmatism. I'm going to hang around for a while to see how long I can keep him on the right track."

"Nothing ever really changes," I said.

"When change is imposed from the top down, I agree," Lum said. "But this . . . this is coming from the bottom up. It's hearts and minds making themselves felt in the upper levels. This kind of change can last."

Didn't believe that for a minute but wasn't going to argue.

I said, "We'll see."

"Maybe you will, but I'll be out of here in a few years. After I put in my time with Brode, I'm heading for Neeka."

"Why Neeka?" I asked.

"Because Jean will be there. She fascinates me. I want to get to know her better. And maybe, if things work out . . ."

He let the sentence trail off.

"She's sterile, you know," I said for no good reason I could think of.

"Of course. But there'll be more than enough of kids around, don't you think? What're your plans, Sig?"

Shrugged. "More of the same."

"No plans for heading Out Where All The Good Folks Go?"

"Not a chance. Born an Earthie, gonna stay an Earthie."

"Want to work for Brode?"

"Not interested," I said. "Don't like politicos, no matter what the wrapper."

"Good for you." He stood and held up his thumb. "Got to run. Where do I pay?"

Waved him off. "It's on me."

We all shook hands and he left. Doc turned to me.

"You mean to tell me you're not even tempted to try a new life on Neeka?"

"Not in the least."

"Even though Jean and B.B. practically begged you to come along?"

"Me? A farmer?"

"There's got to be something there for you. They've got cities—"

"They've got *towns*, Doc. Little towns scattered all over the map."

The thought of all those far horizons and wide open spaces made me shudder.

"It'll be a shame to let her go," Doc said, eyeing me over his vial of vapor.

Took instant offense at that.

"She's nothing to me!"

He laughed. "What kind of a jog do you take me for? You should have seen your face when Lum talked about heading out to Neeka and maybe marrying her!"

"You've been whiffing too much, Doc. You've got permanent brain damage."

He wandered off to the bar and left me sitting there thinking about emigrating to Neeka. Crazy idea. And yet, maybe there'd be something out there for a roguey guy like me. Something other than farming. *Anything* but farming!

It was a thought. A remote maybe.

We'd see.

MAGIC AND *COMPUTERS* DON'T MIX!

RICK COOK

Or . . . do they? That's what Walter "Wiz" Zumwalt is wondering. Just a short time ago, he was a master hacker in a Silicon Valley office, a very ordinary fellow in a very mundane world. But magic spells, it seems, are a lot like computer programs: they're both formulas, recipes for getting things done. Unfortunately, just like those computer programs, they can be full of bugs. Now, thanks to a *particularly* buggy spell, Wiz has been transported to a world of magic—and incredible peril. The wizard who summoned him is dead, Wiz has fallen for a red-headed witch who despises him, and no one—not the elves, not the dwarves, not even the dragons—can figure out why he's here, or what to do with him. Worse: the sorcerers of the deadly Black League, rulers of an entire continent, want Wiz dead—and he doesn't even know why! Wiz had better figure out the rules of this strange new world—and fast—or he's not going to live to see Silicon Valley again.

Here's a refreshing tale from an exciting new writer. It's also a rarity: a well drawn fantasy told with all the rigorous logic of hard science fiction.

February 1989 • 69803-6 • 320 pages • $3.50

Available at bookstores everywhere, or you can send the cover price to Baen Books, Dept. WZ, 260 Fifth Ave., New York, NY 10001.